depths
of blue

LISE
MacTague

Bella
BOOKS

2015

Bella Books, Inc.
P.O. Box 10543
Tallahassee, FL 32302

First Bella Books Edition 2015

Editor: Medora MacDougall
Cover Designer: Sandy Knowles

ISBN: 978-1-59493-433-9

About the Author

Lise MacTague is a hockey player, a librarian, and an author. Her parents had their priorities straight and introduced her to sci-fi at the age of three through reruns of *Star Trek*. Lise has been an overworked art student, a freelance artist, a Rennie, a slave to retail, a grad student, and a slinger of beer. She lives in Milwaukee with two very demanding cats, one who is curled up in her lap even now.

Dedication

For Laces, my four-legged, bewhiskered, twitchy-tailed, constant companion of the past eighteen years. Not much of this book was written without you tromping across the keyboard, sitting in front of the screen or curled in my lap. Any typos are definitely your fault.

Acknowledgments

Thanks must first be extended to my alpha and beta readers: Lynn, Fern, Penny (my mom), Christina, and Shari. Without your feedback and encouragement, these books would never have been finished. Thanks also to Mary Lou, my writing partner for allowing me to bounce ideas, good and bad, off you. Finally, many additional thanks to my editor, Medora McDougall. Without your keen eye there would be just too many crutch-words to be counted. You helped me polish this manuscript from a low luster to a high gleam, and I am forever grateful.

CHAPTER ONE

Jak came awake all at once, sitting up in her narrow bed and pulling the pistol from beneath her pillow in one smooth, practiced movement. She'd been dreaming and the sudden noise confused her. It took a moment before she recalled where she was and the usual despair flooded back to her. She glanced over at the narrow bed on the other side of the room and averted her eyes just as quickly. The pounding on the door continued unabated.

"What the hell do you want?" Jak lowered her voice's pitch and roughened her tone without even thinking about it. Too little sleep after too long a day added further grit to her tone.

The pounding ceased. "New orders for you, Sarge," came the voice through the door. It sounded like Collins, the new private in the unit. Who had he pissed off to get stuck with being the one to wake her? "Captain McCullock says to check your messages."

"Fine, tell Intel I got the message. Now fuck off." She lowered the pistol and ran a hand over the stubble on her scalp. *New orders on less than four hours of sleep. Perfect.* But if it got her out of the camp, she'd take it.

"All right, Sarge." He sounded affronted, and as his footsteps receded, Jak could hear him mutter "asshole." She got up and tested the doorknob. To her relief, it was locked. She'd been so out of it after a twenty-seven hour-shift, a full day on the escarpment, that she hadn't remembered if she'd locked the door or not. At least she'd worn her breastbinder to bed, so even if she'd forgotten to lock the door, her secret would still have been safe.

Her eyes tracked again to the empty bed in the room, and she allowed herself to contemplate it. Her heart constricted, as it always did. She'd looked at it every day for two years, and every day she still expected to see her brother's form sprawled there. Jak had been unable to even bring herself to make his bed. Her side of the room was as tidy as always and his was still the pigsty it had been when he'd been killed. Sorrow tightened her throat, and she breathed hard through the pain for a few moments. She missed him. Johvah, she still missed him.

Bron had run interference for her when he'd been alive. His presence had filled whatever room he was in, and she'd been content to fade into the shadows and watch for threats. Without him, she had to take on everyone face to face.

Since her brother had been killed by a sniper's bullet while they'd been out on assignment, she'd been alone, all alone, with her deception. She was by herself in the middle of a compound full of men who, if they discovered her secret, would—at best— imprison her. At worst, they would rape her and put her on trial for masquerading as a man, something which would likely end with her execution for treason. It hadn't been her choice to join the army, but after their father died it had seemed like the only way for them to survive. When Bron was still alive, she'd been able to be herself with at least one person. She hadn't felt like her own self since he was killed. The strain was getting to her. Some days she felt that snapping at her squad mates was all that kept her sane. It also served to keep them as far away from her as they could get. The more isolated she was, the safer she was with her secret.

She reached behind her and grabbed the cable coming out of the wall above the desk that was shoved against the head of her bed. She pulled enough of it toward her that she could plug it into the jack in the base of her left palm. A slight sensation of vertigo accompanied her immersion into the local net. Some people didn't have to close their eyes to access the data that flowed through their local network, but Jak had always found it easier if she blocked out external stimuli. She accessed her in-box. As usual it was empty except for material related to her missions. There was no one who would reach out to her for any other reason.

"Stowell, you're going deep into Orthodoxan territory, Sector 27 to be exact." Captain McCullock's voice grated on her, bringing his sneering, ginger-mustached face to mind. "Word's come down that Colonel Hutchinson has an offworld visitor you need to take out." She thought she detected a note of glee in his voice as he continued. "You're going in under radio silence and on your own since you refuse to take a partner." *Why should I? They can't keep up with me.* "The insertion team will meet you at 1100 hours." He paused; the usual contempt she heard from him was gone when he continued. "This one's important, Stowell. More important than pretty much any other assignment you've ever been given. Don't fuck it up."

They were all important. What makes this one so much different? She didn't think about it too much. As a sniper, she was a weapon that Command wielded. They pointed her at the target and she pulled the trigger. She accessed the attached files and downloaded the charts and maps for Orthodoxan territory between the fence and Sector 27. Images flooded her consciousness as materials were deposited to her brain.

The long-range weather report caught her attention. There was rain in the forecast. That in itself wasn't unusual; it rained frequently. The strength of the forecast weather systems were what held her attention. They were in for some torrential downpours, which looked like they'd be hitting about the time she would be arriving at Hutchinson's compound. That could complicate her getaway.

The pants and coat of her combat fatigues were folded and draped over the end of her bed. She donned them quickly, then pulled on her boots, stood up and stomped her feet to settle them. She removed the service cap from the small desk at the head of the bed and placed it upon her head. After settling it over the dark blond stubble that covered her scalp, she picked up her rifle, automatically verifying that the safety was on. No one went about without a weapon, even in camp. Raids occurred too frequently to be without one for any period of time. When they happened, every available person was expected to be on hand to repel enemy combatants. She picked her smallest scope up from the table and slid it into one of the many pockets on her fatigue jacket's front. She took a deep breath, settled the habitual scowl over her features, then left her room.

There wasn't much time to get herself kitted up before she had to meet with the insertion team. She nodded to the sentry outside the barracks' front door and made her way quickly down the street. The quartermasters' offices were only one street over. Tall swirls of blue dust blew down the center of the unpaved road. Men in uniforms or fatigues hurried to and fro on various errands. Camp Abbott was always busy, especially during the day. Even though they were grinding their way through their third decade of this civil war, the military never slumbered. It didn't even nap.

The hulking building of the Quartermaster Corps sat on the outskirts of the camp against the three-meter-high wall that made up the perimeter. The wall was tall enough that most people couldn't get over it easily. Someone would have to be plenty tall to be able to leap up, grab the top of the wall and pull himself over. In the time it took to do that the sentries would take him out. That was the idea, anyhow. In reality, the wall slowed down their enemies, but it didn't stop them.

A large enclosure filled with vehicles of all types and sizes lay directly beyond the offices. No one stood guard here. The men inside were not only more than qualified to take care of themselves, they also had immediate access to all sorts of nasty weapons. Jak took the front stairs two at a time and rapped sharply on the main door before she let herself in.

"I hear you're heading out again, Stowell." A grizzled man greeted her from behind the desk. "What do you need this time?"

"Lambert." She nodded in greeting. With Bron gone, she had done her best to stay on even footing with the quartermaster sergeant. It made for less hassle when she had to requisition supplies and a better chance of acquiring rarer and less conventional items.

Some of her compatriots treated the quartermasters with thinly veiled hostility, making their opinion of the noncombatant soldiers well known. Most of them didn't realize that many of the so-called noncombatants had completed their ten years of required service and chosen to stay on to continue their service to their country. Well, if the others treated the quartermasters like crap, it only made her clumsy attempts at affability more effective. The fact that she would occasionally leave them gifts of her fresh kills from hunting didn't hurt either.

"You heard right, as usual. I need supplies for a week."

"I heard you were going after Hutchinson. Good, the man's an animal and he's killed more good men than anyone since Stinson." Lambert spat into the cuspidor next to his desk. Chewing tobacco wasn't frowned on in the service, but dirtying the army's floor with dip definitely was. "You get him good. He commanded the opposing sectors when I was on active duty. Had a habit of sending our boys' bodies back to us booby-trapped with explosives. Killed a lot of good men before we got wise. One of those traps finished me for active duty." He leaned forward and gave his prosthetic calf a dull thunk.

Jak kept her face an impassive mask. It never ceased to amaze her how much Lambert knew about the supposedly classified workings of their intelligence operations. The man had a talent for pulling together small pieces of information into a surprisingly accurate whole. He was a little off on this one, but close enough not to make much of a difference. "I don't know what you're talking about. I'm just heading out that way to do some recon."

"Recon my ass." Lambert snorted. "McCullock had me put together your data dump. Sector 27's three days past their lines. You'll need more than a few supplies. I'm sending you out with a full pack of stims, since I doubt you'll be sleeping when you're in enemy territory. I'm upgrading your jacket. You're about due for a new one anyway. This one has increased insulation and ventilation. It'll keep you warmer or cooler no matter what the weather is. I'm sure you'll need the cooling since you insist on dragging that ridiculous ghillie suit with you. I don't know how you don't get it hung up on every bush you walk past. Those strips of cloth have to make it impossible to move quickly and silently. You know—I could requisition a cloaking unit for you."

"I've told you before," Jak replied wearily. They'd had this argument more times than she could count. "I don't need the cloak. I'm used to moving in it. The suit works better for camouflage and doesn't give me away with that shimmer at the edges of the field. Sure, it's heavier and hotter, but it won't get me killed." Bron had always preferred the cloak to the ghillie suit and had teased her mercilessly for her preference. But she was here and he wasn't.

"Do what you will, you always do," grumbled Lambert. "What else do you need?"

"Do you have any of those infrared scopes?"

Lambert grunted. "You know those are really hard to come by," he hedged.

"If they weren't hard to come by, I wouldn't be asking you," Jak pointed out.

He smirked, then shrugged. "You have a point. I do have one. You can borrow it for the mission, but it needs to come back. Try really hard not to lose or destroy it."

"Got it. I promise to treat it with the utmost respect." She waited impatiently as he heaved himself up from his desk and walked with a slight limp into the back room. While he was gathering the supplies she'd requisitioned, she stared out the front window. She found herself slipping into a state of meditative watchfulness. She let it flow over her. There was no way she could practice that particular skill too much.

Jak dropped back into real time when Lambert returned to the room with a pack and small carrying case. He dropped the pack at her feet.

"A week's worth of food and water, plus the necessary stims. Also, I replenished your first aid kit. Try not to get shot more than a day away from base," he admonished somberly, then spoiled it with a wide grin. "If you find water, there are purification tablets in the first aid kit. It will take care of most of the bacteria and other critters in the water supply. Enough that what's left won't kill you. Probably not, anyway."

He handed her the jacket draped over his forearm. "That's your new jacket. Don't get any holes in it your first day out. And here's the scope. Remember, it's your ass if something happens to it. If it weren't for the fresh meat you 'accidentally' leave here, you wouldn't be getting it at all."

"Thanks, Lambert," Jak said gratefully. "I'll try not to break any of your goodies."

"Try to come back in one piece, that's all I ask. I'll miss the extra meat rations if you catch yourself a bullet."

* * *

The slow-turning blue orb drifted lazily past her window, its brilliant azure in sharp contrast to the deep black of space. This corner of the galaxy was beautiful, she thought. A sizable nebula in brilliant shades of lavender and pink floated in the far reaches of the small solar system. Even though she'd been exploring the edges of the outer systems for years now, she still came across sights that took her breath away. She watched the nebula for a moment longer before turning her eyes back to the planet that was her destination.

Her thoughts strayed, as they often did when she came to a new world, to the first settlers who would have arrived here. Most of the Fringe worlds had been settled in the same way. Passels of settlers had been put into cryogenic sleep and crammed into transport vessels along with plants and livestock from Earth. Typically armed with little more than a basic survey report and the hopes of their people, hundreds of settlement ships had spread out from Earth. In their departure, they'd cut their last ties with the governments there. Those ships had been the first to leave the planet, only able to do so because of newly developed cryogenic technology. They'd ended up on far-flung planets at the edges of the known galaxy. They had to make do with what little they could bring with them and their adopted world's flora and fauna.

Better them than me, Torrin thought. Her role in the galaxy might not be quite as influential, but she was happy with it. She could come and go as she pleased instead of getting stuck on one planet like those poor saps had been.

A few hundred years later, humanity had spread out from Earth again, this time working their way from one star system to the next, spreading steadily outward. Thus the League of Solaran Planets was born.

A strident, high-pitched chirp emanated from the console in front of her. Frowning, she scanned the console's screens. The sensors had picked up another vessel on the far side of the planet. She danced her fingers across sensitive touchscreens as she uttered a low curse. She set a course that would bring her into the planet's orbit but would keep her out of sensor range of the ship. Eyes glued to the display, she scanned for any hints that the other vessel had detected her presence. When her ship slipped into orbit, she sighed with relief. Quickly, she powered down all systems except life support and one console display, then double-checked that her transponder beacon was disabled. According to intergalactic law, it was highly illegal to disable a ship's transponder, but given that the people who'd made that law were the ones she was currently trying to avoid, she wasn't too worried about the ethics involved.

So...what was a League of Solaran Planets warship doing out in this backwater? *She* was there to pick up a lucrative smuggling contract, but the League didn't engage in smuggling, at least not officially. Judging by its position, the ship looked like it was on picket, but her informant hadn't mentioned a League blockade. The League vessel slipped further out of sensor range, the bulk of the planet effectively shielding her from its instruments. She powered on the AI.

"Tien, any communication from the surface?"

"Negative, Torrin." The AI's slightly alien tones echoed around her on the bridge. A small hologram of a diminutive woman in ancient Chinese regalia sprang to life at her elbow. "I do not detect any transmissions."

"Try scanning radio frequencies. It's primitive, but I didn't notice any satellites in orbit. Without those, radio may be the only way they can contact us." If that were the case, she wondered, how had the Orthodoxans managed to get their request out in the first place? They had to have a contact on the League ship, she decided. It was what she would have done in the same situation. Even the high-and-mighty League had its elements who were willing to put aside the finer points of legality and make an easy credit or two.

"Affirmative, Torrin, scanning now." The hologram furrowed her brows in concentration. "I have scanned all twenty-three radio channels that are currently within range. All but one register with static, and that one is repeating a string of numbers. The numbers match Cartesian coordinates on the planet's surface."

The main viewscreen flickered to life in front of her. The outline of Haefen's landmasses appeared. The planet seemed to be mainly ocean, but with two main continents, connected by a narrow isthmus that ran east to west. When Tien overlaid the radioed coordinates on the screen, a pulsating point marked the coordinates on the southwestern hemisphere of the larger of the continents. It was some distance from the isthmus that connected the two continents.

"Bring us in quietly but not right to their coordinates. Pick a spot about forty kilometers away where we can set down." Torrin didn't intend to provide the Orthodoxans with the temptation of seizing her vessel. Even though she was there to negotiate a contract to smuggle materials to them, she had no illusions about what a backwater society with no space assets might resort to if they thought they could procure the items on their own. She'd spent too many credits retrofitting and customizing the *Calamity Jane* to consider placing her pride and joy in needless danger.

She waited as the vessel shuddered its way through the atmosphere and broke through the thin layer of clouds. Everything on this planet seemed to be a shade of blue. Even the clouds were a powder puff blue.

"Tien, is there anything I need to know about the inhabitants?"

The AI was silent for a few moments. Its little avatar massaged its chin as if in contemplation. "Haefonian society is fairly backward by our standards. Their preferred method of transportation is by Earth horse. They scrabble out a living in the arid planet's wastelands. The few resources are a source of constant conflict for the planet's inhabitants, who are broken into dozens of warring tribes."

Torrin had to make allowances for Tien's standards. The AI was rather League-centric, which made sense since she'd been liberated from a League vessel. From the description, Haefen sounded much like other planets on the Fringes.

"It's arid? It didn't look that way from orbit. The planet's blue, for crying out loud. Frozen hells, Tien! The screen shows it's mostly water."

"All I can tell you is what my databanks tell me, Torrin."

"Didn't we just get those updated?" It was unlike Tien to be off in the information she provided. Even though the League data on Fringe planets was a little sketchy, her people spent lots of time in the Fringes and had built up their own database. She'd had the latest updates added during the ship's last retrofit.

"The residents are short-tempered and prone to squabbles and feuds that can last generations," Tien said instead of answering. "You will want to watch what you say to avoid insulting the locals."

Torrin snorted. "This isn't my first rodeo. Is there anything else you'd like to tell me about how to do my job?"

"I merely thought you ought to be prepared, Torrin," Tien replied equably. "You do not want to become the cause of a blood feud."

"I've been doing this a while," Torrin said. "I think I can be trusted not to insult an entire society by accident."

"I only worry that it will not be by accident, Torrin." Tien kept talking over Torrin's irritated exhalation. "We have landed. Perhaps you should attend to your preparations for the trip."

"Snotty machine," Torrin grumbled under her breath.

She unstrapped herself from the pilot's chair and strode out of the bridge and down the narrow corridor to her sleeping quarters. She hauled clothing out of the drawers in her cabinet, looking for an all-weather jumpsuit. The red jumpsuit with black flashing accentuated her hips and breasts, making it perfect to wear during the upcoming negotiations. Torrin grinned. She had some great assets, and she was damn well going to flaunt them if it gave her an advantage. After some thought, she pulled her dark red hair back into a simple ponytail that ended halfway down her back.

Torrin looked at herself critically in the mirror. Satisfied with her ensemble, she belted on a plasma pistol and a lethal-looking military-grade combat knife. She wanted to look feminine but not vulnerable. The pistol and knife should dispel any particular ideas of defenselessness in her hosts' minds. Also, the pistol was a great sample of the type of weaponry she could provide to a feuding backwater princeling to satisfy whatever grudge he had against his neighbors. It was a lucrative opportunity and one she didn't intend to pass up. It was also one with a time limit. Her informant—Neal—had mentioned that there were others interested in the opportunity. Because of their long history with one another, not to mention a hefty bonus, he'd agreed to keep the information under his hat for a little bit. Knowing Neal, that wouldn't last long. The profit in information brokering came from selling the same bit as often as possible, and Neal was a master at maximizing his own profit. She couldn't complain too much; she'd made a lot of money running down his leads.

The door hissed open as she walked toward it. She followed the passage left until it ended at a ladder down to the lower deck. Torrin braced her feet on the outside of the ladder and slid down its length in one smooth movement. The lights came on in the cargo bay as she made her way to the front of the ship. The storage space was small for most vessels this size. She'd sacrificed a lot of room to cram upgraded engines into the ship. The compromise made in storage was more than an even trade for the extra speed the engines provided. In her profession, the ability to outrun and evade the authorities was much more important than how much she could carry. Besides, once she'd struck her lucrative deal, she had access to many other ships to provide delivery of the goods.

Since she was on a fishing expedition, the cargo bay was mostly empty. If the trip panned out, she would be coordinating many more runs and each would be lucrative enough to make her a hefty profit.

"What do you think, Tien?" she queried the empty air. "Do I go with the bike or the antigrav sled?"

"The antigrav sled will not leave any tracks that will lead back to us, but from the power signatures I read while we were in orbit, I doubt the natives have the technological capability for you to recharge it. I recommend the bike, Torrin. If you blur the tracks, this afternoon's storm will destroy any sign of your passage and we should be safe enough from native predations." Tien's voice blared out from a number of speakers and bounced around the empty cargo bay in an unnerving echo.

"Excellent point, as always." Torrin strode over to the two vehicles strapped into place against the far wall.

The AI didn't answer, but Torrin hadn't really expected a response. She disengaged the restraining clamps and lowered the bike from the wall. The sleek, wicked-looking two-wheeler gleamed in the dim lighting. It was low-slung and had enough room on the back to carry a passenger. She'd upgraded the bike herself, adding storage canisters to the rear to increase its speed output and a gyroscopic stabilizer. Short of her taking it over a cliff, the bike wasn't about to tip over. The trip from their landing spot to the coordinates they'd picked up wasn't going to take long. They were far enough removed that no one was likely to stumble across the ship, but close enough that Torrin wouldn't be traveling all day. There was no need to bring an additional fuel cell.

"Tien, the door, please."

The cargo bay door lowered and daylight quickly intruded at the top of the cargo bay and along the back wall. Torrin wheeled the bike over to the top of the ramp and stopped dead.

The planet was so...blue. The view from orbit had suggested as much, but from the ground the intensity of the color was overwhelming. The sky was a vibrant azure she'd never seen before. None of the dozens of skies she'd seen on other Fringe worlds could match it... The clouds were blue, but a lighter shade than the sky. Even the trees were blue. Not as blue as the sky, but the leaves were definitely blue and the bark was a darker, more muted blue that verged on navy.

It definitely wasn't arid, though. There was no way trees could grow that tall unless there was plenty of water. Something was definitely off with Tien's databanks. Torrin hoped she'd come to the right place. If she hadn't, she'd find out soon enough. After that she'd head back to Tyndall, track down Neal and reclaim the bonus with interest. If he'd already spent it, she'd enjoy taking it out of his hide.

She dragged her gaze from the vista before her and wheeled the bike down the ramp. She gave a quick glance around the area, and her gaze settled on a sapling. It was quick work to remove its branches with her knife and carry them over to the vehicle and lash them behind the back wheel. The ground was extremely soft, and groundcover between the trees looked scarce. That would leave a clear trail back to the ship unless she took precautions. After a few miles, she'd be able to remove the branches. Tien's promised rainstorm should obliterate the wheel tracks completely after that.

Torrin adjusted her ponytail and threw one leg over the bike. She opened the throttle as wide as it would go, eliciting the deep roar that never failed to bring a grin to her face, and took off into the forest.

CHAPTER TWO

Torrin sped through the trees; she was absolutely amazed at their size. They towered over her, hundreds of meters above, their canopies so dense that very little light filtered through the leaves. Little to no undergrowth existed to get in her way except the occasional mushroom. It wasn't what she was used to seeing at all. Her home planet had very little in the way of forests. It was very open or at least the habitable parts were. But then, three-quarters of Nadierzda's surface was covered with shifting seas of silt and sand.

The heads-up display in her helmet pierced the gloom under the canopy far better than her naked eyes, and she was grateful for the extra help it gave her as she raced between the trees at speeds in excess of two hundred kilometers an hour. She kept an eye on the map inset in the upper left corner of the HUD. The blinking light indicated that she was almost at her destination. The coordinates had included a time. She was a little late, but it had been terrific luck that she'd arrived with enough time to make the day's meeting window. Her contacts wouldn't have known exactly when she was to be expected. Neal had said something about sending word to expect her, but he wouldn't have been able to give the princeling's people more than an arrival window of a few weeks.

A break in the trees was coming up fast, and she throttled back slightly on the accelerator. She grinned with anticipation; it was almost time for her entrance. The HUD showed a structure and a man-shaped heat signature a short way beyond the break in the trees. As she hit the break in the trees, Torrin cut the throttle and leaned hard to her left, putting the bike into a long skid that ended right in front of the man standing in front of a squat guard tower. The bike's rear wheel threw a long spray of dirt that barely missed the man. As the bike came to a stop, she hopped off it and swept the helmet from her head with a flourish, her hair bursting free from the confinement of the helmet.

Torrin was unprepared for the look of virulent disgust on the man's face. She'd expected surprise or admiration, but nothing had prepared her for the look of total disdain that verged on outright hatred. The man looked at her as if his boot-scrapings had suddenly started talking. He stood there, in his pretty black uniform with its red piping and stared at her in disbelieving revulsion. The twitching little mustache that graced his upper lip looked more menacing than she would have expected for such a ridiculous affectation. He was shorter than she was. She supposed that might account for some of his issues.

The uniform was an incredibly overdone piece of conceit. Apparently the little man's boss had decided to signify his importance to everyone via ridiculous amounts of ribbons and decoration. By the amount of eye-wrenching gaudiness going on, the princeling would be able to afford her fee. That at least was worth dealing with a little rudeness.

"Torrin Ivanov?" The man spoke, incredulous. "*You* are Torrin Ivanov?"

"In the flesh." Torrin grinned to hide her misgivings. She ran her fingers through her hair, displaying her feminine attributes to their best advantage. Once again, his reaction mystified her. Most men couldn't keep their eyes off her unless they, like Torrin, happened to prefer their own gender. She knew most men considered her attractive and had long ago honed that attraction into a weapon. Clearly, this little man couldn't believe his eyes but not in a good way. He wasn't wondering how he'd gotten so lucky to deal with her. He was wondering what in the universe this *thing* was in front of him.

"We've been expecting..." He paused, struggling with his words. "Someone. No one told me you would be—"

"Tall?" she said, flashing him a professional smile. "Red-headed, charming, riding a bike, an excellent blackjack player, vivacious—"

"Sure," he interrupted when he realized she would happily keep throwing options at him. "All of those." He steeled himself visibly, straightened his shoulders and took a deep breath. "I'm Major Miles Yonkman, Colonel Hutchinson's aide-de-camp. The colonel has been expecting you. I have transportation; we'll take that."

"Never mind that," Torrin replied. "I've got my bike. I don't need a horse." Her mind raced. Colonel? Did the backwater princeling fancy himself a military man? And what was the deal with Yonkman? She didn't like the way his last statement became an order or the way his eyes were roaming over her body now that his initial shock had worn off. He made no attempt to hide his appraisal, and his attentions made her long for a shower.

"Horse?" Yonkman looked at her suspiciously, trying to determine if she was making fun of him. "Why would I have a horse? I have a truck."

Apparently, she'd stuck her foot right in it. Though why he looked so put out that she thought he might be making the ride by horseback, she didn't know. That was the preferred mode of transportation down here, wasn't it?

"I won't leave my bike unattended, so I'll follow your vehicle. I hope that will be acceptable." Torrin smiled winningly down at him. She was starting to really dislike the mustachioed little man. She didn't need to like him to work with him, and she was willing to overlook all manner of personal shortcomings in order to turn a profit. However, his part in the local military chain of command only reinforced her suspicion that she wasn't dealing with a normal tribal outfit.

"So I'll follow you?" she prompted when she noticed that his attention was once again drawn to her physique.

"Absolutely. Try to keep up." Yonkman strode over to a truck at the corner of the outpost. Pulling the helmet back over her head, Torrin got back on her bike. He reversed the truck a few meters past the structure, gestured peremptorily out the window for her to follow him, then sped forward to the other side of the small compound. She kept an eye on the outpost's composition and staffing levels as she followed him more slowly. A keen habit of hypervigilance had helped her out of more than one tight spot in the past. The habit was now so ingrained that she was usually barely aware of it.

Things didn't feel quite right, though. They'd been expecting her, so she was in the right place. The big picture was what she'd expected, but the details were all wrong and they were getting stranger. Now the term Orthodoxans was giving her pause. She'd assumed it was a quaint little name for one of the planet's many warring tribes, but what if it was more than that. In her experience, and from what she remembered about galactic history, people with orthodox points of view were rarely the kind of people she wanted to have a drink with. She would have to keep her wits about her on this run. It wasn't the first time she'd gone into a job without all the facts she needed and it wouldn't be the last, not in her line of work.

Four men watched her from the outpost as she drove through; their faces could have been carved in stone. One leaned over and spat to the side as she passed. They carried ugly, squat weapons, fairly primitive compressed-gas projectile weapons unless she was mistaken. If she could see four guards, it was likely that there were at least that many more inside the long, low building at the back of the compound. It had the look of every barracks she'd ever seen. The front of the outpost's compound was the most heavily fortified, though the back and sides were also well defended, which was confusing. It looked like the outpost was facing the wrong way, back into its own territory. Were the natives that afraid of their own people? If the area had been recently annexed from another tribe, it would make sense that they'd experience frequent uprisings. This "Colonel" Hutchinson would need more specialized weaponry if he was fighting his own people. Torrin made a mental note to be ready to discuss crowd control equipment.

As soon as they cleared the small compound, Yonkman sped up further. He was trying to prove something, but she kept pace easily. The truck really was a pile, and she suspected that its top speed was maybe half of what her bike was capable of.

The dirt road leading through the small compound soon met up with a paved road. Both sides of the road were cleared of the majestic trees that she had ridden through on her way to the rendezvous point. The road made for an easier ride, but she'd enjoyed her trip through the cathedral-like silence of the forest's massive trees.

They climbed higher into the hills and Yonkman was forced to slow down to negotiate the increasing number of switchbacks. There were low, tree-covered mountains in the distance. The area was isolated. They passed through the ghostly remains of a modest village at a crossroads. At one time it had been moderately prosperous, but it was now abandoned, doors sagging on hinges. No one had inhabited it for many years. So far she wasn't very impressed by the mysterious Colonel Hutchinson's stewardship over his lands.

They navigated the road for another fifteen minutes, winding up the side of one of the mountains she'd glimpsed, before negotiating not one but three layers of security and checkpoints. The third layer was the most impressive: a wall three-meters tall built out of blue-streaked native stone and topped by an electrified, barbed-wire fence. A boxy, unwieldy-looking home crouched beyond the wall. Multiple levels were piled atop each other, lending it an unfinished look, like someone had started building and had added levels and wings until they got bored and walked off.

After she and Yonkman were waved through by the guards at the wall. Torrin followed him up a winding road to the house's front. Up close, though ungainly, the house towered oppressively over them. Directly to the rear of the building, the mountain continued up, cupping the house between two tree-covered slopes. To the left of the house was a series of much smaller buildings that looked like they'd been erected after the rest of the structure. Also built of the area's native stone, the sheds were surrounded by more electrified barbed-wire fencing. She wondered who Hutchinson had imprisoned there. She could see at least three guards patrolling the area.

Yonkman pulled to a stop in front of the house's wide steps and hopped out of the truck. She swung in next to him. Two guards in plain uniforms stood at attention on either side of double doors. One of them came down the stairs to greet them and almost tripped over the steps when he got a good look at her. The major spoke a few words to him. The guard shot her a sharp, disapproving look, then hurried back up the steps and into the house.

"Leave your bike here. One of the men will take it to the garage."

"I'd rather handle that if you don't mind," she replied. "From what I've seen of your technology, I'm not sure that any of your men could handle her."

"I'm sure they'll manage," Yonkman said shortly, nostrils flared in irritation. "Let's get you inside." He stomped up the stairs.

Left with no choice but to comply, Torrin shrugged and accompanied him up the steps. The remaining guard snatched the door open for the major, who swept through without any acknowledgment. Torrin nodded at the man, who did his best to pretend she didn't exist, though miniscule beads of sweat popped out along his brow at her presence.

The house's interior did not match its exterior. Inside, one room flowed into the other, each outdoing the one before in ridiculous extravagance. Gilt covered every surface even remotely appropriate for ornamentation. The furniture she saw was either plush and overstuffed or elaborately carved and overdone. Overall, the effect was one of oppressive self-indulgence.

Yonkman led her deeper and deeper into the edifice. For the size of the place, there were very few people about; the only ones she saw were more men in military garb scurrying here and there on one errand or another. The major took her around one final corner and stopped in front of a pair of elaborately carved doors that dwarfed him, more than half again as tall as he was. He opened them into an echoing sitting room where overstuffed chairs and settees were arranged in various configurations. A massive mural— apparently a scene from a religion she didn't recognize—dominated one wall. Her glance gave her the vague impression of large, blocky figures in a riot of colors. The painting topped the wainscoting that sheathed the walls halfway up to the high, vaulted ceilings.

"Make yourself comfortable. The colonel's a busy man, but I'm sure he'll be here soon." He pointed across the room. "There's a bar over there. Help yourself to anything you want to." With one last sneer, he left.

Torrin relaxed slightly without Yonkman's suffocating presence. His vacillation between a disgust that ranged on open hostility and barely concealed lust made her very uncomfortable. She reminded herself that she stood to make a tidy profit here and wondered what Colonel Hutchinson would be like. She wandered over to the long bar and rummaged through it until she found a tumbler. After opening a few bottles, she settled on one that smelled a bit like whiskey but was a shade of blue that she'd never seen before in the beverage. All of the other alcohol that she checked was either clear or blue. She poured a finger's worth into the glass, took an exploratory sip and almost choked. It tasted like whiskey all right but was extremely strong. She was known to enjoy her libations, but this one burned fiercely all the way down. She poured a finger's worth of water from a pitcher on the bar into the tumbler to dilute her drink. She would have to nurse the drink; it wouldn't do to enter into negotiations while drunk.

She pressed two fingertips behind her right ear. "Tien, do you read?" There was no response from the ship's AI, not even static. Torrin wandered over to the room's far side and gazed out French doors onto the slope of the mountain behind the house. The mountain's broken peak jutted out of the foliage and clawed at the intensely blue sky.

"Are you there?" She activated the subdermal transmitter with her fingertips again. This time she received some static. There must be some sort of communications dampening field over the place, probably built into the walls. It had to be some kind of electromagnetic interference or it wouldn't have cut her communications with the ship. She would have to be some distance out from the building to be able to reach Tien.

Being cut off from her ship made her a little nervous. Once she concluded the deal, she would ditch this place so quickly they wouldn't even see a vapor trail.

Glancing at the clock in the corner of the room, she settled herself into one of the overstuffed chairs. Or attempted to. The monstrosity had so much cushioning that she felt like it was trying to absorb her. She stood quickly. She tried a few other chairs to the same effect.

"Screw it," she proclaimed to the empty room. She strode back over to the bar and hopped up to perch on its edge. She set one foot on the seat of the barstool in front of her, then brought her ankle up and crossed it over her knee. With her glass on the bar next to her, she drummed her fingers on the high gloss surface. She hated waiting without anything to do, but there was nothing to do for it except settle in until Hutchinson graced her with his presence.

The mural pulled her attention, with its bright colors and large figures and she let her gaze travel around it. Noble-looking men gazed across a bloody field at a group of distorted beings. They looked like they might have been humans at one time. Hovering between both groups a figure with massive white wings and a somber mien pointed accusingly at the dark, twisted humanoids. The painting seemed somehow uneven, as if it had been completed by a number of different people, none of whom had been very well trained. The figures, though impressive, were somehow childish, their proportions off slightly, though in different ways. As she looked at it, she realized that there were absolutely no women among the colorful, noble-looking figures. At first she thought there were no women included in the mural at all, but when she looked more closely at the distorted figures, she realized that some among them were female. Those had been represented the most grotesquely of all. Torrin shivered a bit. Whoever the artists had been, they didn't seem to have much regard for women.

Some fifteen minutes had passed when the door opened and a man entered. He carried a large box, which he trundled over beside a table. After placing it on the floor, he knelt and started taking items out of it and placing them on the table. He was wearing a military uniform like the other men she'd seen so far. It wasn't as ornate as Yonkman's, which meant he was a lower rank than the major. Much lower judging by the almost complete lack of ornamentation. The man continued his work, his back mostly to her.

She hopped down from the bar, and he started, completely surprised to discover that he wasn't alone in the room. He looked back, shock crossing his face, and almost fell over. He managed to keep from toppling completely, barely getting a hand down in time before he hit the floor.

"Who let you in here?" he asked, staring at her. "You know you're not supposed to be out during the day."

"Excuse me?" Who was he to tell her when she could or couldn't be out? She'd been invited here.

He stood up and strode over to where she stood by the bar. Like the other Haefonians she'd seen so far, he was short, barely coming up to her chin. He pushed his head out from his shoulders at her, his face drawn down into a forbidding scowl. Torrin's lips twitched when she figured out what he'd reminded her of. It was a picture that she'd seen in a flea-dip bar on some backwater planet. A group of dogs playing some kind of card game. She hadn't been familiar with the game and she'd never seen an Earth dog in the flesh, but she'd seen a couple of pictures. The bulldog—that was the one he looked like.

"Are you laughing at me?" The man's voice was soft and cold in anger. He grabbed her upper arms. "You know better than that. It's not your place to laugh at me." He flexed his fingers with every other word. He wasn't tall, but he was strong enough that she swayed in his grasp.

That was it. So far she'd held back out of respect for another world's customs, but she wasn't going to let some backwater asshole with little-shit syndrome manhandle her.

"You need to let go of me." She gritted her teeth in what she hoped he'd take for a smile. If he let go of her, maybe she could avoid offending her host. "Now." Her voice was rimed in frost. Menace prickled from her tone, and he ignored it at his own peril.

"You don't tell me what to do."

She smiled, a real one this time. The Haefonian looked at her askance for a moment before yelling in shock as Torrin brought her arms around, striking him on the inside of his forearms with enough force to knock his hands away. She stomped on his instep, and he howled, hopping on one foot.

"Fucking bitch!" He drew back one arm and swung at her, fist balled. She slid back out of his reach and caught his hand on the backswing, using the momentum back to haul him off his feet. He landed on his back with a muffled yelp as the air was expelled from his lungs.

"Stay down," Torrin told him. So far he'd avoided serious injury; all she'd damaged was his pride. From the way his face twisted in fury, she doubted he would take her advice. With difficulty, he got his legs under him. Air wheezed in and out of his lungs as he tried to catch his breath. She waited a moment longer, hoping he'd use his head and stop pushing the issue. He moved to lever himself off the floor, and she struck, raising her foot and bringing it down on the back of his hand. Bones cracked and the man screamed, a high, thin wail that trailed off into sobs. He rocked back onto his rump and clasped the abused hand to his chest, rocking from side to side against the pain.

"What in Johvah's name is going on here?" a voice roared from the doorway. Crossing the floor toward her was a man taller than any she had yet seen on the planet. He had to be almost her height. If he was shorter, it wasn't by more than a few centimeters. Though older, he had a powerful physique and a well-coiffed head of platinum blond hair. The man surveyed her handiwork and grimaced. Yonkman trotted at his side, face pale as he took in the scene.

"This man attacked me," Torrin said. She turned to face him, one shoulder in front. If he was going to take a swing at her for defending herself, she wanted to lessen the profile he had to strike at. "Is this how you treat potential business partners?"

"Miss Ivanov," the tall man said. He grinned and she could almost hear a spangle as his incredibly white teeth caught the light. "My apologies for the welcome you've received. I don't know what this man's problem was, but you have my assurances that he will be dealt with harshly." He extended a hand to her. "I'm Colonel Philemond Hutchinson, but please, call me Phil."

Torrin shook the proffered hand. She kept her face impassive as he employed a vise-like grip. The show of strength was juvenile, and she refused to rise to his bait by wincing.

"Yonkman!" The major saluted in the face of the colonel's fury, his own face still bloodless. "Get this piece of crap out of here. Take him to the stockade. I'll deal with him later."

"Yes, sir!" Yonkman saluted again, then grabbed the still-sobbing man and dragged him forcefully from the room.

"Let's get down to business, shall we?" He took her elbow and led her over to the chairs in one corner and waited while she seated herself. Hutchinson took the chair next to hers and watched her intently. "I understand you're the one to talk to so we may procure some products that would be otherwise unattainable."

Torrin laughed. His attempt at subtlety was more confusing than smooth. "Colonel, I'm a smuggler. You don't have to sugarcoat your request. Let me know what you need, and I'll tell you what it'll cost you."

"Very well. To start out with, we need to upgrade our communications systems, but we don't have the option of satellites. They were some of the first targets the Devonites took out. At this point, we're both reduced to radio signals, and while we've thoroughly compromised their radio communications, I'm afraid they've done the same to ours."

"Took out?" Torrin asked. "Your enemies have some pretty heavy weaponry at their disposal then?"

"They used to. We've ground down their heaviest weapons over the years, but unfortunately they've done the same to ours."

"How long has this dispute been going on anyway?"

The colonel threw his head back and laughed, his voice rolling richly around the room. "Dispute? That's one way of putting it." He chuckled again. "Miss Ivanov, we have been engaged in a civil war with our Devonite brethren for over three decades now. Their aggression has been held at bay for thirty years through the mighty struggle of the Orthodoxan army. We need to break the stalemate and stem the flood of our men's blood."

Torrin sat back and stared at him, completely flummoxed. Tien hadn't mentioned anything like that in her rundown on the planet. Clearly, the information in her databanks was woefully incomplete. Come to think of it, the contract hadn't mentioned anything about a civil war either. From what her informant had said, she was going to be running guns for one side on some kind of tribal border dispute. This sounded much bigger than that. Bigger might actually be to her advantage. Mentally, she added a few zeroes to the amount she'd planned to charge for the job. The League picket made sense now.

"I see," she said, thinking quickly. "Tell me what you're thinking, then."

"As I said, our first priority is in communications. After that—" He was cut off as doors on the other side of the room were flung open and a young Orthodoxan soldier darted into the room.

"Sir!" The soldier saluted with a fist over his heart and a half bow at the waist.

The colonel surged out of his chair. "I left orders not to be disturbed, Private!" he hissed, his face in the young soldier's.

"My apologies, sir." He remained half bowed, eyes cast down. "Your aide thought you ought to know that the Devonites have launched an attack and have captured supply routes behind our lines."

Hutchinson drew back, eyes ablaze. "Which ones?" he barked.

"Routes seventy-nine and ninety-two, sir."

The colonel turned back to Torrin.

"Miss Ivanov, I'm afraid I need to attend to this. Supply routes are my main priority. Without them our brave men will be ill-equipped for the rigors of war."

"Not a problem, Colonel. I'll return to my ship. You can contact me when you'd like to set up another meeting; it's your money that keeps me here."

"Call me Phil, and I'm afraid that won't be possible," he said dismissively as he turned to follow the private out of the room. "Route ninety-two is the one you took to get here from the rendezvous point. You'll be spending some time here with us until I can get this sorted out. Never fear, we have a room set aside for you. You'll be well taken care of." With that he strode out of the room.

"Well taken care of?" This place made her more and more uncomfortable. Hutchinson was certainly charming, but that couldn't quite compensate for the strange behavior and rudeness of his men. Of course, she had very little choice in the matter. As long as she was unable to contact her ship, there wasn't much she could do in a building full of armed men, surrounded by fortifications and still more armed men. This place gave her the creeps. She would bide her time and duck out at her earliest opportunity, profits be damned. The money would be no good to anybody, her or the ruling council back home, if she wasn't around to close the deal.

CHAPTER THREE

Jak bounced up and down in the back of the armored personnel carrier. The springs on this one were definitely going to pot. If they weren't already there. Jak's teeth and bones rattled with every bump and pothole that the APC hit. The twelve men crammed in there with her endured the jostling with the same stoicism she did. She kept one hand in a firm grip on the forestock of her sniper rifle and the other hand clamped around the edge of the bench seat. She didn't want to lose her grip on either one. If she lost her seat, she would be exposed to the ridicule of the others riding with her. Dropping her rifle could knock the alignment of the barrel askew. She wouldn't have the luxury of running a complete diagnostic and resighting the weapon before heading into the field. In the long run that would be even more painful than being the butt of jokes from the dozen muscle-bound meatheads who were there with her.

She knew many of them, most only by sight. Collins was there, though she wished he wasn't. He was the only one of the group who didn't know enough to keep her at arm's length. She wasn't there to make friends. She was only there to do her job and to find her brother's killer.

Jak was thrown into the man next to her as the APC took a hairpin turn. The front was along the base of a long escarpment which was the single biggest reason that the Orthodoxans hadn't been able to punch through their lines over the past thirty years. The top of the escarpment was a perfect place for artillery emplacements and gave Devonite snipers the ability to pick off Orthodoxan soldiers with impunity. The sniper squads all took shifts at various places atop the escarpment and did their best to wreak as much havoc from afar as possible. There was even a scoring system where each rank of enemy combatant was worth so many points, officers being worth the most. At one time Jak had topped the leader boards; second place had gone to Bron. Her point total had dropped off when she had started volunteering for more and more missions behind enemy lines after his death. Points gained during those missions didn't count since there was no independent verification of kills.

"Sorry," she grunted. The man next to her—Walters, she thought—shoved her back into a sitting position. He shrugged and resumed his quiet conversation with the man next to him. She regained her grip on the bench seat and turned her head to gaze out one of the little windows that lined the personnel cargo area. She could see the rock wall of the escarpment whizzing by at high speed. After another hairpin turn, during which she managed not to end up in anybody else's lap, all she could see was sky.

There wasn't much to do except stare through the window at nothing. They had a ways to go before they reached their drop-off point. Jak's mind turned back to the mission briefing. The lieutenant had brought the insertion team together and filled in some of the blanks that had been left out in McCullock's message. She'd already done her homework and had her route and its alternatives plotted out in her mind. It was little different than dozens of other missions she'd carried out behind enemy lines. The only deviation was her target. She'd never gone after an offworlder before. For a moment she wondered how high a score Bron would have seen fit to assign to an offworlder. She had no beef with someone from offworld, but if he was going to smuggle new weapons to the Orthodoxans, he had to be stopped. The smuggler would go down just as quickly as an Orthodoxan with a bullet through the sternum.

Twenty minutes of bumps later, she'd collected a new set of bruises and the APC was slowing as it neared its destination. As it came to a stop, she slid her pack and ghillie suit out from under the bench seat. The doors at the end of the carrier were opened from the outside and bright light shone into its dim interior. She squinted against the brightness and hopped down from the vehicle. As soon as she hit the ground, she slung her pack over her shoulders and started a close inspection of her rifle. She didn't think it had been knocked into, but this would be her last chance to verify the calibration.

"All right, listen up," barked a dark-haired man as he descended from the passenger's seat of the vehicle's cab. Everyone turned to face him. "We don't have much time to get in place before the artillery opens up and the infantry assaults the far pylon. Hump your sorry asses into position."

Jak and the others snapped hurried salutes. Lieutenant Ackerley wasn't a stickler for formality so the salutes weren't as crisp as they would have been with someone like Captain McCullock. Ackerley commanded in the field on a regular basis and was more than willing to let the niceties slide during a mission.

In the distance Jak could make out a brilliant field of shimmering blue. The force field ran the width of the isthmus and marked the outer edge of Orthodoxan territory. As they got closer to their positions, Jak could see the field more clearly. Rising ten meters into the air, it reared up out of the blasted and broken terrain that clearly marked the front lines on the isthmus. Thin poles were driven into the ground every hundred meters to the north and south as far as she could see. Between the poles a bright blue light pulsed slightly. Ahead of them, on the other side of the tree line, was one of the pylons. The pylons were much larger than the guide poles. Each one was wider around than three men holding hands could reach. These structures provided power to that section of the force field. Such assets were usually heavily guarded. This one was far enough from the bulk of the fighting, however, that it was watched less closely than most. The commander of the Orthodoxan unit tasked with guarding Pylon 5 was also tremendously lazy and more than a little corrupt. He'd been in the pocket of the Devonites for the past three years. He would almost certainly turn a blind eye to all but the most obvious Devonite action.

The rest of the unit hunkered down to wait, the men assuming relaxed but watchful positions. Jak found herself a slightly elevated perch and slung the rifle off her shoulder. She laid herself flat on the ground and rested the rifle against a rock protruding from the top of her little hillock. She pulled a silencer and the infrared scope from one of her jacket's front pockets and affixed them to her weapon. She felt more than saw a presence to her right while she peered through the scope into the distance beyond.

"Everything good, Stowell?" Ackerley asked as he squatted down next to her.

"I think so, sir. Just double-checking." She sighted on a Haefonian wild turkey that had alighted atop the pylon. The view through the scope lit everything up in shades of green, disguising the bird's muted blue plumage. "Permission to recalibrate?"

"No time," he said. "The festivities will start shortly."

"Yes, sir." It didn't look off, but she would have been happier if she could have rechecked the alignment of the barrel. She would have to hope that everything was in as good a shape as it looked.

Ackerley checked his wrist chronometer. "If I'm not mistaken the diversion is about to start at any moment." Dull thumps of artillery in the distance echoed his words almost immediately, and the lieutenant smiled.

"Right on time." He raised his voice to be heard by the rest. "Let's give those Orthodoxans some time to notice the shelling. They're a little slow, so we might be here a while."

A subdued chuckle rippled through the men, and Ackerley lifted a pair of binoculars to his eyes and aimed them through a gap in the trees to a barely visible building a few kilometers behind the force field. Jak trained her sights on the far-off Orthodoxan outpost as well, zooming in on the building until it was clearly visible through the force field's blue shimmer. A few minutes after they began watching it, men boiled out of the outpost's doors like ants fleeing an anthill being stirred. Enemy soldiers piled into trucks, followed more slowly by officers who grouped together at the door talking worriedly. One of them glanced warily in their direction. Jak knew he couldn't see them, but she watched closely for any sign of hesitation. The officer jumped into the front of one of the trucks, and she breathed a small sigh of relief. The vehicles lumbered off to the south.

Ackerley waited until the trucks and their accompanying dust clouds must have been out of sight of even his binoculars. Jak busied herself with securing her rifle and scope and getting ready to move out. The rest of the men stayed patiently in their positions until Ackerley nodded.

"Let's go" was all he said, but the men moved smoothly into action. Four men approached the low hill from which Jak and Ackerley had observed the Orthodoxans and set up a couple of two-man mortars. They readied them in case a stray Orthodoxan noticed their movement. Firing through the force field was impossible; they would need to loft projectiles over it. Collins and three other men crouched as they ran forward and took up overwatch positions at the edge of the tree line. They would cover Jak until she made it into the Orthodoxan trenches. The last two men approached the pylon at a run. When they reached the base, one pulled out his entrenching tool and hastily dug at a loose pile of dirt abutting the pylon. The other man watched intently, pistol drawn and a large set of bolt cutters clutched in his other hand. Their position was the most exposed, but they moved with the ease of much practice. The first man reached into the hole he had dug and pulled out a thick wire. From experience, Jak knew that the wire was thicker than her thumb. He sat back and held the wire stretched between his fists. After a quick pause to holster his pistol and slip on a pair of thick, insulated gloves, the other man snipped the wire in half with the bolt cutters. The force field winked out between the pylons.

Ackerley slapped Jak on the shoulder. "That's your cue," he snapped.

Jak took off at a sprint. She dashed down the side of the small hill, hoisting the pack containing her ghillie suit and supplies over her shoulder as she ran.

"Go get 'em!" She heard Collins half shout to her as she passed him. Even had she cared to, she didn't have time to acknowledge him as she ran on. The success of the insertion operation counted on the force field being interrupted for a short enough time that the Orthodoxans didn't notice its absence. As she passed them, the two men who had brought down the field were already fitting the pylon with a replacement wire that looked identical to the one they had just cut and removed. It would be virtually impossible for the Orthodoxans to tell that their pylon had been tampered with if they chose to look, which they rarely did. She completed her sprint by sliding into an abandoned trench a hundred meters from the force field right as the flickering blue light reappeared behind her. She fetched up against the trench's far wall and stayed there for a couple of moments, breathing hard. With her back against the side of the trench, she could see the top of the field above the crumbling earthen edge.

Jak caught her breath, then headed north through the trench running parallel to the force field. The Orthodoxans had abandoned these trenches not long after they had put up their electric wall. From the top of the escarpment, Devonite artillery had pounded the trenches severely after the completion of the fence. The Orthodoxans had been forced to retreat to their bunkers and outposts outside the range of the light artillery. Neither side used heavy artillery often. The shells were extremely expensive and since satellites for both sides had been knocked out of the sky early in the civil war, heavy artillery wasn't particularly accurate. Unless a target could be painted with a laser, using it was at best an expensive shot in the dark.

She moved quickly but cautiously. Jak had occasionally come across evidence of Orthodoxans in their trench system. She didn't want to run into a patrol so she kept her eyes and ears peeled. She would have wagered that she knew these trenches better than the Orthodoxans did. This area was one of her favorite insertion points. Her family's home hadn't been far from this area, just a little further north and east. She just needed to follow the trench system north and west until it met the foothills and she could disappear into the heavily forested hills. She grinned. The forests beckoned her on and she sped up a little bit. In the trees she would be able to be herself in a way she couldn't when she was "home." With still more speed, she ran toward her sanctuary. Bron's absence to her left throbbed in her consciousness. She'd heard that men who lost limbs could sometimes feel them even though they were long gone. Entering the field without her brother still felt wrong, but at the same time, it felt like he was still there. She put his absence out of her mind or tried to. She could think of other things, but Bron's absence always weighed on the edge of her awareness.

* * *

Jak leaned against a tree's trunk, feet planted firmly on the branch stretching out in front of her. She paid no heed to the forty meters between it and the ground. The forest and trees were her second home. As a child she'd spent more waking hours in them than she had in the house in which she'd been born and grown to adulthood. Her attention was on the boxy building in front of her. It had taken her the expected three days to reach the sector where Hutchinson's so-called palace was located. Her tree lay just outside the wall enclosing his compound. She wasn't sure if the Orthodoxans were stupid or lazy, but they hadn't bothered to clear the forest on the other side of the wall. Being days from the front was no excuse to get so lax. Still, if they were going to hand her advantages she would certainly take them. The question now was…which one?

From her vantage point, she could see the back of the main building. A long balcony lined the second floor, and a lavish deck ran the length of the first. Through the infrared scope, every detail was visible even though night had fallen almost completely. When her gaze passed over the series of lonely outbuildings to the side of the house, her mouth tightened. She knew what those buildings represented and they made her sick.

In the back of her mind, Jak was aware that her window of opportunity was rapidly closing. As was typical in the mountains, darkness was falling rapidly. She'd hoped to arrive with more daylight to properly scope out the compound's defenses, but it had taken her longer than she'd thought to negotiate the last leg of the mountains. The forecasted storm would hit sometime in the wee hours of the morning and she wanted to be long gone by then. Even the Orthodoxans, though they were criminally incompetent, would be able to track her through mud. She needed to kill the offworld smuggler and get back to friendly territory in a hurry to avoid the inclement weather.

The branch she was on stretched over the wall, offering one way to get into the compound. The four-story drop didn't faze her, but getting out would be difficult, given the height of the wall and the security measures at its top.

She surveyed the area in front of her more closely and snorted out loud. The undergrowth had been allowed to grow wild from the wall almost to the deck at the back of the house. The

Orthodoxans probably thought that was all right since the plants were less than half a meter high and the ground sloped toward the deck. They'd still left her more than enough cover in which to conceal herself. They were practically begging her to come in and off their important visitor. She smiled mirthlessly; she was happy to oblige them on that count.

From her left she caught a flicker of movement coming her way. Through her scope she watched an older soldier amble along the base of the wall. He was probably about forty years old, which for an Orthodoxan was impressive. Most enlisted men didn't survive that long unless they caught someone's eye. Maybe he'd impressed Hutchinson, which didn't say much for him. She swung her rifle to her right and sighted on another, much younger soldier coming into view from the opposite direction. Exactly forty-five minutes had elapsed from the last time these two passed, and almost exactly forty-five minutes since the pass before that. The men's paths along the outside of the wall crossed, and they stopped to chat almost directly beneath her perch. Even though she was a fair way up the tree, she was able to hear what they said without having to engage her auditory implant.

"All clear, Mercer?" the first one asked.

"Of course it is," Mercer replied. "We're so far from the front that the Devonites can't be bothered to show their faces."

The older man snorted. "They don't have to. We walled them out and ourselves in. They just sit there and take potshots at us over the fence from the top of that bloody cliff and we just have to bend over and take it."

"How long did you serve at the front?"

"Fifteen years. I'd still be there if I hadn't pulled the colonel's ass out of the fire."

"Really?" The unnamed soldier looked impressed. "I didn't know you served with the Adonis. Is it true that he was a hardass?"

"You wouldn't believe what he was capable of by the way he is now. He terrorized those Devonites, terrorized not a few of his own men too. But he got the job done and killed a shit-ton of those bastards while he was at it. Then he had the by-blow of one of the Supreme Congress flogged and got pulled from the front. Probably would have been strung up if he hadn't made himself into a damned war hero. So he got assigned to the middle of nowhere to coordinate troop and supply movements. He thrived under pressure out there. I'm sure he's been going stir-crazy the last three years. Nothing ever happens here."

"Sounds like he'll get some action tonight." Mercer sniggered nastily. "That bitch's been holding out on him for three days now, but the guys in the barracks are convinced he'll close the deal real soon."

The older man nodded. "A good thing too. He's being a pain in the ass. Getting some should relax him. His regular girls can't even keep him satisfied."

Jak marveled that one of Hutchinson's women had been giving him the runaround. She had no clue why he would put up with one of his breeders withholding sex. From what she knew of the Orthodoxans, that kind of behavior usually resulted in a woman being sent back to the breeding pens in the cities. Being a breeder at a compound like this would be no picnic, but being in a city's breeding pen would be infinitely worse.

"Well, I'm crossing my fingers," Mercer said. "Maybe when he's done we'll get a piece. She doesn't know her place, she's uppity as hell and way too damn tall, but that won't matter when she's on her back with her legs spread."

The other man elbowed him. "Keep those hopes to yourself until you're invited. The colonel has special plans for this one, or he wouldn't have gone to the trouble of taking so much time with her."

Mercer shrugged, pivoted on his heel and marched back off the way he'd come. The older man shook his head and went in the opposite direction. Jak waited for them to disappear from sight and slung her rifle across her back. She'd stowed her pack a couple of hours' walk away. She might need to leave in a hurry and she hadn't wanted to worry about it slowing her down if she had to run for it. She had enough rations on her to last her a day, and she hadn't needed the stims yet. Those would be most helpful on her way back to the front. She had snatched some sleep as she needed it here and there on her trek in, but if she was being followed she wouldn't be able to rely on doing that during the slog back.

She shimmied down the trunk. The numerous hand and footholds in the tree's rough bark made for an easy scramble down to the ground. She was careful not to snag the ghillie suit on exposed branches or rougher patches of bark. Leaving chunks of the suit behind could expose her prematurely.

While she'd listened to two soldiers gossiping, night had fallen completely. She could make out the top of the wall by the glowing blue barbed wire. The sky to the northeast was barely tinged with the brilliant blue remains of sunset. She toggled on her ocular implant's night vision capabilities and rummaged along the wall's base. From her perch, she thought she'd seen a likely spot. Her hands came in contact with a pile of loose dirt. Carefully she scooped it away from the wall with her bare hands and exposed a section of duracrete below the surface. She reached into one of the ghillie suit's capacious inner pockets and pulled out a small explosive charge and detonator. She molded the malleable charge into a half circle and placed it against the wall along the top of burrow she'd made. After covering the charge with the dirt she had dug out, she retreated behind her tree. Hopefully, those two yahoos were out of earshot. Gaining entry was usually the most risky part of the operation for her, more so now that she didn't have her brother to watch her back. Jak hunkered down and pressed the button on the detonator.

A muffled thump hit her in the chest, followed moments later by the pitter-pat of dirt raining down onto the leaves under the tree. She froze for a couple of moments and engaged the auditory enhancement feature on her aural implant. When she didn't hear any shouts of alarm or footsteps approaching at a run, she slid back out to inspect her handiwork.

Just below ground level there was now a hole in the wall, one a little wider than she was. She crouched, gathered as much of the loose dirt as she could and shoved it through the hole in front of her, then eeled her way through the narrow opening. She was able to clear it without losing chunks of her ghillie suit, though she did have to excavate a little bit on the other side. Fortunately, undergrowth obscured the hole she'd blown in the base there. Having the vegetation there was sloppy and if it wasn't for the fact that it was making her job a lot easier, she would have been livid.

As soon as she reached the other side, she took the dirt she'd accumulated and pushed it loosely into the hole behind her. She hoped it would disguise the hole she had blown in the hard-packed ground. With a little luck, the soldiers wouldn't know it was there unless one of them stepped in it.

Satisfied that she was unlikely to be discovered that way, she proceeded through the brush toward the back of the house. She moved at a painfully slow crawl, taking pains to ensure that her head, back and rump never broke the line of the plant matter through which she proceeded. Any definable shape silhouetted against the wall could potentially give her away. She crawled roughly parallel to the wall until she was situated directly behind the back of the house, a quarter of the way down the slope that led from the wall to the mansion's back deck. She paused there long enough to unsling the rifle from her back. The deck was about three hundred meters from her current position to the house, an easy shot for her. Toggling off her own night vision, she switched on the scope's IR feature and swept the area for enemy sentries. She counted eight of them arranged around the edifice's flat roof. As she watched, one of the four closest to her craned his neck over the side of the roof and looked down at the deck then nodded to the other three. The four of them wandered to the opposite side of the roof and met up with their counterparts. To her surprise one of them broke out a bottle and they shared swigs of what she assumed was alcohol. She shook her head. She knew they were three days from the fighting and that the Orthodoxans were lazy as hell, but this was getting ridiculous.

She moved her scope down to see what the soldier had looked at before he and his compatriots abandoned their posts. The doors to the deck were wide open and light was streaming through them. Two figures stood against the deck's railing. She dialed in the scope and zoomed in. The one on the right with the perfect hair and broad shoulders was obviously Hutchinson. He stood too close to the other figure, probably the offworld smuggler. Jak zoomed in further to get a look at the man she'd been sent to kill. As Hutchinson casually tried to put a hand over his guest's, he shifted to the side and into full view.

Jak felt like she'd been kicked in the gut. The offworld smuggler was female and she was gorgeous. From the twist of her lips she also had no interest in Hutchinson's advances.

What the hell was she supposed to do now? She didn't want to kill the woman. She'd never killed a woman before. While she had no problems killing Orthodoxans, this was no Orthodoxan. They deserved what they got and she was more than happy to give them a bullet between the eyes. But a woman? Her finger hovered over the trigger, then withdrew for a moment before resting on it again. Her orders were clear: kill the offworld smuggler. But no one had told she was female. Cold sweat broke out on her forehead as she wrestled with her orders, caught squarely on the horns of her dilemma.

There was something about her, a look of disdain for her current company. Jak seized on that detail. Maybe she could turn this around. Her orders were to kill the tall, curvaceous smuggler, but there were other ways to take out an asset. She breathed slowly and carefully through her mental struggle. Her heart hammered so hard it felt like her entire body quivered in time with the beats. She needed to keep her heart rate down. Command and Intel, especially McCullock, wanted a dead merchant, but maybe she could salvage the situation without killing her. They didn't know what the smuggler could offer them, but if it was good enough for the Orthodoxans, it could bring an advantage to the Devonites instead. The longer she argued with herself, the less she wanted to shoot the smuggler. She watched as the woman sidled away from Hutchinson once more. His face had started to harden. Jak knew that he wouldn't let the woman's use to him as a supplier keep him much longer from what he really wanted.

Her mind made up, Jak slung her rifle back over her shoulder and crawled down the slope toward the deck, her pace markedly quicker than the slow and careful stalk she'd taken to the top of the incline. The bright lights that poured through the open door would cause night blindness on the part of anybody inside and she didn't have to worry about the sentries on the roof. When she reached her destination, she pulled out the rifle once again and screwed a silencer to the end of the barrel. Her range was so short that the minor inaccuracy added to the shot by the silencer wouldn't be a problem. She was less than fifteen meters away and this was a shot she could have made blindfolded. She assumed a prone position behind the stump of a stunted sapling and calmed her breathing and her heart rate. Hutchinson came into view in her sights and she centered the crosshairs in the middle of his forehead. She inhaled deeply, then exhaled slowly, sticking the tip of her tongue out between her teeth and biting down gingerly. She squeezed the trigger.

CHAPTER FOUR

Torrin looked down her nose at the sentry in front of her. "Please thank the colonel for his kindness, but I'm afraid I won't be wearing his gift."

She had less than two hours before she would be forced to endure another dinner meeting with Hutchinson. He was unfailingly polite and gallant, a welcome reprieve from the suffocating attentions of Major Yonkman. However, he periodically moved into her space and tried to touch her. Never in a threatening manner but always there. She tried to make allowances for cultural differences. Many planets, especially ones with ample populations, had limited ideas of personal space. Her own preferences tended in the opposite direction. If she could touch someone with an outstretched hand, they were too close. Hutchinson's mannerisms, while a little off-putting, weren't nearly as bad as those of Yonkman and the others. They never looked her in the face, and if they addressed her at all, their remarks were usually made to her breasts.

The boy at her door couldn't have been more than eighteen. It looked as though he'd barely started shaving, though it was hard to tell since his hair was a platinum blond so light it was almost white.

His uniform was immaculately pressed; the boots shone with a mirror finish. His eyes were a pale blue almost as light as his hair and they bored into her with a frightening intensity that revealed a passion that verged on zealotry.

"The colonel would like you to wear this to your 'planning' dinner tonight," he repeated, the quotes practically audible, holding up the hanger again. She supposed they all thought she was sleeping with him. Hutchinson had hinted around the idea but hadn't pushed her on it. Apparently, he still hadn't figured out he was barking up the wrong tree; the thought of having sex with a man was enough to turn her stomach.

She reached out, gingerly slid the proffered dress from the hanger and held it in front of her. While she had no doubt that she would indeed look stunning in it, she didn't care for the dress. The fabric was clingy, and it would have dripped off every curve of her body. Wearing something in the native costume of the planet would put her at a disadvantage in their ongoing negotiations. Her clothing currently served as a reminder that she was different, that she could provide him with goods from offworld that nobody else could.

"Maybe the colonel is concerned that you're starting to stink." The little blond boy sneered as he spoke. He looked her up and down, then leaned ostentatiously away from her.

Torrin had been stuck in Hutchinson's mansion for three days now. The longer she'd stuck around, the worse the locals' behavior had become. She stepped closer to the soldier until she was practically on top of him. She raised her hand to tuck an errant strand of hair behind her ear, and he flinched. Clearly he'd heard about the damage she'd wrought on the soldier who'd accosted her in the sitting room. The colonel appeared to have responded to the incident quickly and sharply; she hadn't seen the injured man since. Still, if she hadn't broken his hand for attempting to do more than gawk at her, she was convinced the others wouldn't be accepting her demurrals of their company now.

The other guard moved forward and shoved his rifle between her and the blond, not so incidentally bouncing the barrel off her ribs as he did so. He was older and while he didn't have the same zealous light in his eyes that his companion did, his face was set in determined lines.

"You should go back in your room" he said flatly.

"Oh, I know. I'm just *so* safe with you here to protect me from those *nasty* Devonites," Torrin gushed and sidled over toward the older soldier. She stopped right in front of him, just centimeters away. She towered over him also. He leaned away from her perceptibly.

"You need to get back in there," he repeated, his voice heated.

"I'm going, I'm going." She probably shouldn't be torturing her guards, but it passed the time and their presence was ridiculous. She was well aware that they were there less for her protection and more for her captivity. After a brief mental struggle where she considered drawing her plasma pistol, she discarded the idea. Though the pistol was more advanced by far than their primitive weaponry, she would be no match for both of them as well as the guards at the end of the hall. Those two watched the confrontation with her guards through disapproving expressions.

Torrin lingered a moment longer to heighten the soldier's discomfort, then swept back into her room, closing the door behind her. The bedroom was large and luxurious; no expense had been spared in its decoration or furnishing. Scrollwork and gilt decorated the wall, the ceilings and every available surface on the furniture. The furniture was very heavy and looked to have been made for a man's taste with its dark, earthy tones. Windows lined one wall, and while she could open them, she'd given up on the idea of using them as an escape route. More of the now-ubiquitous sentries were posted under the windows and though she'd monitored their movements closely, she hadn't yet discovered any weaknesses in their routes or timing.

The windows kept the room from becoming too suffocating, giving her a breathtaking view of tree-covered mountains topped by the stunning blue of the sky. Even the storms in this place were beautiful, she'd discovered; heavy blue-purple clouds piled on top of each other, up and up, until they covered the area in a dark avalanche of cumulonimbus clouds. The lightning's white fire lit them up in shades of electric purple and blue which was fantastic during the day and at night was one of the most gorgeous scenes she'd ever seen on any planet. She shivered at the memory of the storm she'd watched over the mountains the previous night and rubbed her hands briskly over the goose bumps that rose on her arms.

Torrin tossed the dress onto the bed and, peeling off her clothing, she headed for the adjoining bathroom. It boasted a water shower, which had taken some getting used to. She was more accustomed to sonic showers, but there was a definite hedonistic appeal to having warm water running down her body. The soap added a delightful slipperiness to her skin, and she grinned as she contemplated additional uses for the slick substance.

She cranked the shower's spray to a hair below its hottest setting and stepped in. The pulsing jet of water pounded some of the tension out of her muscles. Her back was especially stiff. She leaned forward and planted her palms against the far wall and simply stood there, for how long she didn't know. Eventually, she turned and started in on the business of cleaning herself. She grimaced as she sluiced the water through her hair. The little blond sentry had a point, she admitted to herself. Things had gotten a little ripe. The only solution to that, however, was to change out of the jumpsuit she'd arrived in, and there was no way in hell she was about to do that. She would have to settle for cleaning herself as meticulously as possible.

A good thirty minutes later she emerged from the bathroom, thoroughly refreshed and wrapped herself in a capacious, fluffy towel. She busily toweled off her wet, now very tangled hair. The sonic showers didn't do the number to her hair that these hydro showers did. She would need to comb her hair for at least ten minutes to return her tresses to some semblance of order. If she was lucky. The hated dress caught her eye where it lay on the bed and she scooped it up, crumpled it into a ball and tossed it into the nearest trash receptacle in one motion. Nodding with satisfaction, she turned and headed to the dresser, where she pulled out a comb and started in on the gargantuan task of untangling her hair. Her reflection stared back at her from the mirror. Once again, she had to smooth out her brow, undoing the furrow that kept appearing above the bridge of her nose. This place was going to give her wrinkles for sure.

After an hour spent recovering from her shower and lounging around the room coming up with ways to amuse herself, there was a peremptory knock at the door to her room. It was pushed open abruptly. The two sentries stood in the doorway, glaring at her.

"Colonel Hutchinson requests the presence of your company at dinner, ma'am," said the older sentry. The blond didn't say anything but smiled unpleasantly and turned, indicating with his arm that she should precede him.

"Of course," Torrin replied. She paused on her way out of the room and picked up her plasma pistol off the dresser and started to belt it to her waist.

"You won't need that, ma'am," the older sentry said quickly.

"The colonel's been very interested in it," she drawled back at him. "It's an example of the weaponry that can be provided for your forces."

"The colonel has expressed his intent that this not be a working dinner. He would like to make dinner about pleasure, not work."

"Well, I'll just bring it along in case he wants to talk business."

The sentry's face hardened once more, and his blond companion gripped his rifle and raised its muzzle slightly, not quite pointing it at her. "I'm afraid I'm going to need to insist. The colonel was very clear. No weapons."

"Fine." Torrin placed the pistol back on top of the dresser and accompanied her guards out of the room, her mind racing. These dinners had always been held under the guise of discussing business, enabling her to steer the conversation back to that subject when Hutchinson had tried to engage in more personal topics. She wasn't sure how much longer he was going to allow her to politely fend him off. Her palms started to sweat; she could feel the walls closing in. This wasn't going to end well. She knew she could demolish the man physically, but if she did so his men would kill her. Unless they decided on a more complicated punishment. She was rapidly running out of options.

Dammit, Neal, she thought. *You could have given me much better background on these assholes.*

She proceeded through the house, attended closely by her armed escort. To her eye, everything seemed more sinister this evening. The men she passed seemed to be watching her more closely, judging her and finding her wanting. Once again she wondered at the total absence of any other women. To the best of her knowledge, she was the only female on the premises. She'd assumed that she would see some women as her unexpected stay lengthened, but so far she had seen none.

They stopped in front of the overly ornate double doors to the dining room. Her personal guard nodded to the two men stationed there. The massive doors groaned as the soldiers muscled them open.

"Miss Ivanov for dinner, sir," the one on the left announced. Torrin was not entirely comfortable with the way he phrased his announcement. It made her sound like she was the main course.

At the head of the long table, Hutchinson rose from his chair and walked over to them. He grasped her hand and brought it to his lips, kissing it soundly. Torrin supposed he thought the action was gallant, but the effect was somewhat ruined by the intensity of his grasp. If he was going to be charming, he really shouldn't have tried to crush her fingers. She smiled faintly in response.

"Torrin, my dear, how are you?" he boomed. He waved the assortment of sentries away. They retreated from the room, closing the doors firmly behind them. Torrin tried not to flinch as the latches clicked shut.

"I'm sure you've been extremely busy trying to clear a path to my vessel through those hordes of enemy fighters," she said, not answering his query.

"Of course, of course," he said absently, tucking her hand in the crook of his elbow and escorting her to the table. Its surface was piled so high with food that she could hardly make out any open space. "My men have been working valiantly on your behalf."

"Please be seated." He pulled out the chair directly to the left of his. As she sat, he pushed it in. She preferred this side of the table to the other. The other side put her back to the windows, which not only made her a little twitchy but didn't afford her the gorgeous view. Windows ran the entire length of the room and looked out onto the wide deck—which itself spilled out onto the slope that went up and met the tree line. During the day, the slope was covered by a stunning display of blue and purple flowering bushes.

"You aren't wearing my gift." Hutchinson interrupted her internal monologue.

"Oh, it was lovely, but it's not really to my taste," she replied blithely. "I'm a woman of simple tastes and it was much too ornate for me."

"I'd have liked to seen you in it." He frowned in disapproval, lips tightening. "I chose it especially for you."

"I appreciate the thought, I really do, but I'm more comfortable in my own clothes," she said firmly. "So where are the charming Major Yonkman and his attendants?"

"Miles won't be joining us tonight. We've talked entirely too much business while you've been our guest. I wanted to show you that there's more to us than just work. Hence the feast."

"It's certainly impressive."

"I'm so glad you approve, I had our chef prepare all sorts of local delicacies." He pushed his chair back and picked up her plate. "I'll just serve you up some choice morsels."

"You don't have to worry about that; I'm happy to serve myself."

"Nonsense," he said, waving the spoon in his hand dismissively at her. Specks of the dark brown gravy in which he'd just smothered a slice of meat flicked off the end of the spoon and splatted onto the table. "I know which dishes are which, and it's my pleasure to introduce you to the best we have to offer."

She wished that all of his statements didn't sound so ominous. Her skin was prickling so much it was a wonder that it hadn't crawled off her body. To hide her discomfort she took a sip from the glass at her elbow and choked when she recognized the spirits that she'd first encountered in the sitting room. After a glance his way to see if he'd noticed, she discreetly poured the offending beverage into a soup tureen by her elbow. Fortunately, Hutchinson was much too busy piling her plate high with food to catch what she'd just done. She poured herself a drink from the carafe just beyond it. She hoped the clear, slightly blue-tinged liquid might be water, but it proved to be more Haefonian whiskey.

"And there you are, Torrin." Hutchinson placed the heaping plate in front of her. The odors that drifted off the mound of food did indeed smell delicious. Her mouth should have watered in anticipation, but she was too anxious to summon up even a drop of saliva.

"I see you're thirsty." He nodded approvingly at the glass in front of her. "Drink as much as you want. Tonight's about fun, not work."

"Of course, Colonel," Torrin said. "I must say the food looks and smells wonderful. I hope I'll get to meet your chef. He must be very accomplished."

Hutchinson strode back to his place at the head of the table and dropped his own plate to the table with a thump. Heeding his own advice, he downed a generous swig from his glass. "Our men do not cook," he replied.

"Then I'd love to meet her," Torrin said, intrigued. This was the first indication she'd gotten that there were any women on the premises.

"That won't be possible. She's extremely busy, especially at night." The colonel dug into his plateful of food with a small smirk. "But we don't want to insult her. Dig in!"

Torrin picked up her knife and fork and cut off a slice of meat slathered in brown gravy. The morsel was delicious and almost melted in her mouth, but it was very salty. She quickly sampled each item on her plate, chatting blithely to Hutchinson about the weather she'd observed from her window. She finally found one dish that didn't seem to be as salty as the others and filled up on that. The occasional sip from her glass gave the appearance that she was drinking but in reality, very little whiskey passed her lips. The colonel had no such compunction; she lost track of how many tumblers of the blue liquid he downed. His naturally pale complexion grew flushed and ruddy from the effects of the alcohol.

"So, Torrin..." He interrupted her in the middle of her point on the loveliness of the cloud formations on Haefen. "How does someone end up in a dangerous profession like smuggling?"

"Please, Colonel," she replied with a professional smile. "I'm not sure what you're getting at."

"Please." He snorted and gestured at her with his knife. "Smuggling is a dangerous job. I'm surprised you're not too delicate for that kind of work."

"I assure you that I'm nothing of the sort. I can handle myself, but it's kind of you to be worried on my behalf." She bared her teeth at him in a poor excuse for a smile.

"Damn right it is. What you need is a keeper. Otherwise you wouldn't be getting yourself into these dangerous situations."

A frisson of fear shot down Torrin's spine. "Dangerous situations? You mean the Devonites who have impeded my progress back to my ship?"

Hutchinson guffawed and heaved himself up out of his chair. He swayed a little bit, but only barely. If she hadn't known how much alcohol he'd consumed, she might have missed it.

"You don't have to worry about them," he said. He strode over to her chair, pulled it away from the table and spun it to face him. His handling of her and the heavy chair were very deft. He leaned down toward her and placed his hands on the edge of the chair's arms, effectively pinning her back into the chair. "I'll protect you."

"That's awfully nice," she gritted out past clenched teeth. "But you don't need to worry on my account."

"That's where you're wrong." He tried to close the distance between their faces, but Torrin turned her head and his questing lips only met her jaw. Fear heightened her reflexes and her foot shot out, sweeping one leg out from under him. As he stumbled to one side, she slid out of the chair in the gap that was created.

"Colonel, you forget yourself," she told him icily. "And I have no interest in you or any of your men. In fact, I have no interest in men, period."

Hutchinson laughed, braying his amusement. "A dyke? We haven't had any of those lately. I knew you'd be spirited. I look forward to breaking you. When I'm done with you, you won't even think of women again, you'll be addicted to this." He reached down and cupped himself crudely through his pants.

"You do this and you won't be getting any tech from me," she threatened in desperation.

"That's all right," he shot back blithely, taking a step toward her. "We found your ship earlier today. Once we get into it, one of our old pilots will fly it off this place and we'll get our own tech."

Good luck with that, she thought. Tien wouldn't let them in and would lock the whole ship down; they'd never be able to fly it off planet. Every fiber in her body screamed at her to run, to escape. She sidled away from him, and he closed the distance between them in a leap, any trace of his earlier inebriation all but gone. She needed to get him out the door, but he had her arm in a steel grip. He brought his lips down atop hers, crushing her own lips cruelly against her teeth until she tasted blood and had to open her mouth. His tongue plunged into her mouth, stabbing into its depths while she tried not to gag. His other hand grabbed her by the rump and pulled her closer against him where she could feel his hardness pressing into her hip. When he finally came up for air, she sagged against him as if suddenly faint.

"Wow," she moaned, "that was amazing. No one's ever kissed me like that. I didn't know it could be so good."

"That's because you've never had a real man," he said, full of pride at his prowess. "Once you've been with a real man, you'll never go back to women."

"It's so hot in here," she said, still hanging off him. "I feel like I'm going to pass out. Can we go somewhere cooler? I'd hate to faint and miss this."

"Of course, my dear," he said, magnanimous in victory. He was still pressed up against her, grinding painfully against her. "Let's go onto the terrace."

Perfect, she thought. With an escape route, she'd have a fighting chance. "That would be nice" was all she said as he disengaged from her.

He kept a grip on her elbow and escorted her to the large glass doors that led out onto the deck. He reached past her, not-so-subtly grazing the side of her breast with his arm, and pushed open the door onto the massive deck that ran the length of the back of the house. She preceded him out into the night. The cool air was a welcome reprieve from the oppressive closeness of the dining room. He let go of her to close the door behind him, and she made her way to the railing. She needed to incapacitate him somehow so he couldn't chase her into the night. The fastest route away from the house looked to be up the hill. She couldn't make out the wall in the dark, but she knew that in daylight she would have just been able to see it.

Hutchinson came up and stood behind and to the side of her. He put his hand down on top of hers. She turned her head away from him and grimaced in disgust. He put his other hand around her waist and tried to pull her closer as she leaned away. Feeling her resistance, he jerked her against him and leaned over to whisper in her ear.

"You know, I will have you one way or the other." His breath, heavy with alcohol, made her eyes water. "It will be so much better for you if you can come to enjoy my touch. With me, you would be first among my favored women, but if you can't bring yourself to be with me after we finish, I can always give you to my men. They'll use you without any consideration." He trailed a hand across her arm, up to her shoulder. "Aside from the aberrant dyke streak that I'm going to take care of, I can tell you have strong blood. I can't wait to see the sons you will give me."

She grasped his hand where it rested on her shoulder and looked over her shoulder and into his leering eyes. As she opened her mouth to respond to him, his forehead disappeared in a gout of blood, bone and brain matter. His eyes, glassy and wide in blank surprise, held hers as he toppled slowly backward and hit the deck's planking with a thud.

Torrin stood there, rooted to the ground, shocked. Dazed, she wiped clumsily at the blood that speckled the side of her face. She caught movement from the corner of her eye and looked out into the darkness. Just inside the edge of the light cast by the dining room windows a bush stood up and separated itself from the shrubbery around it. An arm reached out and pushed a hood down and she looked into the grim face of an absurdly young man.

"You need to come with me," he whispered harshly. He leveled a huge gun at her. The muzzle's bore yawned at her and she couldn't rip her eyes from it. "Now."

CHAPTER FIVE

After Hutchinson's sudden death at her side, it took Torrin a moment to follow what the man was saying. He jerked his head to the side, gesturing for her to join him. She wiped again at the blood on her face, then numbly climbed over the rail. Her captor lunged forward and grabbed her forearm, then dragged her up the slope while keeping an eye on the house behind them. Torrin was surprised that the house hadn't swarmed with angry activity when Hutchinson's forehead had exploded, but no one seemed to have noticed. The compound was eerily silent as she was hustled away from it. Her pace slowed when she glanced over her shoulder.

"Keep moving, keep moving," her captor (rescuer?) whispered harshly and propelled her forward with a jostle to the small of her back. He ran easily while she stumbled the rest of the way up the slope. The bushes and undergrowth caught at her feet, always threatening to slow her down or to trip her up completely. He had no such problem, even with the long strips of fabric attached to his clothes. He never seemed to get hung up and constantly pushed and urged her faster up the slope.

"Shit, a blind man could follow this trail," he muttered, and Torrin wondered if he was admonishing her. She was too stunned by the sudden turn of events to do more than wonder. "Can't be helped. They'll figure it out fast enough."

They reached the top of the slope, and he dragged her along the wall, keeping a close eye on its base as they moved.

"Dig here." He stopped and gestured at a mound of dirt. She stared at him numbly, not understanding. Incongruously, she noticed how short he was now that they stood next to each other. She hadn't noticed anybody this diminutive among Hutchinson's men.

"For the love of—" he snapped. "Pay attention!" He kicked the mound and dirt sprayed off the pile. "I can't watch our backs and dig this out. You need to do it. Now!"

The urgency in his voice snapped her out of her daze and she knelt, shoveling dirt out of the way with both hands. Even though it was loosely packed, the dirt caught at her nails and tore them, but she kept digging as if her life depended on it. The mound dwindled quickly to reveal a narrow tunnel, not much more than a hole really, under the wall. She widened it as much as she could before the hard pack of the sides prevented her from increasing its size any further.

"Get through it," he said, gesturing with the muzzle of his rifle. She eyed the opening dubiously. The small tunnel didn't look wide enough even for her shoulders. She dropped to her belly, but he grabbed her shoulder, bringing her to a stop. "Don't even think of taking off once you get through. Run and I'll just let your friends track you down. For all they know, you took out their precious colonel."

"You have no idea—"

"Just get going." Once again, that hand propelled her forward, this time wrapped around her belt and heaving her off the ground. "We don't have time for chitchat."

She snorted but crawled forward into the hole. Of all the nerve, he'd started it. Hell, he'd dragged her along. His target was dead; he didn't need her. Her hair snagged on the tunnel's rough walls and she whispered a curse. With a jerk of her head and a flash of pain, she tore out the trapped strands. She had a moment of difficulty when her shoulders proved too wide for the tunnel's walls. There was sudden warmth along her back as her short captor covered her body with his, and she had a momentary flash of panic until she realized he was pushing her left shoulder down into a small gap.

That did it and she was swiftly freed up and scrambling out the other side. She moved to the right of the opening and leaned her back against the wall, trying to get her bearings and hoping her eyes would soon adjust to the dark. He popped out through the opening and took a quick look up and down the length of the wall.

"I don't believe it. We're still in the clear." In his surprise he sounded less harsh. His voice was surprisingly light. He cleared his throat. "Come on, we can't let up now." The harsh whisper was back, and a hand wrapped around her arm in an unbreakable grip, pulling her away from her resting place. They sprinted into the woods.

It was dark among the trees. He ran on, unconcerned by the impenetrable blackness. She hadn't noticed any night vision equipment and she wondered how he could see. She came back to herself painfully as she tripped and went down hard, skidding a few meters down the slope on her belly. Pain brought her back to reality in a hurry. The further they got from Hutchinson's compound, the steeper and more challenging the terrain was getting.

She wondered if they were far enough from the compound that she'd be able to contact Tien. Having the AI's take on the situation would help, as would any extra information she could supply. Torrin reached for the subdermal transmitter behind her ear and missed grabbing onto a branch to steady herself on the downslope. She crashed into her captor's back.

"Watch yourself," he said. She was beginning to hate the growl of his voice. It goaded her, pushed her. Torrin just wanted to rest, to close her eyes for a few moments and stop moving, but he was always there relentlessly moving her forward. His hands hooked under her armpits and pulled her up to a sitting position.

"Let's sit a couple of minutes," he said. He examined the side of the tree before plopping himself down beside her. Her eyes had adjusted to the gloom some time ago, but it was so oppressively dark that she couldn't make out much beyond the pale oval of his face. She had noticed a narrow triangle carved lightly into the bark of the tree. He'd run his fingers along it as if making sure it was there before he'd joined her.

"Thanks," she panted. "I like to think I'm in pretty good shape, but this is brutal."

He laughed without humor. "This is nothing compared to how brutal your Orthodoxans'll be if they catch us. They'll probably shoot me on sight, but you they'll take their time with."

"They aren't my anything," she sputtered. "They've been holding me captive for three days. I would have been long gone if your people hadn't launched an attack and blocked my way back to my ship."

"We haven't had any major operations behind the fence in years. If someone blocked the way to your ship, it wasn't us."

"Of course," she whispered. "He lied about all of it, just to get into my ship and my pants."

"It's what they do." His growl softened, "Did he—"

"No!" Torrin interrupted quickly. "Not for lack of trying, but I held him off and then you…finished things."

"Good." He stood up and held his hand out to her. "Time to keep moving. The weather's going to take a turn any moment now, and we need to be as far as we can when that happens. When all this dirt goes to mud it'll be even harder to move in. Then even they'll be able to track our every move."

She sighed and grasped his hand and he heaved her to her feet. For such a short guy, he had some muscle behind him. He took her shoulders and turned her, pushing her ahead of him once more. She broke into a stumbling run, trusting him to keep an eye on what was coming up and to guide her around it. The first time she got some time alone, she had to reach out to Tien. She hoped there would be some way to do that without alerting him to her ability. The last thing she needed was yet another group going after her ship.

About thirty minutes later, as far as she could tell, he snagged her elbow and pulled her to a stop. She didn't ask why, just let her legs fold under her and collapsed into a sitting position. The muscles in her calves and thighs screamed at her. The burning was only somewhat alleviated by getting off her feet.

"Wait here," he said roughly. "And don't go anywhere."

"I know, I know, or the Orthodoxans will eat me."

"Just so's you know" was all he said. Torrin heard scrabbling and looked up just in time to see him disappear up the tree, and she shuddered. She didn't know how high the lowest branches were, but from the other Haefonian trees she'd seen, she knew they were a long way up. The idea of being that far from the ground without any kind of safety harness made her vaguely queasy. Being many miles higher in a spaceship didn't bother her at all. She trusted the thrusters and hull of the vessel more than she trusted her own balance at thirty meters. Now that she was on her own in the dark she wished he would come back quickly. The blackness seemed to press in on her. Now that she wasn't running for her life, she could hear all sorts of noises in the dark.

She pressed on the transmitter behind her ear. "Tien, do you read?"

There was a short burst of static and she almost wept to hear the AI's slightly mechanical tones.

"I am receiving your transmission, Torrin. Are you well?"

"As well as can be expected after what's been going on." In low tones, with frequent glances up the tree where her captor had just disappeared she recounted the events of the last few days. "How are you holding up?"

"I am also as well as can be expected, Torrin. The Orthodoxans have located the ship, but their tools are woefully inadequate to the task of penetrating my hull without destroying it. They seem unwilling to cause permanent damage at this point." The AI sounded mildly perturbed but exhibited nothing like real concern.

"Stay put and locked down," Torrin ordered. She was alerted to the return of her unnamed captor by the sound of more scrabbling. "I need to sign off. I'll contact you as soon as I'm able."

He dropped the last couple of meters and landed next to her. He dropped a rucksack by her feet and sat down on the huge root she leaned against.

"Hungry?" he asked.

"Not in the least," she said, feeling her gorge rise in response to the question. "I had quite enough before you blew Hutchinson's head off, thanks anyway."

"If you say so." He popped open the bag and rummaged through it until he found some food to his liking and munched away noisily.

"I wouldn't say no to some water, though."

He unclipped a flask off the side of the bag and tossed it to her. She struggled for a moment with the bottle's unfamiliar spout.

"Just squeeze," he advised. She tilted her head back and squeezed the sides of the bottle. As the stream of water hit her mouth she realized how parched she'd become. Between the saltiness of her dinner and their flight through the woods, she was incredibly thirsty. She greedily gulped down mouthful after mouthful of water.

"Watch it, we only have so much. You'll get a stitch if you drink too much."

She nodded and gasped as she came up for air.

"Thanks, that's just what I needed," she said. "So what's your name, anyway? I could just call you 'Hey You,' but that seems a little disrespectful for someone who pulled my ass out of the fire."

"Wouldn't want you to feel disrespectful," he snorted. "Call me Jak."

"Torrin."

"It's good to meet you, Torrin," Jak replied formally.

"Likewise." She laughed, struck by the absurdity of their formality. "I'd curtsy, but my legs are a little shot."

"I hate to do this, Torrin, but we have to move. We've got a long way ahead of us to get back on the right side of the fence. It'll be way easier if we don't have a mob of pissed off Orthodoxans breathing down our necks."

She sighed and took his hand and allowed him to haul her to her feet. Her legs screamed in protest, but she pushed on into the dark.

They hadn't gone more than twenty paces when a bright flash lit the night and seared an afterimage of the surrounding trees into her retinas. Right on the heels of the flash an immense peal of thunder boomed out so loudly that she could have sworn that her teeth vibrated.

"Oh shit," she heard Jak say. He turned her way to say something further, but whatever he had to say was drowned out by the rain that thundered down through the trees. In a matter of moments her hair was soaked and plastered to her head and neck. Fortunately, her jumpsuit was waterproof, but that didn't stop every inch of exposed skin from being drenched instantly. Jak grabbed her and dragged her closer to him, pulling her down so that her ear was by his mouth.

"You have to follow me," he shouted over the roar of the rain. "We need to stay on stable ground. Our trail won't be as obvious and it'll be much safer. The weather's really going to slow us down, but it'll do the same for them. Walk only where I walk and be careful!"

He started off at a much reduced pace, testing each step before he trusted his weight to it. As soon as Torrin took her first step, she understood his caution. The dirt was liquefying rapidly, and each step was considerably more treacherous than the last. Her feet threatened to slide out from under her constantly. She had more luck when she learned to walk directly in his footsteps, but the length of his pace was shorter than hers, and she would occasionally miss a footprint. When they started heading downhill, she had even more trouble.

Lightning split the sky without surcease and peals of thunder followed so closely that she knew the bolts were right overhead. The driving rain wouldn't let up and even the shortest distances became insurmountable obstacles. Mud alternately sucked at her feet or slipped out from under them. She thought she'd been tired during their frantic dash through the trees, but this tortuous snail's pace ground her down even more quickly. What little night vision she'd managed to gain was wiped out by lightning flashes, but she took advantage of each flash to glance ahead to see Jak's back as he carefully made his way forward.

"Jak," she called when he started getting too far ahead. "Jak!" She shouted louder when he didn't stop. "Dammit, Jak!" He was too far ahead and the thunder and rain were drowning her out. She picked up her pace to catch up to him. As she struggled forward, she realized that his footprints were being washed away and she watched with horror as the last visible print disappeared just as she placed her own foot down on top of it. She froze in place and waited tensely for the next lightning flash. When it came, all it revealed was forest all around her and no sign of her captor. Unsure what to do, she hesitated. Should she stay put and hope he'd come back for her or try to catch up to him in the direction she thought he'd gone? Torn between both options she waited. A particularly close clap of thunder made up her mind. She couldn't hang around any longer. She needed to keep moving. She gritted her teeth and pushed off in the direction she'd last seen Jak.

Between one flash and the next he appeared in front of her.

"What are you doing?" he yelled over the rain. "You're going the wrong way!"

"What am I doing?" she shot back, incredulous. "You took off. I couldn't see you. It's dark, it's raining and I don't know these woods!"

"Here." He grabbed her hand and pulled her along with him. His hand was warm over hers and surprisingly petite. It was also as rough as his voice. No wonder he had no problems climbing trees; his palms practically felt like tree bark. She stumbled along behind him into the darkness again.

They slogged on through the mud and the rain. After a few hours the thunder and lightning slacked off. The rain remained constant, however, and the mud continued to slow their progress. Jak dragged her, sometimes literally, for hours. He was like a machine. He never flagged, always sure of his footing and always there to steady her steps. She wasn't sure which was worse, going uphill or down. Uphill required all of her strength and energy to keep lurching forward, but downhill sapped her remaining reserves as she tried to keep from slipping and sliding down through the trees. She noticed that even in these trying circumstances Jak left very little trail. She, on the other hand, broke off branches, turned over rocks and scraped gouges into the sides of trees. Even the most novice tracker would have no problem picking up her trail. Jak didn't say anything, though he did look back occasionally and shrug as if to say there was nothing he could do about it.

The longer they went, the more resentful she became. This man was the reason for her discomfort and exhaustion. Him and Neal. Next time she saw her informant, she was going to kill him, slowly and inventively. She allowed her mind to wander among the various scenarios she concocoted for Neal's demise.

A trickle of cold water had worked its way down the neck of her jumpsuit and she turned her ire on the real villain of the piece. He'd pulled her out of a warm, dry house and into this cold, wet, hellish existence. His stoic demeanor only soured her mood toward him further, and every time he so much as glanced at a sign of her passage she wanted to scream. When the sky began to lighten, Torrin finally stopped dead in her tracks and dug in her heels. Jak managed to pull her a half meter through the mud before he realized she had stopped.

"I'm not moving another meter," she announced. "I'm exhausted and my legs are ready to give out. I'm soaked to the bone and I'm freezing."

Jak grinned up at her and she reddened in fury.

"I don't give a crap if you can keep going for three days and nights on an empty stomach and no sleep," she spat, cutting him off as he opened his mouth. "Unless there's a bed and a hot meal at the end of it, I'm not moving another step."

"You done?" he asked, cocking an eyebrow at her. He let go of her hand and drew the back of his hand across his forehead, smearing a streak of blue mud into his hairline. "We're almost to the last camp I made on the way to the house. We can hole up there for a few hours and rest up."

"Oh." It was all she could think to say in response. He recaptured her hand and started off through the mud again.

"I have to say, I'm surprised how well you've been keeping up," he said as he forged forward. "You're doing way better than I thought you would."

"What's that supposed to mean? Because I'm female, I couldn't possibly keep up with a big strong manly man like you?"

"Well, no—"

"Because I don't have chest hair that means that I'm less worthy."

"I don't really have any chest hair to speak of mys—"

"You're a piece of work, just like every other man I've seen on this planet. I've run into some misogynistic bastards in the Fringes, but you guys take the cake." She was unprepared for his response when he swung around to face her.

"We're nothing like the Orthodoxans. Our women aren't enslaved and treated like nothing more than breeding stock. We started this fight when they tried to make us live like them, and thirty years later, it's hell, but it's still better than living like that." He practically spat the words at her, his voice growing rougher and more gravelly with each word. "Now come on."

He yanked her after him. Torrin was so shocked by his outburst that she followed him mutely as they climbed up a rocky ridge and walked through a small clearing. At the clearing's far edge, one of the forest's massive trees had come down and had become wedged against another, even more massive tree. Where they met, a natural shelter had been created. As they moved into it, Torrin was surprised at how big the area was and how dry. Another narrow triangle was carved into the base of the tree near the entrance. She doubted she would have even seen it if she hadn't noticed him looking for them on their trek.

"This is nice," she said, looking up at the roof of the shelter a good eight meters above their heads. She noticed he still held her hand and tugged on it. "You can let go now."

"Sorry," he growled and let her hand drop, coloring slightly. He paced to the back of the shelter, set his pack down and rummaged through it. "Hungry."

It was less of a question and more of a statement but Torrin realized she was ravenous. "Yeah."

He tossed her a package and the flask. "It's heats up when you add water. Just pour some in and you'll have a hot meal."

Torrin tore open the package and poured some water into the package and watched with delight as the liquid began to bubble and steam.

"Give these back when you're done," he said, handing her a fork and spoon. "It's the only pair I brought. I wasn't expecting to have to make my way back with one extra."

She dug in greedily. The food was heavenly, and the gulps of water she grabbed between heaping forkfuls of food even more so. As she ate, the knot of resentment in her chest loosened and she found herself hating Jak a little less.

"You weren't?" she asked. "What was your mission exactly then? Were you just there to kill Hutchinson and picking up the offworld smuggler was just a bonus?"

He didn't answer and she looked at him over her package of food. For the first time he looked uncomfortable. He'd killed a man in cold blood, had effectively kidnapped her and then run for hours up and down hills through mud and rain without looking this discomfited.

"I can't answer you, Torrin. It's against regs to discuss a current operation."

"A current operation? It's you and me, Jak. There is no operation."

"Look, I can't talk about it. The less I say before I debrief the better." He still looked uncomfortable, but by the set of his jaw, she knew she wouldn't be getting any further information out of him.

"I need to get out of this suit," Jak announced and stood abruptly. "It's soaked through and feels like it weighs a few hundred kilos." He made his way to the back of the shelter where his rucksack sat and started hauling clothing out of the bag. "How you holding up? You wet?"

"No, my clothing is fine, it's waterproof. But I could use something to dry my hair."

He tossed her a towel. Little more than a washcloth, it was threadbare and almost transparent in places. "Sorry, it's all I have."

She shrugged and did her best to wring the water out of her hair before vigorously rubbing it down with the square of cloth. She came up for air in time to see Jak pulling up a shirt over his shoulders. He had his back to her. She was struck by his slenderness. He was whipcord over bone. The muscles of his shoulders were sharply defined, but his build was almost delicate. He turned around, doing the buttons up almost to his chin and caught her staring. He raised one eyebrow inquiringly in her direction.

"Uh, just wondering if you have a brush or comb?" She wondered at her flustered state. She didn't go for men, never had, but she was stumbling over her words as if she had some sort of schoolgirl crush. Even when she'd been a schoolgirl, she hadn't had schoolgirl crushes. She knew she rode the edge of exhaustion, but it must have been affecting her more than she thought. The pause had gone a little too long. To cover it up she held up a ratted and knotted lock of hair. "My hair has seen better days."

"Sorry." He ran a hand through his own hair, causing it to stick up in all directions. "I don't really need one myself so I didn't pack one." He grinned at her cheekily, and she smiled back in response. *Stop that*, she told herself.

"I'll just have to make do then," she said and cursed herself for the inane response. She ran fingers through her hair, trying to comb out the worst of the snarls by hand.

Jak moved past her toward the mouth of the lean-to, sniper rifle in hand.

"You should rest. I'm going to keep watch," he said over his shoulder. "You'll find a bed of grasses at the back of the shelter. Try to get some sleep." He hunkered down at the mouth.

Torrin stared at Jak, trying to decide how to broach the subject. Finally she decided there was nothing to do but go for it. She'd been getting steadily more uncomfortable and her back teeth were starting to float.

"I need to…see to my necessities."

"What?" Jak turned around to look at her, one eyebrow raised.

"Necessities." Frustrated at his continued look of incomprehension. "I have to relieve myself."

"Oh! I just went when I did the perimeter sweep."

"I'm so happy for you. In case it escaped you, I don't have the same luxury you do."

"I know." He stood up and looked around their shelter. "Well, you can't go here."

"Thank you." Torrin knew her voice was insultingly calm, but she didn't care. She had to go and his dithering wasn't making her any more comfortable. "But if you don't want me to, you're going to need to let me past."

"You're not wandering around out there by yourself."

"And I'm not going to have you standing there like a freak watching me go about my business. Where do you think I'll go, exactly?"

"I have no interest in watching you do your business. I'm not going to let you escape or fall down a ravine or be eaten by one of our local beasties. If you want to go, you're going to have to deal with me being in the area."

"Fine." Torrin pushed by him and back out into the driving rain. She was chilled again almost immediately. She made her way around the deadfall and into the woods. True to his word, Jak followed closely behind. When she headed for a likely bush that was thick enough to provide some privacy, Jak stopped her.

"Take this." He handed her a small trowel. "Dig a hole and go in that, then fill it up afterward."

"Really?" Torrin was ready to go and she couldn't imagine taking the time to dig a hole before she could get some relief.

"Really. We don't want to attract any of those beasties." He closed her hand around the trowel's handle, then moved off a few paces and turned his back. "I'll be right over here."

"Fine." As quickly as she could, Torrin dug her hole. "You'd better not be peeking."

"I'm not peeking." His voice was muffled.

Good, she thought. *He's facing the other way.* What seemed like long minutes later, she stood up and kicked dirt back into the hole.

"All done?"

"You bet." She stomped past him toward their shelter. He caught up with her a moment later. He was probably worried she would make a break for it. All she wanted was to get back where it was dry so she could warm up. Still, if he was going to insist on accompanying her every time she needed to attend to necessities, she was going to scream. Eventually he would just have to trust her.

He stopped being her shadow as soon as they got back into their makeshift quarters for the night and settled himself back in his sentry position at the door.

Trying to untangle her hair, Torrin moved to the back and found the promised pallet and lowered herself gingerly into it. It was surprisingly comfortable. She wormed herself around until she found a position from which she could fall asleep. She glanced toward the opening again and assured herself that Jak was there, looking out into the rain. She hoped the sound of the rain would drown out what she was about to do. Torrin lifted her right hand behind her ear and activated the transmitter.

"Tien, can you hear me?"

"I read you, Torrin."

"Good." Torrin glanced over at Jak's back, making sure he couldn't hear her. "It looks like I'm going to have to go along with the man who rescued me from the Orthodoxans. I'm effectively stranded. I'm going to see how I can salvage this. If I can convince the Devonites that they need me, it'll be in their best interest to get you back to me." She sighed. "Of course, if you could come and get me, I wouldn't have to go through this crap."

"I cannot come and get you, Torrin," Tien reminded her. "You do not permit me access to ship propulsion systems, remember?"

"I know that," Torrin hissed. She mentally cursed herself for not trusting the AI to pilot the ship independently. The AI's League origins kept her from trusting it completely, yet if she had unbent enough to allow it, Tien would have been able to come to her rescue when Hutchinson had first locked her down. She'd have to change that as soon as she got back to the *Calamity Jane*. There was no way she would allow herself to be in this situation again.

"I will wait until you return, Torrin," the AI responded imperturbably. "You are reaching the edge of my transmission capabilities, however. Without a satellite or other communications network, I will be unable to reach you if you move much further west. You are currently fifty-two kilometers northwest of my position. I estimate you will be out of my range in another five kilometers, depending upon the terrain."

"Noted," Torrin replied absently, her eyes drawn once more to Jak at the entrance. "It won't be long then, based on our movements so far. What can you tell me about where I'm headed?"

"Not much, Torrin. My databanks do not match what I have scanned of the planet. On our flyover, I detected two continents connected by an isthmus. You seem to be headed toward the isthmus. There is a large energy reading that runs the width of the isthmus at its narrowest point. It seems to be a barrier of some sort. Beyond that, my readings tell me this area seems to be mostly temperate rain forest, not arid desert."

"So I can expect more rain."

"Affirmative, Torrin."

"That's just great. Sit tight, I'll contact you as soon as I'm back in range."

"Understood. And be careful, Torrin."

"Always." With that final exchange, she deactivated the transmitter. One last glance toward the entrance assured her that Jak remained unaware of her activities. She closed her eyes and sleep rolled her under in an instant.

CHAPTER SIX

Jak carefully scanned the edge of the clearing. If anyone came through the trees, she would have very little time to mount an effective resistance. There was still no sign of pursuit, and she hoped it would stay that way. She sneaked a glance at the back of the shelter where she could barely make out Torrin's form curled up on the makeshift pallet. The tall woman was dead to the world. Jak wished she could close her eyes for a while as well. Their trek had been brutal. She was surprised at how well Torrin had stood up to the rigors of their journey. Not because she was a woman, of course. Jak chuckled as she examined the irony of that particular conversation. It was funny, but she felt more relaxed with Torrin than she had with anyone else since her brother had been killed. She swallowed her chuckle as quickly as it bubbled up. She didn't have the luxury of enjoying someone's company, especially not someone who was for all intents and purposes her captive.

She shook her head slightly. McCullock was going to hand it to her when she got back to camp. There was no way she could have disobeyed his orders any more thoroughly. Hopefully her superiors would see the value of Torrin's abilities and the technology the smuggler could bring back to them. All she had to do now was get them through enemy territory in one piece. It was pretty clear by the wide trail the other woman had left behind that Torrin had little to no woodcraft. All they could do was hope that no Orthodoxans came across their trail. The rain was washing away some sign of their passage, but their footprints were an unavoidable beacon in anyplace untouched by the deluge. They were just waiting for someone to happen across them.

She continued her perusal and pulled up her map of the area. Torrin was doing pretty well, but they were still moving through the woods slower than she would have liked. The rain and treacherous conditions hadn't helped. At their present pace it would probably take them an additional three and a half days to make it back to the fence. That would leave only half a day of wiggle room to rendezvous with the extraction team. There wasn't nearly enough leeway in that equation for her comfort. The rations she had along were only meant for one person. She could stretch the food to cover them both, but they would need to supplement their available rations. She could hunt, but that would mean building a fire to cook whatever she managed to bring down. A fire would be risky on this side of the lines, but she didn't see how they could avoid making one at some point. It wouldn't be easy, but she thought they could manage it as long as nothing went wrong.

She lost herself in the semi-meditative state she assumed when she was stuck in one place, watching. Time passed without her cognizance and she merely concentrated on keeping an eye on the clearing. About three hours later, she heard stirring from the back of the lean-to and Torrin sat up on the makeshift bed. She looked bleary-eyed but had lost a lot of the previous night's tension. Jak watched as Torrin yawned hugely and stretched like an Earth cat. She could almost hear her joints pop. Quickly, she averted her eyes and went back to scanning the perimeter before the other woman realized she had an audience.

"Everything still good?" Torrin asked as she joined Jak just inside the mouth of the shelter.

"So far," Jak replied. "Rain is slowing but hasn't let up."

"I think I could cheerfully do without rain for the rest of my life."

"You get used to it."

"Hmm." Torrin was back to running her fingers through her hair, trying once more to untangle the knotted strands. "You should probably get some sleep. I can take a turn on watch."

"I don't think so." Jak shook her head. Did the woman think she was crazy or just dim-witted? "I'm not giving you a weapon. You're pretty much my prisoner, remember?"

"Oh yeah, how silly of me to forget," Torrin shot back. "Because I'm going to kill you in your sleep, then live out the rest of my days as a hermit in these woods with half the planet out for my blood. I get that you don't trust me, but there isn't much I could do to you out here that wouldn't turn around and bite me in the ass. You look ready to fall over yourself. Let me spell you for a couple of hours."

Jak tightened her lips and prepared to rebuff her again, but Torrin forestalled her.

"You can keep your gun. I'll just make sure no one's sneaking up on us while you're sleeping. I kind of need you to be functioning well so that you can save my skin, got it?"

Jak continued to scan the clearing while she mulled it over. The fact that she was even considering the idea told her how tired she was. Torrin's arguments made sense. Sleep might be a better option than paranoia.

"Fine. You'll find some binoculars in the bag. Use those to keep an eye on things. Wake me if you see anything." She put up her rifle and made her way to the back of the shelter. The surface of the bed was still slightly warm from Torrin's body heat. Jak snuggled down into its yielding softness. It took her a while to unwind enough to let sleep overtake her. Dregs of adrenaline still pumped through her system from their flight through the storm, and her mind kept chasing itself in circles.

As she lay on the pallet ramping down her churning thoughts, she considered Torrin through slitted eyes. Her brother had spread himself pretty thin among the camp's available women. He'd been quite the lady's man. She had never felt any particular attraction to the men she knew, something she'd always counted as a blessing. Sexual attraction would have made it that much harder to keep them at the distance her deception required. She did wonder at her fascination with the tall offworlder. Everyone knew that women were attracted to men, not to other women. Sure, she had never felt that way for a man, but she had good reason. Something about the other woman's strength and fire enthralled her.

It didn't matter. Torrin surely had a man back wherever she called home. Jak was probably only interested in her because she'd never met anyone from off the planet. Yes, that must be it. Torrin was a novelty, which explained why she found her so interesting. It was an academic interest, nothing more. Satisfied with the logic of her ruminations, Jak sneaked one last glance at Torrin, closed her eyes completely and let sleep drain away her awareness.

She awoke with a start an unknown while later. It wasn't the nightmare that woke her, for a change, but she wasn't sure exactly what had drawn her into wakefulness. She cast her eyes over to the entrance of the shelter, then leaped off the pallet in one motion when she realized that Torrin was no longer seated in the entry. She snatched her sniper rifle up from beside the improvised bed and darted into the clearing. The rain had stopped sometime while she slept and the risen sun's rays had broken through the clouds. The air was already humid as the heat after the storm promised to be oppressive.

Across the clearing Torrin stood on the rocky ridge. She turned in time to see Jak erupt from under the downed trees and waved while gazing at her through the binoculars.

"Damn woman," Jak muttered to herself as she stomped over to where Torrin stood. She was halfway to her when a sharp report, like the shot of a gun, rang out through the clearing. Torrin staggered then disappeared from sight with a roar of rocks and mud as the edge of the ridge gave way under her weight. Jak broke into a sprint, hauling her rifle over one shoulder as she dashed across the clearing to the spot where Torrin had disappeared.

She threw herself down on her belly and slid, her head poking over the side in time to see Torrin and half the hillside being swept down the incline and into the river that ran along the bottom of the hill. The river, swollen from that night's deluge, raged in the confines of its banks. Without hesitation, Jak swung herself around and over the edge of the small precipice and pushed herself down the slope to the white water below.

CHAPTER SEVEN

"Shit, shit, SHIT!!!" Torrin blurted as she hurtled down the side of the precipice. Scrubby trees and bushes sprang up in her path and whipped by her before she could so much as reach for them. The white water of the river rushed closer to her before the world dropped away from her. Her arms and legs windmilled briefly before she hit the water's angry surface. All the air was forcefully expelled from her lungs, as much from the cold as from the force of her body hitting the water. The frigid water closed over her head and she struggled to reach the surface, her lungs already burning. She broke the surface with a heaving gasp to fill her lungs with as much oxygen as possible. The river's turbulent course spun her around like a top, but she could see one bank looming close and tried to force herself toward it. She could swim, but she didn't have any experience with water this rough. The rivers and lakes she was used to were calm with only shallow ripples from the wind, unlike this raging, seething beast that was doing its best to kill her.

She threw her shoulder into her stroke and kicked as hard as she could and was rewarded when the near bank drifted closer. Encouraged, she repeated the maneuver over and over, until she felt a glimmer of hope, but she was tiring rapidly. No, she wouldn't think like that. She was going to make it. She hadn't trudged through half the wilderness on Haefen to lose her life to a stupid accident.

Her head exploded in a blinding corona of pain. Limp, she slid off the enormous rock that somehow had sprouted in her path. She couldn't focus; her arms and legs were instantly leaden. She shook her head to try to clear the pain and confusion but sank under the surface instead. Bubbles streamed from her nose and mouth, and she fought to force her arms and legs to propel her back up. With frantic haste she thrashed and generated enough movement that her mouth broke the surface. She gulped in sweet air, but the water closed over her too rapidly and the air turned into water. She coughed, taking more water into her tortured lungs. Still she struggled while the edges of her vision darkened until she looked up at the water's surface through a long tunnel.

What was that shape? she wondered muzzily. The sun looked so pretty, its rays refracting and skipping about. It was so blue, she loved the color, but that shape was blocking it out. She stopped struggling and gazed upward, cradled in the river's embrace. It didn't seem so rough now; it rocked her back and forth, lulling her to somnolence. She couldn't remember why she struggled so mightily. It was so much nicer just to let the river rock her to sleep. She succumbed, sliding down into that deep, peaceful darkness.

She woke to pain, choking and coughing. A weight on top of her used her rib cage like a bellows, forcing water out of her lungs and onto the mud by her face. She retched and dirty river water poured forth from her mouth, splashing into the muck and splattering back up at her. Again and again she vomited turgid water until she could finally breathe enough to talk.

"Enough," she moaned, but the pressure continued. "Enough!" she said more vehemently, trying to turn herself over, to get away from whatever it was that worked her ribs over. Hands grasped her shoulders and flipped her over, pulling her up to a sitting position. Jak's face slid into her field of vision, features creased with worry, eyes terrified.

"You all right?" he asked, shaking her slightly. "You swallowed half the river and you were out for way too long. I was…" His voice faded and he stared at her.

"I'm okay," she croaked. Well, she wasn't exactly okay, but she was alive. She was too miserable to be dead. She hurt all over and felt as if she'd been beaten with a large stick. Her head wanted to split open. She was so very cold and was shaking uncontrollably.

"Crap," Jak said. "You're going into shock. I need to get you warm, but we can't stay here, we're too exposed."

Torrin nodded and tried to push herself up, teeth chattering.

"Hold on." Jak stripped his jacket off and settled it around Torrin's shoulders, then grabbed her by both elbows and pulled her to her feet. She staggered and had to lean on him for support. He didn't seem to mind and reached over and pulled her arm around his shoulders. Once again, she was struck by his strength. He was solid as bedrock and absorbed her extra weight without comment. She looked around and saw that she'd washed up like so much flotsam on a tiny beach at a bend in the river. Small rocks and sand made it hard to keep her footing as small stones shifted beneath her feet. Slowly, they made their way off the river's bank and into the forest looming somberly at the edge.

After only a few hundred meters into the trees, what little strength Torrin had regained began to flag rapidly. Her shivering increased until she felt like she was about to fly apart. Jak scanned the area quickly and settled her down with her back against a fallen log. He pulled open the jacket and reached for the closure of her jumpsuit.

"What do you think you're doing?" Torrin weakly batted his hands away.

"We need to get you out of those clothes." Jak sat back on his heels and considered her. "You're in shock, you need to get your core temperature up and your clothes are soaked. They might have been waterproof in the rain, but I bet half the river ended up inside there. You'll never get warm while you're wearing them."

"I'm not taking my clothes off in front of you," she said. Her fingernails were turning blue, she noticed with bemusement. It wasn't a flattering shade on her. "Besides, you're just as wet as I am. Why aren't you getting naked?" Not that she wanted to see him naked. Seeing a naked man might make her lose whatever was left in her stomach. Still, that might not be a bad thing, since there was probably still more river water in there. She ignored the small frisson she'd felt at the idea of his nudity and turned it into a convulsive shudder. Hadn't she just been thinking that she would probably be sick if she saw him naked? She felt absolutely no attraction to men, but this one was making her consider things she never had. How hard had her head bounced off that rock?

Jak grabbed her chin, alarmed at her increasing vagueness.

"Stay with me," he ordered. "I'm not in shock and I'll be fine. You won't be." Once again he reached for the closure straps of her suit, deftly shedding her hands while she tried futilely to stop him. He fumbled a bit with the unfamiliar closure apparatus but was able to figure it out and slid it down over her breasts.

"You can keep my jacket on if you're so worried. I promise I won't peek," he said and reached into the aforementioned jacket to push her suit off her shoulders. His hands were so hot on her; they left trails of heat on her skin. "You need to help me," he growled, and she worked to pull her arms out of the suit and hold the coat closed against her nakedness. She forced herself to remain stock-still so she didn't arch into his touch as he skimmed the top of the suit down to her waist, those wonderful hands leaving ripples of spreading warmth behind them. "Lift," he grunted when he came to her buttocks. She definitely wasn't paying attention to how his hands felt on her rump. She was most assuredly not lifting her hips into him nor pressing her torso into his. She was merely following his directives so he could get the suit pulled down her legs and off.

As soon as his hands left her skin, she regained some of her senses. What was she doing with this man? Disgusted with herself, she pulled her knees protectively toward her chest and clutched the jacket more securely around her shoulders. She did feel somewhat warmer now that the sodden jumpsuit was no longer plastered to her skin.

"What are you doing?" She jumped as he closed his hands around her ankles. Suddenly terrified and seeing Hutchinson's leering face in her mind's eye, she kicked feebly at him.

"I'm working the blood back into your legs," he said. He recaptured her ankles and started to rub them down vigorously. "We can't risk a fire. The smoke will be a beacon for anyone looking for us. All our supplies are back in the shelter. All I have is what I was carrying, which fortunately includes my rifle, so we'll be able to eat. Right now we need to get you moving again and the best way is to warm you up."

"Oh" was all she could think to say. She wanted to be warm, but she didn't want to deal with the riot of emotions that his touch awoke in her, that strange, visceral attraction and an accompanying disgust that was almost equally as strong. His hands were strong and slightly rough on her ankles, and he moved slowly up her ankles to her calves, kneading and massaging. Maybe if she closed her eyes she could pretend that he was a woman. No! Her eyes popped open almost as soon as she closed them. Desire had shot through her belly as soon as her eyes had drifted shut, leaving a pool of warmth that spread rapidly to the space between her legs.

"I've got it," she croaked, throat dry. She briskly rubbed her hands over her arms, willing warmth into all of her extremities so he would stop touching her. He continued to massage her lower legs and ankles for a few more moments, then closed his hands over her toes. Satisfied that some warmth had returned to her feet, he let go and stood up. His clothes hung damply from his frame, but she saw that he did still have a rifle slung across his shoulders. The hand he slid through close-cropped blond hair made it stick up at all angles.

"Are you going to be all right on your own?" he asked, gazing out into the forest. "I need to get my bearings and figure out how we're going to get out of here."

"I'll be fine," Torrin replied. She just wanted him away from her. His presence confused her. Hopefully she'd be able to clear her head once he was gone. He nodded absently and disappeared into the forest's shadows.

Torrin stretched out a little bit. Wearing only a strange man's jacket had left her feeling more than a little exposed. Fortunately it was cut long or it wouldn't have even covered her waist. As it was, it came barely to the bottom of her buttocks. She wasn't overly self-conscious about exposing her body, but the woods loomed far above and the canopy was so thick very little light could get through. Who knew what creatures were lurking in the darkness.

She shook her head. That line of thinking wasn't helping her at all. Her thoughts were no longer on Jak, but scaring herself didn't really improve her disposition. As soon as she cast her thoughts in her captor's direction the warm glow in the pit of her stomach returned.

"What's going on?" she wondered aloud. She didn't want this attraction, especially not to him, but her traitorous body refused to listen. It had been a while since her last romantic encounter. She typically didn't lack for sexual partners, though she didn't stay long with any one woman. Not being tied down and being able to have new experiences were a big part of what attracted her to the smuggler's life. She treated her love life the same way, and the women she got involved with usually knew what they were getting into and didn't resent her for it. In fact, she was good friends with many of her former lovers. There were a couple of notable exceptions, she ruefully acknowledged to herself.

This line of thinking didn't help much either, so she got up and slipped feet into her boots. She paced along the edge of the downed log, which warmed her a little more. She had to hold the jacket closed across her breasts. Jak didn't have the same endowments she did and the coat's closures didn't quite meet. She lost track of how long she paced back and forth.

Jak appeared in front of her. Torrin gave a startled squeak and hopped back from him.

"Frozen hells, you scared me!"

"Sorry." He grinned. "That was an interesting sound."

"What did you expect, sneaking up on a body like that?"

"I said sorry." He held up his hands in surrender. "You better?"

"I'm starting to warm up."

"Good. There's a clearing a short way ahead. We can set up in the sun and dry off your gear."

"In case you hadn't noticed, I'm not really dressed to gallivant around in the woods."

"If we stay here, by the time your suit dries out the Orthodoxans could have caught up to us. This'll be faster and you'll be way happier, trust me."

"I don't have much choice, do I?" she grumbled under her breath. She ignored him when he quirked an eyebrow inquiringly at her. "Fine, but you go first, I won't have you walking behind me checking out my ass."

"Okay, okay!"

Was it her imagination, or did Jak color when she mentioned her ass? He was so carefully not looking at her that he might as well have gawked openly at her half-exposed body. He seemed as embarrassed as she was. Clearly, he was a very different breed from the men she'd interacted with in Colonel Hutchinson's service. Covertly, she considered him as he scooped her suit up off the forest floor and made his way through the underbrush. It was dark under the canopy, but she could have sworn he was still blushing.

He was moving pretty quickly, and she had to holler at him to slow down. It was slow going as she picked her way through bushes trying to hold the coat closed with one hand while doing her best to avoid branches scratching her exposed legs. Jak waited patiently, his back to her as she caught up.

"You can go," she announced as she drew up right behind him. He forged on again, this time more slowly, giving her time to keep up with him.

They made their way deeper into the forest, away from the river. Fifteen minutes later, at their snail's pace, the trees gave way to a clearing. A stark rock formation forced its way out of the clearing's center. Grass sloped up to meet it in a natural incline. Jak picked a particularly sunny patch and spread Torrin's jumpsuit out in the pool of light. He plopped himself down on the ground in the sun and arranged himself to face it, arms held out a bit from his sides. Torrin realized that he was attempting to dry himself out. Out of her clothes she was mostly dry, except for her hair and the jacket around her shoulders, though surprisingly it too was almost dry. She mentioned as much to Jak.

"It's made from ytterencatte pelts," he replied, eyes closed and face lifted toward the sun. "They're everywhere in the canopy around here. Their fur repels water and is lightweight. We use them a lot for outerwear. In fact, that's how I ended up hooked up with the army in the first place."

Torrin arranged herself in a patch of sun not too far from him. Prudently, she kept herself just out of his reach. So far he'd been a perfect gentleman, but she still didn't trust him even though he'd promised not to sneak a peek.

"How's that?" she asked when he didn't elaborate.

"I used to hunt them with my family and we sold their pelts to the local command post. After my father died, they took us in since we had a bit of a connection to them."

She noted his slight pause over the word "family." His expression gave nothing away; a stone would have been more expressive.

"Who's we?"

"My brother and me. My father had debts we didn't know about. After he died, his debtors took our home and lands. We had no money to pay them off. As oldest male, Bron was headed for military service already, but they didn't turn down one more when we came knocking."

"Bron's your older brother then?"

"Ye-es." Jak seemed hesitant to share. Irrational irritation surged through Torrin at his reticence. This man was dragging her across the back of beyond and kindling unwelcome emotions in her, but he couldn't share a little personal information?

"What capacity does he serve in, then?" she probed. His expression turned from stony to downright forbidding. She dug a little harder. "Is he as prone to kidnapping women as you are?"

"I don't want to talk about him" was the clipped reply.

"Oh, I'm sorry. You two aren't close then?" She bore in further, trying to get at the truth behind his refusals.

He rounded on her, eyes narrowed. "He's dead, all right? He was my spotter, my best friend and my brother. I miss him more than I'd miss my right arm. Every day I wake up and I get to relive his death all over again. When he died a part of me went with him and I don't think I'll ever get that piece back. So when I say I don't want to talk about him, I don't want to talk about him!"

He sat in front of her, jaw clenched and chest heaving. By the time he finished his rant, he was practically screaming at her. Torrin felt terrible. No wonder he was hesitant to talk about his family. He couldn't be that old and in his young life he'd lost his father and brother. There was no talk of a mother, and Torrin assumed that she too was dead. She reached out her hand and laid it gently on his forearm. At her touch, a muscle jumped convulsively in his jaw, but he didn't move.

"Oh, Jak, I'm so sorry. I had no idea. It's hard to lose a family member."

"What would you know about it?" he asked dully.

"I barely remember my biological mother. She died when I was very young. I never knew my father, but that's just as well. If I ever get to meet him, I'll kill him myself."

Jak looked her in the eye, shocked. "Why is that? They didn't get along or something?"

"Something indeed." Torrin laughed hollowly. "My mother was rescued off a slave ship. My father is any one of the piratical bastards who raped her on her way to the slave markets of Ur-Five.

She died when I was four. I was adopted by a couple of women who raised me as their own."

"That's terrible." Jak sighed. "I guess life is crap all over."

"It gets better." She tightened her grip on his arm and leaned forward. "I didn't understand for a long time, and when I finally got it that she wasn't coming back, it hurt for a really long while. It still hurts when I think about her, but the pain becomes part of you and eventually you don't have to think about the loss all the time."

"I don't think that'll work for me," Jak shook his head. "It's been two years and it still feels like yesterday. It's why I take on missions like hauling my ass three days through the woods to kill…" He cut off abruptly. He looked up, his face suddenly suffused with color. "Your jacket is, umm…" He pointed at her chest.

Torrin looked down and noticed that the coat had gaped open in the front, giving him an unobstructed view of her breasts. Snatching her hand off his arm, she clutched it closed.

"Sorry," Jak mumbled, pointedly looking elsewhere.

This was getting ridiculous, Torrin thought. It didn't matter if he could catch a peek at her boobs. If he really wanted to he could take much more than that.

"It's all right," she laughed, a little too loudly. "I'll just go over here a bit."

She slid away from him and arranged herself in the hope of catching some rays. The grass was soft where she lay back into the incline, and she closed her eyes. At peace for the first time since she met her first Haefonian, she allowed herself to drift, not quite asleep but not really awake.

She wasn't sure how long she lay there, but when she came back to a semblance of herself her hair was mostly dry. And knotted. She sat up and reached for her suit, glancing over at Jak. He stared solemnly out into the forest. He was set up with his rifle and occasionally used the scope to scan deeper into the trees.

"Go ahead and get dressed. I won't peek." He must have eyes in the back of his head, she thought. She had no idea how he'd seen her movement since he was facing in almost the opposite direction. To emphasize his promise not to peek he put one eye up to the rifle's scope.

Quickly, she pulled the jumpsuit's legs over her own and turned away to pull up the suit's top. Normally she wouldn't care who saw her naked, but Jak had her in such emotional turmoil that she didn't trust herself. Better to avoid temptation at this point. On both their parts. He must feel some attraction for her. After all, she did cut quite the figure. Well, maybe not in her current bedraggled state. What she wouldn't do for a comb, she decided.

Fully dressed, she made her way over to him. He was sunk in the shadows cast by the trees at the clearing's edge. She looked more closely at his shirt, it looked wet. Pressing a hand to the back of his shoulder, she confirmed her suspicions. His shirt was still very damp, almost sopping.

"You're still wet," Torrin accused. "You really need to get out of those clothes if you're ever going to dry off."

"I told you, I'm not the one who needs the warmth," he said. "But I see you're not in shock anymore. That's good." He twitched his shoulder beneath her hand.

She pulled her hand back a little too quickly when she realized she was still touching him. Now she was coming up with excuses to touch him. Why couldn't he be female? she wailed to herself.

"Now that you're good again, we need to be moving on," he said. Standing, he slung the rifle over his shoulder. "I'll dry off as we keep moving. I've been able to get my bearings. Your unplanned dip might actually help us. They won't be able to track us over the river's course so they'll have no idea where we came out of the water. We're on a course that's further east than I'd planned on so we'll miss my extraction team, which means we get to take the long way around."

Jak started off across the clearing, skirting the impressive formation at its center.

"How do you know where we're going?" she asked. "I've never seen you check any maps. My tablet is back at Hutchinson's compound, but I've never seen you pull one out."

He grinned and tapped his forehead with his index finger.

"It's all right here. I had the maps uploaded before I came out. They don't have great coverage of our current area, but I've got enough from past uploads to navigate us through without too much trouble. I think."

"Wait, you have this information directly uploaded to your brain?" Torrin was astounded. She hadn't been aware of anyone with that technological capability. "What other surprises do you have up there?"

"You mean you don't? I thought everyone had cyber implants."

"Not at all," she said. "You're the first I've heard of, and I've been around the galaxy. Most places experimented with cybernetic implants but abandoned them centuries ago. I don't know of any beyond some prosthetics that have been successful. No one's been able to figure out how to incorporate them internally. I guess there's some disconnect with how they interface with the brain or something. There are some communications implants, but even those work by picking up vibrations and transmitting them. They don't actually hook into the brain."

"I guess that's one upside to us being on our own out here. What I remember from school is our first settlers were very adept with cybernetics and mechanical enhancements. The civil war only increased research and development in those areas."

"That's amazing. Though I notice you didn't tell me about what else you have going on in that brain of yours."

He quirked an eyebrow at her, and she realized how her last statement had sounded.

"You know what I mean!" she said.

"And I'm not going to tell you. I need to keep some things a mystery."

She wondered if Jak realized how flirtatious that last remark sounded. He seemed completely oblivious to her as a woman, for which she was just as glad. *And a little disappointed*, a traitorous little corner of her mind whispered to her.

CHAPTER EIGHT

The woods were getting thicker around them again. The trees butted against each other and clawed for the sky in endless competition for more sun. Now that she was fully dressed she kept up with Jak fairly easily. The ground had dried out since their last trek, which made the terrain much easier to navigate. As they walked under the trees in daylight, she could see the strangeness that made up the Haefonian undergrowth. The canopy was so thick that light filtered through only in occasional rays of brilliant cerulean. The odd hardy shrub or plant thrived here, but in the deepest shadows and recesses of the woods barely luminescent things were abundant.

"Mushrooms," Jak grunted when she asked. "They're the only plants that survive where the woods are thickest. I wouldn't eat them. They won't kill you, but you'll wish they had."

"They make you sick?"

"Not so much, but they cause nasty hallucinations that're pretty intense. People sometimes kill themselves to make them stop. The visions are so bad that there isn't even a market for them, except as some really messed up poisons."

So this beautiful planet had a dark side. Aside from the Orthodoxans, that was. She peered into a particularly deep shadow where the strange luminescence was brightest. The mushrooms ringed the roots of a massive tree and created a series of electric blue steps.

"Why do you do that?" Torrin asked when she noticed Jak carefully cutting a narrow triangle into the trunk of one of the trees. They were the same ones he'd followed the other night.

"So we can retrace our steps if we need to," he replied as he finished. "I can use the maps in my head, but they're not that detailed."

It made sense. Torrin started paying close attention whenever he stopped to mark a tree or shrub. After a while, she thought she understood what his various marks meant.

They continued deeper into the forest until the rays that split the perpetual gloom came more and more infrequently. Jak displayed no difficulty in navigating the continuing darkness. Torrin was only able to keep up with him because the deeper they went the less undergrowth there was. The path cleared up considerably, which was good since it was almost impossible for her to see. The glowing mushrooms were more abundant as well, but their luminescence was so dim it only illuminated a small pool around each group of fungi.

Torrin lost track of how long they walked. Eventually her stomach decided to remind her that it had been quite some time since her last meal. Apparently, almost drowning in the raging river had given her quite the appetite.

"What are we going to do about food?" she asked finally.

"I'm keeping an eye out for any game, but there's not that much where it's this dark."

"Not many animals like the darkness, I take it?"

"It's not that. Just not many game animals here." Jak sounded vaguely amused. "There are a number of animals who think we're game, though."

All of a sudden, the woods seemed much more sinister. Shadows pressed in on her, and the hair on the back of her neck raised as if she could feel malevolent eyes on them.

"Are they dangerous?" She hurried to get closer to him. If she'd had her usual armament she knew she wouldn't feel nearly so vulnerable. She cursed the guards for making her leave her plasma pistol behind in her room. It wasn't in her nature to let someone else take care of her. Under ordinary circumstances, she didn't care for being this dependent on another person, but most especially not on a man.

"Yup," he responded blithely. "But the Orthodoxans won't expect us to cut through here for exactly that reason. They almost never make it this deep into the forests."

"You still have your sidearm, right? Why don't you let me have it?"

He stopped so abruptly that she bounced off his back. He spun around and caught her upper arms just in time to keep her from tipping over.

"Are you kidding me? What're you going to do with my pistol?"

"Use it to protect myself is what," she shot back indignantly. "I don't need you to watch over me. I can protect myself."

"Let's just forget for a second that you're my prisoner and I'd be a complete idiot to arm you," he said, his voice tense. "How about the fact that you can't see a damn thing in this darkness? How about that you're wound up so tight I can practically see you shaking? I don't need you shooting me in the back because you decided to make a break for it or because you thought I was a big bad beastie come to eat you."

"I'm not a moron! I have nowhere to go except with you. I can see that even though I don't like it." *And at this moment, I don't much like you*, she thought fiercely at him. "And if I'm shaking it's because I'm hungry. I almost drowned back there, remember?" *Sure, that's why you're shaking*, the little voice piped up in the back of her head. *It has nothing to do with the fact that he's holding on to you.*

"Oh yeah, I remember. I swallowed about a liter of water hauling your ass out of the drink."

"Whatever…" She wrenched her arm out of his grip. "You need to trust me. I don't have any choice about my circumstances."

"Fat chance. I bet you can handle yourself quite well, no matter the circumstances. If I give you a centimeter, you'll take every one I've got and probably come back for more." His voice tightened. "And while we're standing here arguing, a very large aetanberan is coming up on us."

"What are you talking about, there's a wha—" The rest of her words were cut off when he shoved her down in front of him. His face lit up and thunder crashed in the darkness above her. The flash from his rifle revealed a face set tightly in concentration, tip of the tongue gripped by white teeth. When the noise mercifully stopped, her ears were ringing and she felt as much as heard the crash of something large hitting the ground close at hand. Very close at hand. She turned, but what night vision she'd gained in the deep shadows had been mostly wiped out. Even though she was almost blind, she could barely make out the massive bulk of something almost as tall as Jak was. Lying down. The harsh smell of the rifle's projectiles hung in the air almost, but not quite masking a strong gamey odor.

"What the hell was that?"

"An aetanberan. They're large mammals, native to the planet. They're extremely territorial and they'll happily rip apart anything that wanders into their territories."

"How did you know it was headed our way?"

"I saw it. Well, after I smelled it. One of my extra advantages is the ability to see in the dark." Jak shrugged uncomfortably. "Still, there's no point letting all of this go to waste." He strode over to the rapidly cooling carcass and pulled a large knife out of the sheath at his belt.

"You can't be serious." Now that the smell of the projectiles had faded, she could smell the beast. Smell it, hell. She could practically taste it, the odor was so strong. No wonder Jak had noticed it by the stench; the animal had an extremely pungent odor about it, sour and vaguely caustic.

"As you pointed out, we need food. Aetanberan meat tastes way better than you think, seeing how bad it smells." He cut a slit into the fur on the creature's back and peeled it aside. "I need to move quickly on this, though. Soon the smell will attract even nastier things."

"Knock yourself out," Torrin said and moved off a little way, hoping to find a patch of air that didn't reek so badly. Was it just her imagination or could she hear things moving around in the darkness? The ringing in her ears was slowly easing. "Hurry up!"

"I'm almost done," he replied calmly to her hissed order.

True to his word, Jak moved quickly. Before long, he was wrapping a bloody hunk of meat in a piece of material he'd pulled out of one the many pockets in his pants. The wrapped hunk went back into the same pocket.

"Let's get moving," he ordered. "When we get far enough from the carcass that we're no longer in danger, I'll roast this up and we'll get some real food." He slid a hand into hers and pulled her along behind him. She didn't object; she just wanted to be away from the corpse of the hulking beast.

They walked at a much brisker pace than he'd set since she went into the river. It wasn't the run with which they'd left the compound, but it was still urgent. They must have gone another few kilometers when the ground began to slope downward more consistently. They'd had as many struggles uphill as down, but the descents were becoming more frequent and lasted longer. Thankfully, the trees began to thin and sunlight poked through the canopy with increasing frequency. The sun was also much lower than it had been when they ventured into the deepest part of the forest. By Torrin's estimation, it was well into late afternoon.

"Let's stop here," Jak decided, casting a look around and eyeing a small deadfall nearby. Torrin regarded it dubiously.

Jak looked at her and raised an eyebrow. "You look like you were expecting a palace and someone offered you a shepherd's hut instead."

"It's not that," she protested. "I've slept in much worse!" *Including a couple of prisons*, she thought. But those hadn't been her fault, no more than her current situation was.

"Don't worry," he said, eyebrow still raised. "I'll be able to make it bigger. Why don't you get some wood for a fire and I'll work on where we'll sleep for the night. Don't go too far. We aren't out of danger from wildlife yet."

As she picked up likely sticks and twigs she realized that this was the first time she'd seen any evidence of a sense of humor from him. She rather liked it, though with that crooked smile he looked even more ridiculously young.

When she returned to their camp, he had ringed the deadfall round with large branches and interspersed them with smaller twigs to form woven walls on three sides. He'd dug a fire pit in front of the shelter and was lining the outside with stones.

"Aren't you worried that a fire will give away our position?" She dumped the armload of branches next to the pit.

"It could," he admitted as he continued to pile up stones. The muscles in his forearm stood out in sharp relief as he moved the heavy rocks. "I'm not too worried, though. The Orthodoxans don't usually come this far into the woods, and the canopy will break up the worst of the smoke."

He started sorting through the wood she had gathered, laying the smallest and driest twigs into the fire pit first. He quickly built up the rest of the twigs around it and sat back on his heels to survey the construction critically.

"Good thing the firestarter usually works even if it gets wet," he said, reaching into one of his many pockets. From his jacket he produced a cylindrical device not much longer than his palm. He pressed down on one end and the other end glowed red then white-hot. He touched it to one of the branches at the base and it immediately burst into flames. After he repeated the maneuver in a few more places, the fire burned away merrily.

Torrin crowded in on the fire. The warmth and dry heat felt nice. She realized just how cold she'd gotten now that she'd stopped moving. Maybe her hair would finally dry out. She dropped gracefully into a seated position, legs crossed and palms held out toward the flames. Jak pulled the hunk of meat out of his pocket. He washed the blade of his knife off with the contents of a flask that he unclipped from his belt, then held the knife over the flames until the metal started to smoke. He carved the chunk of Aetanberan flesh into four pieces and skewered them on some long branches that he'd set aside. He passed one over to her.

"Make sure it's well cooked," he said. "Most of the gaminess cooks out that way, but if it's rare it'll taste real funky."

Torrin nodded and went about the task of cooking her dinner. Jak propped the other three skewers up against a stone near the fire so they hung over the flames and he didn't have to constantly tend to them. Reaching back, he snagged his rifle from where it leaned against a tree trunk and started pulling it apart. She watched with great interest. She rarely dealt in propulsion weapons, preferring instead the plasma-based ones. By his practiced motions, she could tell he was very familiar with the process and his weapon.

"How long have you been a soldier then?" The question popped out of her mouth. She cursed herself mentally. She was still irked with him and hadn't meant to engage him, especially since he was being so stubborn in his refusal to let her have a weapon.

Seemingly unaware of her internal struggle, Jak answered as he continued to tend to his weapon. "About four years. I was…

sixteen when I joined up with Bron. They saw we were good at marksmanship pretty quick and we were fast-tracked into sniper school. They never have enough snipers. We get killed off at a good rate." There was that pause again. He was lying about something, but nothing in that statement was really worth lying about. Still, that put him at twenty, which was a few years older than she would have guessed.

"That's understandable, I soppose," she said. "How can you stand to be out here all on your own? It would make me crazy. I don't do well without someone to talk to."

"It wasn't so bad when Bron was still alive." He still stripped and cleaned the rifle with mechanical motions, but his motions had lost their earlier crispness, becoming stiff and jerky. "He would spot for me, so we were always going out as a pair. Sometimes I can't concentrate on anything beyond our targets, and he would keep me safe by watching our surroundings while I took the shot. He got me in and out of the kill zone in one piece and I got the job done."

"It's a miracle I survived this long," Jak sighed heavily. "The survival rate for single snipers is about half that of pairs." He didn't sound sad or worried about his chances, just resigned, almost as if he didn't really care if the worst happened to him. She couldn't imagine being so close to someone that even two years after they were gone, such emptiness could still gnaw away at her insides. She'd never allowed any lovers to get close enough to her that any sort of void would be left when they went away. There was her sister. She knew if Nat died that she would feel terrible, but the kind of emotional chasm that his brother's death had torn in Jak was beyond her comprehension. The closest she could come was the anguish she'd felt after her biological mother died. But she'd moved beyond that with the help of her adoptive mothers. Her heart went out to him. He obviously didn't have anyone to help him move beyond the pain.

"Well, I guess that explains some of your roughness," she informed him, trying to lighten the mood a little.

"Roughness?" He eyed her over the rifle barrel he was cleaning out.

"Certainly. Your coarse demeanor. You're obviously partially insane from the forced isolation out here." She got into her theory and pointed her skewer at him for emphasis. "Mind you,

you were probably already somewhat unstable since you chose to do this job. Sneaking around in the woods, shooting people who don't know you're there, then disappearing again." She waved the dripping chunk of meat in a sweeping motion through the fire. "Very mysterious. I'm sure you have women dropping at your feet." Where had that come from? She didn't care, she really didn't care. *Really.*

"That's your theory? That I'm crazy for doing this, but mysterious so I must have women falling out of the trees." He looked faintly amused. "If I'm that nuts, then women should be running the other way, no?"

"Oh, you'd be surprised at what women will find attractive," she replied blithely. "So do you? Have women falling over you, that is?" If she didn't care, why was she pushing it, her little mental voice asked more than a little snidely.

"No. That was Bron's department," Jak said. "He was tall, handsome and outgoing. I'm short, scrubby and for some reason I don't get on with people real well."

"It's that roughness I was telling you about," Torrin replied. She hummed a little as she waved her meat slowly over the flames. She was inordinately pleased by his relationship status or lack thereof, more so than she should have been since she had no interest in him whatsoever.

The smells that came off the cooking meat were surprisingly good especially compared to the stench that had come off the beast after Jak dispatched it. Her mouth watered and her stomach growled loudly. She glanced quickly over at Jak to see if he'd noticed, but he was staring out across the fire, lost in thought. He must be thinking about his brother, she thought. She wasn't sure if the moroseness was an improvement over the anger he'd exhibited the last time she'd brought Bron up or not.

"Your meat should probably be turned," she said, following her own advice with her hunk of meat. Jak gave a little jerk at the sound of her voice and slid his glance down to touch the flesh that roasted on the skewers. He reached over and flipped them around with an economy of movement that spoke of much practice. He was clearly no stranger to acquiring and cooking his own food. A useful talent, especially in this situation. She knew that if she were wandering out here on her own she would be long dead. Or recaptured by the

Orthodoxans. She shuddered; death would be preferable to being in the clutches of those assholes.

"You all right?" Jak asked, wondering at her reaction.

"I'm fine." She waved him off. "Tired, hungry and my hair is a snarled mess. Aside from that, everything's peachy."

"Hungry we're working on, fixing tired'll come. I'm afraid the only thing I have to help with the hair is this." He held up the knife.

"Absolutely not," she huffed. "There is no way I'm letting you near me with that. I don't need a haircut like yours."

He looked wounded out of all proportion to the gibe. "There's a good reason for my haircut," he muttered, sliding a hand through the short strands. They stuck up at all angles and looked vaguely like a haystack she'd seen in an agricultural history book. As a farmer, one of her adoptive mothers had developed an obsession with ancient agricultural history and had acquired all sorts of texts on twentieth century farming.

"I'm sure there is. It looks fine on you, but I don't think I could pull it off."

"You'd be surprised what you can pull off when all your choices are shit." He stood up abruptly. "I'm going to take a look around the perimeter."

"Okay..." Had she offended him? She thought she'd paid him a compliment, but he seemed to disagree. Well, she wasn't about to worry about it. She'd told him he had a roughness about him. Something was bringing the edge of his personality closer to the surface. It couldn't be easy, dragging a strange woman across the countryside. She still wondered why he'd bothered. He'd really stuck his neck out for her and for no good reason that she could see.

A few minutes later Jak came back to the fireside. The sunlight that broke through the canopy was rapidly dimming as the sun started to set.

"We'll have to share the knife." He sat back down, removed his pieces of meat from the fire and wrapped two of them with some broad leaves he'd brought back from his trip around the camp's perimeter. He blew on the third piece to cool it down and carved a rough slice off of it.

"It's still hot," he warned as he handed over the knife.

"Got it," she said. Frankly, she was surprised that he hadn't planned to cut the meat for her. Who knew what trouble she could get into with his knife? She might just take him hostage and then… *Then nothing*, she told herself firmly, wondering why all she could think of was the bare expanse of shoulders she'd glimpsed the other day. She would hold him for a small ransom, then get off this blasted planet.

Their dinner passed in silence. She was in no mood to talk, not after his earlier abrupt departure, and he made no effort to engage her. If he wasn't going to try, then neither was she. As they were both finishing up, rain started to fall.

"Right on time," Jak said. "It rains most afternoons or evenings in these parts."

"Of course it does. Why should we get a break now?"

"It's all right. That's what the shelter is for." Jak stood up and kicked dirt over their fire. A cloud of smoke rose from the pit as the fire was quickly snuffed. Torrin made her way over to the tiny haven and ducked inside. The interior was a bit bigger than she thought, but they would be packed in cheek to jowl. Jak entered right behind her. With his height or lack thereof he didn't have to duck far to clear the opening. He settled himself cross-legged with the rifle across his knees and faced out the entry. Torrin eyed him ruefully. The way he was positioned she would either have to sleep half out in the rain or curl herself around him. She didn't want to get soaked again, not now that she finally felt like she'd dried out completely. There was nothing for it, and she settled herself down.

"Don't mind me," she murmured, shaping herself around him. He shifted slightly to give her a little more room. His body heat made up nicely for the absence of the fire. Slowly she relaxed and eventually gave up trying to avoid leaning into him. As she finally unwound and gave in to her fatigue, her last awareness was of Jak's body relaxing against hers. She smiled.

CHAPTER NINE

Jak had to wait until Torrin's breath lapsed into the regular rhythms of sleep before she could allow herself to relax. The woman was driving her to distraction. Torrin was constantly watching her. Her own obsession with Torrin was disturbing, but it all paled in comparison to the panic she'd felt when Torrin had gone over the side of that precipice. She hadn't thought at all but had just thrown herself into the water after the tumbling woman.

Watching Torrin struggle against the river and almost break free of its grip only to be thrown into the rock had been excruciating. When her head disappeared below the level of the water, Jak had swum after her with a strength she hadn't known she possessed. She'd always been a competent swimmer, but she knew she didn't have the skill or strength to rescue somebody from whitewater rapids. Her body had taken a pounding during the rescue attempt.

The tightness in her chest disturbed her. It was probably from inhaling river water during the rescue. She hoped it wouldn't slow her down. At this point it was mostly an annoyance, but she couldn't afford to let on that something might be wrong.

The other woman showed a lot of interest in her though they'd only just met. Jak wasn't entirely certain how to deal with her inquisitiveness, especially when it touched upon topics she wasn't prepared to discuss. Her bringing up her family had definitely been a mistake. Still, she shouldn't have melted down when Torrin pushed her on Bron. Even after two years that emotional wound refused to heal.

Slowly her tense muscles released, and she leaned slightly into Torrin's warmth, contentment seeping into her. When the sun had gone down she'd switched over to night vision and she could clearly see Torrin deep asleep every time she glanced down. She looked so peaceful, so different from the way Torrin's eyes had blazed into her own when Jak had told her in no uncertain terms that she wouldn't be getting her hands on a weapon. Jak chuckled quietly as she recalled the indignation written across Torrin's face and in her voice. She found that she actually enjoyed seeing the other woman riled up. The fire of her personality was marvelous to see.

Also marvelous to see had been the curve of Torrin's buttocks from beneath the much-too-small jacket Jak had given her to wear. Then there was the inner slope of her breasts, rounded and firm... Jak felt a little guilty for looking when she had promised not to, but it wasn't like she'd meant to.

Her attraction still made no sense to her. She'd never felt any attraction to women before. That sort of behavior was an aberration; the Devonite scriptures surely condemned it. Of course, she'd never felt any kind of pull toward any of the men she knew, but it wasn't like she'd had much contact with women either. She glanced down at Torrin's prone form again and reached out to smooth a lock of auburn hair away from her face. She froze a second before touching her skin. It hadn't been her intention to do that. Her hand trembled slightly where it hovered over Torrin's brow. She only wanted to touch her, to feel that smooth skin under her fingers, to connect with someone as she hadn't been able to do for far too long. Unable to resist any further, she gently stroked the auburn strands back from Torrin's forehead.

The other woman stirred slightly and sighed, leaning slightly into Jak's hand. She allowed her hand to linger a little longer, then pulled it back with regret. Women didn't have these kinds of feelings for each other, and there was no way she wanted Torrin to know how she felt. She didn't want to see disgust on Torrin's face when she realized what kind of a deviant Jak was. It was better for both of them if she could only throttle down her immoral urges. Still, Torrin's skin had felt so soft and supple. She imagined she could feel Torrin's warmth clinging to her fingertips, and she brought them up and ran them over her own cheek.

With an emphatic shake of her head, she sat up straight and pulled herself away from Torrin's sleeping form. Torrin scooted in and pressed herself back against Jak's side. She sighed and held herself up as rigidly as she could, determined not to get too comfortable around the other woman again.

She sat that way for a while, shifting only when her legs started to cramp. She tensed and released each muscle group individually, exactly as she did when she was waiting for a target to expose itself on a long stalk. Her eyelids were sliding closed of their own volition and she caught herself nodding. After the third time she almost nodded off, she pulled the packet of stims from the breast pocket of her jacket and popped one under her tongue. Fortunately they were stored in a watertight container and hadn't been destroyed in the river. With the stimulant racing through her bloodstream there was no worry that she might fall asleep. She tried not to think about the side effects and instead concentrated on keeping an eye out for any danger. She wasn't too worried about Orthodoxans. Their unanticipated trip down the river had actually been a great way to throw those bastards off their trail. However, the wildlife in these areas was ferocious and the predators hadn't had enough human contact to have learned to fear them. Animals like the aetanberan would view the two women as food.

The stims were taking effect; she was becoming more alert by the minute. The biggest obstacle now was staying still. As the stimulant flooded her bloodstream, immobility was becoming almost excruciating. This was far from the first time she'd used the drug and she was well aware of the effects. If she needed to, she could keep absolutely still even as adrenaline coursed through her system, but she didn't really need to at this point.

It still rained outside, but she saw a likely chunk of wood not too far from the shelter. Carefully, she disengaged herself from Torrin's slumbering embrace and slipped out into the rain. She grabbed the piece of wood from the ground near the now-extinguished firepit and ducked back into the shelter. In her absence, Torrin had shifted and now slept on her back, arm flung out into the spot Jak had occupied mere moments before. Jak gently shifted her arm over and sat back in her spot. To her disappointment, Torrin no longer snuggled against her. She missed the warmth and the contact. She'd had no extended physical contact in the two years since Bron had been killed. She hadn't known that she'd missed that feeling of physical closeness to another human being until she had it again. Did it really count if the other person was unconscious? she asked herself. Either way, it made her feel better and she decided to go with it.

She turned the piece of wood in her hands, examining it from all angles. It was weathered from its time exposed to the elements and was an appealing dark grayish color. It was slightly longer than her hand and a little wider. As far as she could see without starting carving, it was perfect for her purposes. She pulled the knife from its sheath at her belt and stuck the tip of her tongue between her teeth, bit down and started to whittle. As she carved away the outer layers, she could see that the wood was shot through with brilliant blue streaks. Excellent, the wood was Haefonian oak; it would hold up well to what she was planning.

As the night passed, she alternated between keeping watch into the rain and darkness and whittling. The combat knife wasn't exactly the appropriate size for serious woodcarving and she came close to slicing her fingers open on more than one occasion. Torrin slumbered away through it all, oblivious to Jak's muted movements and the muffled oaths she uttered whenever the blade nicked a finger. To her relief the rain stopped a couple of hours before dawn. The ground would be damp, but not as bad as it had been during their flight from the compound. The area would recover quickly from the saturation of that night and would be much more stable.

When the sun started to peek through the canopy, Jak slid out of the shelter. Torrin had spent most of the night curled around her. It had felt nice, but after a while it was all Jak could do to keep from touching her again. Whittling had helped to keep her mind off Torrin's close proximity, but eventually even that couldn't distract her from the woman. She unwrapped one of the hunks of aetanberan from the broad leaves in which she'd wrapped it and removed some slices in preparation for breakfast.

She heard Torrin moving around in the shelter and grinned in anticipation.

"Where did you get this?" Torrin asked as she left the shelter. She held up a wooden comb.

"I didn't get much sleep last night so I made it," Jak said offhandedly. "You were all worried over your hair and didn't like my other idea."

"You made this? It's beautiful!" Torrin held it up to get a better look at it and ran a finger over the wood.

"I'm glad you like it, but it's no big deal. When you spend a lot of time hunting, you find stuff to do to occupy your time. And the thing about hunting in forests is that there's a lot of wood around, so it's kind of natural." Jak cut herself off abruptly. She was babbling.

"Well, it's a big deal to me. This is the most thoughtful gesture I've ever had from anyone."

"You mean aside from rescuing you from some big hairy man who was gonna do awful things to you?" Jak asked wryly.

"Well, yeah, I guess." Torrin plopped herself down on the ground and started dragging the comb through her hair. Her auburn hair had gotten very tangled over the last two days. Based on the effort that Torrin was putting into it, the grooming was going to be difficult. Jak would have gone the knife route herself, but she had to admit that Torrin's hair was an excellent feature. Not as excellent as those hips certainly or that ass. Unbidden, a view of Torrin's bare breasts popped into her head. Her face heated instantly. She popped some aetanberan meat into her mouth and chewed, hoping Torrin wouldn't notice her flaming cheeks. Being so fair-skinned wasn't all it was cracked up to be. Embarrassment always painted itself across her face in bright strokes for all to see.

They sat in companionable silence for fifteen minutes or so while Torrin struggled with her hair and Jak silently ate her breakfast.

"You want something to eat?" Jak asked when Torrin eventually stopped worrying at her hair. It was quite a transformation. The redhead's hair had taken on a life of its own, curling down around her shoulders in gentle waves instead of hanging in limp hanks. Jak's fingers itched to reach out and touch it, but she proffered a slice of cold meat instead. Torrin accepted the offer gratefully. Jak couldn't help but notice that she'd slipped the comb into the top pocket of her jumpsuit.

"I'm going to have to really push us today," Jak said regretfully. "We have a lot of ground to cover and since we're taking the long way around, it's going to take some time and it won't be easy."

"Has any of this been easy?" Torrin asked around her mouthful of aetanberan. "Whatever we need to do, I guess. So have you reconsidered on lending me your pistol?"

Jak sighed. This woman just didn't give up. "No, I'm not giving you a gun, sorry."

"Had to give it a shot. So to speak." Torrin smiled at her cheekily. "I thought maybe a good night's sleep would put you in a better frame of mind."

"My frame of mind is perfectly fine, which is why you're not getting a gun. Besides, the last time I gave you a piece of equipment, you dumped it in the river."

Torrin grimaced at her and seemed to be on the edge of sticking out her tongue.

"I think we better get going," Jak said quickly. She walked over to the shelter and quickly dismantled it, spreading the branches over a wide area. There was no point in advertising that they'd spent the night there. It would be fairly evident to a trained eye, but the Orthodoxans didn't seem to have too many of those.

As they set off she brought up her map of the region. They were moving out of the area for which she had detailed maps. They needed to keep north on a parallel path to the fence all the way to the coast and swing west from there. The fence didn't quite extend all the way to the ocean, but the ends were especially well defended. Over the years, what little development had happened in the way of watercraft by either side had been quickly destroyed by the other, given the chance. Both sides still kept up strong presences against further incursions from the water. The Devonites still had some seaworthy vessels, but those never got anywhere near the front. The Orthodoxans might have had some of their own vessels, but Jak hadn't heard any confirmation of their existence. Sneaking through the fortified zone was their only hope, and it was a pretty slim one.

Their way north was relatively uneventful as they traveled over slowly changing terrain. By the end of the day they'd descended from the mountains and were making their way through rolling foothills. They were able to make up a lot of time on the less challenging slopes. Jak was encouraged by their pace, and though she was usually rather dour when in the company of others, she found herself being unaccountably chatty.

"So you know what I do," she said as they made their way up the side of a low hill. "And I know you're a smuggler. What do you move, exactly?"

"I procure hard-to-get items for people in difficult situations."

Jak snorted. "That tells me nothing."

"I mostly smuggle illegal items for people who aren't supposed to have them." Torrin rolled her eyes, annoyed at having to spell it out.

"That's better. I know what that means."

"In my line of business it's not always smart to spell things out so openly. Given that it's usually at least partially if not completely illegal, it can be dangerous to advertise too openly. Those who need what I offer understand that."

Jak felt mildly insulted by Torrin's last flippant statement. Apparently, the smuggler thought her too dim to understand what she did. "Well, if it's so illegal and dangerous, why even bother?"

"Well, for one it's good money. There's way more money to be made by these activities. That's why *they* call it profiteering, I suppose."

"They? Who're they?"

"The League of Solaran Planets. They're one reason I do this. Any chance I can get to stick it to them only makes the profit sweeter at the end of the day."

Jak was confused. She knew Central Command had been in contact with the League. The people she knew viewed the interaction as a promising development. League support would mean stability and as far as she was concerned that could only be good.

"Why are you so down on the League?" Jak asked.

"For good reason, as it turns out. They come into situations like yours in Fringe space and wait until they see which side is going to come out on top. Then they throw in their support with that side. When peace is restored, the grateful populace soon decides to join the League because they promise peace and prosperity. And they get complacent, but they also get cultivated by the merchant families of the inner systems, and before you know it, any viable businesses or industries are bought out by those families and they become the only game in town. And the best part is it's those damn merchants who are usually responsible for the destabilization of the planet in the first place. They put people's lives at stake simply to make a few bucks, and it's disgusting. They refuse to help anyone if it doesn't advance their own interests."

"Well, they didn't have anything to do with what happened here," Jak told her, taken aback by Torrin's vehemence. "The Orthodoxans started this mess on their own, and the only reason it's still grinding on is because we decided we weren't going to roll over for them."

"Are you so sure of that?" Torrin asked. "The League is sneaky and underhanded. Any kind of financial shenanigans are a sure sign that they were involved."

Jak laughed hollowly. "Financial shenanigans? You think that's what started all this?" She shook her head. "Far from it. The Orthodoxans decided after decades of treating their women like crap that everyone should be treating females like livestock. My people had been doing well for themselves in our own territory, and we weren't about to go following in the Orthodoxans' footsteps. The first sign that things were going seriously wrong was when the Orthodoxans attacked the Devonite settlements in the east and took all our women. They shot anybody who resisted—men, women, even children who were only trying to get back to their moms. They took anyone female, down to and including infants, and turned the men out of their own cities, naked and without any supplies. I guess they hoped the wilderness would finish them off. Well, some of the men made it back to the west in time and told them what had happened. When the Orthodoxans showed up with their army and tried to get past the isthmus into our lands, we stopped them and turned them back. They didn't expect our men to fight so hard to keep them out. I think they thought our men would see the rightness of their path and fall right in line. They have some whacked-out religious beliefs that came when our ancestors first settled the planet. On their own, their beliefs kept getting weirder until they felt their best option was enslavement of half the population to their wants and needs. When that didn't work, they settled for making us pay."

She smiled bitterly. "Well, look who's paying now. We still have all our lands and our laws. They poke and prod at us, but they can't break us. I'm pretty sure that they die faster than we do, but with their breeding pens, they can bring in new men faster than we can. So if the League comes to us and says they can help us out and that's what they want in return, it's better than the alternative."

Torrin stared at her in horror. "So all Orthodoxan women are slaves?"

"That's right. The 'lucky' ones get bought by a man and only have to service him and bear him children. But getting your own woman is expensive, so most men go to the breeding pens where hundreds of women are kept for the sole purpose of having babies. They're forced to have sex with man after man until they become pregnant. Once they give birth, they go back to the pens to start over. The boy children of the breeding pens go to the army, the girl children grow up and go into the pens unless they're lucky enough to be bought as a 'wife.' The girl children of married unions are confiscated at birth and brought up for the breeding pens. The boy children grow up to become craftsmen, merchants or officers."

"That's...insane! It's barbaric and just..." Torrin's words failed her and she struggled with the truths Jak had thrust upon her. "I've been to some pretty backward places," she said slowly, "but this place wins the prize by a long shot. I've seen women mistreated and called property, but never on such a massive scale or with such, such...mass production."

"The League doesn't seem so bad now, does it?" Jak asked.

Torrin looked at her. She looked like she might throw up. "The League might be a better alternative, but it's not the only alternative."

"What do you mean?"

"If you have two choices and they're both crap, it's time to look for a third one. If you can kick some sense into the Orthodoxans without getting League help, then your people won't feel beholden to them. They have a blockade around this planet because they don't want anyone else tipping the balance. Well, I can tip the balance. I can get your people the supplies and technology that you need to finish them off."

Jak stopped in her tracks and eyed the other woman. She'd been hoping that Torrin would see her way to dealing with them instead of the Orthodoxans. Hoping that what Torrin could offer would make up for the fact that Jak had broken from her mission and hadn't taken out her target. Not that anyone would mind that she took Hutchinson out instead.

"That would be really helpful. It could be a hard sell, but I know you don't like to give up. But just so's you know, it's not all sunshine and roses for women with the Devonites."

"Oh?" Torrin drew her eyebrows down and stared at Jak through them.

"It's not like that," she protested. "We don't enslave our women, but they don't have all the rights that the men do either. They can choose who they want to marry, and no one is allowed to force themselves on them." She hated the way she was describing the social dynamics of her people. The fact that she kept on referring to the women as "them" made her feel like a giant hypocrite. "They can't own property, and there are only certain jobs that are considered suitable for them."

"I see." Torrin eyed her dangerously. "Women can't be trusted with important jobs, I take it? No head for numbers, and who knows about their judgment. It's probably better if you big, strong, so-much-more-intelligent men take all that on."

"Look, I didn't make the rules. I don't even agree with them," Jak assured Torrin earnestly. She wondered where she had lost control of the conversation. It was no surprise that Torrin had reacted badly to the realities of the situation, but she needed to get her back on track. "I can't change the way things are, but I wanted you to know what you're up against before you got neck deep in it."

"Thanks, I guess," Torrin replied. "I wouldn't go about getting any ideas about asking me to do your laundry or cook your food. I know what kind of tasks men think women are good for, and you won't catch me doing any of them, especially not for you." She shook her head. "It's not as if I'm not used to having to come in and be better than everyone else, just to level the playing field. And when it comes to this, I'm definitely good at being better than anyone else." Torrin laughed. "Your bosses won't know what hit them."

No, they probably won't, Jak thought. *I really hope I'm there to see it.*

CHAPTER TEN

"We should start looking for a place to spend the night." Jak squinted. The sun was nearing the horizon. "It looks like we have about an hour of light left. It hasn't rained today, so it probably will tonight. I want to get under some shelter before that happens." The tightness in her chest hadn't improved much, and she didn't want to spend any more time out in the elements than she had to.

They continued on for another twenty minutes before they came to a river. Jak tossed a twig into the water and watched as it was whisked downstream.

"Current's too strong here," she said. "We'll have to follow it until we find someplace we can cross."

Torrin just nodded and kept plodding forward. Jak could tell her strength was flagging. She hated to keep driving her forward, but they really needed to find somewhere to bed down for the night. The forest was much sparser in this area, so finding a well-concealed site to hunker down in was of utmost import. Unfortunately, it also meant that a fire would be extremely ill-advised. For herself, she was much more comfortable in deep woods with majestic trees and deep shadows, but there was no help for that now.

As they continued along the river's edge, Jak noticed bushes with edible berries. She picked as many as she could without slowing. The dark berries nestled amidst long thorns and by the time she had a decent handful she was nursing the effects of multiple thorn-pricks to her fingertips. They rounded a bend, and she saw a taller stand of trees a little way in from the river's edge.

"Over there," she said, pointing. "We should be able to find some decent shelter in that stand."

Torrin stopped in her tracks and turned woodenly. Exhaustion was obvious in every line of her body.

"Here, have some of these," Jak said, taking one of Torrin's hands in her own. She turned Torrin's hand over and poured most of the berries into the woman's palm, saving a few for herself. Butterflies mated madly in her stomach at the contact. "They're perfectly safe to eat," she said and popped a few into her mouth. The sweetness of the juice was so welcome her tongue practically tingled in tastebud overload. Torrin popped a few in her own mouth, and her eyes widened in appreciation.

"These are really good!" She gobbled down the rest of the handful. Her tongue flicked out to lick the dark juice that stained her lips. "Do you have any more?"

Jak stared at Torrin's tongue for a moment. "Sorry, those are all I could pick on the move. We'll probably find more tomorrow. There're usually bunches of them along the river."

"Pity. I suppose we have more meat for dinner."

"You got it, but we won't be getting any dinner at all if we don't get moving."

"Picky, picky." With renewed vigor Torrin struck out toward the small copse of trees.

The stand of trees provided some protection from prying eyes but not nearly enough protection from the elements. There were no conveniently downed trees for Jak to use as the basis of a shelter. She settled for stripping some of the scrubbier saplings and branches to create a woven mat. She lashed one end to a couple of small shrubs and let the other drag on the ground. The last time she had created a blind like that had been in the company of her brother, and she felt the usual pang of sadness when she thought of him. Torrin watched her intently as she worked.

"If you want to help out, put the branches I cut off the saplings over the open sides of the blind," Jak called to her.

"Sure thing." Torrin picked up the branches and closed off the sides of their shelter.

"No fire tonight. We're too exposed. We might as well send up a flare for the Orthodoxans."

Torrin nodded. "You know how much I've been looking forward to a meal of cold meat. Thanks for not disappointing!"

"That handful of berries is the highlight of tonight's offerings. Don't forget to tip your server."

"Oh, I'll tip my server!" Torrin cut herself off and looked mortified. "Uhhh, never mind." She blushed and bent over, tidying up the edges of their shelter unnecessarily.

What had that been all about? Jak studied Torrin, who glanced over at her from where she crouched. When she met Jak's eyes, she gave a little start and blushed even brighter. Jak was surprised at her embarrassment. If Torrin blushed any harder she would set the nearby trees alight. Not sure what to make of Torrin's mood, she fell back to what she knew and unslung her rifle from her shoulder. She took up a spot in front of the shelter where she could keep watch in the direction of the river and started dismantling her rifle.

Torrin kept herself busy for a little time longer, then slithered under the blind. Jak could feel the weight of her eyes on her back while she worked.

"Your night vision must make caring for your weapon much easier at night," Torrin ventured after a long silence.

"I haven't turned on my night vision yet. It's kind of nice to do this by feel. In sniper school we were expected to be able to do this blindfolded. Night vision doesn't help much then." Jak continued to field strip her rifle.

"Do you have to do that every night?" Torrin asked before a massive yawn cracked her jaws.

"It doesn't hurt anything. All I have to count on out here is my rifle and my wits. Stripping and cleaning it puts my mind at ease that I'll be able to continue to count on it."

Torrin flipped over onto her back and slid an arm over her eyes. Her breathing was already slipping into the steady rhythms of sleep.

"That sounds really lonely," she said so quietly Jak had to strain to hear her.

It is, Jak thought, *it really is*. She finished cleaning her rifle in silence and slid into the blind next to Torrin as rain began to fall.

The other woman sighed and snuggled up against her, throwing an arm over Jak's back. At her touch Jak felt the now familiar warmth spreading through her body, kindling an ache between her thighs. She reached into her pocket and pulled out the package of stim pills and deposited one under her tongue. Sliding her rifle up in front of her, she kept an eye on the trees outside of the shelter. She ached to touch Torrin back, to run fingers through her hair, to slide her thumbs across those full lips. Peering through the scope, she settled in for a long night.

When morning came, she slipped out of the blind and headed down to the river to fill up her canteen. It was good to get out of there. Torrin had spent most of the night snuggled up against her, often with an arm, leg or both thrown over her. Jak had spent most of the night burning for the other woman and hating herself for it. When the canteen was full, she headed back to the berry bushes. She filled as many of her pockets as she could. The inch-long thorns caused her some problems, and as she headed back to their camp, she sucked on one of many holes on her fingers.

Torrin was already up and moving around the camp, pulling apart the blind and spreading the branches out across the copse of trees.

"Good call," Jak said.

"You did it the other morning, so I figured I should return the favor. It gave me something to do while I waited for you to come back."

"You looked so peaceful, I couldn't wake you. I went and got us some breakfast. Berries and water."

"That's great. Better that than cold meat." Torrin held out her hands, and Jak started pulling berries out of the various pockets in her jacket and pants. "That's an interesting way to carry food."

Jak shrugged. "It worked. Have some water."

Torrin drank her fill and handed the flask back to Jak, who took a drink and started in on her own breakfast of berries. She accessed her maps of the area to check on their progress. They'd actually done better than she'd anticipated. There was still a long distance to cover, but they were about halfway back to the front.

"Following the river to the coast is our best bet, but we need to cross somewhere. The river widens a lot more the further out it goes. By the time it gets to the ocean, it'll be too wide to cross. Our goal for today is to cross the river, then get as close to the coast as we're able."

Torrin nodded and gulped down the last of her berries. Jak stood, shouldered her rifle and scarfed downed her last few berries. They left the small stand of trees and made their way back to the river, where Jak refilled the flask, and they struck out, following the river's bank north.

By noon the river was considerably wider than it had been where they'd made camp the previous night. They took a quick break to rest their legs. The terrain wasn't nearly as challenging as the mountains they'd encountered around Hutchinson's compound, but they also weren't nearly as well fed. Jak was starting to tire more rapidly than normal, and she suspected that Torrin had similar issues. She chafed at any delay to their progress but also knew they had to conserve their energy. They needed to shorten their route, and the easiest way to do that was to walk in a straight line between the loops of the river as it meandered through the foothills. When they started out again after a breather, she walked with her rifle held at the ready in front of her chest. If they saw anything resembling game, she would bring it down.

As they ventured further north, however, the terrain got flatter and flatter, the trees became shorter and sparser and by early afternoon they were trudging across rolling grasslands. Jak felt exposed without her woods around her. The skin between her shoulder blades itched. The grasslands were showing signs of cultivation, which made her even more nervous. All they needed now was to be seen by some farmer who would alert the Orthodoxan forces to their presence. Whenever they crested a hill, she hunkered down to survey the area before allowing them to proceed. If they stood at the top of a hill, they would be perfectly silhouetted, immediately visible to anyone looking their direction. Torrin responded well to her whispered instructions, not arguing or questioning the need for caution. A few hours before sunset, Jak discovered their way across the river and the first sign of human habitation.

They crested another low, rolling hill near a bend in the river, and Jak quickly hunkered down, motioning to Torrin to get down as well. Below them was a road which led to a bridge across the river. The river was fairly wide, and there were low buildings on either side of the bridge. Jak surveyed the structures through her scope. Each structure was built just to one side of the road, and a barrier extended from the side of the building across the road. On their side of the river, beyond the small building with the barrier, was a bigger building. Jak watched as a door opened in the side of the larger structure and a uniformed man exited, closing the door behind him.

"Shit," she hissed.

"What is it?" Torrin whispered, concerned, sliding in next to her.

"Orthodoxan military post. I think it's a toll bridge." Jak pulled away from the crest of the hill a bit and rolled onto her back. "We need to get across that bridge, and I have no idea how many of their men we're up against."

Orthodoxans! Torrin instinctively flattened herself as far as she could until she literally hugged the ground. It was a little ridiculous, she told herself. There was no way they could see her over the hilltop, but she couldn't help herself.

"So what's the plan?" she asked.

"I don't have enough intel to make a plan." Jak shook his head. "Without knowing how many we're up against, we're screwed."

He crouched and made his way down the hill, motioning for her to follow. The further they got from the hill's crest, the more Torrin's nervousness eased. The cold hand that had reached inside her chest at Jak's words slowly loosened its grasp around her heart. There wasn't much she was afraid of, but her encounter with the Orthodoxans, especially the last part with Hutchinson, had unnerved her more than she'd realized.

"So, you must have some idea of what we should be doing," Torrin prompted when they stopped at the bottom of the hill.

"I don't like it, but we need to take the time to find out how many of them there are. Here." Jak pulled a rifle scope out of one of his jacket pockets. "Try not to lose this one."

"How many of those do you need, exactly?" Torrin chose to ignore his dig.

"I use different ones for different distances. Trying to use a long distance one for short or medium distances is pointless."

"They make digital ones, you know. Those can handle varying ranges. I'm sure I can get hold of some for you. And the Devonites, of course."

Jak shrugged. "I'm fine with these. It's not smart to rely too much on digital equipment out here. If it stops working and you don't have a backup, you're in big trouble." A spasm of pain crossed his face. "Trouble gets you killed."

"Bron?" Torrin laid a hand across the back of his. He nodded.

"He preferred a cloak device to the ghillie suit I like. His projector developed a glitch that caused a slight ripple in the air. It's not unusual with cloaks and the Orthodoxans have obviously been trained to look for it." He closed his eyes and put his other hand over hers. "He took a sniper's bullet in the throat."

Torrin grimaced but said nothing. Jak's hand gripped hers hard enough to hurt, but he looked like he was about to cry. She really wanted to throw her arms around him and hold him, but she wasn't sure if she'd be able to stop herself from going further. The past few nights of close proximity had done nothing to blunt the attraction she felt for this man. It was an attraction that she shouldn't feel, didn't want to feel, but she couldn't help coming back for more.

She must have made a noise because Jak opened his eyes and looked down at their hands. He let go of her hand with alacrity, almost throwing himself backward.

"Sorry," he muttered, face pink.

"It's okay. If you need to talk, I'm here. Remember, I know a little something about losing someone."

"Sure, sure," he said. He was dismissing her, she was sure of it.

"Hey, I mean it. Talking about it can really help. Have you talked to anyone about it since it happened?"

"There's no point in talking about it. Actions count for more than words, especially out here." He looked at her, and she stepped back at the dead look behind his eyes. The warm blue eyes shouldn't have been capable of looking so cold. It was clear he thought he didn't have anything to live for. Unless…

"You're trying to find him," Torrin accused. "You want to find the man who killed your brother and take him out."

"So what if I am? No one has as much right as I do. My brother isn't the first one he took from me."

Torrin rocked back on her heels at the revelation. "What? Really? How do you…"

"We don't have time for this," Jak cut her off midsentence. Torrin sat there with her mouth agape for a moment, then snapped her jaws shut.

"You're right," she said. *But don't think I'm going to let that one lie,* she thought. *There are so many layers of wrong happening here.*

He looked at her, eyes flat. "I know you won't drop it. I wish you would. We have bigger fish to fry right now."

"I said you were right."

"I need you to go back up the hill and watch the closest tollhouse. Try to count how many of them are in there and see when their shift change happens."

"I can do that. Where are you going to be?" She hoped she didn't sound too worried.

"I'm going to see if I can find a better line of sight across the river. I'll be doing the same thing. Make sure you stay down. If you stand up at the top of the hill, anyone looking over will see you silhouetted against the sky."

"Got it." Torrin stood up, crouching. He reached out and grabbed her wrist.

"We have no communication devices, so meet me back here in a couple of hours." He pointed at a point in the sky not far above the horizon. "When the sun gets past that point, come back down."

"Okay," she said, impatient to get started. She tried to get her arm back from him, but he tightened his grip and pulled her back down half a step. Surprised, she looked at him. He looked unsure and chewed on his lower lip.

"I really shouldn't do this." He let go of her hand and undid his belt, sliding it out of the loops in his pants.

"Ummm, what are you doing?" She looked at him askance. What was he thinking by taking off his pants?

"You're the one who's been on my back for a weapon. Do you want my pistol or not?" His voice was peevish.

"Oh." That made more sense than him taking his pants off, but the men on this planet had some seriously messed up priorities. No one could blame her for jumping to the wrong conclusion. At that moment, she was struck by just how far outside her comfort zone she was. While she was no stranger to conflict, she hadn't been a soldier in a very long time. She had no hard feelings for the military. She'd known more than one soldier and not a few of them intimately. She'd been one herself, if only for a short time. Actually, when she thought about it, she seemed to have a propensity for military lovers. Maybe that was why she was so drawn to Jak. But this wasn't her milieu. She was a negotiator. She loved to wheel and deal, to get the best bargain for herself and her people. There was no way to bargain her way out of this position. Her whole world had been turned upside down, and there would be no way to right it until she got off this hellish planet. It was a pity that a world this beautiful was rotting like fruit on the vine.

"Here," Jak said, and she started, coming back to the present. She took the pistol from him and clipped it to her waist. Fortunately the holster went on much like the one she'd had for her plasma pistol. The holster was oily leather and unrelieved black. There was a flap over the top that stopped her from getting at the gun.

Jak reached over. "You open it up here." He pressed on a point part of the way down the holster and the top popped open. Torrin felt at the spot he'd pressed on and could feel a slightly raised nub. She pressed the spot back into the holster, and it clicked closed. When she ran her fingers over it again, it popped back open.

"Have you ever used a weapon like this?" Jak asked. She shook her head, and he reached into the holster, pulling out the pistol.

"Here's the trigger," he started.

"I'm not a complete neophyte," Torrin interrupted, somewhat irritated by his assumption. "I've just never used an explosive-based propulsion weapon before."

He nodded. "The safety is here. Make sure you engage it before you holster the pistol. When it's flipped up, the safety is off and you can fire. Now this is just a pistol, but it's a powerful one and the recoil is a bitch."

Torrin cleared her throat at the pejorative term.

"Sorry. The recoil's a pain in the ass, kind of like you." He grinned at her. "Is that better?"

She glared at him through narrowed eyes. He was trying to convince her that the fragile, haunted man was gone. She knew when someone was shining her on. He grinned and he joked, but the dead look still lingered in his eyes.

"I guess not." He shrugged. "Just remember that this is going to kick back and plan for it. You need to resight your next shot or it's going to go high and wide. If we had some time, I would have you take some practice shots, but we don't need to let the Orthodoxans know we're here."

Torrin turned the pistol over in her hands, running her fingers over it, familiarizing herself with the shape and weight of the weapon. Jak pulled a couple of magazines out of one of his pants pockets. He reached over and took one of her hands off the gun and placed it along the top.

"Feel the slide there?" He pressed her hand down on it. "Pull that back to pop the magazine out. It'll engage when you pull it all the way back. Then take one of these and replace the empty one." Demonstrating, he pulled her hand back and the slide released the ammunition clip. It fell to the ground, where he picked it up and handed it back to her. "Put it back in. You'll have to really slam it in there to get it to catch."

As usual, his touch on her skin awoke conflicting feelings within her. She didn't know if it was because they were about to head into a potential combat situation, but she was very aroused. If he'd been female and they hadn't been on the other side of a hill from who knew how many enemy combatants, she would have jumped him. She couldn't remember the last time she'd been this turned on. The warmth in the pit of her stomach and her loins was so intense that it was almost painful. If she'd been alone, she could have brought herself some relief, but she couldn't think of a more inappropriate time for that.

She took the clip and fumbled it back into the gun. Her hands were less than dexterous, and she almost dropped the clip back into the grass. It took her three tries to slam the clip home.

"I've never done this before," she explained, trying to cover for her sudden clumsiness.

"Here, I'll help you through it." Jak reached for her hands.

"No!" He looked a little hurt at the strength of her denial. "I can get this. Just let me run through it." She didn't want his hands on her again. His touch completely clouded her ability to think and function. Without his help, she ran through the motions with confidence and was able to get it down.

"I'll head around the hill that way," Jak said, pointing to his left. "Fire the pistol three times in a row if you get made. I'll make sure that I have a line on you wherever I set up."

She nodded and started back up the hill, holstering the pistol. He had a line on her thoughts, and she needed to get away from him. The more time she spent with him, the harder it was to keep her hands to herself. When she got back to Nadierzda, she was going to tumble the first available and willing woman. Apparently she'd gone way too long without a good romp. And now here she was, heading up a hill into a life-or-death situation where she would be facing off against men with rifles while she had only a little pistol and a scope. Her priorities were messed up. She could easily die here, and all she could think about was sex. She sighed and pushed on toward the hill's crest.

CHAPTER ELEVEN

Torrin crawled the last few meters to the top of the hill and lay prone, her head barely cresting the top. As soon as she saw the small outpost, her rambling thoughts sharpened. She pulled out the scope Jak had given her and trained it on the structures below. There was one man in the small building by the road. Craning her head, she took a look at the sun to gauge how much time she had left. She checked out the rest of the area. There were no other Orthodoxans in evidence, but the biggest building looked big enough to house a dozen men. She really hoped that wasn't the case and wished she knew exactly where they were in Orthodoxan territory. Surely if the outpost was far enough behind the front lines, they wouldn't staff it with too many men. Sadly, that didn't match what little she knew of the Orthodoxans. The outpost where she'd met Major Yonkman, though far from the front, had been heavily manned.

"Tien, are you there?" A little extra intel would come in handy, but all she got in return was silence. It had been too much to hope that she was still within range of her ship, but she had to try. Maybe she would get lucky and the signal would bounce off some low-hanging clouds and she'd be able to get in contact with the AI.

Not having information at the ready to answer the smallest inquiry was driving her nuts. Who knew she could have missed a weather report so badly?

Her perusal of the area on the near side of the river complete, she turned her attention to the other side of the bridge. There wasn't anything that she could make out there, and her scope wasn't powerful enough to bring up any meaningful detail. She tried to pick Jak out but couldn't. That was no real surprise. She was pretty sure he could disappear into a fold in the ground and no one would know he was there unless they stepped on him. Knowing where he was would have made her feel a little better. He'd said he would set up where he could see her, and the thought reassured her somewhat.

After she checked out the surroundings, she returned her attention to the buildings below her. The man in the tollhouse looked extremely bored. He'd rocked his chair back on two legs and balanced while bouncing up and down. Every now and again he would turn his head back into the tollhouse. Apparently, he had better things to do than pay attention to the road. He was more focused on the inside of the building than the outside. She could have done naked cartwheels at the top of the hill and he wouldn't have noticed.

She crawled sideways, trying to get a better view inside the building and noticed another pair of boots. From her angle, they were all she could make out. So there were two of them in there. From the size of the small structure, if there were more men in there, they would have been shoehorned in. Satisfied with her deduction, she checked the angle of the sun. To her disappointment, the sun had barely moved at all. It was going to be a long afternoon.

As she watched, she went over the events of the past few days in her head. She still wasn't sure why Jak was dragging her across the back end of beyond. He had no ties to her, no responsibility for her. He hadn't indicated that his people wanted to trade with her. He seemed hopeful that they might but had warned her that it would be a hard sell. His sensitivity to women was amazing, especially given that his society was little better in their treatment toward her gender than were the Orthodoxans. In her experience, men raised like that saw women as little more than chattel. They might give lip service to the idea that women were intelligent and capable human beings, but they didn't really believe it. Their feelings of superiority would be severely threatened if they realized that women could be as good as them, if not better, given the opportunity. Jak wasn't like that, though. She was sure of it. Maybe it stemmed from the fact that he was so slight. He'd probably fought all his life to be taken seriously. She knew what that was like. When someone else decided that you were less than they were, for any reason, you had to work twice as hard to be twice as good just to get on a level playing field.

He certainly worked hard. His hands were incredibly strong and he was extremely self-assured. The only chinks she saw in his armor related to his brother, and that armor wasn't nearly as strong as it had been a couple of days ago. It wasn't that he was softening, exactly, but she wagered that he'd let her see parts of who he was that nobody had seen since his brother died. Maybe even before. She considered the fact of his being out here without a spotter. His was an extremely solitary way of life, and she didn't know how he stood it. If it turned out that he was out here for a purpose beyond the mission he'd been given, though—that could compensate for a lot of the solitude. She didn't know how he thought he would recognize the sniper who killed his brother, but he seemed to think he could track him down.

What are you doing? Once again, she was thinking about Jak. She needed to stop that. She had plenty else to be thinking of. How about the different equipment she could provide for the Devonites to help them defeat the Orthodoxans? Their current situation really drove home how much they needed a secure communications system.

She glanced over to where she thought Jak might be, wondering what he was up to. *Stop that. You're prepping for your next big sale,* she admonished herself sternly. There were all sorts of weapons that she could supply for them. She would have to keep the size of the shipments down so as not to attract the League's attention right away. Eventually they would realize that someone had been meddling, but she hoped she would be long gone by then. She had no desire to spend any more time in a League prison even though their prisons were fairly mild compared to the couple of jails she'd ended up in on the Fringes when a customer or two had realized how badly they'd been outbargained. Some of the Fringe worlds were little more than feudal societies, and when the wrong person got pissed off, they had free rein to do what they wanted to.

A dust cloud came into view over the horizon while she sat there trying not to think of Jak. She trained the scope on the cloud and brought a vehicle into focus. It drove along the road toward the tollbooth. The dust kicked up as it sped along the dirt road made it difficult to see. From what she could make out, though, it didn't seem to be a military truck. She watched with interest as it pulled up in front of the small structure and the soldiers stepped out to greet it. One of them talked to the truck's driver and took possession of some papers while the other one walked around to the truck's exposed bed. Mounds of round vegetables were heaped in the bed of the truck. They had the blue Haefonian tinge that she'd become familiar with, but they looked like Earth cabbages, a staple vegetable on the Fringes as it grew well almost anywhere.

The soldier poked the muzzle of his rifle between some of the cabbages. Satisfied with his inspection, he helped himself to an armful of the leafy, round vegetables. He called something out to his partner, then took his prize back to the tollhouse. His partner waved the vehicle through.

That wasn't good news. If the Orthodoxans were checking papers and searching vehicles, then she and Jak wouldn't be able to commandeer a car to make it through the checkpoint. She hoped Jak would have a better idea of how to proceed. The river looked much too wide to cross without a boat, and besides that she had no desire to get back in the water so soon after her last swim.

She checked the horizon and grunted in disgust when she realized once again that not much time had passed. If only she had something to do. She really disliked being at loose ends. How did Jak do it, she wondered, all by himself for so long with nothing to do but watch. Obviously she wasn't cut out for the life of a sniper. With a grimace, Torrin forced herself back to the surveillance.

The next thirty minutes passed painfully slowly. As soon as the sun was in the remotest vicinity of the area of sky Jak had indicated, she scrambled down the hill. Jak was nowhere to be found. She entertained herself by pacing back and forth in the shallow valley. The enforced inactivity of surveillence had reminded her of how hungry she was. While she was sick and tired of their meager meals of aetanberan meat, to her cramping stomach even that now sounded great. Turning on her heel to stomp the other way, Torrin bit off a scream when she almost collided with Jak.

"Holy hells!" she hissed. "You just about gave me a heart attack."

"You need to pay better attention to your surroundings. I could've been a patrol of Orthodoxans for all you know."

Torrin rolled her eyes. "Well, how lucky for me that you weren't."

"Yeah, it is lucky." Jak's voice heated. "You aren't taking this very seriously. Those people want to kill us or worse."

"I'm being plenty serious, but I can't keep up the constant vigilance like you can. I'm a merchant, not a soldier. Those days are far behind me."

"Just be more careful. And pay attention!" Jak looked at her soberly. "Just because I haven't seen any sign of patrols doesn't mean they won't send one. Did you see anything useful?"

"They have two men in the booth, but I didn't see anyone else. A farmer drove by and had his truck searched and his papers checked. If you're thinking of stealing or hijacking a vehicle to get through there, think again. They're searching whatever passes to see what they can help themselves to, not just in the interests of being thorough."

"I was afraid of that. The other side of the river has a couple of men also. We're going to need to do more surveillance. I need to see what their shift change looks like." Jak chewed at his lower lip in thought. "We need at least one shift change, but two would be better to get a decent count of their total numbers. We're already outnumbered two to one, but they're Orthodoxans so we still have the upper hand."

"So what does that mean for food?" Torrin was very conscious of just how empty her belly was.

"We can finish up the last of the meat. It's too dangerous to hunt out here, though. It's going to be a hungry day." He contemplated his hands for a few seconds. "We should eat now, I think, then get back to watching."

He pulled the very paltry chunk of meat from one of his pockets and unwrapped the leaves from around it. Torrin happily accepted the thin slice that he cut off for her and he helped himself to a small piece. What was left was barely more than a thick slice.

"At least we have breakfast," Jak said as he wrapped the meat back up again. He wolfed down his piece in a few bites. Torrin's slice was long gone by this point. The meat had blunted her hunger a little, but she could still feel where it gnawed at her backbone.

"Back to it," he said, wiping his hands on his pants, then started up the hill.

"Do you want me to go watch the other side, then?" Torrin asked.

"I've seen all I need to over there. We need to see exactly what we're up against over here."

They clambered back up the hill. The shadows had started to lengthen, and clouds moved in front of the setting sun casting them in brilliant hues of orange and pink. They glowed from behind, and Torrin was struck by the contrast between the blue of Haefen's landscape and the orange flames of the sky. The setting sun glinted off a distant object, and she tapped Jak on the shoulder. He had his rifle trained on the buildings below.

"What's that over there?" She pointed off in the direction of the glint. "The sun was shining off something metallic or glass."

Jak swung around in the direction Torrin pointed. "Get down, as low as you can!" With his rifle and scope trained away from the buildings, he scanned the landscape. The tip of his tongue protruded from between his teeth. Torrin realized that he was ready to pull that trigger; his entire body vibrated with tension. She flattened herself against the ground.

"Someone could be out there with a high-powered scope," Jak said. His voice was distracted, most of his attention on the far hills. "Slide over to my right and pull out the scope from my top jacket pocket. Carefully. I don't think he's seen us, but if he's out here, he's looking for somebody."

Torrin barely breathed as she carefully slid down the hill and around Jak. She slipped a hand into his jacket and pulled out the scope and went to hand it to him. He shook his head slightly without taking his eye from the scope on his rifle.

"I need you to help me spot. Check out the area where you remember seeing the glint. Also, check on the toll bridge every now and again. The last thing we need is for someone to stumble on us because we're looking for a sniper that may or may not exist."

Torrin swallowed hard as she raised the scope to her eye. The hair on the back of her neck prickled, and she felt like she was about to crawl out of her skin. As she perused the far hills, looking for anything that might be a person Jak pulled in his rifle and slid down the hill a couple of meters. He screwed a device onto the end of the gun's muzzle.

"What's that?" she asked, attention on the hills in the distance.

"Silencer and flash suppressor. I hate to use them since they'll lessen my effective range, but we can't let the Orthodoxans down there know we're here." He crawled back up the hill and took up his position.

"Anything?" he asked.

"Nothing yet. The shadows are making it hard to find anyone." She was getting frustrated, and her own tension was ratcheting up exponentially. By contrast, Jak was entering a more relaxed state.

He scanned back and forth with the rifle. "Look for shapes that don't belong. Lucky for us, this guy isn't too good, or you never would have seen that glint. The setting sun might outline him, so look for that too."

She had to strain to hear his murmured instructions. He slowed his breathing and allowed calm to wash over him.

Once again, she trained her scope where she thought she'd seen the shine of light and considered the terrain, keeping his advice in mind. Every stump and rock looked like an enemy. Her eyes almost slid past one rock formation before she moved back to it. This rock formation had a branch sticking out of it that looked a little too straight to be found in nature. It was deep in the shadows cast by a taller hill.

"I think I found something," Torrin said.

"Talk me over to it," Jak instructed. "Let me know the major landmarks and then talk me in."

"Okay. It's the shorter hill in front of the tall one with the exposed rock formation at the top that looks like a broken fist. Two-thirds of the way to the left is a stunted sapling."

Jak adjusted his aim, following her instructions. "You're doing great, keep going," he said in a soothing voice when she paused.

Torrin knew her instructions were likely to end with someone's death. She had killed before but always in self-defense or other justified reasons. The other person had always known it was coming. Stalking someone and delivering death before they even knew what was coming didn't sit well with her.

She took a deep breath. "Follow the top of the hill from the right of the sapling. There's a small rock formation there that doesn't look right."

"I see him!" Muted excitement colored Jak's voice. "He has no idea where we are. He's actually facing the wrong way, back the way we came."

"How do you know he's looking for us? He could be a local out hunting or something."

"Not likely. That's a military grade sniper rifle. Some farmer out hunting wouldn't use a weapon that would blow large holes in his dinner. That and most people don't wear helmets to go hunting."

Torrin watched through the scope with trepidation and heard Jak exhale. She knew what was coming but couldn't look away. Now that she'd been watching the spot for a while, she could make out the different parts of the man she'd mistaken for a pile of rocks. His head was covered by a helmet with a piece of cloth coming off the back, creating a line to his shoulders. It disguised the silhouette of head and shoulder with some effectiveness. Coming off the front, she made out the long barrel of a high-powered rifle. He was indeed facing the wrong way, but she could tell from the way he moved that he was doing what they just had. He was definitely scanning the area for someone or something.

A spray of red bloomed on his shoulder. Torrin jerked. The silencer did its work well. She'd barely heard anything. The force of the bullet's impact rotated the Orthodoxan sniper around to face them. She saw the look of surprise on his face before it disappeared in a mist of crimson. His body collapsed and disappeared behind the far hill.

"We got him!" Jak's voice was fierce in triumph.

Torrin felt nauseated. Her gorge rose, and she had to force it down around a lump in her throat. She knew they had had no choice, but killing in any state other than the heat of the moment didn't sit well with her. It seemed unfair. She slid a few meters down the hill and lay there looking up at the rapidly darkening sky. This was a fine time to discover a sense of fair play. The stars were coming out, and they twinkled down at her, unconcerned by her moral quandary.

Jak dropped down beside her. "Are you all right?" he asked. "You did really well. You're a natural."

"I don't know how I feel about that." Torrin laughed bitterly.

"You never killed anyone before?"

"That's not it. I've just never killed anyone who didn't know it was coming." She placed her head in her hands. "It feels a lot different this way."

"Does it help to know that if you hadn't seen the sun off his scope, we would be dead? If not now, then very soon. He would have found us and one or both of us would be gone, with a bullet in the brain."

"I know that." Torrin sighed, frustrated. "If only I could believe it." She moved down the slope, away from Jak.

Jak wasn't sure what to do. She wanted to talk to Torrin, to find out why she was so upset, but she also knew they needed to take care of the situation with the bridge. The enemy sniper had been about three kilometers away, close enough to reach. He probably had supplies that would help them survive longer out here. She'd seen precious little in the way of wildlife. This area was more desolate than she was used to in her forests.

She cleared her throat. Torrin looked up at her, eyes hooded. "You're not going to like this, but we need to retrieve what we can from the body."

"Are you serious?" Torrin's eyes widened in disbelief. "Won't that be dangerous? What if he has a partner?"

"If he had a spotting partner, the guy would've been there with him. Another rifle and the supplies he'll have on him will help our chances of survival." She slid down next to Torrin. "It's no easy thing that I'm asking, I know, but I wouldn't suggest it if it wasn't important." She put her hand on Torrin's shoulder and felt unaccountably wounded when she twitched out of her reach.

"Well, I'm going," Jak said, more harshly than she intended. "You can come along or stay here on top of the Orthodoxans."

Torrin shot her a dark look. "That's a low blow. You know I'm not going to stick around where they can stumble over me."

"Good, it's decided then. Time to move out." She made her way down to the bottom of the hill and started off in the direction of the dead Orthodoxan. After a few moments she heard Torrin following her. She suppressed a smile; Torrin still had no idea how to move quietly.

CHAPTER TWELVE

Their journey to the dead sniper was uneventful and quiet. Torrin refused to engage with her and Jak was no good at drawing people out. She hadn't been good at engaging others before her brother died. After two years of self-imposed solitude, she was even worse at it. It wasn't long before she decided it was too much work and stopped trying to talk to Torrin. Whatever crisis she was in the middle of, she'd made it clear it was one she would weather on her own. Jak just had to leave her to it.

Jak cast her mind back to her first human kill. For years she'd been hunting and was no stranger to dealing death, but it was different when it was a person, even an Orthodoxan. Though she'd known the other soldier would have happily killed her, it had been difficult to reconcile taking a human life. Her first time had been much like today's kill, at an uncomfortable remove through the scope. When she'd made the kill, Bron had been so excited. The only way he would have been happier was if he'd pulled the trigger himself. Back then, it had been clear that he was the better spotter and she the better sniper, but he'd definitely preferred taking his own shots. It had taken most of their first year before he'd stopped demanding his fair share of time on the trigger. In fact, he hadn't been convinced until she'd almost gotten them both killed because she'd been so focused on their target that she missed the enemy patrol that had passed within three meters of them. After that, he'd understood that his part was to keep them both alive to get the job done.

In her mind's eye she could still see the hapless soldier's head as it exploded in a fountain of blood. She'd wanted to cry, but in the face of Bron's enthusiasm and their instructor's approval she hadn't been able to do anything except grin and try to ape her brother's excitement. When they'd gone back to camp, she'd cried herself to sleep and sworn that she would never kill a human being again. At the first opportunity, she'd planned to slip away from camp in the night and live out her life deep in the woods where no one would find her.

Two days later an enemy sniper had gotten their instructor, and she never cried over an Orthodoxan again. She threw herself into their training and concentrated on getting the Orthodoxans before they could get her people.

It had been years since she'd thought of her early days as a sniper. The idealistic, naive girl who'd joined up was gone. She and Bron might have joined up because they had no other options, but she'd believed in what they were doing. As the shine wore off, she'd gained a grim satisfaction in being the best at her job. That satisfaction had hardened into a single-minded resolve for revenge that had glowed white-hot in her mind since the day Bron had taken a bullet through the throat. The appearance of Torrin in her life threatened to shatter that resolve. She should be strong enough to move past the irresistible pull she felt for the woman, but no matter how hard she resisted, she could feel Torrin setting up camp in her head. The longer it went on, the less energy she had to fight it, the more natural it felt. She felt equal parts hope and terror over Torrin's unexpected reaction to the death of the enemy sniper. Hope that Torrin might decide that Jak was too horrible to deal with and leave. Terror that Torrin might do exactly that.

"Stop it," Jak growled.

"What was that?" Torrin asked.

Shit, had she said that out loud? "Uh, nothing. Trying to figure out where we are, that's all." She scowled and hoped that her excuse didn't sound as hollow to Torrin's ears as it had to her own.

Night had fallen and the clouds that had provided such a spectacular sunset now blocked out the moon and stars. She'd already had to engage her night vision. Torrin kept up pretty well, but Jak had to slow occasionally to let her catch up.

"We aren't far, I think." She looked around. The hill with the broken fist was right in front of them, and it was all she could do to make out the sapling at the hill's crest. "Up there." She pointed and Torrin gave her a look. "That's right, you probably can't see that far. Sorry. If you want to stay here, that's okay. I can get what we need on my own."

"That would be okay." Torrin sat down quickly with a sigh of relief.

Jak climbed the hill, angling toward the back where she'd seen the man disappear after he went down. He laid in a crumpled heap a third of the way down the hill. She made her way over to his still form and flipped him onto his back. The upper third of his face was gone, exposing the sinuses and brain. Insects already crawled in and out of his wounds.

Exhaling heavily to clear the stench of death from her nostrils, she pulled a data cord from her pocket and plugged one end into the jack on her hand. She pulled open the collar of his shirt and exposed the top of his chest. Digging around, she located the dataport set into his right collarbone. Her people had their input devices in their hands, but they were accustomed to sharing information. The placement of the Orthodoxan jacks seemed designed to discourage sharing. It was fortunate that her first shot had hit him in the other shoulder. If she'd hit him in this shoulder, his collarbone and port would have been gone.

"I hate this shit," she muttered as she plugged herself into his system. It was the only way to retrieve his orders, but rummaging through a dead man's data was extremely disorienting. There was no way to access the thoughts or feelings he'd had while alive. If he'd still been alive, the neural activity along his nerves would have allowed him to prevent external access to whatever data packages he'd uploaded. Now that he was dead, the information was ripe for accession. Everyone stored their internal data a little differently, so it took her a little bit to find his last set of orders. Her heart sank as she scanned them. He'd been sent out after them specifically. The Orthodoxans had at least some inkling that they may have headed out this way. The orders didn't note an exact location for them, however, so it was possible they'd sent out as many men as possible to cover all likely routes. She hoped that was the case; it would give them a fighting chance.

The orders confirmed, she spent a little time pulling any additional information she could find. Maps were always good; those she could turn in to Command when she got back. Intel would pore over them and hopefully be able to make use of them. There wasn't much else of interest. He'd obviously had a mind wipe recently. It was important to move out obsolete and irrelevant data periodically. The human mind only had so much capacity for artificially acquired information. It was possible to internalize data uploads and hold on to the information that way, but the actual data packages needed to be removed before they either filled up all the available space or became corrupted.

Satisfied that she'd gotten all the information she could, Jak moved on to his pockets. She rifled through them and found some small, useful pieces of equipment. Another fire starter, a length of flexible cable, three scopes of varying strengths, some trail food, a couple of glowsticks and another knife. Looking around, she spotted his rifle a meter or so away and picked that up as well. Critically, she examined his jacket, but the shot to the shoulder had torn a huge hole through the fabric. It was covered in blood, the collar stained with what could only be chunks of brain matter. There was no way she would be able to convince Torrin to wear it. That was unfortunate. Torrin's red outfit was nice on the eyes, but the color didn't blend well into their surroundings.

She retraced his tumble back to the top of the hill and looked around to see if she could locate his pack. It was unlikely that he had been there without some additional equipment. From his orders, it was clear the Orthodoxans hadn't known precisely where they were, so he would have covered some distance. A few meters past the hill's crest, she located the bag nestled among some rocks.

"Good deal," Jak whispered exultantly. She snagged the bag and headed back down to Torrin.

"Any luck?" Torrin asked as she got closer.

"Jackpot," Jak said, holding up the bag. She broke open a glowstick. It gave off a sickly green glow that cast enough light to see by, but not enough to ruin her night vision and unlikely to attract unwanted attention, nestled as they were between the two hills. "Let's see what we have," she said and opened it up. Torrin leaned in so she could see.

At the top of the sack was a set of folded fatigues. She handed them to Torrin. Next she pulled out a pair of binoculars. "Not as nice as the ones you threw into the river, but better than nothing," Jak said. Torrin flung the clothes back at her, but she easily snatched them out of the air.

"Nice catch," Torrin groused.

Jak tossed the fatigues back to Torrin and reached deeper into the bag.

"Yes!"

"What is it?" Torrin asked, intrigued by Jak's jubilation.

"Food!" Jak pulled out a bunch of Orthodoxan military ready to eat meals. "They won't be as good as the ones made by my people, but at least we won't starve. There's a few days' worth there and more in the bag. It looks like he was planning on being out here for a while. If we're careful, this'll be enough to get us back on the other side of the fence. If we're lucky, we'll be able to stretch this with some hunting and we won't be hungry at all."

"Well, that's good news, anyway."

"Unfortunately, that's all the good news there is," Jak said, still reaching around in the bottom of the bag. She didn't feel anything other than more meals and a large canteen. It would be worth it to go through the bag again in daylight to make sure she hadn't missed anything, but she was glad she'd made the call to recover what they could from the corpse.

"What do you mean by that?" Torrin prompted. She seemed annoyed at having to ask.

"Hmmm," Jak replied helpfully, shoving what she'd pulled out back into the bag. When she finished, she looked Torrin in the eyes. "The Orthodoxans have men out looking for us. I don't think they know for sure we've gone this way. The orders read more like they're covering their bases. That's the good news. The bad news is that it looks like they sent out a lot of snipers to hunt us down. They're really pissed that we killed Hutchinson and they're out for our blood."

"Oh, crap!" Torrin couldn't believe their luck. With everything else that had happened, it had been easier to just hope they would be able to get away without any more problems. "Wait, what do you mean by 'we' killed Hutchinson? You pulled the trigger. I had nothing to do with it."

Jak gave her a hard look, his face bathed in the green luminescence of the glowstick. The color lent a ghoulish cast to his features.

"Would you rather I'd let him keep on with what he was doing?" he asked. "Not that it matters much now. We're both in this mess together. We just got to be more aware, and it's going to slow down our return from behind enemy lines. No more cutting across hills. We're going to have to skirt them. The last thing we need to do is make ourselves any more visible than we have to."

"So how long before we can make it out of here?"

"Once we get past that toll bridge, I think we can make it in about two and a half days. Maybe half a day to a day more, depending if we have to detour around a lot of hills or not."

Torrin noticed that Jak looked exhausted. There were circles under his eyes she hadn't noticed a day ago. His eyes looked like they glittered at her from the bottom of a well.

"Do you plan to go the entire time without sleeping?" she demanded. "You look like shit, and I haven't seen you sleep for the past two days. There's no way you'll make it at this rate."

Jak shook his head. "Don't worry about me. I got it covered. It's not my first time trapped out behind enemy lines for longer than I planned."

"Can we at least make camp here and you can take a nap? I'll keep watch."

"No way. We need to head back to the bridge so we can find out exactly what we're up against and come up with a plan." He stood up and shouldered the pack, then picked up the dead sniper's rifle and tossed it to her. "Try not to shoot me with it."

Torrin snagged it out of the air and struggled to her feet. Her legs were tired from all of the walking they'd done over the past few days. She wasn't used to all this exertion. While the rolling hills were a welcome break from the mountains and forests, she still wasn't getting the rest she needed to recover, and of course Jak didn't flag at all. Even though the dark circles under his eyes were so pronounced that he looked like he'd been beaten about the face and he looked like he was seconds from falling asleep on his feet, his stride was as even and purposeful as ever.

"Leave the glowstick," he said over his shoulder when she stooped to reach it. "I know it's not much light, but it could give our position away, especially if there are more snipers out here."

How did he know she'd been about to pick that up? He must have eyes in the back of his head. A disturbing image, to be sure. She smothered a snicker as she imagined two blue eyes blinking at her from under short blond hair. She was really getting punchy. If she was lucky, there would be some sleep for her when they got to wherever Jak decided they should watch the Orthodoxans from. With a smothered groan, she forced her legs' burning muscles to keep on after the sniper.

True to his word, Jak skirted them around hills and kept them to the lowest ground he could find. Their trip back to the rise that overlooked the bridge took significantly longer than their first trek. It was a little easier since she didn't have to negotiate the varying slopes, but the walk took twice as long.

"I'm not moving any further." Torrin sat down next to a boulder that jutted out of the hillside at an odd angle. If it rained, she could probably fit most of her body under the overhang. *If* it rained. She gave a mental snort.

Jak continued a couple of paces before her statement registered. "We're almost there," he said, turning back to face her and continuing to walk backward a few paces before stopping.

"I don't give a rat's ass. I'm not moving another centimeter. You keep on. I'm perfectly happy bunking down for the night by this rock." Torrin folded her arms and glared at him, jaw set. "You may be used to trekking around the back of beyond with no food and less sleep, but I'm not."

"Fine, stay there if you want to. I'm going to keep going and set up an observation post at the top of the next hill. I'll come back for you in the morning."

By his tone, she could have sworn he was rolling his eyes. "That's fine by me."

Lying back against the grass, she sighed in relief and closed her eyes. Immobility had never felt so good. She could have fallen asleep right there, except that she could feel him standing, waiting for a response. She cracked one eye open and glanced over at him.

"I'm fine, go do your observing. If you get tired, we can switch places, and I'll watch them while you sleep."

Jak shook his head once more. "I told you, it's taken care of. See you in the morning." Torrin closed her eyes and waited to drift off to sleep.

Sleep was slow in coming. Without Jak's presence, the surrounding countryside brimmed with life. Before she knew it, every little rustle and chirp was making her jump. A while later, she convinced herself it was *too* quiet and something awful was sneaking up on her. She pulled herself up to a seated position and leaned her back against the rock, cradling the Orthodoxan rifle to her chest. Satisfied that she would have at least a fighting chance if some wild animal decided to attack her, she eventually drifted off into a light doze.

She woke when something closed over her elbow. Swinging the rifle blindly, she connected with a mass that gave an explosive "oof." She opened her eyes just in time to see Jak folded over the butt of her rifle.

"Sorry, sorry, sorry!" She snatched the rifle back from his midsection.

"It's okay." He wheezed, struggling to fill his lungs. Torrin watched him work to breathe for another few moments until he was able to struggle upright and fill his lungs. "Heh, you really had something behind that."

"You scared me. Next time, call out or something to wake me."

"Now you tell me," he groaned, rubbing his abdomen. "Next time I will. I might not live through waking you a second time."

"I *am* trained in self-defense. You're lucky that you grabbed me by the elbow. If you'd taken my shoulder, I probably would have broken your arm." It was the truth, but she could tell by the way he nodded that he didn't believe a word she said. There was no reason he should. It wasn't as if she'd proven her mettle to him. He'd had to rescue her from the clutches of a power-hungry, misogynistic rapist. Then he'd shepherded her across the countryside and saved her from drowning in rivers and being eaten by giant bear-things. She wouldn't have believed her either.

"So what's our situation?" Torrin asked. If she pushed her knowledge of self-defense, it would only look like she had something to prove.

The sky was still dark but beginning to lighten in the east. The local wildlife knew daybreak approached and the air was filling with the chirps of birds, punctuated by the occasional strident, grinding shriek. She hoped that was also a bird. Jak didn't seem concerned by the noise so hopefully nothing within earshot was interested in eating them.

"We're up against eight men, split into two shifts. They just finished up their shift change and from what I can tell our same friends from yesterday are out there again now."

"So we're outnumbered four to one?" Torrin was worried. Those didn't sound like good odds at all. "Maybe we should find another place to cross the river."

"It's not as bad as it sounds, especially now we have two sniper rifles. This is our best bet to cross the river. It only gets wider downstream. I really don't want to have to backtrack for a ford that might not even exist."

"Does this mean you finally have a plan?"

Jak nodded. "I have the beginnings of one. We're going to attack them at this time tomorrow morning while they're switching up their shifts. I just need to iron out some of the kinks." He looked excited about the prospect. Torrin noticed that all traces of the previous day's fatigue were gone. The deep circles under his eyes were barely a shadow and he moved with a crispness that she hadn't noticed was gone until it was back. She wondered how he kept doing that.

"So you woke me up even though we have twenty-seven hours before we even think of launching our attack?"

He had the grace to look a little embarrassed. "I thought you might want to know what's going on."

"Never mind," she said, a little exasperated. "I'm going to sleep a few more hours. You look bright-eyed and bushy-tailed. You can keep watch."

"Fair enough," Jak replied calmly.

She lay back down on the grass and closed her eyes. He started moving away, back up the hill.

"Where do you think you're going?" she asked, not bothering to open her eyes.

"To keep watch. It'll be easier from atop the hill."

"Go ahead and stick around here. You can make sure that one of the beasts from this planet of yours doesn't attack and eat my sleeping body." Her tone was light, but she really did want him to stay. She knew she'd sleep better in his presence, knowing that he watched over her.

"There really isn't too much in the grasslands that's big enough or has a taste for humans."

Torrin opened one eye and looked over at him, standing a few meters away. "Please?" she asked simply.

Jak looked surprised but came back down the hill and seated himself near her. "Since you asked so nicely, I suppose."

Closing her eyes, she relaxed. Sleep came very quickly this time.

CHAPTER THIRTEEN

Jak was floored. Torrin's request for her to stick around had caught her off guard. She hadn't lied. It really would have been much more effective to keep watch from a higher vantage, but when Torrin had asked she'd been disarmed by the simple request. The lines of sight down here were crap. It wouldn't be hard to move a whole mess of people on top of them without being seen. The idea made her skin crawl. Not being able to keep an eye over a sizable area was kicking her fear into high gear.

To keep her mind off it, she reached over and picked up the Orthodoxan rifle Torrin had been carrying. It probably needed a good cleaning. She started breaking it down. To her surprise, the rifle was fairly new and seemed quite well taken care of. She cleaned and oiled it as a matter of course. The magazine held enough bullets for twelve shots. That was a greater capacity than her rifle; she was limited to eight. It usually didn't matter, since she typically went after single targets and was almost always able to kill with one shot. One shot, one kill had been drilled into her and Bron by their instructors in sniper school. The sniper from yesterday had required two because he'd been wearing a helmet and had been facing away from them, not to mention the long distance. Three clicks was a long way, even for her. Not her longest kill, but it was up there. As she'd anticipated, the impact to the shoulder had spun the Orthodoxan around, enabling her to administer the kill shot.

There was an extra clip of ammunition in the stock of the rifle, for a total of twenty-four bullets. She looked around for the supply pack and saw that Torrin was using it as a pillow. Searching through the pack in daylight would have to wait until she woke. She hoped there was additional ammunition in the bag. For her own rifle, she was limited to what she had in her pockets. Half her extra ammo was with her own supply pack at the top of that ridge in the forest all those kilometers back. The Orthodoxan rifle took a different size of ammunition from hers, but between what she had in her pockets and what was in her rifle, there was more than enough to clear the bridge of enemy combatants. The sticking point was that she had no idea what they would face closer to the fence. She would have to be judicious with her ammo expenditure.

Her eyes strayed back to Torrin's sleeping face. She wanted to take the smuggler into her arms and hold her. She looked so vulnerable and the way she'd asked for Jak to stick around while she slept made Jak feel…something. Valued, maybe. It was an emotion she couldn't readily identify, but she knew that if someone or something came around the hill with the intent of harming Torrin, she would protect the sleeping woman at the expense of her own life. The intensity of the emotion scared her. After only a few days, it was getting hard to imagine a life without Torrin. She would have to let her go eventually. Torrin had to return to her own life on her own planet. There was no future for them together in any case. Down that path lay only misery—and disgust when Torrin realized that Jak was female and harboring unnatural feelings for her.

If only Torrin had been a man, she would be able to feel for her without having to hate herself. Jak's lips twisted as the seething turmoil of emotion threatened to overwhelm her. She clamped her eyes shut, but tears squeezed out from under the lids anyway. She couldn't keep watch with her eyes closed. Angrily, she dashed the tears on the back of her hand, then scrubbed it across her face, destroying any remaining tracks.

Even though she had told Torrin that she would stay close by to watch over her, she moved halfway up the hill. The vantage would allow her to survey a larger area and the physical distance from the source of her emotional turmoil should help to clear her mind. She longed to be back down there, pressed against Torrin. She had a sudden mental flash of her skin against Torrin's. It was so strong that she could almost feel her bare belly and breasts pressed to the length of Torrin's naked back. A bolt of heat seared through her loins and spread between her legs. The feeling was so intense that she moaned and closed her eyes. The illicit peeks she'd taken of Torrin's nakedness fueled her imagination. Her imaginary self reached around Torrin's side and cupped the bottom of her breast, running her thumb lightly over an erect nipple that hardened further at her touch. Dream Torrin moaned deep in her throat and rocked her hips back, pressing her buttocks into Jak's pelvis.

Jak's eyes snapped open, breaking her out of her lustful reverie. Her hand was down the front of her pants, fingers tangling in damp hair and parting the slick folds of her sex, touching herself in scalding wetness. She snatched her hand back as if burned. Her face flaming, she sneaked a glance down the hill to make sure Torrin hadn't woken up and witnessed any of her aberrant behavior. To her relief, Torrin still slept soundly.

She needed to put more space between them. She climbed further up the hill until she was almost to the top. Raising her rifle, she surveyed the surrounding countryside. She hadn't forgotten about the possibility of enemy snipers, and keeping an eye out for them would keep her mind off the woman below and off her own despicable feelings.

It took longer than usual to sink into the meditative semi-trance she employed when she surveilled an area for an extended period. When the trance finally did come, she almost sobbed with relief at the clarity it provided and the end it brought to her tangled thoughts, if only for a while.

She stayed that way for the next couple of hours, safe in the meditative state where she didn't have to think or feel. A touch to her elbow broke her out of her reverie.

"Do you want to get some sleep?" Torrin asked.

"I'm all right," Jak replied, shifting away from the smuggler. Even that featherlight touch threatened to throw her back into the maelstrom of emotions. She really was all right, at least on the sleep front. Another stim was all she'd needed to beat her earlier fatigue. She'd need another one before their operation against the Orthodoxans at the bridge, but she had enough for that and hopefully to last her until they got back across the fence.

"I'm going to get some food. Do you want anything?" Torrin started back down the hill. After a final study of their surroundings, Jak followed her. When Jak got to the rock, Torrin was preparing one of the ready to eat meals. Jak pulled one out of the rucksack for herself and dug in. It was good to have some real food for a change. The meals tasted like crap, but they were better than a steady diet of aetanberan. After wolfing down her meal, she cleared the tough, resilient grasses from a square of earth and starting drawing out their plan of attack.

"They only have eight men, four who work each shift," Jak started. "That means they'll all be out of their barracks for shift change. We're going to pin them down, and I'll pick 'em off, one at a time, until we've wiped them out."

"That seems like overkill." Torrin shifted in her seat, looking a little uncomfortable. "Do we have to kill all of them?"

"If we leave any of them behind, they'll be able to send people after us. That'll only confirm our presence in the area, and we'll have to deal with way worse."

"Won't an outpost full of dead bodies confirm that just as easily?"

"We won't be leaving them lying around. If we dump them into the river, no one's ever going to find the bodies." Jak was confident. This close to the coast, there were some large predators in the water; they would make quick work of any corpses that went into the drink.

"So you don't see any other way of getting this done?"

"No, I don't. I'm open to any suggestions you got."

Torrin shook her head, troubled.

"Tell me now if you don't think you can do this. I can't have you cracking under the pressure while we're trying to get it done." Jak did her best not to sound impatient. She didn't understand Torrin's reticence. It was obvious they had to get past the Orthodoxans, and beyond retracing their steps, they were out of options.

"I've got this," Torrin assured her.

"Good. We have a lot of time until we launch our attack. I think we should inspect and clean our equipment and keep an eye on them. Oh, and you need to change out of that suit of yours and into something a more low key. The fatigues in the sack should fit."

Torrin went from looking reluctant to looking mutinous. "There's nothing wrong with my suit," she snapped.

"It's very nice, but the red doesn't exactly blend in with the scenery. If this is going to work, then they can't pick us out. The camouflage fatigues will make that harder. You got to change."

"If I change, you can't watch." The argument sounded ridiculous as soon as it left Torrin's lips, and from the way she reddened, she thought so as well.

"For crying out loud, I don't need to watch you!" Of course she didn't. She'd already seen most of Torrin's salient bits and could easily bring them to mind. Just like she was doing right now. Her face was suddenly very hot and to hide her unexpected embarrassment, she picked up the sack and rummaged through it. She pulled the fatigues out and tossed them over to Torrin. She pulled everything else out to see if she'd missed anything. In addition to the items she'd found the night before, she discovered some extra ammunition clips for the sniper rifle and an ultra-thin coil of rope. That was nice to see. Who knew when rope might come in handy?

"Well, go on and get changed," Jak tossed over her shoulder as she continued to rummage through the bag. She resisted the urge to sneak a peek as Torrin flew through her wardrobe change. Feeling virtuous, she busied herself with packing the items back into the bag.

"I'm done." Torrin sounded irritated and Jak understood. The fatigues weren't exactly flattering. The man for whom they'd been fitted hadn't been quite as tall as Torrin. The pants were a little short; the sleeves exposed an expanse of wrist. Her full breasts pushed against the fabric of the jacket, making creases that drew attention right to all the right—or wrong—places.

"I'm up here," Torrin said dryly.

Jak tore her gaze from Torrin's chest. "Sorry. Your jacket doesn't fit very well."

"You don't seem to think so," Torrin said, head cocked to one side, glaring a challenge at Jak.

"Well, at least you won't stick out so badly now. That's something." Jak shrugged uncomfortably.

"I'm so glad," the smuggler said waspishly. "Remind me not to let you dress me ever again. Your fashion taste leaves a little to be desired."

Jak snickered. Torrin threw her an irate look which sent her into gales of laughter. By the time Torrin crossed her arms and started tapping her foot, Jak was laughing so hard that tears coursed down her face. She rolled over into the grass, clutching her sides.

"Wait, let me get this straight," she gasped out around guffaws. "You're getting on the case of a soldier for not having decent fashion sense?" She wiped tears off her face. "Do you think we get a say in the cut of our combat jackets? Maybe you'd like some ruffles along the hems of our coats? No, wait I have it. Stripes of glitter down our pants to matching boots!" Jak dissolved into guffaws once more.

Torrin unbent enough to uncross her arms and grin. "When you put it that way, it does sound a little ridiculous." She started laughing herself. "You'd look really pretty in hot pink, though. It would really bring out the rosiness of your cheeks."

Jak snorted and tried to regain some control of herself. The idea of dressing in hot pink threatened to make her lose it all over again.

"I don't remember the last time I laughed that hard, thanks." She liked seeing Torrin smile and hoped she'd be able to get her smiling again soon. First they had to get across the bridge. With the reminder, her mood sobered quickly. "Let's head back up to the hill overlooking the toll bridge. I wanna make sure that we don't have any surprises when we launch our attack."

Torrin nodded and tossed Jak her fitted jumpsuit. "All right, but you can put this in your bag."

Jak put the suit in the sack, inhaling surreptitiously as she did so. She could smell Torrin's unique scent, deep and sweet, with an underlying bite. It was unlike that of any she'd ever experienced. Most of the time, she was surrounded by sweaty men. She longed to fill her lungs with the aroma but resisted. Nothing would scare Torrin off like some strange man burying his nose in her clothes.

"Let's go," Jak said abruptly, standing and jerking the bag onto her shoulder. Without waiting for Torrin's response, she took off toward their viewing post in the hills.

Torrin jogged after the sniper. For someone with such short legs, he could certainly move when he wanted to. The ridiculous camouflage uniform bunched in all the wrong places and wasn't nearly as comfortable as her jumpsuit. She tugged on the wrists of her shirt in a vain attempt to make them a little longer.

Why did so many of her interactions with Jak end up with him running away from her? Every time she thought she'd exposed a chink in his armor, he clammed up tighter than before and practically raced to put physical distance between them. He couldn't know the unfortunate effect he was having on her. Maybe he simply wasn't used to having a woman around and she confused him. He'd admitted that his brother was the one who had a way with women. With the way he acted, she doubted he'd had much interaction with females. It didn't really change much; it just left her chasing after him across the grasslands and hills of the Haefonian wilderness.

By the time she caught up with him, he was setting himself up at the top of their hill. His sniper rifle rested on a small tripod and he was attaching one of his many scopes to it. She was still more than a little uncomfortable with the idea of killing so many men in cold blood. They wouldn't get over the river any other way, but she didn't have to like it.

"What should I do?" she asked quietly.

"I need you to take your final position over there." Jak pointed off to his left. "Scout out a good position that looks over the barracks and will let you cut off their access to it. When you're done, let me know and I'll check on it."

"You do know that I've never shot one of these before. I'm not just talking about propulsion weapons, but also long-range ones. I'm used to weapons that allow me to get more up close and personal."

"Don't worry. You don't need to be able to shoot the wings off a fly. Just to keep them pinned down so I can take care of the rest."

"All right, you're the expert." Torrin had serious reservations about her ability to be helpful. She shouldered her weapon and slid below the level of the hill before edging around in the direction Jak had indicated. The turnabout was a little strange. Just the other day, she'd practically had to beg to get a sidearm from the man, and now he'd not only let her hold onto his pistol, but he'd also set her up with a high-powered rifle. *What changed?* she wondered.

At the top of the hill, she set up her spot and glanced at the intended target through the rifle's scope. The vantage was decent. but the angle was off. She moved further to the left and checked again. Still off. She moved two more times before she was satisfied with both the angle and the vantage. True to his word, Jak came over and checked her setup.

"Huh." He didn't say anything else, just moved the rifle a hand's width to the right and said nothing else.

"That's all you have to say? I did good." Torrin was proud of herself. She hadn't been exaggerating. Her weapons of choice were a plasma pistol, a vibroknife for close quarters and her hands for when she didn't want to kill, which was more often than not. Taking the time to plan a meticulous strike from hundreds, even thousands of meters away wasn't exactly in her wheelhouse. For her, killing was a reaction to a situation gone irretrievably wrong, not an activity to be planned out and strategized over days beforehand. Pulling the trigger wasn't anything she looked forward to, but she could appreciate the craftsmanship that went into it.

"Yeah, it's not bad," Jak said noncommittally. He slid a meter or so to her right and took out one of his scopes to survey the buildings below the hill. Torrin noticed that he occasionally surveyed the surrounding countryside and the hills behind them. Ever since they'd taken out the other sniper, his focus had been razor sharp. He was so tense he practically vibrated. She wasn't sure how he could keep it up.

They spent the rest of the morning and afternoon watching the toll bridge. The only break in the monotony came when another farm truck rumbled through. Torrin's repeated attempts to engage Jak in conversation were rebuffed with monosyllabic responses that went nowhere. She didn't know why he'd suddenly decided to distance himself from her. The longer his silence dragged on, the more she wracked her brains to discover what she could have done to offend him.

"You should get some sleep while you can," he finally said to her. Darkness had fallen, and rain had started coming down about an hour earlier, a soft drizzle that coated them with a thin layer of dampness. Torrin hadn't realized she was soaked until the gentle rain had seeped through to her skin. She'd really wished for her jumpsuit then. Even if it hadn't been waterproof, it would have been more comfortable than the fatigues.

"Great" was all she said in return. There was no point in offering him the same courtesy. He would just turn it down as he had every night since her unscheduled dip in the river. Still, she was exhausted and even though she was wet and in some discomfort, the idea of sleep was extremely appealing. She slid a short way down the hill and closed her eyes.

The dual discomforts of rain and ill-fitting clothing kept her from truly restful sleep. She roused at every sound or movement from Jak. It wasn't his fault and he was very still, but in her sleep-deprived state she was becoming very irritable. Finally, when she heard him rustle about in his pockets then pull out a canteen, she couldn't stand it anymore.

"Do you think you could—" Torrin cut off midsentence, not sure what she was seeing. "What's that?"

Jak stared at her in the midst of popping something in his mouth. He took a swig from the water bottle and washed it down.

"What was what?"

"What you just ate." She eyed him suspiciously, propping herself up on her elbows.

"You don't need to worry about it. It's just a little something I need right now." He wouldn't look her in the eyes and took up his surveillance of the area again.

"Is that what's keeping you awake? Is that some sort of pharmachem?" She wanted to know what he was taking. Her life was in his hands, like it or not, and she didn't want to have to worry that some drug-addled man was about to screw up their escape.

"It's perfectly safe. It's a stimulant. It keeps me awake for long periods when I need to be, like now." His attempt to sound nonchalant didn't quite ring true.

Torrin was more than a little suspicious. "So there are no side effects. You're not going to turn into some sort of raving sex freak?" She sat the rest of the way up and looked him right in the eye.

"I don't think you have to worry about that," Jak replied gravely with a hint of amusement. "There are no instant side effects. I need to keep taking them now until we get out of Orthodoxan territory. Once I stop taking them I'll sleep for a few days, but that's pretty much it."

"How about some of those for me, then?"

"I don't have enough for both of us. Besides, only one of us has to be awake at a time. I know you'll cover my back once I wake you up, so it's all good."

"Oh." Torrin was mollified and inordinately flattered that the sniper trusted her to watch his back. If she wasn't mistaken, he hadn't trusted anyone that much since his brother died.

"Now go back to sleep. Things will go better if you're well rested."

"Sleep would go better if I weren't getting rained on," she groused, lying down and turning over. A moment later, she felt him place his water-resistant jacket over her, stopping the relentless mist of rain on her face. The jacket smelled faintly of him, like the deep woods. It reminded her of the forests they'd traveled through. The scent was surprisingly light and not at all unappealing. With her head finally sheltered from the rain, she faded quickly and tumbled headfirst into a dreamless sleep.

CHAPTER FOURTEEN

Too soon, Torrin woke to Jak shaking her shoulder.

"It's showtime," he whispered. "Get up."

Sleep had left her groggy and she shook her head to clear the cobwebs. "I'm up."

"Good," Jak said. "You know the plan. You don't start shooting until they make a break for their barracks. Don't try to take them out, just make sure you lay down a field of fire so they can't make it into the building."

"I'll do my best." She was still uneasy but was ready to do her part to see Jak's plan succeed. Her discomfort must have translated to her voice because Jak patted her on the shoulder then gripped it. He squeezed reassuringly.

"You'll be fine. Just stick to the plan." He let go of her and ghosted away into the darkness.

Torrin took her place behind the rifle and looked through the scope. It wasn't the one that she'd last seen on the rifle, but when she looked through it she realized that unlike the other scope, this one had night vision. Through the viewfinder she could see the barracks as clearly as if it were full noon. Details stuck out in sharp relief, objects contrasting more than they normally did. Next to the rifle, Jak had left a pile of ammunition clips. It seemed like she had enough ammo to kill an army, not just eight men. Men who were unaware of what was about to rain down on their heads. For a moment she felt sorry for them. Then she remembered the treatment she had received at the hands of the Orthodoxans. They would happily have taken the two of them out without any warning or second thoughts.

She lay there and watched the buildings below for what seemed like hours. Her adrenaline spiked when four men trundled out of the barracks. Two of them started across the bridge, both yawning hugely. The two who had been stationed on the far side must have been itching for their chance to turn in and came out to meet their relief halfway across the bridge. The two in the near tollbooth exchanged pleasantries with their relievers.

Come on, get on with it, Torrin thought at them. She worked to calm her breathing and willed them to move faster so she could get this over with. Eventually the two in the near building started toward the barracks. Halfway across the bridge, the first of the men fell, missing half of his skull. There was no sound, the side of his head just exploded in a curtain of red. The three men with him stared in disbelief and two more collapsed in the time it took for them to gape at their fallen companion. The fourth man took off at a mad dash for the near shore, screaming at the others.

The other four reacted immediately, the two at the tollbooth ducking into the dubious safety of the small building. The other men were halfway back to the barracks and broke into a sprint for the larger building. Torrin opened up on the strip of ground between them and the barracks. The rifle thundered beside her head as bullets kicked up little geysers of earth where they struck the hard-packed earth. One of the men tried to keep running and was struck in the leg by a round. The force of the impact snapped his lower leg, and he dropped like a stone, blood fountaining in a scarlet arc. His partner came to such a sudden stop that he laid out on the ground in a long slide. Feet and hands scrabbling, he got his legs underneath him and bolted back toward the booth.

The injured man lay in the open ground between the buildings, screaming. Even from her distance, Torrin could hear the thin wail of his voice. She divided her attention between the three men left in the tollbooth and the man lying on the ground. There wasn't enough room in the small building for three men; she could clearly see a shoulder and part of one of the soldiers' backs. At random intervals, one of the soldiers would stick a gun through the doorway and blindly fire off a few rounds. They must have seen muzzle flash from her rifle as they fired vaguely in her direction. None of the bullets came remotely near her.

Torrin swung the gun back to check on the man with the injured leg in time to see him trying to pull himself toward the barracks. She fired a few more rounds into the ground near him, and he came to a stop and started dragging himself the other way. Checking on the bridge, she saw the fourth man from the far side had collapsed facedown just short of the near bank. A rapidly growing crimson pool expanded beneath his head.

"Perfect," Jak said, appearing right at her elbow. Torrin bit back a squeak. She kept her eye glued to the scope and her eye on the situation below though she really wanted to glare at the sniper. He was completely oblivious to her irritation and set up his own rifle. Faster than she thought possible, Jak lined up the shot and took out the man whose body was visible through the toll booth's doorway. He tumbled backward out of the building with a crimson flower blossoming in the small of his back.

"Keep the other two pinned down in the building. I've got to work my way around to line up a shot on them. Just fire down at the door occasionally, but really rain the bullets down if they try to make a break for it," Jak instructed.

"What about the wounded one?" Torrin asked.

"Don't worry about him. He's done." Unaware of the bomb he'd just dropped on her head, Jak disappeared back into the darkness.

Torrin fired a few bullets into the ground in front of the small building and reloaded as quickly as she was able. Numb, she checked on the man she'd hit in the leg and saw that he had stopped moving and was lying on the ground just a few meters from where she'd last seen him. Quickly she slid the scope's focus back to the doorway of the building. A hand snaked around the side and fired a pistol at her. They'd gotten a better fix on her position. Bullets whizzed over her head.

She returned fire, shooting first into the ground as instructed and then into the side of the building. The hand and gun disappeared back inside with alacrity. She watched and waited, firing into the ground often enough to keep them from making a break for it.

A short eternity later, another man tumbled part of the way through the doorway. She saw nothing else until Jak slunk into the scope's range. He moved quickly, crouching low to the ground and fetched up against the side of the toll booth. Rounding the corner, rifle held in front of him, he disappeared into the structure. Moments later he reappeared, waving his arms over his head.

Torrin exhaled slowly and leaned her forehead against the back of her rifle. She was glad it was over. The death and pain they'd rained down on the Orthodoxans had been way too easy. Death should never be that easy, she thought. Even for those who deserved it.

She got up and collected the rifle and knapsack. Slinging each over a shoulder, she hurried down the hill to where Jak stood. As she got closer, Torrin could make out the iron-heavy scent of blood. There was a charnel house aroma in the air, with hints of human excrement. Some of the men's bowels had voided where they'd died. It had been bad enough at the top of the hill but surrounded by their handiwork, Torrin wanted nothing better than to get across the bridge and away from this place of death.

"Nice shooting," Jak greeted her as she jogged up to him. "One of the slugs you put through the walls killed the eighth guy."

She turned a sick smile on him. "So glad you approve," she muttered back sarcastically. "Let's get out of here."

"Give me a few minutes to get what I can from inside the barracks. Stay out here and keep an eye down the road. Holler if anyone comes."

"Wait, what? Let's just go!" Torrin didn't want to spend any more time here than she already had.

"I need to do this. It won't take long." He took off at a run for the barracks, leaving her with none but the dead for company. She had no choice but to watch the road. Her hands shook, and she was having problems actually seeing the road. The Orthodoxans probably could have driven a convoy past her and she wouldn't have noticed. True to his word, Jak wasn't gone long. He came back dragging the body of the man who had died as a result of the slug Torrin had put through his leg.

"Help me get these guys into the water. I've muddied what happened here, best I could." He passed her, headed for the river.

Torrin looked over at the pile of bodies in and around the tollbooth. Swallowing a mouthful of bile, she pulled the top body out of the small structure. It was still warm to the touch and slick with blood. She had to hook her hands under the corpse's armpits and pull it backward to get it into the river. She dragged the body slowly out onto the bridge and heaved it up on the railing before pushing it into the water below.

The sun had just started to crest the horizon, lending the entire scene a soft light starkly at odds with the grimness of their task. Torrin toiled in silence, numbly pulling bodies to the bridge and tipping them into the rushing current where they were mercifully swept out of her sight.

On her way back for the last corpse, she noticed smoke pouring out of the windows and doors of the barracks building. That must have been what Jak had meant. Not very subtle, but she hoped that everything they'd done there would buy them the time they needed to make it to the front. Otherwise, the deaths they—she—had dealt would be for nothing.

The last corpse was over the edge and bobbing down the river where she watched it float facedown until it disappeared below the surface with chilling rapidity.

"You don't want to know what's down there," Jak murmured, suddenly standing next to her.

"You're right," Torrin replied coldly. "I don't."

Jak shot her a wounded look but didn't push it. Torrin knew it wasn't his fault they were in this situation and that she owed him her life. It was unfair, but she couldn't let go of the feeling that he was somehow responsible for the distasteful task she'd just undertaken.

When she didn't respond to his look, he pushed himself away from the railing.

"Let's go," he said shortly and strode off. Torrin let him get a fair way ahead before following him.

Behind them, the rising column of smoke was silhouetted against the rising sun. Birds called back and forth while insects buzzed from stalk to stalk in the surrounding grasses. The grasslands around them buzzed with life, but none of it touched the stillness of the void that yawned within her.

* * *

They crouched at the edge of a ridgeline. Two days of hiking cross country had gone without incident, and they'd made pretty good time. Jak was relieved that they were so close to the front. When she looked to the night sky to the south, she could just make out the blue glow of the fence. The ground here was harsher than the rolling hills of the grasslands had been. It was broken here and there by jagged ridges cutting across rugged earth. The terrain was made rougher by the crater holes that had been created by decades of artillery shells. Below them was a series of trenches. Beyond those were a narrow strip of no-man's-land and beyond that Devonite territory. They were almost there. She could see the escarpment as an inky blot, rising into the stars. All they needed to do was get past the trench system and they'd be home.

She snorted. *Home.* She wondered how long it would be before she couldn't stand it anymore. Before she had to get out of the camp and back to the woods. The cycle kept repeating itself. She simply couldn't stay in that place for long. The longer she was cooped up inside it, the more she felt the urge to go back to the forest, to search for her brother's killer. Homecoming was a little different this time, though. Torrin was coming back with her. She had no illusions that the other woman would stay long, but she felt more at ease in Torrin's presence.

Torrin had been taciturn for the first day or so after the toll bridge. She seemed to be coming around now. After a day of responding only in monosyllables, if at all, she was now talking in full sentences. Sadness still clung to her, but the dark veil that had descended over her had mostly lifted.

Jak had been impressed with how the smuggler had handled herself during their operation. She'd held herself together until after their task was over and she'd been very effective. She'd chalked up two kills, very impressive for someone who professed little experience with a long-range weapon. She knew better than to congratulate her, however. Torrin seemed content to pretend it hadn't happened. Jak was happy to oblige her if it meant she got to talk with her again.

Torrin was stretched out on her belly next to her, the night vision scope to her right eye. Jak lifted the binoculars to her own eyes and activated her implant's night vision.

"There's a lot of them down there," Torrin commented.

"Yup."

"I don't think we can kill all of them."

Jak disagreed but kept her peace. Disagreeing was a risky move with Torrin's mood of late and she sounded like she had more to say.

"We need a way to draw them off somewhere." The smuggler spoke slowly like she was talking her way through an idea that was just taking form. "If we can get them out of the way, do you think you can get us through the trenches?"

"Probably. I've spent enough time in Orthodoxan trenches to know how they're usually laid out. What you thinking?"

Torrin swept her scope out to the north where the ocean lay.

"There's no way we can make a trip out there. Our oceans have some freaking huge predators in them. The ones that took care of the corpses at the bridge?" Jak winced at bringing up the toll bridge. She took a deep breath and hoped Torrin hadn't noticed the lapse. "Well, the ones out at sea make those look like thimblefish." At Torrin's inquiring look, she held up two fingers a few centimeters apart. "Little fish about this big. What's out there would snap us up as easy as snacking."

"That's not what I'm thinking." Thankfully, Torrin gave no indication that she'd noticed Jak's slip. "But if we can make them think something's going on out there and they turn their attention to it, we might be able to sneak by."

Jak was intrigued. "It would have to be pretty big."

"I don't think that'll be a problem." Torrin turned toward her, face lit up with enthusiasm. "The bullets that your people use, they contain an explosive charge, right?"

Jak nodded.

"So they'll go off if they're subjected to high enough heat?"

"Yeah."

"So let's make a raft, pile it high with our ammunition, set it adrift, then set it on fire. The fire alone should get them to notice it, but if they think they're being fired on, they'll want to take it out."

"It could work." Jak mulled the plan over in her mind, examining it from all angles. "We don't have that much ammo, which means we'd probably have to send all of it on your raft. If it doesn't work, then we'll be stuck without any."

"So we put in the Orthodoxan ammunition and you hold on to your own. I know you picked up extra at the bridge."

"I did and a few other surprises that might help us out." In addition to ammunition and maps, she'd grabbed as many hand grenades as she could cram into the knapsack. It wasn't a huge number but enough to set off a few attention-grabbing explosions. "We need to find a way to get down to the beach. There should be plenty of driftwood out there. If we time this right, we'll be able to send it out when the tide comes back in and the water will pull it out into the middle of the bay." Jak slithered away from the edge of the ridge and started retracing their steps. Torrin followed her quickly, and together they picked their way across the sharp rocks and gravel that littered the landscape.

"We passed a ravine about thirty minutes back," Jak said. "It heads the right direction, maybe it'll take us out to the shore."

They traveled back along the path and down the ravine. It had a few more twists and turns than Jak had accounted for. She noted with some alarm that the high water marks along the walls of the narrow gully were well above both of their heads. If a storm came up and dumped a lot of water on them, they could be in some real trouble. She really missed having access to reliable weather reports. Not knowing what the weather would be like didn't help her plans at all.

Eventually the ravine came out of the rocky hills into a series of sand dunes.

"It looks like the tide's coming in right now," Torrin noted, disappointed.

"That's perfect. It means that we'll be able to launch this raft of yours tomorrow under cover of darkness. That gives us the morning to gather the supplies we need and the afternoon to build."

"I was just hoping we could get past them tonight." Torrin sighed and ran a hand distractedly along the back of her neck, pulling her hair to one side. Jak thought she looked particularly fetching that way. The wind off the ocean tugged playfully at the loose curls. "I'm really tired of sleeping on the ground, out in the open."

"Just one more night. If we can pull this off, we'll be home free."

"I guess." Torrin looked ready to fall over. The excitement of her plan had worn away, leaving exhaustion in its wake. Without adrenaline to keep her going, she'd faded rapidly.

"Let's make camp here. The dunes will protect us from the wind and we'll have the rocks at our backs. No one will be able to sneak up on us from there." Jak looked around for some materials with which to build a shelter. A line of driftwood looked promising. "Stay here," she instructed and went to gather building materials. She was able to find some longer sticks and used the length of rope from the Orthodoxan sniper's bag to lash them together at one end. She leaned the tied ends against the rock wall and layered smaller sticks at right angles. Satisfied, she ducked into the makeshift shelter. The ground was soft, but not as loose as the sand of the dunes. Some stubborn grasses held the ground together.

"Come on in," she said, sticking her head out of the lean-to.

Torrin stumbled in and lay down on her side. Jak settled herself next to the exhausted woman. As usual, Torrin snuggled up against her as soon as she fell asleep. The now familiar thrill ran through her, leaving fire in her veins and excitement in the pit of her stomach. She smiled and shifted until the smuggler's head was pillowed in her lap. The feeling of arousal that Torrin's touch brought no longer felt alien. It didn't soothe her, but she felt alive in a way she never had before.

Pulling the package of stims out of her pocket, she examined it closely. She had two left; one for tonight and one for tomorrow. They absolutely had to get across tomorrow night, because once the stims ran out, she would be useless. Given how long she'd taken them on this trip, she would likely sleep for days once the medication was purged from her bloodstream.

Still, it had been worth it. Even if they got killed trying to make the border the next night, she'd had the best week of her life since her brother died. She popped a stim pill into her mouth and washed it down with a swallow of water. The adrenaline rush hit her almost immediately. She resisted the urge to get up and move. Instead she stayed there with Torrin's head in her lap until the sky started to lighten in the east.

When there was enough light to see without the use of her implant, she carefully eased herself out from under Torrin's head, taking care not to wake her. A long line of dried driftwood lay just on the other side of the dunes. She started combing through the detritus to find wood suitable for raft making. About an hour later, Torrin joined her, looking much refreshed.

"Sleep well?" Jak asked as she dragged a bulky log over to her pile of raft materials.

"Surprisingly, yes," Torrin replied, stretching luxuriously. Jak tried not to notice how nice Torrin's breasts looked pressed against the material of her jacket. "Apparently sleeping in the sand agrees with me." She eyed Jak up and down, eyes critical. "I won't ask how you slept, since you just medicate that particular need away."

Jak shrugged. "One of us has to stay awake, it might as well be me."

Torrin shook her head in response. "I'll get breakfast," she said, digging through the knapsack and pulling out two ready to eat meals. She mixed in some water and brought Jak the already steaming packet.

"Oh boy," Jak said with a decided lack of enthusiasm. "Pork or chicken?" The Orthodoxan ready-to-eat meals lacked serious imagination.

"Not that you can tell by the flavor." Torrin laughed. "They may as well be the same dish. No wonder the Orthodoxans are so cranky."

Jak smiled at Torrin's sally and shoveled food into her mouth as quickly as possible. When she finished, she turned back to her pile of materials. Not only had she scavenged some large pieces of wood, but she'd also managed to find a fair amount of seaweed. It was dried in long strands and she thought it would work well to lash together the pieces of the raft.

"We need to drag this stuff closer to the water," she said. "The tide should be going out soon, but we need to make sure that we won't be working anywhere that's visible to the Orthodoxans."

"Makes sense," Torrin replied and grabbed a large piece of wood by one end and started hauling it toward the water. "You check on the Orthodoxans. I'll get this moved up."

"Sounds good, but leave the big stuff and I'll help you with it."

Torrin stopped dead in her tracks and shot her a look. She batted her eyelashes outrageously. "Oh, would you be so kind as to lend a hand to a poor, helpless woman?" she said in a high falsetto. "I would be ever so grateful if you did!"

"You're about as poor and helpless as an aetanberan," Jak snorted. She laughed out loud when Torrin's expression wavered back and forth between pleasure and irritation at the backhanded compliment.

"Thanks, I think," Torrin finally said. "Don't praise me with faint damns or anything." She grabbed hold of the driftwood log and started heaving it toward the waterline. "You can help me with whatever's left."

Left to her own devices, Jak followed the rock wall around toward the beach. They were in a natural bay, but the rock face curved in at a sharper angle than the waterline. When she got to the end of the rocks, she crouched and looked around the point. The rocks curled away from her and formed another half moon on the other side of the bay. The opposite side was bigger than their side and at the far end of the beach she could see one of the Orthodoxan buildings. She trained her binoculars on it and made out men and movement.

Swinging around, she surveyed the top of the cliff for more men. She saw a couple likely machine gun emplacements, but they didn't seem to be manned. Apparently the Orthodoxans weren't worried about attacks from the ocean. It made sense, there hadn't been any need for those emplacements for decades, but she and Torrin were about to take advantage of their complacence. They really couldn't have asked for a better setup. Even if the current took the raft out to sea, at night it would be visible for kilometers. If they were really lucky, the current would run the raft right past the Orthodoxan outpost, which would give them more time to get past the men stationed there.

"We're good to go," Jak said when she rejoined Torrin, who carried a large armful of driftwood. She'd made quick work of the pile and was bringing up the last of it.

Torrin grunted in response and deposited her load on the sand. She stretched, knuckling her back. "That's good," she replied absently. The stack of wood looked daunting, but she started sorting it quickly into piles of like sizes. Her face had an intense look that Jak found absolutely enchanting.

"Are you going to help?" Torrin asked acerbically. Jak blushed, embarrassed to be caught staring.

She hurried forward. "You looked like you had it handled," Jak muttered.

"So here's the plan." Torrin was all business. "We create a frame out of large pieces of driftwood and lash it together using ties made of seaweed. If we soak the pieces in the ocean, the ties should shrink when they dry, holding it together better." She pointed without looking up. "Put that one over there."

Jak moved as directed. Torrin had taken the bull by the horns, and she was happy to work at her direction. She only had the barest idea of how to go about constructing a raft and was glad that Torrin seemed to have it figured out.

"You know it doesn't have to last forever, right?" Jak needled the other woman.

"Do you want it falling apart before it does us any good?" Torrin wasn't the least bit amused. "Because that's what you'll get if we don't do this properly."

"Okay, okay."

"And don't try to mollify me. I'm not going to screw up our chances to get out of this hellhole."

"I get it," Jak said placatingly. "Don't worry, we'll get out of here." She almost wished they didn't have to. Going back over the fence meant the mask would go back on. Even though she hadn't told Torrin her secret, it was a lot easier to be herself around another woman, especially one who didn't know how she was supposed to act.

Over the next few hours the raft began to take shape. Jak had to admit that Torrin knew what she was doing, even though she was more than a little officious at times. Bossy even. By sunset the raft was pretty well assembled and the tide was rolling back in. The beach was so long and shallow that it would take some time for the water to be deep enough to carry the raft, but they had to start moving.

"It looks good. We need to get it outfitted," Jak said when it became clear Torrin would continue to fiddle with the raft.

"Let me just—"

"We need to get moving now or we won't have time to get in place to make a break for it." Jak cut her off firmly. The knapsack lay neglected to the side of their barely seaworthy vessel. Jak pulled out all the Orthodoxan ammunition and most of the grenades. Between what they'd used and what they'd recovered at the bridge, they had more than she'd anticipated.

Torrin had ignored Jak's instructions and was constructing a frame over the top of the raft. She grabbed two handfuls of ammo and started lashing the cartridges to the sides of the frame with strands of wet seaweed.

"It'll keep the ammunition up there from going off at the same time as what we put in the bottom," she explained to Jak's quizzical look.

Of course, that made perfect sense. At the moment, the ocean's waves weren't raging, but they were high enough that the fire needed to be protected. Jak quickly built up walls around the center of the raft and insulated them with rocks and sand interspersed with seaweed. She laid an intricate network of damp seaweed radiating from the raft's center, then created the structure for a huge bonfire.

"So how will we start the fire?" Torrin had the look of someone who'd just poked a large hole in her own plan. It was well past dusk and there was barely enough light to see by naturally. Jak switched over to night vision and pulled the length of rope and the fire starter from one of her pockets and held them up. Torrin squinted at her in the gloom.

"We'll throw the firestarter in there in an open position," Jak said. "If we douse the area in water, it'll take a while to start the main fire, which will hopefully give us time to get back to the trenches."

"Couldn't the starter get extinguished?"

"Probably not. They're designed to be able to set fire to the wettest wood and to work after being submerged. This one went into the river with us and it still works fine. With it being stuck open, there's the possibility that it will fail completely, which would set everything in the vicinity on fire." Jak shrugged. "That'll work too. Now let's get the rest of the ammo in there and get out of here."

Torrin grabbed the rest of the bullets and sprinkled them over and around where the bonfire would be.

"Great, now let's go." Jak tossed in the firestarter and took off at a sprint, trusting that Torrin would be close on her heels.

CHAPTER FIFTEEN

They crouched behind a low sandbag wall, closer to the border than they'd been yet. A knot the size of an Earth cat had taken up residence in Torrin's throat. It had taken them far less time to return to the trenches than it had to leave. She'd followed on Jak's heels, worried that she would lose him in the darkness. It had to have been about fifteen minutes since they'd arrived, and she was growing increasingly nervous as each moment passed.

Surely the raft should have been visible by now. What if their plan failed? How would they get across without some sort of distraction? There were just too many Orthodoxans.

She put her mouth to Jak's ear. The sniper jerked as if he'd been bitten. "Do you hear anything?"

"No. For the third time." His reply was testy. He made a good show of being unconcerned, but if he wasn't at least somewhat nervous, he wouldn't jump every time she whispered in his ear.

"It won't work," Torrin fretted.

"It will work," he said. She could practically hear his eyes roll. "It's a good plan. We'll be fine."

"How can you be sure? There's so much that could go wrong. What if—"

"Shhhhh, do you hear that?"

"Don't shush me and don't think I'll fall for that," Torrin huffed. She couldn't believe that he would try to shut her down like that. Her eyes bulged and she grew even more indignant when he clamped a rough hand over her mouth. She was about to bite his hand when she heard distant shouts and, beneath that, sharp explosions.

"It's working." Even in the dark, Torrin could see Jak's eyes gleaming. "Let's get this done."

Jak pushed himself up from his crouch and peered over the low wall. He looked down at her and gestured her to follow, then vaulted over the wall in one smooth motion. She pushed herself up and looked north. The distant horizon was fitfully lit by distant flashes. Searchlight beams sliced through the darkness toward the source of the disturbance.

"Come on," Jak hissed at her from below. The walls of the trench went down for a meter and a half and he crouched low at the bottom, waiting for her. She pushed herself over the wall with far less grace than he had and landed with a splash. Mud flew everywhere and splattered all over the two of them. The bottom of the trench was covered by centimeters of wet muck. The trench stretched away into darkness on either side of them. She put her hand out to steady herself on the nearest wall and came back with a handful of mud. It was all over everything. She tried to shake it off and instead succeeded in flinging it all over herself. Giving up on cleanliness, Torrin wiped her hand on the front of her jacket with a grimace.

Jak tugged at her elbow and started off cautiously, taking care to make as little noise as possible. When she followed, he looked back with reproach at the amount of noise she was making. She forced herself to slow down and consider every step she took. Soon she was almost as noiseless as he was, though she didn't move as quickly. He was attuned to her progress and held up to wait for her whenever he got too far ahead.

They followed the trench as it curved gently northward for a couple of hundred meters and then split into a T-junction. Jak held up his hand, stopping her in her tracks. He took her by the elbow and leaned in close.

"Pull out your pistol, but only shoot if someone sees us," he whispered in her ear. Shivers skittered down her spine. She tried to ignore the sensation and pulled out her sidearm in response to his directions. Jak stuck his head out into the gap, glanced both ways and pulled it back in.

"We're clear," he breathed. "Follow me." It was strange, she thought. The sniper rifle that she'd rarely seen out of his hands was slung over one shoulder. In his right hand, he gripped the great big combat knife that she'd seen him handle but rarely.

He took the right branch at the junction and she crept along in his footsteps. Hopefully, he knew where he was headed. He acted like it. There was no hesitation in his movements. The trench branched again after only a few meters and Jak took the left branch without pausing to consider.

They followed along the path without seeing a soul for quite some time until they came around a corner and ended up face-to-face with an Orthodoxan sentry. Before the man could do more than gape at them, Jak closed the short distance between them. He slammed his hand over the soldier's mouth and his momentum sent the two of them back into the trench wall. In a flash, Jak drove his knife up beneath the sentry's rib cage. He leaned into the thrust, questing with the knife's tip for the sentry's lungs. The hapless soldier spasmed as the knife found a lung; dark blood seeped around the knife where it protruded from his chest.

Jak stepped back, pulling the knife out and letting the Orthodoxan slump to his knees then keel over to one side. He lay in the mud on the trench bottom, twitching. Torrin stood rooted in place, shocked by the swiftness of Jak's savage attack. The other man hadn't had a chance and hadn't realized that he stared death in the face until it was much too late. Her own experiences with this type of combat were from so long ago that her instincts were too rusty to be counted on. Her most recent tussles had been of the nonlethal variety, convincing some meathead that his advances were unwelcome or persuading a would-be thief that another shipment would be less trouble.

Jak fingered a patch on the upper arm of the downed soldier. He breathed hard through his nose, trying not to pant. He bent quickly and wiped his combat knife on the hem of his fallen foe's jacket, then started rifling through the bloody uniform. He grunted in triumph when he pulled out a piece of folded paper and unfolded it, perusing it quickly. "He was a lieutenant, and this is a map of the defenses. With this we can avoid the tangle wire emplacements and even better the minefield." Jak turned the map and traced a finger over it, lips moving as he thought. Satisfied, he folded up the map and slid it into a pants pocket.

"Time to move on," Jak whispered hoarsely. "They'll come looking for him soon. Some poor enlisted bastard wouldn't be missed, but an officer…It can't be too much farther now." He took off down the trench again. His motions were quicker now, and he seemed less concerned with stealth than with speed. Torrin could still hear gunfire to the north. The raft was doing its work well. The diversion had been more successful than she'd imagined possible.

She followed Jak through another couple of branchings and over another hundred meters before he once again held up his hand. He poked his head around a corner and withdrew it with a muffled curse.

"There's a bunker ahead and it has men in it." He sounded frustrated. "We need to take it out with a grenade. There's no way we can risk them coming out on top of us. Once we do that, we're going to have to haul ass. The noise'll bring everyone in the area down on top of us."

"Got it," Torrin replied and tightened her grip on the pistol.

"You need to keep heading west if something happens to me. If you keep going in that direction you'll get to the end of the trenches, then it's up and over. Once there, you run until you hit the barbed wire barricades. Your best bet there is to flatten yourself and squeeze under them." He stopped and regarded her. "The minefield is right behind that. There's a clear path two-thirds of the way between the barbed wire clusters. It's only about a couple of meters wide, so you need to be careful to stay on a straight course."

"Why are you telling me all of this?" Torrin demanded.

"If I get taken out, you need to know how to get out of here. What we're about to do now is more dangerous than anything we've had to do since we hooked up. I want you taken care of best I can." Jak lifted one shoulder and let it drop. "I owe you at least that much for getting you into this mess."

"It's a better mess than the one I was in. At least here we still have a chance." Torrin wondered what had gotten into him. Jak looked her right in the eye and then raised a hand to caress her cheek. The touch sent sparks dancing across her skin, even here when they were moments from death, dismemberment or worse.

"Just do your best to get away if something happens to me," he said, cupping her chin and drawing his thumb over her lower lip.

Mute with surprise over the blatant display of affection, all Torrin could do was nod. He smiled and set his shoulders.

"Let's do this." He pulled two grenades out of a capacious pocket and pulled the pins, arming them. In no particular hurry, he walked around the corner. Torrin flanked him, pistol raised. In front of them, light spilled from the doorway of the bunker. She could see the men inside, men who even now stared in frozen horror or scrambled for weapons as they noticed two figures descending on them from the gloom.

Jak tossed first the one and then the other grenade into the bunker with the soldiers. The grenades followed a slow, lazy arc through the air, then bounced off the wooden floor. Chaos erupted as men scrambled after the rolling, bouncing grenades. Jak continued on past the rectangle of light, pulling Torrin after him. The grenades went off as they cleared the doorway.

Even though they were clear of the door, the double shockwave hit Torrin in the chest with a pair of staggered thumps and she exhaled explosively. A gout of fire and earth shot through the bunker's door with a roar and Torrin threw up an arm to protect her face from the rain of mud and dirt. Through it all, Jak kept moving, pulling her away from the scene of carnage.

"Come on!" Torrin could barely hear him; her ears rang from the blast. She turned, feeling like she was underwater. He yelled something else she couldn't quite make out and pulled on her hard. The air was heavy with the acrid tang of explosives and burning flesh. He was running, pulling her along, stumbling behind him. Off balance, she snatched her hand out of his and sprinted along in his wake. They ran full tilt for the last fifty meters before stopping at a dead end. Jak pointed up frantically, and she jumped, grabbing the top of the trench wall and pulling herself up. Reaching back, she grasped his hand and hauled him up to the top of the trench wall.

Bullets whined past her ear. Even though the searchlights were still pointed out to sea, at least some of the Orthodoxans were aware of their presence.

"Over there," Jak yelled, adrenaline raising the pitch of his voice. He pointed out into the darkness and sprinted toward the line of barbed wire barely visible in the darkness. Torrin followed at his heels as he squeezed himself between two strands of the tangled wire. He was small enough to get through without any damage, but by the time she'd made her way between the strands she bled from half a dozen scratches and punctures. She didn't slow down, though. Yells and shots rose behind them as they tried to make good their escape.

Torrin stumbled as a line of fire blazed over her left bicep. "Shit," she cried and clapped her hand over the arm. Her fingers came back bloody and her arm throbbed.

"You all right?" Jak yelled over his shoulder. He was ahead of her once again, throwing himself into a slide at the base of a tangle of wire.

"I'm fine," Torrin shouted back. "It was just a graze."

"Good, then get your ass under there!" Somehow he was holding up an entire section of wire. Without having to be told again, she dived under the barbed wire mess and waited on the other side as he let himself through.

"We just have the minefield, and we're home free," he said as he emerged, panting with exertion.

"Good. Their shots are getting closer. We're running out of time."

"I need to get my bearings." Jak started muttering to himself. "The minefield starts...and the strands of wire are there and there. That means the path must be...there!" He strode over to an unremarkable patch of ground. "We need to take the path straight through there. I'll go first. If I blow up, try to the right a bit."

He started forward cautiously and looked over his shoulder after he'd gone about ten paces. "We're good. Follow me and walk only where I've walked."

Torrin took a deep breath and followed him out into the darkness. Bullets buzzed by spitefully, some of them close enough that she felt the air move in their wake. Jak moved deliberately, and she suppressed the urge to scream at him, to force him to move faster. Their pace seemed far too slow, though she knew one wrong move would end in disaster for one or both of them.

Halfway through the intervening area, the night around them burst into full noon. Jak cursed and squeezed his eyes shut. The soldiers manning the searchlights had gotten wise to their break for it and had the lights trained on the two fugitives.

"I can't see," Jak said through gritted teeth, his eyes still screwed shut. Tears traced clean paths through the grime on his face. "My night vision is shot. You have to get us through the rest of the way."

He stood stock-still in the minefield, not daring to move. Torrin grabbed his arm and pulled him behind her.

"Stay on this line." Jak was insistent. "If you go too far one way or the other, we're done."

"I've got it," she replied. "We're almost through, just trust me." Moving carefully but swiftly and trying to pay no mind to the bullets that passed by them, she navigated the final fifteen meters to the barbed wire on the far side. The searchlights gave out more than enough light for her to see by, and she could make out a break in the fences and a wall of sandbags beyond that. She pushed Jak in front of her through the gap and over to the low wall. Hands reached up and grabbed him as she maneuvered him over the edge. The same hands took hold of her and dragged her down into the trenches.

"Well, you guys are a beautiful sight." Torrin lay on her back staring back up at a group of men in fatigues who gazed down at them in a combination of awe and consternation.

It had been an incredible stroke of luck to stumble into a Devonite patrol as they broke through the enemy lines.

"Who's in command?" Jak demanded, consciously roughening her voice now that she was back among her people.

A tall man pushed his way through the men clustered around them. He pushed a helmet back from his forehead and considered her closely.

"Sniper Sergeant Stowell, back from a run. I'm based out of Camp Abbott." She pulled her dog tags out from her shirt, detached one and handed it over to him.

The tall man inspected the tag closely. "Corporal White. Glad you made it back." He tossed her the dog tag. "We're a hell of a haul from the Abbott crossing."

"Tell me about it," Jak replied ruefully. "I missed the extraction window, so we had to take the long way around. I'm about a week and a half late coming back."

White whistled in disbelief. "Let's get the sergeant and his prisoner back to the lieutenant. Eldred, Singer and Waddell, you're with me. The rest of you spread out, pass the word. The Orthodoxans could try something."

Jak could hear bullets still whizzing above. It sounded like there was at least one machine gun in action. She was glad the Orthodoxans hadn't been able to get their shit together with that one during their dash across no-man's-land. Beams of white light slid through the night above their heads, still looking for the fugitives.

"Let's move before they decide to start shelling us," she suggested.

White smirked. "It's unlikely they'll try that. They don't want what they'll get in response. We still have one of the big ship-killers here, and they know there's nothing to stop us from shelling the hell out of them with that fucker. Still," he said, "no point in sticking around any longer than we have to." He led them away into the darkness. Jak and Torrin followed behind him, the three Devonite enlisted men taking up the rear.

"I'm not your prisoner," Torrin whispered angrily in her ear as they walked. "Are you going to clear that up for him?"

"No," Jak replied firmly. "He doesn't need to know the details. I won't clear it up for anyone until we get back to Camp Abbott."

The strange group wended its way through the maze of trenches for twenty minutes before entering a bunker that was eerily similar to the one they'd destroyed not an hour previous. White motioned them to wait and stepped through the door, saluting. Jak could hear voices low in conversation, but they were too quiet for her to make out what was said. Moments later, White stepped back out and directed the two of them to enter.

Jak stepped through the doorway and saluted. "Sniper Sergeant Stowell, sir!"

A slender young man seated behind a rough table at the back of the room looked up at the announcement. The table was littered with papers and documents and a partially shuttered lantern sat at his elbow. His face had the harried look of someone who had too much to do in too little time. The light brown hair on his head stood in irregular peaks as if he frequently rubbed his hand through it. He stood and returned her salute. His uniform was no different than that of his men. She approved of such caution this close to the front. Most lieutenants his age were inordinately proud of their rank and didn't understand that the display of any of the accoutrements of rank was tantamount to asking for a sniper's bullet. On more than one occasion, she had taken out young Orthodoxan lieutenants with such tendencies.

"At ease, Sergeant," he said laconically. "How did this happen?"

"Mission went a little sideways on me, sir. I had to come back through hostile territory with a civilian. We ended up off course and behind schedule, so I thought taking the long way around was best. My extraction team would be long gone, so we didn't head back to the Abbott crossing."

"Your IO should have informed all of the posts that you were out there and late." He quirked a thin eyebrow at her, inviting an explanation. Jak wasn't surprised that McCullock hadn't reported her failure to return. It was just like the bastard to try to get her killed or captured by leaving her stuck behind enemy lines. Even after all these years, she wasn't sure from where their mutual antipathy had sprung. One of these days it was going to get her killed.

"Can't say, sir," was all she could say. "It's urgent that I get back to Camp Abbott. The civilian needs to talk to Base Command."

"About what, soldier?"

"Can't say, sir. It's classified." Command would be surprised to know it was classified, but she figured he would appreciate the discretion. There was no point in getting anybody's hopes up that they might acquire some new technology, something that could swing the war's momentum decisively in their favor. Besides, Torrin was pretty volatile, and Jak knew there was no guarantee that Command would be able to negotiate a deal with her.

"The civilian has a name," Torrin interjected. "Torrin Ivanov, Lieutenant. Pleased to make your acquaintance." She pushed herself in front of Jak and extended her hand to the young officer.

"Ma'am," he said, eyeing her hand for a long moment. The wait stretched uncomfortably until he grasped the proffered hand and shook it. "Lieutenant Dixon." He shot Jak a look of surprise. It was clear that he was unaccustomed to interacting with strong women. They didn't come much stronger than Torrin, and Jak carefully hid her amusement, her features a bland mask.

"We can have you on a transport at first light," Dixon said. "It'll be about half a day's drive to get you back to Abbott."

"Thank you, sir."

"White!" The lieutenant raised his voice.

"Sir?" White ducked back into the bunker.

"Get Sergeant Stowell and his...guest back to transport. Put them on a truck at first light. Get Abbott on the phone and let them know the sergeant is heading back their way."

"Sir!" White saluted.

"Dismissed," Dixon said, returning his attention to the papers on the table. Jak saluted, and White gestured for them to leave the bunker ahead of him. As they passed in front of him, Jak didn't miss the admiring glance White gave the smuggler's backside. She glowered at him in warning, and he held up his hands in mock surrender.

"Follow me," White said, pushing his way between the two of them. Jak decided that it was an excuse to touch Torrin and bridled silently in response. She knew the men on the front lines didn't get many chances to mix with women beyond the whores they hooked up with when on liberty. If they thought they would treat Torrin like some sort of prostitute, she would have to disabuse them of that notion...with extreme violence. Torrin seemed oblivious to the corporal's attention, but Jak knew what was happening.

He led them through the trenches for a long time, until they were well removed from the front lines. A short set of stairs took them from the confines of the trench and into an open field, littered with massive boulders and rocks. A hike of another thirty minutes brought them to a compound full of vehicles of every size and description.

"The Transport Corps Depot," White said when she looked around. "You'll wait in there." The corporal indicated a low building with a fenced lot behind it. Passenger vehicles large and small were parked within the enclosure. He closed the distance to the squat structure and opened a door and indicated that they should precede him inside.

"Quartermaster Sergeant," White addressed a balding, rotund soldier behind a desk in the capacious interior room. "These two need to be on a transport to Camp Abbott at first light. Dixon's orders." Having discharged his duty, White turned to Jak and Torrin. "Good luck Sergeant. Ma'am." He held out his hand to her, and after a second's hesitation, Torrin took it. White shook it and executed a half bow. "Pleasure, ma'am," he said. He left the room with frequent glances back over his shoulder at Torrin. For her part, Torrin gave no indication that she'd noticed the corporal's admiration.

"First light's not for a few hours and you two look like you've been dragged through a knothole backward. There's a couple of cots through that door. You can rest until dawn." The bald man looked sympathetic. They must look awful, Jak thought.

"Thanks," she said and went through the indicated door. True to the quartermaster's word there were cots in one corner of the room. Torrin plopped herself down on the nearest cot with a sigh of pleasure.

"This is the closest thing I've had to a real bed in a week," she said blissfully. "I'm going to sleep like a baby."

"Good," Jak grunted. "You look like hell." She was in a foul mood that she couldn't account for. They were back in Devonite territory and she should have been happy to be home, but she already felt hemmed in and confined. Usually she didn't start feeling trapped until a few weeks after the completion of a mission. Maybe it was that she knew she couldn't sleep yet. She had one stim pill left and she would need to take it soon. She could already feel her reactions slowing as sleep threatened. It would be so nice to sleep and she actually considered forgoing the last pill. But once she stopped taking the stims, she would need days of sleep to recover.

"Real nice," Torrin said in response. She was lying on her back, an expression of bliss on her face. Within moments, she had dropped off into a deep slumber.

Jak pulled the last stim out of her pocket and washed it down with a gulp from her canteen. She lay on the cot until she was certain that Torrin was in a deep sleep, then got up and started pacing. It hadn't really occurred to her that they would ever get this far. It had always been the goal, but the odds had been stacked so heavily against them that she hadn't planned for their success. In less than a day, she would have to defend the choice she'd made to break from the mission. Back and forth she paced, deep in thought while she planned her defense of the mission and Torrin. If she didn't get this exactly right, Torrin could be killed. She herself could be exposed, which would likely end in her own death for treason, but that wasn't particularly important. She knew how much her life was worth, and it would be more than an even trade to keep Torrin alive if it came to that. So she paced for hours, running through arguments in her head one by one and discarding them.

CHAPTER SIXTEEN

Torrin craned her neck trying to see out the window as the truck bounced over ruts and rocks. She and Jak had been crammed into the rearmost seat of a small transport vehicle. Two rows of front seats were taken up by three Devonite soldiers and a driver. The men were careful not to watch her. Jak was his usual taciturn self. Since they'd made it back from Orthodoxan territory, he'd retreated so far back into his shell that she barely recognized him. He snarked at everything she said and glared at his fellow soldiers, especially if they seemed to be paying her any attention at all. She pretended not to notice his changed mood, but it was getting harder and harder to hold her tongue. Why he was so irritable, she didn't know; surely he'd relax now they were no longer behind enemy lines. He was even more wary of the men who were on his side than he'd been of her when he'd first dragged her out of Hutchinson's clutches.

The transport's windows were tiny and the glass was pitted and scratched to the point that light barely made it through, never mind allowing her a good view of the passing scenery. She was used to high quality, scratch-resistant polymers or, better yet, force fields. These windows were downright primitive compared to what she knew. It constantly amazed her to see how widely technology could vary on the Fringe worlds. The Devonites and Orthodoxans lived without many of the technologies she thought of as essential for a certain level of comfort. Oddly, not only did they get by, they thrived. Beyond that, they'd developed tech that outstripped developments on other worlds, including some of the so-called core worlds. The strides they'd made in cybernetics were nothing short of amazing. If she could get her hands on the specs for that tech, she could become a very rich woman.

They'd been on the road for three or four hours and they still had a ways to go. Try as she might, she was unable to so much as glance at either of the vehicles that escorted them.

"You should be pleased," Jak said to her out of nowhere. His voice was much gruffer than it had been while they'd trekked through the wilderness. It reminded her of how rough his voice had been when they'd first encountered each other. It had lightened up as they'd spent more time together, but now that they were with the Devonites, it had roughened further and dropped in register. Perhaps it was nerves. She wondered what he had to be so nervous about.

"How do you mean?" One of the men in the seat in front of them glanced back at her. Torrin smiled at him and he quickly looked away, an odd response to her attempt at politeness.

"It's quite a compliment, how many men they're sending to escort you to talk with Base Command at Abbott," he explained matter-of-factly. "When I've come back from missions on my own, it's me and a driver, that's it. They must really want to talk to you."

"Sarge?" The soldier up front interrupted.

"What is it?"

"We're not heading to Abbott. Orders are to convey you to Central Command at Fort Marshall. They're kicking you up the chain."

Jak's eyebrows climbed up his forehead in surprise. Torrin couldn't remember ever having seen him that surprised, not even when she'd disappeared over the edge of that cliff.

"Are they now? That's...good, I guess." The sniper mulled that over. "Thanks, soldier."

"No prob, Sarge." The man turned away from them again.

"This is good. Real good. They must see something, so maybe…" Jak muttered to himself, then trailed off into silence. He glanced over at her and an emotion like guilt crawled over his face before he quickly shut down all evidence of feelings.

"So who are they taking me to see, then?" Torrin queried.

"You're going to see the Central Command Council. They're in charge of all our military forces. Sounds like they're serious about seeing what you can offer."

"Excellent. It's better than having to work through intermediaries. I'd rather deal directly with the money people."

"You should be very happy then." In contrast to his words, Jak didn't seem especially happy. His eyes had taken an inward cast, and he plucked worriedly at his lower lip.

Torrin allowed things to slip back into silence. They continued without speaking for another three hours. Eventually, the transport came to a halt, and they were allowed to leave the vehicle. Torrin was happy to stretch legs made stiff from hours of sitting. They'd stopped in front of a small building, where the transport was being refueled. From the smell, it was some type of petroleum product. That surprised her. She knew that much of the planet's technology had reverted to a time many centuries earlier, but she hadn't realized how far back the clock had turned. It had probably been five or six hundred years since fossil fuels had last been used on Earth. Most of the other Fringe worlds she'd traded with hadn't resorted to them either. Of course, none of the other planets had been in the midst of a decades-long civil war.

While she was checking out the fuel situation, she noticed Jak off to one side talking to a couple of soldiers. She observed as items changed hands before Jak came back to rejoin her.

"What was that all about?"

"Just stocking up on some necessary supplies. If I'd known we were going to get rerouted, I would have stocked up back at the front line depot."

"Anything I should know about?"

Jak's only answer was to lift one shoulder and turn away. His evasion irritated her, and she stared at him, lips pursed. By now he should know that one way or another, she would get to the bottom of things. She was about to push him on it further when she noticed the other Devonite soldiers watching them closely. A few of them stood in a cluster off to one side and were engaged in an animated discussion. The way they kept turning and looking at the two of them, it was obvious that they were discussing her.

"Do I need to be worried about these guys?"

Surprised, Jak looked her in the face, then looked over the men around them. "Probably not. I outrank most of them, and that should keep them in line. Devonite men aren't like the Orthodoxans." He sneered slightly. "Of course, there are always some assholes. Just make sure you're not caught out by yourself with any of them."

"So nothing's really changed then, has it?" Torrin said accusingly.

"What do you mean?" Jak looked confused.

"Just like in the wilderness, I still need to rely on you to keep me safe." Torrin wasn't happy with this turn of events at all. One of the reasons she worked alone was because she valued her independence more highly than almost anything else. It was sometimes dangerous and often lonely, but she didn't have to rely on anyone but herself. Her constant need to rely on a man for the past week had irked her intensely. "I can take care of myself, you know. I don't need some guy who thinks with the hair on his chest to be watching over me."

"Oh, I know," Jak replied. By the slight quirk of his eyebrow Torrin knew he still had more than a few doubts in that department. She hadn't had much opportunity to prove to him that she could handle herself. She looked forward to changing his mind.

"Let's go! Wrap it up!" The shout came from their little convoy's lead vehicle. The men bustled about, securing weapons in the trucks. Sighing, Torrin allowed herself to be led back to their transport. She clambered into the backseat and was sitting there with her arms folded when Jak joined her. There was no way she was pouting, she told herself. She was planning, pure and simple. That and looking forward to wiping the sly little eyebrow quirk off Jak's face when he discovered exactly how well equipped she was to take care of herself. In her current black mood, he was about to find out firsthand how skilled she was at watching her back.

She had the biggest bargaining session of her life coming up. This one could literally mean the difference between life and death. It wasn't the first time she'd had to trade as if her life depended on it. Torrin took a deep breath and pushed the aggravation away from her. It wasn't a productive emotion. She didn't understand how her emotions for Jak could flit between arousal, affection and rage so quickly. Obsessing over the sniper wasn't productive either. She tried to put him from her mind.

From a pocket, she produced the comb that Jak had whittled for her a lifetime ago. As she pulled it through her hair, she mentally composed a list of what she could offer. She already knew what she would ask for in payment. If she played her cards right, she could end up not only with her life but with the biggest score of her career.

* * *

The second leg of their journey was almost over, and Jak was getting restless. She was glad that she'd been able to procure more stims. With luck she wouldn't need the entire week's supply she'd managed to pick up, though her body was needing the pills more frequently now. Instead of taking them every twenty-seven hours, she was down to twenty-three hours between doses. She'd never had to take them for this long. Addiction was no worry with the pills, but the other side effects were going to be brutal. She hoped she wouldn't have to deal with any complications beyond vast amounts of sleep. In training, the doctors had given them some medical gobbledygook about immune system compromise if the pills were taken for too long. If that meant she ended up with a cold as the price for living on stims for a week and a half, then so be it. A little stuffiness and cough would serve her right.

She smiled ruefully. Torrin would be pissed if she knew that Jak had picked up more of them. She needed to make sure she didn't find out. It shouldn't be too difficult. Since their refueling stop Torrin had been withdrawn and distracted.

The bouncing of the truck's wheels over well-traveled dirt roads was replaced by the hum of concrete under their tires. They were close to Fort Marshall if they'd hit paved roads. The end to the bouncing and shuddering of the vehicle over the rough roads was welcome, and though motion sickness was no longer a threat, her stomach clenched with concern. One way or the other, she was about to face the piper. She hoped it would go well, for Torrin more than herself.

After another fifteen minutes the truck slowed and came to a stop. The men disembarked, leaving her and Torrin. The smuggler stood, hunched over to avoid the low ceiling. Jak took her arm.

"Good luck," Jak said. Torrin turned to regard her and gave her a little smile.

"Thanks." Her smile widened. "I think your commanders are the ones who need the luck, though."

Torrin seemed a different woman; she radiated confidence. Seeing her like this, Jak knew that Central Command was in for a shock. The smuggler's confidence cheered her up. As she followed Torrin out of the truck, however, she spotted the last face she wanted to see glaring at her from the surrounding crowd. Her knee buckled when she landed, and she jostled into Torrin.

"Look out there, tiger," Torrin laughed, righting her with a quick grab of her upper arm. When Jak didn't respond, Torrin followed her gaze to the ginger-mustached man gazing at them. "What's the matter?"

"That's my Intel Officer, McCullock." Jak groaned. "We don't see eye to eye. I was hoping that by being routed here I wouldn't have to deal with him. He's not going to be happy with the way the mission turned out. In fact, not only did I botch it, I managed not to get myself killed."

"How did you botch the mission? You killed Hutchinson."

"Hutchinson wasn't my target." She looked Torrin in the eye, considering if she should tell her. The smuggler was going in to deal with Central Command. If Torrin knew that they'd wanted her dead, she would have a serious edge over them. As she deliberated with herself, Torrin waited, getting visibly nervous.

"Hutchinson wasn't my target," she repeated, her mind made up. "You were."

* * *

When Torrin was eleven, she'd begged and pleaded until her adoptive mother had gotten her a wild plains pony to gentle all on her own. She had loved that little pony, but breaking her to saddle and bit had been a struggle. The pony had kicked her in the chest once as she'd passed behind to saddle her. That powerful little pony's hoof to the sternum had knocked the wind out of her, but it hadn't hurt nearly as much as Jak's revelation. Her ears roared, and for a moment her vision darkened. Now it was Jak's turn to reach out and steady her.

"You see why I couldn't tell you?" Jak asked. His eyes were deeply concerned, begging her to believe him.

"Uh, yeah." Her voice was unsteady, and she had to force out the response. Her breath caught, and she forced herself to breathe normally. "You could have picked a better time to drop that bombshell, though." She needed to avoid any sign of weakness, and she pushed herself away from his steadying grasp. "I'm fine." While she understood why Jak hadn't told her sooner, she was still unaccountably hurt by his admission. He could have told her before this. It wasn't like he hadn't had plenty of opportunities.

"You need to use this to your advantage," Jak pressed. "Make them pay for wanting you dead." His gaze was intense. Surely she was imagining it, but an emotion akin to fury seethed in the depths of his regard.

"Don't you worry," Torrin said. Her anger rose to match his. They wouldn't know what hit them. She smiled again. Jak stepped back half a step, and she wondered what her face had looked like. Quickly she got hold of her emotions and calmed herself. It wouldn't do to have the Devonite Central Command Council know she was onto them.

"Stowell." The ginger-haired, mustachioed man pushed his way through the crowd and settled himself in front of them, arms akimbo. He was a couple of inches shorter than Torrin but still loomed over Jak.

"Sir," Jak responded, a match for his tone in coldness. He waited just a shade too long before he saluted, and McCullock's face darkened at the calculated insult.

He pushed his face right into the sniper's. "You've gone too far this time." Spittle flew from his lips, and his voice dripped triumph and venom. "You'll be cashiered for this little stunt."

"I don't know about that, sir." Jak's gaze didn't waver, eyes driving into McCullock's like nails. "They're getting an opportunity they wouldn't have if I'd actually followed your asinine orders."

"So you admit disobeying a direct order!" McCullock's voice rose in victory. "I'll see you court-martialed and tried for treason. You'll be facing a firing squad before you know it."

Jak just stared back at him. He stepped back and watched the wild-eyed officer, who was breathing so hard the ends of his mustache trembled. McCullock became aware that a deathly quiet had descended over the crowd, and he glanced around shiftily to see a crowd of soldiers staring at them.

"What's worse, sir?" Jak asked. His voice was loud enough that those watching could hear him clearly. "Bringing back an asset to the war effort or not letting the border posts know that there was a soldier out on a run on the other side of the fence who hadn't come back on schedule?"

Torrin had only thought it was deathly quiet. It shouldn't have been possible for things to get any quieter, but they did. No one moved, and she was pretty sure everyone stopped breathing.

The officer drew himself up, visibly tamping down his emotions. "I don't know how that happened. I gave the order to notify the trenches and border posts. It must have gone astray somewhere." Torrin found his display unconvincing. Jak just nodded.

"Of course, sir," he replied evenly.

A short man, barely a couple of centimeters taller than Jak, appeared next to McCullock. His hair was gray at the temples, and he was clad in rumpled fatigues that looked as if they'd been recently slept in. By contrast, McCullock was dressed to the nines in a peaked cap, pressed uniform, with medals and service ribbons decorating the front.

The disheveled man glared at McCullock. "I believe your presence is needed elsewhere, Captain."

McCullock jumped and paled. He gave a half bow, bending slightly at the waist. "Of course, General. I'm sorry, I didn't see you there. I meant no disrespect, sir."

"Just go, McCullock. We'll discuss this later. Dismissed." He turned away from the disgraced captain to Torrin. "My apologies, Miss Ivanov. Some of my subordinates can be more than a little overzealous. I am General Callahan. Some call me Central Command." The corners of his eyes crinkled when he smiled, she noticed. He had a calming presence. He exuded so much steadiness that she would have sworn he could have kept his balance while balanced on the wing of a ship while it navigated an asteroid field.

"No problem, though if anyone needs an apology, it's this man." She indicated Jak with a wave of the arm. If she could mitigate some of the punishment he feared was coming, then she wanted to do so. Even though he should have told her the truth about his orders days ago, it didn't change the fact that he'd saved her too many times to count over the past weeks.

"Certainly," Callahan said. "Sergeant Stowell will be dealt with in accordance with his actions." He smiled, the grin splitting his face. He must have been hoping that she would miss the part where he guaranteed nothing about Jak's treatment, for good or for ill. He needed to get up earlier than that to pull that sort of obfuscation over on her. She made her trade with words; he would find out soon enough why she was so good at her job.

"Why don't we get you somewhere where you can get cleaned up?" Callahan said. He glanced over his shoulder and motioned to someone in the crowd. A man separated himself from the crush of soldiers who'd been watching with open interest as events transpired. This soldier was better dressed than the general, though not as snappily as McCullock. He had the look of an officer to him, which was confirmed by the way the Devonite enlisted men parted for him.

"Come along, let me show you the showers," Callahan said.

A shower! As heavenly as that sounded, she kept an eye over her shoulder as Jak was escorted in the opposite direction. She caught his eye and sent him what reassurance she could. His pale face looked like he needed it. Callahan threaded her hand through the crook of his elbow. It should have been awkward, given the difference in their heights, but it felt surprisingly natural. He chatted amiably to her as the crowd evaporated around them. The new officer trailed behind them at a respectful distance.

CHAPTER SEVENTEEN

Jak glanced back at Torrin as she was escorted away. Torrin caught her eye and winked.

"Time to debrief, Sarge," the soldier to her left informed her. "Sorry, we can't stop for anything." Jak glared at him, her irritable persona firmly in place now that she was back among her people.

"Is there something you're trying to tell me?" Jak demanded hoarsely.

"No! Not at all, Sarge! Just if you were hungry or thirsty or… wanted a shower or something like that, we can't stop." The poor man looked extremely uncomfortable. If Torrin had been there, she would have been in stitches over the uneasy soldier's discomfort while he struggled with to find a graceful way to tell a non-com that he stank.

"Fine," she said while inside she chuckled. Neither of her two escorts attempted any further conversation as they accompanied her through the fort. Their destination ended up being a singularly unprepossessing building. It was of middling size and of indefinable color. Everything about the building screamed that it was unimportant. In Jak's experience, that meant there was no doubt it was extremely important.

The two men accompanied her into the building and up to the second story where they left her in front of a plain wooden door. She pushed open the door and was greeted by two officers…and McCullock.

"Stowell," he sneered. Both men turned and looked at him with such disdain that he seated himself in one of the chairs along the wall, muttering to himself all the while. The men were both colonels. From the looks of their uniforms, one was Operations and the other Intelligence. In stark contrast to McCullock, they both wore fatigues instead of dress greens. The Ops colonel walked forward with his hand extended.

"Sergeant Stowell," he greeted her warmly. "Congratulations on taking out Hutchinson. We missed a few opportunities to nail the bastard back before he got taken off front line operations." His grim smile exposed slightly crooked teeth. Grasping her hand, he shook it firmly. "Whatever else happens, remember that you avenged the deaths of hundreds of Devonite soldiers."

Whatever else happens? That didn't sound promising.

"Wait," she said, cottoning to the other part of what he'd said. "How did you know—?"

"That Hutchinson is dead?" The Ops colonel thumbed his right earlobe. "Good news travels fast. Besides, we have friends in all sorts of places. The Orthodoxans think their force field holds us out, but you know better than most how porous their fence really is."

The other man, a little shorter than Ops, came over and took her hand as well. "I just want to add my congratulations to Colonel Elsby's. So good job, Sergeant. Now let's get started."

Elsby grinned at his colleague. "Wolfe is impatient to debrief," he informed her conspiratorially. "His kind are always after the next piece of intel. You and I know it's all about what you can do, but he's all about what he can learn."

Wolfe had seated himself in one of the chairs behind the long table that dominated the far end of the room. One chair faced the table, and he gestured toward it, indicating that she should sit.

"It's because of what we find out that you know what to do," Wolfe said, straightening the papers in front of him and opening a plain white folder. His voice held the weariness of an argument often debated.

"That's fair," Elsby admitted, crossing the room to take one of the other seats behind the table. They left the middle chair empty. Jak waited for McCullock to take the third chair, but he showed no signs of moving.

Wolfe caught her glance over at the still muttering captain. "He's not part of the debrief. He's only here to give us background on your original mission parameters."

"That's right, the original mission parameters," McCullock repeated with heated emphasis. "Since you strayed so far from the original mission as to leave it completely unrecognizable."

"And now we have an unanticipated opportunity" came a voice from behind them. Recognizing the voice, Jak came rigidly to attention. General Callahan closed the door and crossed the room to take the empty chair. All three men came to attention and saluted. Callahan returned their salutes. "At ease," he told Jak as he sat.

Jak snapped off her best salute and dropped into parade rest.

"Take a seat, son," he told her in a fatherly tone. "I'm sure you've been through a lot."

"Sir," Jak agreed and carefully sat in the chair.

"Now tell us what happened out there. Take your time, but be thorough. We need details only you can give us so we know how to proceed."

Jak wondered what kind of information they were looking for. Intel on the Orthodoxans or on Torrin? Probably both. She swallowed hard and launched into her account of events. She needed to spin this just enough that they realized how great an asset Torrin could be. Maybe they would overlook the part where she'd gone completely rogue on her assignment. That would require glossing over quite a few details, but if she stuck to the bare bones of her account and let them draw their own conclusions, she might get away with this. She hoped.

Torrin was happily ensconced under a stream of water. It was just a hair away from scalding, and she was glorying in the heat. Muscles that had been stiff for so long that she'd forgotten they could feel any other way were finally loosening up. She shampooed her hair a fourth and final time. As for the mud crusted under her fingernails and ground into the pores of her hands, she'd given up trying to eradicate those final bits of dirt. She would have to take the skin off her hands to be rid of the last of the persistent grime.

As she rinsed her hair, she pulled apart some of the worst of the tangles in it. Jak's comb had helped to keep the snarls down, but she'd still managed to amass a collection of knots and tangles. She toweled herself off, then attacked her wet hair with a vengeance. A comb and brush had been provided to her, but she used the comb Jak had made for her. It worked every bit as well and was a small touchstone in this strange place, evidence that someone on Haefen had cared enough to make something for her with his own hands.

The surroundings were alien to her. The shower room was both spacious and spartan, designed so that multiple men could use it at once and about as far removed as it could be from the splendor of Hutchinson's mansion and still be indoors. The bare walls were some kind of concrete composite. They appeared to be extremely hard and durable but were an unappealing dark gray that sucked the light out of the light panels on the surrounding walls.

When she'd been let in, she'd been handed a bundle of clothing. She opened it up now to see what they'd provided for her. Tutting softly over the contents, Torrin grimaced. She really should have inspected the bundle before she took it, but the prospect of being clean for the first time in weeks had pushed all other considerations from her mind. A plain blouse in muted plaid was complemented by a long skirt of dark blue. This would never do. The outfit didn't suit her at all. She would rather have worn the too-revealing outfit the Orthodoxans had provided for her than this monstrosity. There was no way she was going to be seen in public looking like a housewife. Not to mention the psychological advantage it would impart to the Central Command Council when they got down to negotiations.

Torrin balled up the offending outfit and stuffed it back into the bag. Cringing, she donned the filthy, bloody fatigues she'd arrived in and slipped Jak's comb into the top pocket. Her skin almost literally crawled where it came into contact with the filthy material. She grimaced, trying not to think of how dirty the clothes were.

"These won't do at all," she announced as she exited the shower room. General Callahan was gone, and two enlisted men accompanied by an officer waited in his place. Torrin glanced at the officer's insignia in an attempt to determine his rank, but she had no familiarity with Devonite uniforms and couldn't make a determination. She hadn't even known that Jak held the rank of sergeant until he'd been addressed by one of the men. Come to think of it, she hadn't seen any rank markings on any of his clothing. She supposed that made sense for someone operating behind enemy lines.

"What seems to be the problem, Miss Ivanov?" The officer seemed amiable enough. "The clothes you were provided are what most women of good breeding around here wear." He watched her blandly, one eyebrow slightly raised. His features were eminently forgettable, and there was a grayness about him. She had the feeling that most people had to think very hard to recall any distinguishing characteristics. Everything about his mannerisms, his look, his lack of remarkableness, screamed "spy" to her. To most people, he would have just been an unremarkable individual. If she'd had some free credits, she would have bet that he'd carefully cultivated that aspect for years.

"I'm sure you can find something more appropriate for me," Torrin said. "I'm not one of your women, and it won't do for me to try to masquerade as one of them. I, for one, am not in the habit of hiding who I am."

The officer quirked a dry smile at her, not acknowledging her dig. "I can see that, Miss Ivanov. Is there something I can provide that would be more to your liking?"

"Sergeant Stowell has the clothes I was wearing when I arrived on Haefen, but they aren't fit to be worn at the moment. They need a cleaning as badly as I did."

"Indeed." *Cheeky bastard. He didn't have to agree with that,* she thought.

Wrinkling her nose, she continued. "Some clean fatigues like your men wear will do. If you can find some that fit a little better than these, I would be in your debt, officer…"

"Lieutenant Smythe," he replied with a sudden smile. "I'll do my best, but our uniforms typically aren't tailored for someone with your—endowments." He had a great smile which instantly transformed him from forgettable to memorable. Torrin surprised herself by laughing out loud.

"Point to you, Lieutenant," she acknowledged, still chuckling.

"Hold tight while I find you something a little cleaner," Smythe told her. "As soon as you're feeling presentable, I have orders to bring you in front of the Central Command Council."

Smythe left, leaving her alone with the two men. They did their level best to ignore her, but neither of them could stop themselves from sneaking glances when they thought she wasn't looking. She felt like a freak on display from the surreptitious way they watched her. When the lieutenant returned, he was a welcome sight.

Torrin took the folded fatigues from him and went back into the shower room to change. The uniform was still a little tight across her breasts and hips, but the length of the legs and sleeves was much better. She released a heavy sigh. Being in clothes that were as clean as she was made her feel like she'd obliterated most of the cares of the past weeks. It was probably just as well there were no mirrors in the shower room. She didn't want to think about how little the fatigues flattered her. The fact that she was worrying about how she looked for the first time in well over a week was a welcome change. Now if only she could find a decent outfit on this planet.

She emerged from the shower room and rejoined the three soldiers. They'd been conversing quietly, but they clammed up as she exited, the enlisted men coming to attention. At a nod from Smythe, one of them relieved her of the filthy clothes that dangled from her hand and dropped them down a nearby chute.

Torrin patted the front breast pocket of her jacket and turned too late to stop him.

"I needed something from in there!" She trotted over to the soldier by the chute, but he shook his head.

"Sorry, ma'am. It's gone."

Smythe watched her closely as she turned back to him in a mild panic.

"There was a comb in there that I'd like to have back," she explained to the lieutenant.

"You're attached to that, I take it?"

Torrin tried to laugh it off. "You never know when you'll need a good comb." Indicating his closely cropped receding hairline, she continued. "Well, you might not, but I do. This mass is hard enough to tame without the proper tools."

"I see." The lieutenant walked over to a panel in the wall. He tapped on the panel's surface, and a few moments later a tinny voice issued from the adjacent speaker. "The laundry room has just received a set of dirty Orthodoxan fatigues. Please see to it that any effects left in the pockets are returned to me." The speaker spit out a watery sound of acknowledgment. Torrin couldn't make out words, but she recognized the tone.

"We should be able to get those back for you soon," he said. "I hope that will suffice."

At her nod, he gestured to the two soldiers. They closed ranks right behind her, and she looked back, startled.

"Don't worry about them," Smythe hastened to assure her. "They're mostly there for your protection. A lot of people want to know more about the woman from off planet. Also, since Central Command hasn't made an official statement about your status, we need to demonstrate that we're keeping a close eye on you."

He started down the hall, and she followed at his side. They left the building by way of a side door, and he walked her through the fort. It was larger than she'd expected, based on what she'd seen at the front and at the refueling station. This so-called fort was actually a small city. Everything she could see was militarized, and uniformed men bustled to and fro. The place was awash with soldiers.

As they walked, Smythe asked her questions. They started innocently enough, but she had to work hard to keep her answers light and not betray anything that might hurt her negotiation chances or that might get Jak in trouble. Finally, she started answering his questions as if she was a brainless ninny and his probing slowed. From the penetrating look he gave her, he was no more fooled by her act than she'd been by his. Torrin was sweating from the effort of not showing her cards, but she kept right on with the act.

After a long walk, they stopped in front of a hulking building, more massive than any she'd seen so far. The concrete of the edifice was so dark it was almost black. There was nothing elegant about the structure, but its sheer size and bulk lent it a powerful mien. It crouched above them, promising to crush anyone unfortunate enough to cross the might of the Devonite army.

"We sometimes bring high-ranking Orthodoxan prisoners of war here." Smythe's comment was offered out of nowhere.

Torrin blinked at the unanticipated tidbit of information. "Most of them leave under a death sentence for war crimes. Your friend Hutchinson would have been among them if we'd ever gotten our hands on him." He looked over at her, pinning her to the spot with his eyes. The affability was gone as if it had never been. In its place was a gaze harder than steel. "And there's your sergeant." Smythe skewed his glance past her.

She pivoted in time to see Jak being escorted by two men through a door halfway down the building's south side. He didn't see her, and she made no attempt to get his attention, not while she was under the eyes of the much-too-perceptive Lieutenant Smythe. His last set of comments had completely thrown her. Was he implying that she was being associated with Hutchinson and that she might share the fate that had been in store for him? Maybe he was trying to get her to worry about Jak's plight in an attempt to rattle her. Whatever he was after, she couldn't let him know that she was shaken. She tore her gaze from Jak's back and smiled as blandly at him as he'd ever smiled at her.

"The architecture is impressive," she said. He smiled. "A little primitive, though," she finished blithely, and the grin froze on his face. *Match point*, she thought and smirked at him.

"Let's go inside," Smythe said, ignoring the gibe.

Two men separated themselves from their positions on either side of the side doors. One of them held open the left-hand door and the other approached her.

"Ma'am," he said. This was an impressive physical specimen, she thought. He was tall, extremely tall for a Haefonian, and he towered over her by about fifteen centimeters. Under his carefully pressed uniform, his muscles were enormous. The entire package was topped by a fiercely chiseled face. She passed in front of him through the door, and he followed closely behind her. It was pretty clear to her that she hadn't become suddenly heterosexual. For all that he was probably one of the prettiest men she had ever seen, she felt no attraction to him whatsoever. Jak was still the only man she couldn't stop thinking about. Even now, when she had more important considerations, the thought of his touch on her skin sent heat shooting through her belly. She quickly dismissed the image. Nothing could distract her from the task on hand.

"He needs to search you before you go any further," Smythe said.

"You've been with me this whole time," Torrin protested. "You know I don't have anything."

"You're going to be in the presence of the Command Council," Smythe explained, voice reasonable. "The court guards take their jobs very seriously. If it makes you feel any better, they'll be searching me as well."

"What about those two?" Torrin indicated her two shadows with a nod.

"As your guards, they will be permitted to keep their sidearms. But yes, they'll be searched for any additional weaponry."

"All right." Torrin looked at the pretty soldier who'd waited patiently through the exchange.

"Over here, ma'am." He guided her to one side of the door and had her lean her hands against the wall and spread her legs. Quickly and professionally, he ran his own hands over her body, checking every inch. To her intense relief, his touch roused no interest in her. She couldn't wait for the ordeal to be over. She was only mollified by watching Smythe and her two bodyguards go through the same procedure.

When they'd been thoroughly searched, Smythe led them through a series of high, echoing hallways. The inside of the building was as imposing and austere as the outside and just as dark. They wended their way deeper into the colossal edifice until he stopped outside a wooden door that was taller than she could reach.

"You'll wait here," he said.

"You won't be accompanying me?"

"I need to go report to my superiors. These two will stay with you, though. To keep you safe."

She'd heard that explanation before, recently as a matter-of-fact. Shaking her head, she went through the door. A roomy waiting area greeted her, replete with backless benches. At the unpretentious reception desk directly to the right of the door was the first Haefonian woman she'd seen since arriving on the planet. The woman worked over the leaning stack of papers on her desk. She had a lighted wand plugged into the jack at the base of her hand. After running the wand over each paper, she would turn the paper over onto another stack. The door closed behind Torrin, and the woman looked up and greeted her with a pleasant smile.

"Miss Ivanov, I was told to expect you. Can I get you anything?" She stood and tucked a strand of hair behind her ear. The rest of her hair was pulled back in a severe bun. She smoothed the front of her uniform skirt and watched Torrin, her regard expectant.

Torrin shook her head, unsure how to address the woman. The general disdain in which the people of this planet held their womenfolk made her hesitant to be too familiar.

"Very well, Miss Ivanov. Please make yourself comfortable. The tribunal will be with you when they're ready." The uniformed woman seated herself and resumed her task.

Tribunal? Torrin looked around the room before settling on a bench against the far wall. *I thought I was supposed to meet with the Command Council. Maybe tribunal means something different here.* From her seat she could see the entire room, including the door she'd entered through and the room's only other door. She assumed it led to council chambers; she didn't want to be caught unaware when someone entered. Her shadows settled themselves in seats directly across from her.

Time passed at a glacial pace. The council must be making her cool her heels in an effort to impress upon her how little they valued her time. It was an old negotiating tactic. If they'd admitted her as soon as she'd arrived that would have indicated her schedule took precedence over theirs, signaling an eagerness to deal on her terms. Of course, she knew what they were up to. She had employed the same tactic on more than one occasion herself. They would have to do better than that to throw her off her game.

Left to her own devices, for a while she watched the receptionist, whose routine never varied. She just kept waving that wand over the stack of papers in front of her. Paper seemed ubiquitous to human civilization, mused Torrin. Notwithstanding all of the technological advancements she'd seen on so many different worlds, every society employed paper of some sort. There simply didn't seem to be a more efficient way of disseminating information in a short term. Sure, digital files worked well for long-term storage, but when knowledge needed to be accessed by multiple people for an abbreviated period, use of paper still cropped up regularly.

Haefonian paper, from what she could see from her seat, looked pretty innocuous. It was blue, like almost everything else on the planet but wasn't especially thick or overly textured, not compared to some varieties she'd seen.

I really must be bored, she thought. *Ruminating on varieties of paper between planets? Maybe I should write a research paper.* She laughed aloud at the absurdity of the idea, and the other woman looked at her inquiringly.

"Sorry," Torrin said, trying not to laugh harder. "I had a funny thought," she concluded lamely. There was no way she would be able to explain herself, so she simply let it go and tried to quell her laughter. The harder she tried to contain herself, the more she had to laugh. Finally she had to stomp hard on one foot to stop the fit of giggles.

The room's other door opened, quashing any further urge she had to laugh. Lieutenant Smythe stood in the doorway and looked at her, his face inscrutable.

"We're ready for you," he said. Torrin pushed herself off the bench and strode over to him.

At a glance from the lieutenant, the two soldiers took Torrin by the upper arms and marched her across the room toward the opposite doorway. "What are you doing?" she demanded furiously.

"My apologies, Miss Ivanov," Smythe said behind her. "It seems this may not end up the way you wanted it to."

CHAPTER EIGHTEEN

Jak sat high up in the courtroom's crowded gallery. Why Central Command would be meeting with Torrin in a court, she didn't know. Especially with all these people in attendance. A full military tribunal sat awaiting the smuggler, and they didn't look happy. Jak's debriefing had gone so well she'd assumed Torrin's meeting would be a breeze.

A door opened on the other side of the courtroom, and Torrin was deposited in a chair by two enlisted men. The five members of the tribunal looked on in disapproving silence. Torrin's military escorts took up positions on either side of her chair.

From Jak's vantage point, it was difficult to see Torrin's face. She was far from the action on the floor and slightly behind Torrin's seat. Jak keyed in her implant and zoomed in on Torrin, but the best she could see was the line of her jaw and the curve of an ear. Jak could tell Torrin was nervous from the way she held herself, though she doubted anyone who hadn't spent a lot of time with her would have known.

"The accused will stand," intoned the tribunal chair, pointing his gavel at Torrin.

Accused? Accused of what? Jak was even more confused and her breathing hitched. Torrin had given a little jump when the gavel was leveled at her, but she stood smoothly.

"Miss Torrin Ivanov, you stand accused of espionage and indecent behavior. How do you plead?"

"Excuse me?" Torrin was dumbfounded by the accusation.

"Espionage and indecency, Miss Ivanov," the tribunal chair replied acerbically. "What is your plea?"

"Not guilty, of course," Torrin spluttered. "You can't possibly think I'm a spy."

"That will be determined by the evidence against you. You may be seated."

"Don't I get a lawyer or something?"

"This is a military tribunal, Miss Ivanov, not a civilian court. Since the imposition of martial law thirty years ago, military courts are not subject to the same niceties as our civilian counterparts." The tribunal chair smiled wolfishly, his expression little more than a baring of teeth. "We are perfectly capable of being impartial, never fear."

Jak was floored. This couldn't be happening. The colonels and General Callahan had been so congratulatory and understanding when she'd been debriefed. She thought for sure she had convinced them of the wisdom of taking advantage of Torrin's services. Nothing about the debrief had prepared her for a trial on the charges of espionage.

One of the five tribunal members stood up and addressed Torrin.

"Can you explain your relationship with the Orthodoxan Colonel Hutchinson?"

"I had no relationship with him. We met purely for business reasons."

He nodded and consulted a paper in the folder in front of him. "You were planning to supply him with military technology, is that right?"

"We discussed procurement of a number of different items." Torrin was hedging, and the prosecutor's face tightened in response.

"But many of the items had potential military applications, isn't that right?"

"I'm sure you could make that argument of many items."

"Yes or no, Miss Ivanov."

"Yes, then. He could have used the items for military purposes." Torrin's voice was growing heated. From where she sat, Jak could see the tension in the smuggler's shoulders increasing.

"You are aware that this planet is under a League of Solaran Planets blockade." The tribunal prosecutor was making a statement, not asking a question. The tribunal chair leaned forward and fixed Torrin with a hard stare.

"I didn't know that until I entered the system. The ship was a little hard to miss, though." At her sarcastic admission, the gallery buzzed with whispers.

"And you decided to proceed regardless?"

"Yes."

"Traitor!" The shout came from the other side of the gallery. Jak looked around to see where the accusation had come from but couldn't make out the culprit. Murmurs rose amongst the spectators. The noise level in the room rose rapidly.

"Order!" With a booming thud, the tribunal chair slammed his gavel down on the heavy wooden table. "Order or I'll have the room cleared." At his threat, the buzzing subsided but didn't abate completely.

"The picket is in place to prevent war profiteers like yourself from artificially tipping the balance of the war toward one side or the other."

"I didn't sell him anything." Torrin raised her voice in protest. "He practically attacked me."

"Your intent was clear, Miss Ivanov. You wanted to make some easy money. Well, we're the ones who would have been most affected by your actions."

"What does this have to do with being a spy?" Torrin asked. She struggled to keep her tone reasonable. "So far, all you've proven me to be guilty of is having a strong business ethic." A shocked titter rolled through the watching crowd, and Torrin's shoulders relaxed slightly. She appreciated an audience, but Jak's heart sank as the faces of the men behind the long table hardened.

"It goes to the root of our argument that you will do anything for money. Tell us the truth," the tribunal prosecutor said silkily. "You allowed yourself to be 'rescued' by Devonite military personnel so you'd have the perfect cover to spy on our troop movements and weapons capabilities."

"What? No!" Torrin jumped to her feet. At a quick signal from the tribunal chair, the soldiers on either side of her each grabbed a shoulder and arm and wrestled her back into her chair. She struggled against them in vain while glaring at the tribunal. "That doesn't even make any sense! If that's what you think, you're clearly insane."

"Isn't it true that you were carrying on a sexual relationship with Colonel Hutchinson?"

"No! He tried to force himself on me. The only relationship I was interested in carrying on with the man was a business one."

"So you admit to conspiring to supply him with military technology."

"I already admitted to that." Torrin's face was growing steadily redder. "I'm a merchant. I make my living by selling merchandise."

"I see." The Devonite prosecutor stroked his chin while he watched her with the same horrified attention he would have given a repulsive insect he'd discovered under a rock. "So you sell things. Does that include your body?"

"It most certainly does not and I resent the accusation. Hells, if I'd known what kind of people the Orthodoxans were, I never would have come to this planet at all." Torrin glared at the prosecutor. Jak could tell that she was worked up and hoped she wouldn't say anything stupid.

"Did you know that women are not permitted to own businesses on Haefen? It is the duty of their men to keep them from such onerous duties. By law, your sale of goods is illegal unless you have male supervision."

"I don't need some man to report to. I'm more than capable of running a business on my own. From here, you don't look any better than the Orthodoxans," Torrin railed. Jak cringed. The tribunal wouldn't like that at all. "At least they're up front about their bigotry."

An angry murmur rippled through the courtroom, building in intensity. The spectators had not liked Torrin's characterization of their society any more than the tribunal had. The tribunal members leaned in to whisper amongst themselves and the prosecutor joined them. The whispered conference went on for quite some time, long enough for the trial spectators to quiet themselves without further threats. A tense silence blanketed the courtroom. Finally the members of the tribunal straightened in their chairs, and the prosecutor moved to address them from in front of the table.

"Fellow tribunal members, this woman stands accused of espionage and indecency. She admits to the lesser charge of indecency through the operation of a business without male guidance. Her explanations about her contact with the Orthodoxans are obviously thinly veiled lies. Coupled with her admitted guilt for the first charge, I move that you have no choice but to find her guilty on all charges. She condemns herself from her own mouth. How say you?"

Torrin watched the prosecutor's speech, mouth agape. Her stunned gaze moved to take in the four remaining tribunal members. The first one stood.

"Guilty."

The second tribunal member stood. "Guilty." And so it went down the line. With every guilty verdict, Jak slumped further in her seat. Death sentences had to be unanimous decisions by the tribunal. To save Torrin's life, all it would take was one not guilty verdict; she would merely be imprisoned for life. After the fourth guilty verdict, all eyes turned to the prosecutor. He turned to the silent courtroom and cast his eyes out over the crowd.

"I too find Torrin Ivanov guilty of espionage and indecency. The verdict is unanimous. She will be put to death by firing squad."

"What? No!" Torrin tried to jump up and was again wrestled back into her chair by the two soldiers. "You can't do this to me! I've done nothing wrong!"

"Take her away," the prosecutor said to Torrin's escorts and they dragged her, still struggling, from the room. For a few moments, the spectators sat, stunned by the speedy conclusion to the trial. After a long silence, first some, then a flood of people began filing out of the room.

Jak stayed where she was, staring at the chair Torrin had occupied. She wasn't sure she could trust her legs if she stood up. *How did this happen?* Her debrief had gone so well. There had been no indication that events would deteriorate so quickly. The trial was clearly a sham. The tribunal had never planned to acquit her of the charges. And the charges! They made no sense. Torrin wasn't a resident of the planet. How could she be expected to abide by either Haefonian society's legal or moral structure?

The longer she sat, the angrier she became. Rage boiled in her chest. She'd given her life to the military. They didn't even know who she really was. She'd served them faithfully even though she had to conceal a major portion of herself whenever she was around anybody else. She was half a person because she'd quashed a huge chunk of her personality. And for what? For them.

When it came to Jak Stowell, she wasn't even sure who that person really was. Her time with Torrin was the closest she'd come to discovering her identity. They were about to take that away from her also.

Jak clenched her fists until sharp pain bit into her hands. She looked down. Her nails had broken the skin and she had half a dozen punctures in her palms. She watched, numb, as the crescents filled with blood.

"Problems, soldier?" Jak jumped at the voice from behind her. She craned her neck and leaped to her feet when she saw Colonel Wolfe seated directly behind her. He'd approached so quietly that she hadn't heard him.

"Sir?" Her voice cracked, betraying her emotion.

"Worried about your…captive?" He watched her closely.

"I didn't save her ass, then drag her across the back end of beyond to have you shoot her." She glared at him. "Sir."

"I understand your frustration, Sergeant, but this is all for the best."

"How is that possible, sir?" Jak turned anguished eyes back to her hands. She struggled not to show any weakness in front of the man, but recent events were starting to sink in. Panic rose in her breast and threatened to choke her. "You don't understand. She can help us, and if she's dead that won't happen." Jak sucked in a shuddering breath. *She can't help us. She can't help me.*

"Your part in this isn't finished," Wolfe said, standing. "Come along."

"What do you—" Jak froze. They meant for her to pull the trigger. That was all he could mean. Stricken, she stared at the colonel. "Sir, I can't…you can't want me to…"

The colonel glanced around. Aside from them the gallery was empty. "We can't talk here," he said even though they were the courtroom's only occupants. "You need to come with me."

* * *

Torrin's mind churned as her escorts dragged her from the courtroom. She'd been in some really sticky situations before, but she'd never been condemned to death. On this planet her only allies were the AI on a ship that was locked down and a sniper who had chosen not to follow his orders to kill her. After all that, Jak had just managed to prolong her life, not save it. There was no way she could count on either of them. Tien was unable to come and get her even if she could somehow get a message to the AI. Jak's motives were a complete unknown, possibly even to him. The only way she was going to get out of the situation was on her own. As usual, the only one she had to rely on was herself.

She slowly reduced her struggles as if she were losing strength. She let her body grow slack and started to sob. If the Devonites truly believed women were too helpless to run a business, maybe she could use their preconceptions against them. The two guards were forced to take on all of her weight. She felt them shift to take on her extra mass.

They practically carried her through an exterior doorway toward the back of a waiting truck. This was it. She needed to break out now. Maybe she could lose herself in the crowd of soldiers. With the fatigues she still wore she might blend right in.

Torrin dropped her left shoulder and tucked it, and the Devonite on that side stumbled. She braced herself against him and pushed off, ripping her arm free from his grasp. The other soldier's grip on her right arm acted as a pivot, and before he knew it, she was flying right at him. She ducked her head and smashed her forehead into his nose with a satisfying crunch. Blood spurted from the nose now flattened across half the man's face. He stumbled back, hands coming up to protect himself.

An arm snaked around her neck. The other soldier had regained his feet and was trying to trap her in a sleeper hold. Torrin seized his arm with both of her hands and with a twist dropped to one knee, using his weight and her momentum to flip him over her shoulder. He landed on the ground with a grunt as the air was forcefully expelled from his lungs. He tried to roll over to regain his feet but was hampered by his inability to breathe. His face turned ruddy with his efforts to inhale.

The other guard came at her, arms outstretched. Blood still flowed freely from his nose and dripped down the front of his fatigues.

"Shit," Torrin said. The soldier yelled as he came for her, alerting others to her escape attempt. She grabbed one wrist with both hands and spun, lifting her hands and backing into him, throwing him over her shoulder. He hit the ground and lay there without moving. As she turned to run for the gap between buildings, something grabbed hold of her ankle. She stumbled, landing awkwardly on her hands. She looked over her shoulder to see the other soldier with a hand around her ankle, pulling her toward him. She twisted in his grasp, flipped onto her back and swung her other leg at him, clipping him on the side of the head with her heel. He collapsed into a boneless heap. Satisfied, she pushed herself up and turned to run. Lights exploded in her field of vision and were swallowed by blackness. She vaguely felt herself falling before everything went away.

She came to on a bed, one arm shackled to the frame. Her vision blurred and she blinked to clear it. Light slashed through her skull in shards. She must have taken quite the blow to the head. Slowly the room coalesced around her. She was in an infirmary of sorts. The room was surprisingly open. There were no bars on the windows, and no visible restraints beyond the band around her right wrist.

Lieutenant Smythe smiled at her from his seat beside the bed.

"You son of a bitch," Torrin snarled. He leaned back as she tried to take a swing at him. Fortunately for him, her near arm was the one that was restrained and she had to reach awkwardly across her body to try to strike him.

"Calm down, Miss Ivanov." Smythe raised his hands in a mollifying gesture. "Let me explain the truth of what's going on here."

"I know what's going on," she growled. "You're trying to have me put to death. Well, fuck you, there's no way I'm going quietly. I'm taking as many of you bastards with me as I can."

He blinked at her, surprised. "You really have no idea what's happening? I thought for sure you would have seen what was developing."

"Oh?" Torrin glared at him, still trying to reach him with her free hand. "Enlighten me."

"You won't be put to death."

"So life imprisonment instead? That's so much better."

The lieutenant gave her an exasperated look. "If you keep interrupting me, I'll never finish my explanation." He watched her, and she clamped her lips together, still glaring. Perhaps if she glared at him hard enough, he would burst into flames. The thought cheered her up a little, and she kept her eyes on him as if the weight of her gaze alone might cause his head to explode. Smythe blanched a bit at her look; he saw his own death gazing at him out of her eyes. *Good,* she thought. *He has reason to be worried.*

"What happened in the courtroom was an elaborate ruse. We needed to convince the Orthodoxans that we weren't going to use you. They have some idea of what you can offer, and if they knew that we intended to retain your services, they would plan accordingly. If they think we're putting you to death, they don't need to worry about the new tech you're going to sell us. They'll figure things out eventually, but this way we can buy ourselves some time."

Torrin sat back and considered him. The explanation made some sense, but she couldn't bring herself to trust the innocuous little man.

"You could have let me in on the charade," she accused.

"We determined that it would be better if you didn't know," he said, his eyes apologetic. "Your reaction was extremely convincing. If you'd known it was all a ruse, you might not have been able to pull it off as well."

"That was the shittiest thing you could have done. If I'm not in any trouble, why am I shackled like a criminal?"

"After your impressive escape attempt, it was decided that you should be restrained until the situation could be explained." Smythe produced a key from his pocket and held it up. "I'm prepared to release you if you promise not to try to kill me like you tried to kill your guards."

Torrin nodded and grimaced when more pain shot through her temples. "If I'd wanted the guards dead, they would be."

The lieutenant made a noise of agreement in his throat as he released her hand from the restraint. "I have no doubt that is true. Your skills in that area are impressive and unanticipated. Our debriefing with Sergeant Stowell didn't indicate that you had any type of hand-to-hand training."

Torrin massaged her wrist. "It didn't really come up. He's not the only one who can play his cards close to his chest."

"If you're sufficiently recovered, allow me to conduct you to a real meeting with Central Command."

"Your Central Command can wait until I shed this headache. What happened anyway?"

"Sorry about that." The lieutenant had the grace to look embarrassed. "I had to knock you out to keep you from escaping. The fastest way I could think to do it was to pistol whip you on the temple."

Torrin raised her hand to the side of her head and encountered a tender lump that rose out of her temple. This one did its best to live up to the term "goose egg." Even the gentlest touch sent more pain lancing through her head. She snatched her fingers away, stood, crossed the room and checked her reflection in the small mirror over the room's sink. A large purple knot swelled from the side of her forehead.

"That's just great. But until the headache is gone, I won't be meeting with anyone, especially not your precious Central Command."

"The general made it clear that he wanted to see you as soon as you were awake."

"I'm not entering into negotiations when my head is ready to split open. For all I know, this entire episode has been one long hustle for you people."

Smythe smiled faintly. "That's a little paranoid, don't you think?"

"Just because you're paranoid doesn't mean you're wrong." Torrin fixed him with a level stare. "You haven't exactly given me much reason to trust you."

"I see your point. I'll find some painkillers for your head, then we can go to the general."

Torrin carefully inclined her head and seated herself on the edge of the bed while the lieutenant called out the door for a nurse. She closed her eyes against the glare of the lights and listened as Smythe carried on a quick, hushed conversation, then closed the door. Torrin cracked open an eye when a few moments later the door was opened by a woman in an unfamiliar uniform.

"Thank you, nurse," Smythe said and took the offered pill bottle. The woman curtsied and left with alacrity, tossing a scandalized look back over her shoulder at Torrin. "Here you go." Smythe handed Torrin a couple of pills. She waited while he poured a cup of water at the sink before handing them to her.

"So tell me about the stim pills your people take," she said, before dropping the pills into her mouth and tossing back the water.

"There isn't a whole lot to tell," Smythe said, a little disconcerted by the sudden change of topic. "Many of our soldiers take them while on assignment, especially the ones who venture behind enemy lines. I'm sure I don't have to tell you how dangerous it can be to sleep while in enemy territory. Most of the men only take them for a few days. When taken for too long there is the danger of side effects. I take it that Sergeant Stowell was taking them while rescuing you from the Orthodoxans."

Torrin nodded. "Side effects? Jak mentioned that he'll probably need to sleep for a few days once he stops taking them."

"That's true, though the need for sleep is only one of the side effects he needs to worry about. Did he take them the whole time he was with you?" At Torrin's nod, Smythe's face grew grave. "The stims can have grave consequences in immune system response." At the puzzled look on Torrin's face, Smythe explained. "He could become gravely ill. He'll be susceptible to almost any pathogen. If he ends up sleeping for a number of days, then he most likely won't be exposed to anything. He should be all right, but he'll have to be extremely cautious."

Torrin fiddled with the collar of her jacket while she digested Smythe's explanation. She would need to make sure that Jak wasn't exposed to anything, but how? He could be infuriatingly stubborn.

"How's your head?"

She shook her head experimentally and was relieved to feel almost no pain. Nor could she tell that the medication was dulling her thought processes. "I'm good. Let's get on with this."

"Excellent. The general's been anxiously awaiting this opportunity."

CHAPTER NINETEEN

Colonel Wolfe sat across from Jak, eyeing her intently. Elbows planted on the table, he watched her over steepled fingers. They were in the inner room of a large office. Papers were strewn about, and a huge monitor dominated most of one wall. The small conference table would have comfortably seated six, though by the chairs in the corners and along the wall, it looked like the room had hosted meetings for as many as eighteen.

"Torrin Ivanov will not be put to death. The entire trial was put together to prevent Orthodoxan spies from discovering our real intentions."

This was the opposite of what Jak had expected to hear, and she released a pent-up sigh of relief. She straightened and did her best to reassume a mantle of indifference, though she suspected it was too late. "That's good, sir. I didn't drag her across half of Orthodoxan territory just so you could kill her."

Wolfe chuckled. "That's certainly one way of spinning it." He watched her knowingly. "You have feelings for the woman, don't you?"

"No, sir!" Jak burst out. "I don't like having my hard work wasted is all." Her anger at the accusation was transparent, even to her.

"It's all right, Stowell. She's one damn fine-looking woman, but you're probably barking up the wrong tree."

"Sir, the only interest I have in Ivanov is what she can do for the war effort."

The colonel looked unconvinced but didn't push her any further. "Regardless, you will be instrumental to her insertion back into enemy territory."

"Sir?"

"She will need to return to her vessel, which lies deep behind Orthodoxan lines. Of all the men, you are best acquainted with that territory. I want you involved in the planning of the operation to return her to her ship."

"Got it, sir."

"It's also of highest importance that no one knows who she is or why she's around. You and one other will know her true identity. Captain McCullock is the other, by necessity, though for no other reason."

"McCullock, sir? He hates me." Jak didn't see the wisdom of that choice at all.

"Yes, he does." Wolfe furrowed his brow. "What did you do to piss him off, anyway?"

"Me, sir? Nothing! Wish I knew, but I can't think of anything."

"It doesn't matter. You might not like him, nor he you, but he's a good soldier and an excellent intelligence officer. He won't jeopardize the mission. He's also the only one of the group who's been vetted and who we know for sure isn't an Orthodoxan spy."

"You seem awfully worried about spies, sir. Is there something I should know?"

The colonel ran a hand through his hair. The gesture betrayed weariness and deep concern. "The Orthodoxans have been a little too good at pinpointing their raids recently. They've been striking too often where we're weakest. We've also had a number of sniper groups and lone operatives disappear on their side of the lines."

"We always have people disappear, sir. It's part of the job. We all know the risks."

"They're disappearing with alarming frequency. Somebody is feeding the Orthodoxans sensitive information. I'm sure we'll find the source eventually. For now, we need to get Miss Ivanov off the planet safely before the Orthodoxans figure out what we're doing."

Jak snapped off a sharp nod. She'd had no idea the situation was so dire. They didn't hear much from other outposts and camps. Each camp was fairly isolated unless it was involved in an operation that required personnel from multiple camps. There had been very few of those lately. It made sense with what Wolfe had told her. There was no point in launching a large operation if the enemy knew it was coming. That would only accomplish getting a lot of their own soldiers killed.

"You can count on me, sir. I'll make sure we get her home safely."

"Excellent." Wolfe grinned. "We're going to let the insertion team know that she's an assassin whose target is a top Orthodoxan general or maybe their president. We haven't decided which one yet, but we'll hash the details out when you start planning. Ostensibly, you'll be taking her across the border to get her in place to launch the attempt. At that time, you'll both head for the ship instead."

"Sounds good, sir."

"Also, no one will know that she's female. We'll be disguising her as a man. With her height, it shouldn't be too difficult. We'll just need to convince her to shear off that hair and strap down those gorgeous breasts. It's a shame. She's quite the looker. If I thought I had a chance, I might see if I could catch her eye."

At least she was uniquely qualified to help with that, Jak thought. Wolfe had no idea how apt their decision was; she struggled to keep her surprise off her face. Wolfe continued to wax eloquently on Torrin's charms in gradually more graphic terms.

"Is there anything else, sir?" Jak cut Wolfe off when he began a paean to Torrin's ass. Now that she was paying attention to what he'd been saying, a slow anger grew inside her. Torrin wasn't some piece of meat to be ogled. She was a beautiful, amazing woman with more fire and spirit than any ten men she knew. Combined.

"Almost." Wolfe cut himself off and came back to reality. "We will be televising Torrin's 'execution' in a few days' time. Don't fly apart again when you see it. Or at least, try not to be overcome by righteous indignation at us wasting the opportunity you dropped in our laps." He winked at her.

Jak smiled ruefully. "Understood, sir. I'll do my best."

Wolfe gestured at her in dismissal. "Off with you then. You have plenty of work to do."

Jak stood and saluted, then left the room, her mind spinning with the irony of the situation.

* * *

Sweat dripped from Torrin's brow, and she ran a hand across her forehead to keep it from running into her eyes. She'd been locked in negotiations with General Callahan for an hour already. He seemed so affable, but beneath the genial surface lurked the mind of someone with the business acumen of a corporate raider. She knew she was more than up to negotiating with him, but it hadn't been easy. Though if he'd expected her to be rattled by the trial and death sentence, he must be disappointed. Her very real anger at the whole charade had lit a fire under her that his charm wasn't up to quenching.

They were alone in his office. It wasn't as large as she'd expected for the supreme commander of the entire Devonite military. It was unlikely that he spent a whole lot of time in there. He must be constantly busy with meetings and other important functions. While nicely appointed, the room was impersonal and held a faint aura of neglect.

At the start of their negotiations, he'd been sitting in the chair behind his desk, but that hadn't lasted long. Callahan seemed incapable of staying still, and he paced back and forth behind his desk as he explained to her at length, again, why her price wouldn't work.

"This is what it comes down to, General," Torrin answered calmly. She lounged back in her chair and put her feet up on the corner of his desk. She exuded relaxation but resting her feet on the desk was a calculated insult. "You want what I can provide and I deserve to get paid for the trouble I'll be going through to get it. This doesn't even start to cover the trouble I've been through to get to you, not to mention the insult of that trial."

"You can't expect us to just give up generations of research into cybernetics, Miss Ivanov."

"Why not?" Torrin raised one eyebrow in question. "You know I won't sell it to the Orthodoxans. I won't be dealing with them ever again." She scowled as she felt Hutchinson's fetid breath along the side of her neck and shook her head to dispel the phantom sensation. "You have no market offworld, and even if you venture back into the galaxy once your dispute with the Orthodoxans has concluded, it will be decades before you'll have the capabilities to do so. By the time you get offworld, I'm sure you will have surpassed the technology you're about to give me."

Callahan eyed her dubiously, still pacing. His stance was starting to weaken, she could tell. Time to go in for the kill.

"Look, General. I'm not interested in researching or developing on what you'll be giving me. I just want to be able to patent and sell what you've already developed." She placed her feet back on the ground and leaned forward, clasping her hands together on the desk. "By the time the Haefonians are ready to reach for the stars again, there will already be a market, and you'll be primed to bring in top-of-the-line enhancements."

The general glanced at the ceiling and then back at her. "You make some valid points, Miss Ivanov, but when it comes to business, I don't trust you farther than I can throw you." He moved behind the desk and placed his palms on the surface, leaning toward her. "I want you to sign a noncompete contract against that eventuality. When Haefen joins the intergalactic marketplace again, you turn the cybernetics market over to us."

Torrin chuckled. "My dear general, I can do you one better. When you break the surly bonds of your planet, I'll sign over a controlling interest in the company that I'll found using this technology. Your government will get a controlling interest. Say, fifty-one percent. I'll keep forty-nine percent."

Callahan shook his head vehemently. "Absolutely not. That's much too high a division. We won't go for anything less than an eighty–twenty split."

"I'll be putting in a hell of a lot of work into this. I won't go for less than forty-five–fifty-five."

"Hardly. You'll be doing work on the backs of generations of Haefonians. How about seventy–thirty?"

"Tell you what. I'll agree to sixty–forty, but only if you agree to let my company supply you when you're ready to develop space travel again."

"You've got yourself a deal, Miss Ivanov." The general extended a hand to her. Torrin grasped it, and they shook on the bargain.

Callahan jerked open the door and barked to his assistant, "Get Lieutenant Smythe." He walked back behind the desk and plopped himself into the chair.

"That was exhausting," he said and pulled open one of the desk drawers. "You are a formidable opponent." He produced a glass bottle and two tumblers and splashed a bright blue liquid into each glass. Pushing one over to her, he leaned back in his chair.

"Aren't you breaking your own laws by entering into a contract with me?" Torrin asked, picking up the glass. "Don't think I've forgotten that particular charge. Indecency for practicing business without male supervision? What the hell? That was even more insulting than the espionage charge."

Callahan lifted his glass to her and took a healthy swig. He grimaced and shook his head as the effects of the alcohol hit. "That's a good year. And you're absolutely right. The laws are going to have to change, aren't they? I think we can manage to introduce legislation that pushes through the legalization of female-owned and -run businesses. While we're at it, I suppose it might be good to introduce legislation making it legal for women to own property."

"You think?" Torrin asked sarcastically before sipping carefully from the glass in her hand. The liquid in the tumbler had quite a kick to it but was smoother than the blue whiskey she'd consumed in Hutchinson's mansion. It felt like a few years had passed since that time, rather than a little more than one week.

"This means we really need to crush the Orthodoxans. They won't like this turn of events at all. It'll really send them off the deep end." Callahan guffawed and raised his glass again. "Confusion to the Orthodoxans," he toasted, still laughing.

"I can drink to that," Torrin said, lifting her own glass in his direction and downing another swallow. They were interrupted by a knock at the door. Callahan's assistant, a young clerk, stuck his head in.

"Lieutenant Smythe is here as you requested, sir."

"Excellent! Send him in."

The lieutenant entered the room and took a casual look around the office. Torrin would have wagered her last centi-cred that his quick glance hadn't missed a thing.

"Looks like good news, sir," Smythe said, indicating the mostly empty tumblers.

"Very good news, Smythe," Callahan responded expansively. "I need you to write up the terms of our agreement as we lay them out for you. Then Miss Ivanov and I will sign the contracts, and you will act as witness."

"Very good sir. Then Miss Ivanov and I can discuss the preparations for her return to her vessel."

"That would be great, Lieutenant," Torrin chimed in. "I'll do whatever I need to return to my ship."

Smythe smiled crookedly. "I hope you still feel that way after the details are explained to you."

"Of course I will. I'm up for pretty much anything at this point," she said. "Why?"

Smythe smiled enigmatically and set himself up at the table. Torrin and Callahan chatted amiably while the lieutenant replayed a recording of their negotiation and took down the pertinent points, entering them into his tablet. Twenty minutes later, the document was finished and had been perused and agreed upon. Smythe finished their contract and produced a small electronic device which he plugged into the jack in his left palm. Smythe passed Torrin the device. There was an oval indentation in one end.

"By pressing your thumb into the reader, you'll be agreeing to the terms of your bargain as negotiated with the general."

Torrin pressed her thumb down. She felt a twinge as her thumb was pierced and a small point of blood pooled into the device. The pain wasn't unexpected. DNA was a common way of signing a legal document. Some places took it in saliva, others in blood. Smythe passed the device over to Callahan, who repeated the procedure. He took the device back, disconnected the cord from his wrist and reconnected it to the tablet.

Torrin hadn't forgotten her earlier question. Finally she pushed the tablet to one side and got in his face.

"What aren't you telling me, Lieutenant?"

He looked back at her defensively. "It wasn't entirely my idea, but it's been decided that for your safety and ours, it's best to disguise you as a Devonite soldier."

"Oh no," Torrin said. She knew exactly what he was driving at. "No, no, no! You're not cutting my hair." Her hands flew protectively to the sides of her head. There was no way she was about to let these Haefonian assholes butcher her best feature.

Short hair made her look looked rawboned and unfinished. She needed something framing her face, softening it.

"Ma'am, it's the only way this will work. You have to be absolutely unrecognizable as Torrin Ivanov, the offworld merchant."

Torrin cast desperate eyes over at the general, who nodded to her gravely. His eyes danced over the rim of his glass as he took a final swig.

"You bastard," she railed. "If I'd known this was part of your plan, you would be looking at a forty-nine–fifty-one split for sure."

"That's why a good negotiator always keeps something back," he replied.

* * *

Once again they were back in a small transport, but this time they were finally headed back to camp. It wasn't really home and probably never would be. Jak certainly couldn't let her guard down there, but she would finally be able to get some sleep. After three more days of dosing, the stims were working their way out of her system. Torrin had found out that she was still taking them, and some idiot had told her all about the possible side effects. The lecture she'd gotten as a result had blistered her ears. It had only ended when she pointed out that men didn't scream at other men, especially not in so shrill a tone. Not that Torrin had admitted to screaming, but the accusation had cut her off.

Torrin sat across from her, pointedly not looking at her, and Jak took the opportunity to watch the smuggler closely. Her hair was completely shorn away, leaving only an auburn buzz cut. Jak didn't understand how anyone could think she was a man. Even with short hair and bound breasts, Torrin was given away by high cheekbones, full lips and eyes so deep she could have drowned in them. Jak missed the long strands, but she understood the need for secrecy. Even though she missed her long hair, Torrin still exercised a powerful attraction over her that she could no longer deny.

"Are you quite finished?" Torrin asked waspishly. "You don't have to make a big deal of it. The hair's gone. I look like a lout."

"The hair is gone," Jak said, looking away. "You don't have being a guy down, though. Not really." Still, Jak supposed, she was proof that people saw what they wanted to. At least with Torrin's height and broad shoulders she was somewhat believable as a soldier.

"What would you know about it?"

Quite a lot, as it turns out. "It's the mannerisms. You don't have them quite right," Jak explained earnestly. "Stop trying to prove that you're not a girl. You're a guy now, and you don't have to prove anything."

"What do you mean?"

"Well, like your walk. You're rolling your hips when you walk. Try turning your feet out and swinging your shoulders when you walk, instead of your hips."

"Oh sure," Torrin snorted. "It's as easy as that. I'd like to see you try to pull off being a woman."

So would I, Jak thought. It had been more than ten years since she'd been Jakellyn Stowell. Even then, her father had teased her about having more of a boy's nature than a girl's. He hadn't cared, though, and when he'd decided that it was too dangerous for her to retain her true identity, her boyish tendencies had worked to their advantage.

"You're right, I don't know the first thing about passing for a woman," Jak admitted truthfully. "I'm not sure I could pull it off." *And how sad is that?*

Torrin seemed slightly mollified and went back to her epic sulk. Jak settled herself into the transport's wooden seat and prepared to take a light nap. Though the stims had started to work their way out of her system, they hadn't dissipated to the point where she would be able to get any sustained sleep. Hopefully, if she napped a little, she wouldn't have to sleep for so long when they got back to camp. She'd timed her last dose to wear off a couple of hours after their return.

"You finally stop taking those damn stims?"

"I had my last one about twelve hours ago," Jak replied without opening her eyes. "When we get back, I'll have to sleep for a few days. Try not to piss anyone off."

"Me?" Torrin seemed genuinely surprised. "I get along with pretty much everyone."

Jak snorted. "Sure you do. Everyone who doesn't have a penis."

"That's not true. I get along quite well with some of the men. General Callahan and Lieutenant Smythe, for example. Once they got over threatening to kill me, they were quite…agreeable."

Jak could hear the smirk in her voice and cracked an eye open just wide enough to see Torrin leaning back with a smug smile like a banner across her face. She looked supremely self-satisfied. The negotiations must have gone well. Jak found herself grinning in response. Torrin caught her watching and blushed, quickly averting her gaze. That was interesting.

"You know we'll be bunking next door to each other." As soon as the words left her lips, Jak kicked herself. Why had she even mentioned that? What did she think she was doing, trying to set up a date? That would work well. Even if Torrin was interested, and she was getting signals that she was, it would all fall in on her when the smuggler discovered she was no man. No, it would be better to try to foster some distance between them. She was the primary planner for Torrin's insertion into enemy territory. She would have to be all business to pull off the operation.

"Sure, sounds like fun," Torrin said. "Maybe we can have a slumber party."

Now it was Jak's turn to blush and avert her eyes. A mental image of Torrin dressed in pajama bottoms and camisole bloomed in her imagination. A powerful surge of arousal blew through her, leaving her speechless.

"Pillow fights, truth or dare. I know, we'll do each other's hair," Torrin gushed, either not knowing or not caring about the effect she was having on Jak. "Of course that part won't take very long."

"Umm, sure," Jak said. She slouched down in her seat until her chin touched her chest. Those feelings were again wreaking havoc within her. Torrin's irresistible pull and the guilt of her upbringing clashed. Her loins throbbed painfully. She just wanted Torrin's touch on her. In her. Anywhere. Everywhere.

She yawned ostentatiously and closed her eyes. To all appearances she looked like she was napping, but her mind churned. Guilt and intense arousal kept her from napping for the rest of the ride.

* * *

Jak had dozed most of the way back to the camp. Torrin was glad to see he was getting some sleep, finally, but she missed having him to talk to even though she couldn't seem to stop herself from snapping at him every time he opened his mouth. They'd been the only ones in the back of the transport, and there had been very little to see. She didn't do especially well with boredom so when they finally pulled into the camp, she was more than a little irritable.

The back door was opened by that idiot with a mustache, McCullock. She brushed past him with a disdainful glance. She hadn't forgotten how he'd tried to railroad Jak by not calling in on the sniper being overdue. He smiled at her, showing a little too much teeth.

"Stowell," he bellowed, sticking his head through the door. "Get your ass out of there now!"

Jak blinked at him sleepily and roused himself from the corner of the transport's cab. "Coming, sir." He sketched a salute in the air and pulled himself out of the vehicle.

Camp Abbott was much less impressive than Fort Marshall had been. From where they stood, Torrin could make out the tops of the walls around them. They looked like they'd originally been built to be temporary structures, but necessity had dictated that they serve long beyond their intended lifespan. Masonry had cracked and was flaking away in more than one place, revealing the structure beneath. The interior roads were set up on a strict grid, but they were all packed dirt. The wind blew gusts of dust from one side of the road to the other. The whole place had the overall air of a shelf in desperate need of tidying. All the objects were placed just so, but they'd been abused for so long that her primary impression was one of neglect.

Soldiers roamed the streets here as they had at the fort. These soldiers had seen military action and recently. Some of them sported bandages and the too-pink patches of newly regenerated skin. They weren't nearly as buttoned down and pretty as the ones she'd seen at the fort. Most of them wore combat fatigues that had seen heavy and repeated use. They weren't slovenly, just worn. The only one who looked like he'd recently pressed his uniform was McCullock. By the looks the passing soldiers gave him when he wasn't looking, they felt as much disdain for the captain as she did.

"Let's get you to the barracks." McCullock led them to a long, low building at the corner of a complex made up of a dozen similarly shaped buildings. He walked up the steps and held the door open for her.

Jak rolled his eyes. "We're supposed to be treating Corporal Compton like any other soldier, sir." McCullock just sneered at him and gestured Torrin through before letting the door close in Jak's face. He stared at McCullock through the door's screen before pulling it open and following them.

McCullock led them most of the way down a long hall and indicated a door. "That's your room. Stowell is located right next to you, on the end. Typically, men bunk two to a room in this unit, but given your 'special circumstances' we thought that would be asking for trouble."

Jak had already opened the door to his room and was stepping through it.

"That goes for you, Stowell," McCullock called after him. "No fraternization."

Jak paused, then regarded him levelly. "That would be disgusting and illegal sir."

"And don't you forget it," McCullock blustered in return.

Jak turned to face her. "Two soldiers from another unit were caught—"

"Fucking!" McCullock spat, spittle flying from under his mustache. "They should have put the two deviants to the firing squad, but the judge was 'merciful.'" He sneered. "They'll spend the rest of their days performing forced labor. Keep them too busy for that kind of bullshit."

Backward much? Torrin rolled her eyes mentally but kept her face impassive. Like it was any of his business who they had chosen to sleep with. More than ever, she was glad she would soon be leaving this provincial little backwater.

He glared at Jak. "I won't hesitate to make sure that you get the same or worse. So keep your hands off h-him." Mustache twitching, he gave Torrin a broad smile. "Don't worry. I'll make sure he doesn't bother you."

Was he trying to impress her? Protect her, maybe? He was working very hard at being charming to her, but his treatment of Jak was disgusting. For his part, Jak just stood there and took it.

"That's…great, Captain." She smiled at him wanly. "Now if you don't mind, it's been a long few days and I want some sleep."

"Of course, of course. And please, call me Jagger." He smiled at her again. If she hadn't seen him rip into Jak moments ago, she wouldn't have believed he was capable of such venom. "Don't let me keep you up. I will have your duty rotation brought to you. You will be engaging in some light training duties. The men will talk if you're closed up in your room the entire time you're here." He gave her a funny little bow, glared again at Jak and left.

"You look like you're about to fall over," Torrin said.

"Stims are almost out of my system. I can barely keep my eyes open." Jak looked terrible. The circles under his eyes were so dark that he seemed to be staring at her from two black eyes. His skin had taken on an unnatural pallor, and he leaned on the doorframe of her room. "I won't be able to look out for you for the next few days. You need to play this one smart."

"I'm all about smart. I can take care of myself." Jak slid gently forward along the wall and Torrin reached out to steady him. "I took down two guards and almost made a break for it."

"I heard." Jak yawned hugely. "One of those guys still couldn't breathe through his nose when we left, even after the doctors fixed him up." He gave her a tired smile. "You left an impression."

"Now I know you're in trouble. The Jak I know would never make such a terrible joke." Actually, the Jak she knew would never in his right mind make any kind of joke, let alone one that bad.

"All right, I'm out. Remember, be good." He pushed away from the wall and slouched over to his room.

"You have no idea," Torrin said to his retreating back. *But I want you to.* A weary wave was the only response to her sally. Opening the door, she entered the room that was to be hers for the next while. It was beyond spartan. Two narrow beds lined the walls on either side of the room. Two very small writing desks stood at the foot of each bed. A cable came out of the wall above each desk. She picked one up and turned the end over in her hands. There was no way she'd be able to use it without some sort of input jack on her body. There was nothing for her to do. First things first. She really did need a nap. Once she'd rested properly, she could check out what else this little dump of a camp had to offer.

CHAPTER TWENTY

"So what the hell are you thinking, anyway?"

Jak looked over in time to catch Bron's cheeky grin. He dropped the spotter's scope to his chest and regarded her with great amusement. His face was distinct, crisp, but the background looked faded and smudged, indistinct. The blond of his hair and brilliant blue of his eyes were the only color. All others colors disappeared into a faded tone of sepia.

Not again, she thought. *I can't do this right now.*

"I don't know what you're talking about," she said. *Wake up, wake up*, she screamed inside her head. Dimly, she could sense her body thrashing, but it was as if it belonged to someone else.

"That girl." Bron raised the scope back up to his eyes and scanned a far-off ridge. "She's nothing but trouble."

"She's fine."

"You bet she's fine!" Still looking through the scope, Bron whistled. "That's the problem. All you see is that fine ass and those boobs."

Glowering, Jak ducked her head to look through the scope on her rifle. She knew what was coming. Every time she had this dream it ended the same way, but that never stopped her from trying to end it before it ran its course. Somewhere out there was the sniper who was stalking them.

"You need to turn on your cloak," she replied acerbically.

"Don't try to change the subject." He reached around to the front of his neck and twisted on the control for the cloaking device. Abruptly, he disappeared from view. All she could see was a faint shimmer, like the air over a hot roof in the summer. "She's not for you or you for her."

"Your cloak's glitching out. You should reset it."

"I'm fine. Stop trying to change the subject." She heard his grin widen and ducked her head to peer through the scope again.

"Would it be so terrible if I wanted her? She's amazing, and I feel alive when I'm with her. For the past two years, it feels like someone took my emotions, locked them away at the bottom of a trunk and then dropped the trunk into the deepest part of the ocean. With her I feel things. I feel things for her."

He snorted. "It's not right, you know that. What would Dad say? He'd be destroyed that you took all he did for you just for you throw it away on someone who doesn't even have the right equipment."

"That's not fair," Jak protested. Was that a flash of red among the trees? She dialed in on the area. For the first time since she'd started having the dream she could finally make out details other than trees through the scope. Her heart thundered in her ears, and she willed her galloping pulse to slow. "I can't help it. I didn't want this to happen, but since the first time I saw her, there was something…" She continued to scan the far foliage. "Know what I mean, Bron? Bron??"

He didn't answer. She slowly turned her head, knowing and dreading what was going to happen next. She made eye contact with him just as his throat disappeared in a fountain of gore. Red drowned the landscape. Gone were the blond of his hair and the electric blue of his eyes. A fine mist of blood slicked her face. She could taste it; it coated the inside of her nostrils.

"Bron. Bron!" Jak screamed.

"BRON!" She sat straight up in bed, naked chest heaving. Panicked, she pulled the blanket up to cover her breasts. She couldn't remember getting into bed, let alone getting undressed.

Apparently she'd been so tired she'd taken everything off, including her shirt and breast binder. After a quick glance at the door, she heaved a sigh of relief. At least she'd had the presence of mind to wedge a chair under the door handle. Over the years, she'd learned that she had to take the breast binder off on occasion or she experienced some fairly nasty consequences. Whenever she did so, she made sure to barricade the door in addition to locking it.

She slapped a palm over the light panel next to the bed and looked around. Her eyes fell on the mess on Bron's side of her room and her throat constricted. Tears prickled in her eyes and she cleared her throat angrily. Two years in and it still felt like he'd been taken from her the day before. With Torrin, some of the pain had receded. She'd finally had something else—someone else—to worry about. The room suddenly felt much too small. She had to get out and find Torrin.

First things first, though. Four days of sleep had her thirsty as hell. The supplements she took before the stim-crash kept her hydrated enough that she wouldn't die, but she always felt like she could drink a few liters of water when she woke up. Without bothering with a glass, she drank directly from the receptacle of water that was on the desk next to her bed. She drank deeply for a few moments before she came up, gasping for air.

Jak leaned over the side of the bed as she tried to figure out where her breast binder had ended up. It wasn't readily visible. She grumbled as she slid her legs over the edge and stood. Sleep had really helped; she felt more rested than she had in weeks. *What day is it?* Pulling a clean pair of underwear out of the footlocker at the head of the bed, she pulled them on, followed by a pair of fatigue pants. The location of the binder continued to elude her.

As she was getting on her knees to check under the bed, she heard a loud thud as a substantial object hit the wall next to her. Whatever it was made an impact hard enough to shake the bed. Jak stared blankly at the wall.

"Torrin's room!" she blurted aloud. "What the hell?" She grabbed a fatigue jacket with one hand and her pistol with the other. While she was kicking the chair out of the way of her door, she heard raised voices. Something else hit the wall with a smaller thud than the first one. She pulled the jacket on and ran out into the hall, taking care to clutch the coat closed in one fist.

* * *

Torrin sat at the desk in her room. Someone had rustled her up a computer that could interface with the cable in the wall. Apparently they kept them around so that people who received an injury or experienced a hardware malfunction would still be able to access the local net. She surfed around what passed for the Internet on this planet. It was hard to access on a physical screen. She could tell from what she saw that by not being able to physically hook in she was missing out on a lot. Still, it was better than sitting around doing nothing.

The past four days had been boredom piled upon boredom as Jak slept off the after-effects of those damned stims. She'd alleviated some of her ennui by sparring with the Devonite soldiers. However, when they'd realized how good she was at hand-to-hand combat, they'd started steering clear of her. A few of them had asked for some lessons and she'd obliged, but most of the men avoided her like the plague. Apparently McCullock had been spreading rumors that she was a trained assassin with a questionable grip on sanity and a hair-trigger temper.

A diffident knock sounded on the door.

"It's open," she called, breaking her attention from the screen.

McCullock poked his head around the door, a wide grin plastered on his face. He always looked so pleased to see her.

"It's just me," he said and slid into the room, closing the door behind him. Torrin heaved an inward sigh. His nightly visits were becoming uncomfortable. He did his best to charm her and woo her, but he seemed to have no idea that she wasn't interested. The only man she'd ever felt any attraction for was next door, and he still slept. Torrin really hoped he would wake up soon. It had been four days already. Not only did she miss him, but none of the planning could start without him. On the third day, she'd cornered a doctor in the camp hospital. He'd assured her that there was nothing to worry about at this point. Jak had taken so many days' worth of stims that his body would require a lot of sleep to balance out his circadian rhythms and clear out the toxins that had built up in his brain.

"This isn't his first stim-crash, Corporal," the doctor had said. "There's not much to do but let him sleep it off."

"Shouldn't he be here where you can monitor him?" Torrin hadn't been satisfied with his unconcerned response and couldn't help pushing.

"Many of our soldiers do come here, but he insists on doing for himself. He's not the only one. Most of the snipers are independent sorts. His room was stocked with hydration supplements before he got back. He'll be fine."

There had been little else she could do. The doctor wasn't nearly as concerned as he ought to have been. Maybe that was what usually happened, but surely he could see that this was a special situation.

Torrin hadn't had any better luck checking on him. Jak's door had been securely locked every time she'd tried it, which had been twice a day for the past four days. She'd heard occasional sounds of movement from next door, but that was it. If he wasn't up by the next morning, either she would drag a doctor back or she would batter down his door. She was still split on which one would be the better course of action.

"How are you?" McCullock cleared his throat, and Torrin realized that he'd repeated himself to get her attention.

"Sorry, mind wandered. I'm fine," she replied curtly. He was really being very sweet, but she wasn't going to give him what he wanted. Since he couldn't take a hint, maybe it was time for a more direct approach.

"Excellent!" He settled himself in the room's second chair and scooted it next to her until his thigh almost touched hers, not close enough for skin but close enough that she could feel the heat from his body. Torrin shifted her weight away from him and opened a small gap between their legs. He slid closer again.

"Captain, please give me some room."

"Miss Ivanov, you wound me." He flashed her that charming grin, white teeth peeking at her from under the ginger mustache.

"That can be arranged." She smiled at him sweetly.

He laughed, a full belly laugh of delight. "Don't make promises you can't carry out, my dear." He moved in on her again, eyes sparkling. "Speaking of promises, you've been watching me with those beautiful eyes for four days. Your mouth tells me to go, but your eyes tell me another story altogether."

If she hadn't been so tired of his advances, smooth though they were, she might have been flattered. As it was she was just tired. Tired of his misplaced attentions, tired of waiting for Jak to awaken, tired of being stuck on this miserable hellhole.

"My mouth is telling you everything you need to hear," she said, her tone flat, offering him no encouragement whatsoever.

"I can't resist you any longer," he intoned. He gripped her hand and drew it to his mouth, placing a soft kiss on the back of it, then turning it over and placing another kiss in the middle of her palm.

Gently, Torrin removed her hand from his grasp. "Jagger," she said, "it's not that I don't appreciate your attention. I think you're a wonderful man." The lie wasn't going to hurt anything, and she didn't want to piss him off, not when he was directly involved in getting her back to her ship.

"What are you saying?" He sat up straight in his chair, eyes wounded.

"I'm just not interested. I'm sorry, but I can't be who you want me to be."

"Is it Stowell?" His nostrils flared; he looked ready to spit. "Were you carrying on with him? Because I'm way more of a man than he is. He's a weedy little thing. He can't take care of you like I can. I'm well-connected. He's a no-account nothing who's going to get killed behind enemy lines, just like that pissant brother of his."

"It has nothing to do with him," Torrin said through clenched teeth. "It's just that...you're not my type. At all."

"I'm sure that I can change that. Just give me a chance."

What was it with men thinking they could change her with that...thing between their legs? There was nothing to do for it except go in for the kill. Clearly he wouldn't understand anything else. Torrin took a deep breath to calm herself before starting.

"Captain McCullock, let me be perfectly clear. I have no interest in carrying on any kind of relationship with you, physical or otherwise. If you continue to push the issue, I'm going to have to report you to the camp commander for improper advances. I'm sure a man like you doesn't want the others thinking you might be into them."

McCullock's face twisted into a snarl and color rushed to his cheeks. "Why, you little bitch," he growled and leaped to his feet, swinging a fist at her face. Acting purely on instinct and taken aback by the ferocity of his attack, Torrin grabbed his forearm and turned, using his momentum to throw him into the wall, hard. He slid down slowly, leaving a dent from the impact.

He struggled to his hands and knees, wheezing for breath. "You, you whore!" He screamed the last word at her. "Deviant filth. I'm gonna give you what you need. Don't think I won't."

"You need to catch me first," Torrin taunted. McCullock's face darkened and he reached for her. She danced back out of his grasp and into the chair behind her. The seat caught her legs behind the knees. They folded and she careened into the far wall.

"Gotcha, you cunt!" McCullock advanced toward her on his hands and knees. As he crawled up her body, she tried to send a knee into his groin but it glanced off the outside of his thigh with little effect. "What the hell?"

The door from the hall burst in with enough force that the handle punctured a hole in the duracrete wall. Jak stood in the doorway, pistol in one hand, the other holding his jacket closed.

"Get away from her!" he ordered, pointing the pistol unwaveringly at the captain. McCullock froze where he was, his face slack with fear. "I said move," Jak snapped again.

McCullock rolled off Torrin and slowly got to his feet, hands raised. From where she lay, Torrin could see him bending his knees, getting ready to spring.

"Look out!" She kicked out as the captain leaped. Jak swung his pistol in time to catch McCullock under one cheekbone. The man tipped sideways, his trajectory altered by Torrin's kick, and his hand tangled briefly with Jak's, pulling his jacket partially open.

Are those breasts? Jak pulled the jacket closed so quickly Torrin thought maybe she'd been mistaken. The panicked look he—she!— shot her way said in no uncertain terms, however, that Torrin had seen exactly what she thought she had.

The captain was oblivious to what had just happened; he writhed on the floor clutching the side of his face. Jak carefully kept his— no, her—jacket closed as she crouched down next to him.

"You need to get out of this room and never come back. We'll get Torrin out of here, then you'll put in for a transfer."

"No one will believe you," McCullock said mushily around his hands. "It's your word against an officer's."

Jak smiled hungrily, and McCullock leaned back from the venom in her eyes. "I didn't say I would report you. Just know that one way or another, you'll catch a sniper's bullet and you won't see it coming."

McCullock gaped at her. "You won't get away with that. You'll be caught."

"Does it really matter?" Jak shrugged. "You won't care, you'll be dead. Besides, it's not like I have anything to lose." She stared down at the man and an open grave yawned in her eyes. Torrin's heart ached at the bleakness she saw there. McCullock blanched and scrabbled away from the sniper. He pulled himself up with as much dignity as he could muster and left without so much as a glance behind him.

Torrin stood and held Jak's gaze with her own. Jak turned hastily to leave, but Torrin beat her to the door and closed it quickly, locking it. Jak backed away from her, pistol sliding from nerveless fingers to land on the floor with a clatter. She flinched at the noise, face awash in wariness and confusion. Torrin stalked slowly toward her, and Jak backed away until her back hit the wall.

"I can explain," she said, her voice muted. She flinched when Torrin reached out toward her. Torrin just shook her head and gently parted the front of her jacket. Before her was a magnificent pair of breasts, round, firm and topped by dusky rose nipples. A bolt of arousal shot through her abdomen, and Torrin's knees almost buckled. It made so much sense now. All those days of soul searching over her attraction to a man and Jak had been a woman all along. On some level she must have known that Jak was female, gloriously so judging by the most perfect pair of breasts she'd ever seen.

"Torrin? Would you say something?" Jak's voice was light and clear in a way she'd only heard hinted at. No wonder she growled everything between clenched teeth. Her natural voice was nowhere near a man's register and was almost musical.

Torrin reached out a hand and gently cupped one breast, running her thumb over Jak's duskiness. It fit into her hand like it had been made for her. The nipple pebbled instantly at her touch and pulled a moan of pleasure that was almost a sob out of Jak's throat. Emboldened by her response, Torrin reached out and slid her other hand around the small of Jak's back. She pulled the shorter woman toward her and bent her head, greedily covering Jak's mouth with her own. Her lips were warm and willing, and they parted easily beneath Torrin's questing tongue. Jak arched into her when Torrin pressed her tongue past soft lips.

She didn't know how long they stood there, tongues intertwining, her hands roaming over Jak's front before Torrin reached down to cup her rear and pull Jak hard against her body. She walked Jak back toward the bed until the back of her legs hit the side. Not breaking her lock on Jak's lips, she reached behind Jak and pulled the covers back, then guided her down to sit on the mattress.

Breathing hard, she came up for air. Jak leaned her head against Torrin's chest. She gasped for air as hard as Torrin did.

"I can't," Jak mumbled into her chest. "I can't do this."

"You could have fooled me," Torrin laughed shakily. "Just a second ago you were giving as good as you were getting." She lowered her head and nibbled on the exposed side of Jak's neck. The sniper gasped and shivered.

"It's n-n-not right," Jak stuttered.

"Really?" Torrin murmured, kissing her way up the side of Jak's neck. "Have you ever felt anything this right?" She nibbled around Jak's earlobe and gently tugged on it. Once again Jak gasped. She turned her head toward Torrin and recaptured her mouth. Now it was Jak's turn to slide an insistent tongue between Torrin's lips.

Torrin took the jacket and slowly slid it off Jak's shoulders. Jak shivered as the air hit her chest and slid her own hands inside Torrin's shirt, fingers pulling it out of her waistband.

Torrin pulled her mouth away and laughed. "I take it that means keep going?" Jak grabbed the front of her shirt with both hands and jerked, sending buttons flying as she exposed Torrin's torso. Torrin shivered at the display of strength and the sudden chill of cool air down her front. Arousal built in her belly; she felt wetness between her thighs. She laughed again and pushed Jak back onto the bed.

"So hasty?" She lowered her head to Jak's nipple and enclosed the hard tip with her mouth, tongue swirling around it, teasing it to an even harder point. Jak threw back her head and moaned, lifting her hips toward Torrin. Her hand captured Jak's other breast and squeezed gently, the hardness of her nipple pressing into her palm. Jak's head thrashed on the pillow.

Sitting up, Torrin quickly doffed what was left of her shirt, which disappeared into an unknown corner of the room. Jak's hands reached up to capture Torrin's breasts. A tingling ache grew in the sensitive tips and sent points of heat through her body. Torrin groaned and arched her pelvis into Jak's. She almost came at the pressure of her sensitive center against Jak's hips. The friction of her pants against her engorged clitoris was almost more than she could bear. Her head swam. She needed to see more of what Jak had to offer.

"Pants," she gasped, tugging at Jak's waistband. Jak relinquished her hold, leaving an aching void behind and hastily undid the fasteners. She lifted her hips and Torrin hooked the pants and her underwear and skimmed them both off. "I'm so glad you're not wearing boots."

"No kidding," Jak rasped. "Your turn, smuggler."

Torrin laughed at her demanding tone but quickly obliged. She ached to feel Jak's skin pressed against hers, sweat-slicked and warm. Jak's fingers felt so good against her flesh as she pulled Torrin's pants down her legs. Torrin swore and kicked out as the pants got fouled in her boots. Disposing of them, she quickly rolled over and covered Jak's body with her own, sliding a thigh between Jak's legs. Jak painted Torrin's thigh with her essence where she writhed against her, groaning and arching into her tightly muscled leg. Torrin leaned down and kissed her way up between Jak's breasts. She squirmed against Torrin, eyes open and unseeing.

"Oh Johvah," Jak gasped. "I feel…"

Torrin grinned and thrust her thigh against Jak's center again. For a second she thought she'd gone too far, but Jak clamped her legs around her and rode her to ever increasing heights of passion. When she pulled back, Jak groaned in disappointment. She lifted her head to stare into Torrin's eyes in a mute plea to continue. Torrin was thrilled at Jak's responsiveness.

A wicked smile crept across her face, and Torrin slid a hand down between their bodies. The curls she encountered were wet and warm; she grinned at the evidence of Jak's readiness for her. Slowly and with deliberate care, she spread swollen labia, sliding a finger down Jak's slick wetness. Her questing fingers found Jak's clitoris and encircled it. Jak practically levitated off the bed.

"What do you feel, baby?" Torrin breathed, swirling her finger around Jak's sensitive clit.

"I feel like…" Jak's answer was cut off when Torrin chose that moment to slide a finger into her. Torrin plunged the digit deep and almost came right then when Jak's inner muscles contracted around her. Jak was so tight and quick to respond. Slowly Torrin started thrusting her finger in and out of Jak's opening. Jak's eyes were open, but stared at something beyond the ceiling. Her body twitched in response to the pleasure Torrin was bringing her. Torrin picked up speed and slid in another finger. Jak's hips were now lifting to meet her. Torrin leaned forward and captured one of Jak's nipples between her teeth. It was so hard she thought she could have cut glass with it. Torrin smiled and bit down gently on the trapped nipple while continuing to plunge her fingers deep into Jak's wetness. Jak's eyes rolled back into her head and she let out a breathy groan.

"Oh, Johvah. Torrin!"

Hearing Jak's voice calling her name in such rapture sent a bolt of arousal like lightning through her. Torrin's skin prickled and she gasped. She was close to coming, but Jak came first.

Her hips thrust hard against Torrin's hand. Inside, her muscles clamped down on Torrin's fingers, holding them in place as contractions rippled through her. She came hard and a flood of wetness drenched Torrin's hand. As she shook, Torrin held her.

Slowly, Jak descended from the intense euphoria Torrin had drawn from her. Torrin decided she was more than a little pleased with herself. For a first lay, this one ranked off the charts. She smiled to herself as she contemplated how much better their coupling would get with practice.

"What was that?" Jak asked, her voice exhausted.

"That would be an orgasm," Torrin replied smugly.

"So that's what one of those feels like. I guess I understand why my brother chased after anything he could find in a skirt."

"Wait, this was your first time?" Torrin was astounded.

"It's not like I've exactly had the best opportunities," Jak said ruefully. Torrin stretched out next to her, and Jak curled into her, placing her head on Torrin's chest. "It's not like I've ever really had an interest in any of the men I knew, and I certainly couldn't approach them."

"Why?" Torrin asked.

"Duh, I was dressed as a man," Jak explained unnecessarily. "No guy was ever going to look at me twice. Not unless there was already something wrong with him."

Torrin looked down at the top of Jak's head. She threaded her fingers through short, blond hair. It was barely long enough to grip, but Torrin tightened her fingers and tilted Jak's face up toward her. They kissed hungrily. Torrin broke off their kiss and regarded her soberly.

"What do you mean 'wrong with him'?" she asked. "You do know, don't you, that there's nothing wrong with a man who loves men or with a woman who loves women. It happens all the time. On most planets, except the most backward and repressed ones, it's perfectly natural. You can't help which gender you're attracted to. It just happens. Love wants what it wants."

"I can't help what I feel for you, that's for sure." Jak avoided her eyes and trailed the fingers of her left hand lightly over Torrin's rib cage. Jak's fingertips left expanding pools of fire behind them as they traveled inexorably toward her nipples. "All I know is that I had one of those orgasms, but you didn't." She grinned up into Torrin's eyes and rubbed a palm over her breast. Torrin inhaled sharply and closed her eyes. Jak was a quick study.

Jak lay on her side, facing away from Torrin, who spooned against her, one arm around her rib cage and a leg draped over her knees. She couldn't get over how good it felt to have Torrin pressed nude against her skin. She hadn't realized how much she'd craved contact until she suddenly had it. When Torrin's hands had danced over her body, she'd felt like an instrument being played by a master musician. Torrin had known exactly what to do to send her into heights of rapture. Jak smiled. She thought she'd surprised the smuggler a time or two herself. This might not be her area of expertise, but she was definitely enjoying the chance to learn.

But why then, if everything was so good, was she lying there awake when by all rights she should be in exhausted slumber like Torrin? She was still bone-tired, probably from her stim abuse and the unanticipated exertion. Her clit tightened at the mere thought of their activities, and she could feel wet warmth radiating from the apex of her thighs. All over again, she ached for Torrin.

If only she could believe what Torrin had told her. Other planets had people who loved each other regardless of gender? How could that be possible? Here, to be caught making love with someone of the same sex was tantamount to suicide. Try as she might, Jak couldn't shake the feeling that they were engaged in acts both forbidden and unforgivable.

She closed her eyes tight against the darkness of her thoughts. Despite her best efforts, dampness leaked out between her eyelids. The harder she tried to stop the harder she cried. Before long she was suppressing deep sobs. Torrin's arms tightened against her for a second and Jak froze, worried she'd woken her lover. The deep rhythms of Torrin's breathing didn't change, though, and Jak relaxed. Even the unconscious show of tenderness from Torrin didn't help. If anything she felt worse.

Why was she crying now? She'd barely cried since Bron died. For the first time in two years she had someone who knew about her deception and didn't care. By all rights she should be happy, but she couldn't reconcile what they'd done with what she'd been taught. One way or another it wouldn't last; they would be caught and put to death or worse. Women who were caught in homosexual acts were often subjected to punitive rape. For some reason, men seemed to think they only needed to be shown the error of their ways. She really didn't want Torrin to have to go through that on her account. Hell, she didn't want to go through that herself. The best-case scenario was that Torrin would leave before they could be caught. But…then she'd be alone once again with her secret.

Eyes shut, Jak bore down on her emotions, walling them away. Crying wouldn't solve anything, only action would. Why couldn't she determine which course of action was best? Finally dry-eyed, she contemplated her limited options long into the night.

CHAPTER TWENTY-ONE

"You are so beautiful," Torrin whispered, running a finger up the side of Jak's torso and over to her breast. She couldn't believe her luck. Jak was turning out to be a wonderful lover. In just a few days, she'd set about discovering all she could about Torrin's body and what made her scream. Since their first night together, they'd been snatching what little bits of time they could between meetings and training sessions. Jak's fingers were pure magic, but that was nothing compared to what she could do with her tongue. "Your breasts could have been made with me in mind."

Jak looked up shyly and met Torrin's eyes. Her skin had flushed at Torrin's praise. It was true, though, Torrin thought. Though the skin of Jak's face and arms was bronzed from the sun, her torso and legs were a luminous alabaster. Her own hand looked dark against Jak's rib cage. Unable to resist, she drew her nails across Jak's ribs, glorying at the goose bumps that rose in the wake of her fingers. Jak gasped and wriggled on the bed.

"Stop it," Jak whispered. "That tickles!"

Torrin grinned widely. She knew very well that it tickled. That was why she'd done it. That Jak was ticklish was a delightful and unexpected vulnerability. She liked seeing Jak's human side. She usually projected an aura of frightening competence. That Jak was able to share her vulnerability made Torrin happier than she could express.

"I know," Torrin teased. "So what are you going to do to stop me?" She brought her other hand into play, running them along both sides of Jak's ribs.

Jak tried to curl herself into a little ball. She had to laugh even as she tried to stifle the chuckles. There was nothing masculine about her laugh, and Torrin knew Jak worried about discovery. Worried, hell. She obsessed about it. Torrin knew she had good reason to fear discovery of her true nature, but she wished that it didn't have to extend to their few stolen moments of intimacy. Their end of the barracks was mostly empty. Most of the sniper pairs who inhabited the barracks were out on various assignments. Torrin hadn't seen any other soldiers in their end of the building for a few days.

Finally, when Jak couldn't stand it any longer, she reached out and grabbed Torrin's wrists. Torrin grinned at her, and Jak leaned forward to capture her lips.

"If that's how you're going to stop me from tickling you, I'll have to do it more often." Torrin surfaced, breathless from the passion Jak poured into her. As usual, Jak's slightest touch sent her into a spiral of rising arousal. The full-on assault of Jak's lips had her ready to come all over again. She could feel the heat where Jak's breasts pressed against hers. Her nipples ached where they rubbed against Jak's skin.

"You should sleep here tonight," Torrin said.

Jak lifted a shoulder and Torrin shivered at the movement against her chest. "We'll see" was all she said before leaning down to cover Torrin's mouth again. As their tongues locked, she relinquished her hold on one of Torrin's wrists and slid her hand down between them, covering Torrin's mound. Torrin moaned into Jak's mouth. She felt Jak's lips spread as she smiled at the enthusiastic reaction.

"Look what I found," Jak said when their lips parted.

"Oh, I know exactly what you found," Torrin replied and pressed herself harder against Jak's palm. Agile fingers deftly slipped between her damp labia and into the wet warmth beneath. Fingers circled her erect clit and she cried out, only to have her mouth taken again by Jak.

"Hush," Jak said against Torrin's mouth as her fingers continued to circle and tweak Torrin's throbbing clit.

Torrin gritted her teeth. She'd always been a noisy lay; it went against every instinct to muffle the sounds of her passion. Jak slid her fingers down further, teasing her by rubbing them gently over the entrance to her pussy. Slowly, she slid a finger in to the first knuckle, then back out again. When she moved her fingers, slick with Torrin's juices back up to her clit, Torrin couldn't take it any longer.

"Take me," she ordered hoarsely, opening her legs. Jak sat back for a moment, staring with unabashed admiration at her exposed pussy.

"You're so wet," Jak said. The tip of her tongue snaked out between her teeth, and she bit down on it slightly. Torrin exhaled heavily through her nose. She recognized that look. Jak meant business; she was locked on target.

With a tenderness that made Torrin's heart ache, Jak covered Torrin's exposed mound with her hand and settled between Torrin's legs. Her weight pushed Torrin deliciously down into the bed and she groaned in appreciation. She undulated her hips against Jak's hand. The friction on her clit pushed her higher, but she wanted more. She wanted Jak inside her, to fill her up, to take her completely.

"I want to come with you," Jak whispered, staring into Torrin's eyes. Torrin's clit pulsed at the words, and she bit down on her lower lip to keep from coming right then. She shifted a leg over and Jak straddled it, grinding her wet center against the clenched and quivering muscles of Torrin's thigh. Jak threw her head back, breasts heaving as Torrin worked her leg against her. Her hand clutched convulsively at Torrin's pussy.

"I'm almost there," Torrin gasped, sensation overwhelming her.

"Me too," Jak groaned. She rubbed Torrin's clit with the heel of her palm and rode her thigh. Torrin jerked her hips against Jak's hand, drawing another moan from Jak.

"Give it to me," Torrin growled. She reached down and drew a fingertip across Jak's clit as Jak pressed two fingers against her opening. The answering jerk of Jak's hips plunged her fingers deep inside Torrin. Being taken so utterly almost shattered the last of Torrin's control. She had just enough presence of mind to pull the pillow over her face. Jak withdrew both fingers before pushing them back into her, slowly at first, then picking up speed. She rocked on Torrin's thigh in time with her thrusts. The feeling of Jak's fingers moving within her pushed Torrin higher and higher until she couldn't hold back any longer. Light burst behind her corneas as her release crashed through her. She screamed into the pillow. Above her, Jak continued to rock on her thigh for a few more seconds before stiffening over her. She slowly collapsed against Torrin's still-heaving chest.

Torrin gathered Jak in her arms and held her as they both rode out their aftershocks. She ran fingers over the blond stubble of Jak's scalp and murmured nonsense words in her ear.

Too soon, Jak rolled out of her embrace and lay on the bed, her hand in Torrin's. She stared at the ceiling and Torrin propped herself up on one elbow and watched her profile closely. Sometimes Jak went somewhere else after they made love. It hurt her to see the distance wrapping around her lover like a blanket, muffling the intensity of the experience.

"Where's your mind going?" Torrin stroked her free hand down the middle of Jak's chest. She couldn't imagine the constant discomfort that Jak must be in having her breasts bound. Torrin had made love to women with larger breasts, but Jak wasn't exactly poorly endowed.

"Hmm?" Jak looked over at her, eyes still distant. "Oh, nowhere. Just feeling, I guess."

"Feeling good, I hope."

Jak cracked a smile and Torrin's heart soared in her chest. She rarely got smiles out of Jak, but every time she saw one, she felt like maybe a relationship was possible. Sure, they had a lot stacked against them, but if they could connect on a meaningful level, then they could conquer any obstacle. She really liked Jak and didn't want to lose her. Maybe more than liked. But such feelings were moving much too quickly for love-'em-and-leave-'em Torrin and she focused on the curve of Jak's neck instead.

"Feeling great," Jak said lightly. "How could I feel any other way after all that?" She waved a hand expansively.

"How, indeed?"

Silence lapsed between them again.

"I'm glad they were made for something," Jak said out of the blue.

Torrin glanced over at her, confused. "Glad what?"

"My breasts. You said you thought they were made for you. I'm glad they were made for something. Or someone. I never felt like they were made for me. For the longest time, they've just been in the way. I didn't see the point of having them. If I could have gotten rid of them I would have."

"That would have been a crime against humanity. To deprive the world of a pair of such perfection."

Jak blushed hotly at her words. "For the record, I'm reconsidering."

"Good."

"I mean, now I've discovered what they're good for." Jak smiled and Torrin's heart fluttered once again. Torrin smiled back, completely enchanted.

Silence descended, but this time it felt more comfortable.

"So what did you want to do with your life?" Torrin asked before Jak could use the silence as an excuse to leave. "Before you had to become a man and join the army, that is."

Brow furrowed, Jak stared at the ceiling. She mulled the question. The silence stretched even further, and Torrin began to worry that she'd caused offense with her off-handed question.

"It's okay, you don't have to answer if it makes you uncomfortable."

Pushing herself over on her side to face Torrin, Jak smiled at her briefly. This one didn't touch her eyes.

"It doesn't make me uncomfortable," she said. Torrin got the feeling Jak was trying to reassure her. "I just haven't really thought about it."

"How could you not have thought about it?" Torrin asked, confused. "Surely you had something you wanted to be when you grew up."

"Not really," Jak confessed. "I mean, I started going out with my father to help him hunt when I was ten. Before that, I helped my mom around the house. She died when I was seven and after that it was up to me to take care of my brother while Dad made sure he could feed us. We spent time with the neighbor family down the valley, but a lot of the time it was just me to take care of Bron. I had to grow up pretty quickly."

"So no dreams of your own, then?"

"Not really. Not unless you count dreaming about blowing out the brains of the sniper who killed my brother." The bleakness was back in full force and staring out of Jak's eyes. Torrin didn't doubt that she meant it.

"So what are your plans after you blow away your brother's killer?" Torrin tried to inject some levity into the question, but it fell flat.

Jak stared at the ceiling again. "I don't know. I haven't thought that far ahead." She was quiet for a long time, long enough that Torrin thought perhaps she'd fallen asleep. "It's like I can't really see myself after that happens." Her voice was so quiet Torrin had to strain to hear her.

A chill ran through Torrin, freezing her marrow. "What do you mean?"

"I don't know. For the past two years, pretty much all I've thought about is putting a bullet through that bastard's brain. Once that's done, I'm not sure what's left for me. Like everything I have to live for is gone once he's dead." She paused. "This is all I've known for so long. Some days, I feel like I was made for killing. I mean, I'm good at it. It's hard-wired into me. Did I tell you about boot camp?"

Torrin shook her head. This was the first time Jak had volunteered something about herself. Anything else Torrin had learned about her past, she'd had to glean from comments Jak made in passing. She barely breathed, not wanting to throw Jak off, to distract her from the moment.

"The other boots were really welcoming." Jak barked a laugh devoid of all mirth. "You might not have noticed, but I'm really short. I mean, not so much for a girl, but really short for a man. Some of the other boots thought that made me a weakling." Her face softened from the bitter lines it had settled into. "Bron tried to stick up for me, which made things worse. The shit only got worse when he wasn't around. Worse and harder to pin down. Some of the guys thought they were great practical jokers, and they had a lot of fun at my expense.

"I put a stop to it after they pulled some crap that almost exposed me." Her eyes got a distant look to them, and Torrin wondered if she was reliving the moment. Whatever she was seeing didn't make Jak happy; her eyes had gone hard again. "I put a bullet through the left knee of the leader of the little band of bullying assholes. No one could believe I'd done it. Just to make sure he didn't get any more ideas, I told him if he ever messed with me again, I'd put one through first one testicle, then through the other. While he was writhing around on the floor, bleeding like a stuck pig, I buried a slug in the floor two centimeters away from his family jewels. They never bothered me again."

"Did you get in trouble?"

"No, actually. I worried for days that they were going to rat me out, but they told the CO that the guy's weapon had discharged while he was cleaning it. So in exchange for making my life a living hell, he spent a few days in sick bay and then recovered from the wound for two months. He watched his cronies go through the hell of boot camp instead of going through it himself."

"But not you?"

"We got picked out for our marksmanship a few days after I shot him. The higher-ups found out that we were the best in our class, better even than a lot of the snipers they already had. We got fast-tracked into sniper school and missed out on the fun the other grunts had to go through." She laughed again. "Just think, if I'd waited a couple of days, I wouldn't have needed to shoot that guy. He got killed a few years later, defending a trench single-handedly after the rest of his platoon was killed, but he held out long enough that we were able to reinforce the position. After all that, and he turned out to be some kind of a hero. Just goes to show, you never really know what anyone's capable of."

Torrin stared at Jak's profile. Her eyes stared at nothing.

"I think you're capable of more than just killing." Torrin rested her hand on Jak's bare chest, between the swell of her breasts. She could feel Jak's heart racing. Telling her story had been hard. "You're damn good at loving, you know."

Jak smiled, but her heart wasn't in it. "I don't know if I can give you what you deserve. I don't like to think that far ahead."

"I think we can work on that, don't you?" Torrin said tentatively. "I'd like to think you'll be around for a while."

The smile on Jak's face was shy, but this one looked genuine and relief washed over Torrin.

"I can't promise anything, you know. For all I know, I'll catch a bullet tomorrow or next week. You learn not to plan too far ahead around here."

"That makes sense, I guess." A deep sadness filled Torrin. It occurred to her that she had very little perspective on Jak's life. She had no idea how anyone could survive the kind of uncertainty and loss that Jak had endured. That she was still alive and sane was a testament to her mental and emotional strength. Torrin felt downright shallow by comparison.

"It's nice to have you here now," Jak said, looking back over at her. Clearly, she sensed something was wrong and was trying to let Torrin know she was okay. "I really enjoy spending time with you."

"Even if all we do is fuck like bunnies?" Torrin meant the question to be funny, but it came out a little bitter.

"There's nothing wrong with fucking like bunnies," Jak said seriously, then, "what are bunnies anyway?"

"They're small, furry Earth animals that are known for their powers of reproduction. Apparently, they have long ears and little cottontails and incredible sex drives. I've never seen one except in holopics. They are kind of cute."

"Well, as long as they're cute."

The giggle that bubbled up surprised Torrin. Jak watched her gravely, but a twinkle lurked in the back of her eyes. The hidden amusement made the conversation even more absurd, and Torrin rolled over to bury her face in the pillow so she could let out a full belly laugh. When she finally stopped, she looked up to catch Jak watching her with surprising tenderness, a satisfied smile playing about her lips. Her serious nature hid a dry sense of humor, one that kept Torrin on her toes.

"It wasn't that funny," Jak said.

"I know, but the look on your face. 'As long as they're cute.'" Giggles threatened to overwhelm her again.

"Well, I wouldn't want to be fucking like something that was hideous."

"An excellent point."

"So how about you?"

"How about me, what?" Torrin was confused by the sudden change of direction.

"When you were little, what did you want to be when you grew up?"

"Would you believe that I wanted to be rescued from a perilous situation by a gorgeous stranger who would then have her way with me?"

"No."

Jak's flat denial struck her as hilarious and she had to fight down another attack of the giggles. "Fine," Torrin said, once she'd regained some composure. "I wanted to be a whole slew of things. When I was really little, I wanted to be a stunt rider in a rodeo. Then I wanted to be an interstellar explorer. After that, I thought maybe being a soldier would be exciting." Jak wrinkled her nose at the statement. "I know, what was I thinking? I forced myself to stay in that gig for too long before bailing. Too much uncertainty and bullshit. Plus, I never learned how to deal with those who didn't make it back."

"I hear you on that," Jak murmured.

"So after the soldiering gig, where I had to actually grow up, I decided to become a merchant. I could indulge in the explorer part of my nature, see new places, that sort of thing. Plus, I also discovered that I'm really competitive." Jak turned a shocked look on her, and Torrin smacked her on the shoulder. "Behave." Jak looked deeply wounded, and Torrin smacked her again.

"So I have another question."

"What's that?"

"What's a rodeo?"

Torrin sat bolt upright in bed. "Are you kidding me? You don't know what a rodeo is?"

"I don't think we have too many of them around here."

"A rodeo is a ton of fun. There's only one on Nadierzda. It comes by Landing every few years. Half of the town turns out to see it. It's like a carnival but with livestock."

Jak looked even more confused.

"People show their prize stock, and there are competitions for whose animals are the best. There are also contests over who can do the best riding and who can perform all sorts of farming-type chores the fastest." Torrin had to slow herself down. She was chattering faster and faster as she got more excited in her recounting. Like a remembered echo, she could feel the excitement she used to experience when the rodeo was coming to town. Even her mother got excited and would have her prize goats ready to compete. "My favorite was the stunt riders. Those women could do anything on their horses. I had a pony that I trained myself and I used to set myself to all sorts of tricks and maneuvers in the backyard. Well, until my mother would come and get me for chores. Mama understood, but Mother never did."

"Wait, women riders? And how many mothers did you have?"

"Oh sure. Those women were amazing. I had a crush on about a dozen of them, growing up."

"And your...mothers?"

"The women who adopted me were a couple. I had my mama and my mother. Mother was always the stricter of the two. I'd go running straight to Mama after being punished by her. On Nadierzda, my planet, the only couples are women."

"So you've always liked women then?"

"Yep. But I like you best." Torrin grinned cheekily at Jak, who blushed in response.

They chatted on into the night. For the first time in the four days since they'd first made love, they took things slowly. For now, Torrin felt like they were all alone in the world. All that existed was the room and each other. There was no war going on outside the walls and no reason for Jak to be sent into harm's way. She learned more about Jak in the last few hours than she had in the past almost three weeks. Even then, she felt like she'd only scratched the surface. Whenever she tried to probe more deeply, Jak gave her a pat answer or turned the question back on her.

She tried to be understanding. Years of disguising her true self would have made even the most open person guarded and distrustful. There was an amazing person that lurked beneath Jak's tough exterior and Torrin looked forward to peeling back the layers to get to know her. It wasn't that Jak was reticent, at least not exactly. She didn't volunteer much about herself, but she answered most of Torrin's questions. It was easy to tell when Torrin was skating on the edge of something Jak didn't want to talk about. She just shut down—the way she had the time Torrin had suggested they duck into her room to fool around.

Torrin had only seen the inside of the room once, and that had been in passing. She knew Jak had the room to herself, but the quick glance she'd had inside had revealed that half of it was a messy state that didn't fit at all with Jak's buttoned-down self. When she'd asked about it, all expression had been wiped from Jak's face. Only one topic could shut her down that quickly and Torrin realized that it must be Bron's stuff strewn across half the room. It was no wonder Jak had problems moving on from her brother's death, surrounded as she was by the last remnants of his life.

Getting to know Jak completely, if she ever could, would be a time-consuming process, she realized. Strangely, that didn't bother her, and since she'd just decided they had all the time in the world she concentrated on having a good time.

When Jak fell asleep in her arms instead of slipping out and heading back to her room, Torrin held her and gloried in the feeling of skin on skin. She could easily have stayed entwined that way forever. It wasn't long before she felt herself drifting off to sleep. With Jak in her arms, it was easy to let the night take her without worrying about all the obstacles they still faced.

Jak woke abruptly to a cramp in her calf. Torrin's limbs were entangled with hers, one leg thrown over her hip, the other sandwiched between her thighs. Her belly clenched at the feel of Torrin's leg so close to her pussy. For a moment, she considered waking Torrin. There were many ways she could do so, but she couldn't decide which one would be best, so she just watched Torrin sleep.

In repose, her face looked so innocent. Thick lashes framed Torrin's eyes and hid the wicked glint she'd seen so often. She had the lightest dusting of freckles across her nose, Jak realized. They were enchanting, she decided, contemplating them for a while.

It was really too bad that she'd had to shave off her hair. Jak really missed those long locks. She wondered what it would be like to thread her hands through them while they made love. The thought sent arousal coursing through her again.

The resurgence of the cramp in her calf decided for her. As comfortable and happy as she was to be there with Torrin, she needed to move. It was no mean feat to disentangle herself from Torrin without waking her. Slowly, she was able to extricate herself, all while watching Torrin's eyes to make sure she didn't awaken. She was cold where she'd been pressed against Torrin's skin and she mourned the loss of contact. The loss felt more than skin deep.

Not wanting to dwell on that thought, she felt around on the floor for her clothes. They'd ended up all over the room and for once she was thankful the rooms were so tiny. Flattening breasts that ached for Torrin's touch was an unpleasant experience, but she crammed them into the breast binder anyway.

With one last look at her slumbering lover, Jak slipped from the room. She stopped by her room to pick up her rifle, then slipped out of the barracks.

Camp Abbott was still quiet. The clock in her room had read a little before 0630 hours. She would have to hurry to make the garden before daybreak. Dawn wasn't more than a few minutes away, and the camp would be stirring soon. It wasn't completely still, of course. Sentries manned the tops of the walls while here and there runners dashed from one building to another.

On her way to the produce garden, Jak stopped to contemplate McCullock's quarters. He had a single-family house to himself. It was little more than a shack, but compared to the quarters most of the rest of the camp made do with, it might as well have been a castle. The camp commander's house was a little bigger but also housed his entire staff.

McCullock's room was in the southeastern corner of the house. She knew for a fact that he slept in a bed right under the window. A high-powered rifle with a penetrating round could easily punch through the thin wall. As she did whenever she saw him or his home, she calculated the best way to kill him. Before he'd attacked Torrin, she'd disliked him intensely. That dislike had crystallized into hatred as relentless as the tide. It occurred to her that if she had to make a choice between taking out her brother's killer or McCullock, she'd have a hard time deciding which one to use the bullet on.

The thought disturbed her. She'd promised to avenge Bron's death, not only to herself but to him. Torrin was pulling her focus away from the goal that had kept her going for the past couple of years. Try as she might, she couldn't reconcile her promise to Bron with her fledgling relationship with Torrin. To have one, she would have to give up the other.

With a violent shake of her head, she pulled her thoughts away from the dilemma. This was why she didn't think about the future. All she had was the present and she needed to take what she could from that.

The low keening of a horn broke the morning stillness. While she'd been standing there absorbed in her thoughts, dawn had broken. Around her, the camp was coming to life. She looked up in time to catch McCullock's frightened face staring at her through his bedroom window. With two fingers to the brim of her cap, she tossed him a lazy salute, smiled, then started walking. Let him think she was keeping an eye on him.

She nodded to a few of the men as she crossed the camp. While she was pretty sure that very few of them actually liked her, she was secure in the fact that she had their respect. Her sniping skills alone had assured that. She thought they also appreciated the fact that while she didn't take any crap, she didn't dish it out. *How would that change if they knew my secret?* It was a question she dwelled on periodically. Besides the very real legal concerns discovery would bring with it, the possibility of losing the men's respect weighed heavily on her as well.

The garden was empty. That in itself was no surprise. It would have been bustling with men a couple of hours before, but any food that had been harvested was now being prepared for the camp's breakfast. She wasn't interested in vegetables. What she wanted was at the garden's far edge, where local volunteer wildflowers had sprung up between the cultivated earth and the camp's outside wall. Over the years, more than one soldier had gone courting with blossoms from the unofficial flower patch.

Even if she didn't have a future with Torrin, she still wanted to make her happy in the present. The comb had been a big hit, but Jak didn't have the time to make her anything else. The relentless meetings around Torrin's insertion into Orthodoxan territory and the constant training she subjected herself to severely limited any free time. Free time that was also taken up by the time she was spending with Torrin. She grinned and blushed as she ran her mind over what they'd been doing together.

The bouquet looked nice enough when she assembled it. Not wanting to parade through the camp a bunch of flowers in hand, she tucked them carefully into the front of her jacket. Hopefully the flowers wouldn't be too damaged before she could get them back to Torrin's room.

Her trip back to the barracks was uneventful, but she was glad she'd thought to hide the blooms. The camp's streets were awash with men on their way to the mess for breakfast. She nodded to a few of the members of her insertion team as she entered the barracks. They stood in the long hallway, chatting idly. When they showed no sign of moving on, she scowled at them. Her reputation for surliness prompted them to move along out of the barracks.

"Have a beautiful morning, Sarge," one of them said over his shoulder as they left through the front door. The two men with him laughed and followed him quickly out the door. The men of her unit took her bad temper in stride. A couple of the braver ones occasionally tried to tease her about it, but everyone still remembered or had heard about what had happened to the man who'd pushed her too far in basic training.

She slipped back into Torrin's room once the coast was clear. Torrin lay curled on the bed in the same position that Jak had left her in with her hand lying palm down in the space that Jak had occupied. Carefully, Jak pulled the flowers out of her jacket and fluffed them up a little bit. They hadn't been too badly mangled by their trip in her coat. It was probably a poor substitute to waking up next to a person, but it was the best she could offer. Gently, she deposited the flowers on the pillow where her head had been less than an hour before.

Torrin deserved better than someone like her. She needed someone who could commit to her. Between her promise to Bron and a war that would probably kill her sooner rather than later, Jak couldn't give her that. It was hard to keep Torrin from getting too close. With a sinking feeling, she realized it was probably too late already. For both of them.

CHAPTER TWENTY-TWO

Jak stood calf-deep in muck and trained her rifle on the fence of shimmering blue in front of her. Men crowding the trench to either side radiated a nervous tension. Intel had come down that the Orthodoxans had a raid planned and this section of the fence would be dropping. McCullock had decided she should be in the trenches when that happened.

She bared her teeth at her recollection of the meeting where he'd given her the orders.

"Stowell, this will be our best bet for gathering actionable intelligence for what's happening on the Orthodoxan side. I want you there to count men as they come through the downed portion of the barrier." He'd smiled at her. To anyone else, the smile probably looked genuine. She and Torrin knew better. McCullock was doing his best to get her killed. Letting him catch her lurking outside his home had perhaps been a tactical error. "You're the best we have, so I want you there in the front lines."

"I think the better vantage would be at the top of the escarpment for the raid, sir," she'd offered.

"We have plenty of men who could do that," McCullock had countered, voice oh-so-reasonable. "You're the best, so your job will be the hardest."

Faced with his orders, delivered in such an agreeable tone in front of a room filled with witnesses, she'd had no choice but to agree. McCullock no longer met with her alone to pass on orders; he'd taken to issuing them in front of the group of men who'd been put together to prepare Torrin's insertion into Orthodoxan territory. They thought they were sending in a black ops soldier to take out the leader of the Orthodoxans. Jak had to admit the ruse was a good one. The mission was highly compartmentalized because of the supposed assignment's high stakes. It had the added advantage that no one really expected it to work. When Torrin didn't come back, they would assume that she'd been captured and that the Orthodoxans had hushed up the assassination attempt on Supreme President Weller.

The planning group consisted of ten men, Torrin and Jak. McCullock probably thought that he'd gained the upper hand with his new tactics. Idly, Jak wondered whether she should just be done with it and put a bullet through his brain anyway. She still had some Orthodoxan ammo and the rifle. She could pick a perch to which no one would be able to track back the shot. He'd never see it coming. As much as she would have liked that, she had to admit that she'd have to feel a much stronger threat to Torrin before murdering the bastard in cold blood.

The man next to her coughed wetly, a deep tearing hack. He leaned over and spat into the morass at his feet. Jak leaned imperceptibly away from him. Disease was rampant in the trenches. With so many men in such close quarters in the filthy conditions, it was almost impossible for the camp doctors to stay ahead of the various viruses and bacteria that called the trenches and the men who inhabited them home.

"Get yourself to an aid station, soldier," she ordered curtly.

"I'm fine, Sergeant," he protested. "I want to stay."

"Not going to happen," she replied. "You need to get your ass to the doctor before you infect the rest of your squad with whatever creeping crud you have in your lungs. I'll inform your platoon commander."

The soldier sighed, which prompted another coughing fit. He pushed his way past the massed men, still hacking, and made his way to the back of the trench system. Jak had no way of knowing if he would actually follow her order. He could easily join up with another group waiting to repel raiders and she'd never know. She smiled ruefully. In his shoes, she would probably have made the same decision.

She went back to scanning the fence for any hint that it was about to drop. Her mind wandered back to the sendoff she'd gotten from Torrin that morning. Her face heated as she remembered how the smuggler had pinned her against the wall of her room and slipped a hand down her pants. As usual when Torrin was around, she'd already been wet and ready. She snatched her mind away from the memory. Every time Jak left Torrin's bed, she vowed it would be the last time. And every time Torrin came near her again, Jak's resolve crumbled and she stepped willingly back into her arms. She was so confused, her mind and upbringing telling her one thing but her body and heart dragging her in the opposite direction. She'd thought it would be easier, that she would be absolved of some of inner turmoil when Torrin knew the truth, but it had only gotten worse.

Her eyes prickled with unshed tears, and she blinked rapidly to clear them before they could spill over. She concentrated on the view through the scope. There was movement on the other side of the fence. It was difficult to see through the shimmering blue curtain of energy, but something was definitely happening.

"Heads down, boys," she grated. "Things are shaping up."

As if on cue, mortars whistled over the barrier, exploding with sharp concussions. Soldiers to either side of her ducked their heads, allowing their helmets to shield them from flying shrapnel. An artillery shell exploded directly over their heads, shaking the ground all around them as the shock wave hit. It drove the breath from her lungs, but she kept her eye trained through the scope. There were definitely men massing outside the fence.

Over the concussions of exploding shells, she heard far-off reports as their own artillery returned fire. The Orthodoxans hunkered down on the other side to wait out the answering barrage. She watched them through a gap in the sandbags, her rifle at ground level while the metal roof of the shelter rattled with the shrapnel's angry rain. One of the men to her left went down with a yell as hot metal sliced through his shoulder and out his back.

"Medic!" one of his compatriots screamed as he knelt in the muck next to the fallen soldier, one hand trying to stanch the flow of blood while the other scrabbled in his pack for first aid supplies. The soldier's blood mixed with the blue mud, dyeing it a crimson-streaked muddy purple.

The barrage continued for an eternity, men around her succumbing to explosions and shrapnel. The injured men were removed by medics and stretcher-bearers who had to shoulder their way through as more soldiers pressed forward to take the places of the fallen.

"Heads up," she yelled hoarsely as the blue barrier dropped. "They're coming!" The barrage of mortars quit as abruptly as it had started, and a wall of men rushed toward the trenches. Jak mechanically squeezed off shot after methodical shot as Orthodoxan soldiers filled her scope, but her attention was trained on the opening in the barrier. If their intelligence was right, this assault was merely cover for enabling a team of Orthodoxan raiders to slip through to wreak havoc behind their lines.

Devonite soldiers had their weapons out and were firing over the walls of sandbags at the oncoming men. Orthodoxan soldiers dropped in waves as walls of rifle and machine gun fire raked their ranks. Still they came on, the fallen men trampled into the churned mud by those behind them.

Jak kept her eyes peeled for any small groups peeling off the main charge or sneaking through the fence behind them. She hoped she would see what she was looking for before the charge hit their position. Once the charge arrived, she would be too busy to keep watch.

The ground behind the front ranks of Orthodoxans began to explode, heaving men and earth into the air with equal abandon. The charge faltered slightly, then redoubled, the Orthodoxan soldiers realizing that the Devonite trenches were the only place they might find relative safety. In a distant part of her mind, Jak wondered if it was their artillery or the Orthodoxans' driving the men on. If it was the Orthodoxans goading their own men on with artillery shells, it wouldn't be the first time.

There! A group of maybe eighteen men skirted between the edge of the kill zone and the fence. They were well camouflaged and moved quickly through the downed portion of the barrier. Shockingly, the barrier went up behind them, blocking any retreat for the Orthodoxan soldiers still on the Devonite side. She'd never seen that before. Why on earth would they trap their own men on the wrong side of the lines? Were the Orthodoxans insane or just that desperate?

She didn't have much time. The much-reduced mass of men was nearing the trenches. They'd slowed as they negotiated the razor wire obstacles, but she didn't have long. In her sights, she focused on the first man of the raiding group as he turned to urge the men behind him on. Hopefully he was an officer or at least a non-com. Exhaling, she bit down on the tip of her tongue and took her shot. The Orthodoxan raider collapsed as a bullet obliterated his right kneecap. One of his men ran over to pick him up and went down with a bullet through the forehead. Panicked and with nowhere else to go, the rest of the raiding party broke into a run for the nearest cover. Calmly, Jak picked off two more before they could get to the dubious shelter of a small artillery crater.

She barely had time to react when a blur filled her viewfinder and she pulled the trigger through sheer reflex. An Orthodoxan soldier dropped right above her, his ankle mangled by her shot. She pulled her eye away from the scope and looked through the gap in the sandbags as she lined up for the kill shot. Her second shot caught him in the chest and he stopped trying to crawl away.

The Orthodoxans topped the Devonite trenches a heartbeat later. She had time to sling her rifle over her shoulder and to pull out her pistol and combat knife.

"Come on, boys," she hollered. "Let's give 'em hell!"

Teeth bared, she squeezed off a shot with her pistol, stopping an Orthodoxan soldier in his tracks at the top of the sandbags. He tumbled headfirst into the trench to lie motionless in the mud. Two more Orthodoxan soldiers took his place, and she took out one before the other launched himself over the edge. He slammed into her, his superior weight driving her backward into the muck and slime with a splash. The soldier sat on her rib cage and raised his rifle over her. Before he could bring the butt down into her face, she drove her knife into his side. He froze, gaping at her, giving her time to pull the knife out and sink it in again, desperately seeking out his vital organs with the knife's tip. A Devonite soldier, noticing her predicament, brought his trench club down on top of the Orthodoxan's helmet. The man spasmed, his eyes blank as he slid sideways to lie twitching at the bottom of the trench.

Jak pushed the man's remaining bulk off her and tried to push herself up. She slid a little in the muck before righting herself. Over the shoulder of the Devonite soldier who had just saved her ass, she saw an Orthodoxan raising his rifle.

"Get down," Jak yelled. The Devonite dropped and she put a bullet into the left eye of the enemy combatant.

Abruptly, it was all over. A deafening silence fell across the battlefield, broken quickly by the moans and cries of the wounded. Here and there a single shot rang out and a voice raised in pain was silenced. Wounded Orthodoxans who were too badly injured to treat were being put out of their misery. Some of the wounded men could have probably been saved, but in the heat of the moment after the battle had concluded, men tended to follow their instincts and not their conscience. Any moment now, the area would be flooded by medical personnel.

Jak traded nods with the man whose life she'd saved and who'd saved her. She recognized him as Collins, the overly friendly soldier from her insertion team. He didn't seem like such a bad sort now. It was in rare times like these that she felt a kind of connection with other Devonite soldiers. They'd been through the same horror and had both come out of it because they could count on each other. Cautiously, she poked her head over the top of the trench wall, ready to duck if anything out there moved. The ground in front of the sandbags was littered with corpses and wounded men. Already the air had taken on the charnel house smell of a battlefield. The combined scents of blood, excrement and burned flesh were unmistakable. Jak grimaced at the stench. Normally, she wasn't anywhere near these kinds of scenes. She dealt death in a much more clinical, surgical way.

There was still work to do and she looked back down into the trench.

"You, you and you," she said, pointing at Collins and the two uninjured men closest to him. "We have work to do. Come with me."

Not waiting to see if they followed, she heaved herself out of the trench. The rifle would be more use on the battlefield than the pistol and knife so she holstered them and went back to her preferred weapon. The three men crawled over the trench walls with her.

"We have some prisoners to pick up," she told them. "Keep sharp. Let's not lose anyone out here."

"Got it, Sarge." They nodded and followed her, eyes moving constantly, examining everything, discarding it as a threat and moving on to the next object of suspicion.

They moved slowly over the broken battlefield. Jak noticed the dispassionate stare in the eyes of the men and supposed that her face must look the same. Later the horrors of the day would come back to haunt her, but for now she had a job to do. She led her small band deeper into the battlefield toward the pathetic group of Orthodoxans marooned in a shell crater.

* * *

Torrin stood at the top of the battlement walls. She ran her fingers over her cold cranium. Her long, beautiful hair was gone, reduced to mere stubble, and she mourned its loss like the loss of an old friend. If she was being honest with herself, she would have acknowledged that she was obsessing over her hair so as not to go insane with worry over Jak. It was bad enough thinking of the sniper deep behind enemy lines, but she knew from firsthand experience that Jak was very much at home in the woods. Jak had admitted to her, though, that she hadn't spent much time in the trenches. It certainly seemed more dangerous than stalking prey that didn't know she was there.

She stretched as high as she could to peer past the trees. The road into camp was swallowed by the gigantic trees that were ubiquitous to this part of Haefen. Trying to see through them was an exercise in futility, but that didn't stop her from giving it a go. Turning, she paced back and forth and tried to work off some of the nervous energy that kept her going.

"Didn't figure you for a nervous one," the corporal at her side said conversationally. She'd seen him around a few times in the sparring salle. He was one of the few who would still spar with her, though he typically got the worst of it. "You're supposed to have ice water in your veins."

Torrin laughed. "You'd think so, wouldn't you?" She returned to pacing. "I don't want Sergeant Stowell to get himself killed before he can get my mission off the ground."

The corporal nodded wisely. "You won't have much longer to wait," he said. "There's a big dust cloud heading our way. That'll be our boys heading back in." He grinned, but the humor didn't reach his eyes. "If it was the Orthodoxans, we wouldn't see them coming."

Peering over the wall, Torrin could see the cloud. She barely confirmed its presence before heading to the stairs. It wouldn't do to appear too eager, so she restrained herself from bolting for the gate to watch for Jak. Instead, she walked back to her room at as sedate a pace as she could manage.

Waiting made her feel like her skin was too tight. She didn't wait especially well at the best of times, but not knowing if Jak was dead or alive gnawed at her from the inside. How did other people deal with this constant worry? This was why she didn't get closely involved with her lovers and moved on before either of them could form any meaningful attachment. Being this emotionally dependent on someone else was torture. And yet, she already couldn't picture her life without Jak. They'd only been physically intimate for a few days, but they'd formed a bond during their time of interdependence in the wilderness. In some ways she felt like she'd known Jak all her life, though there was plenty she didn't know about the woman.

Finally she heard the door to the next room open, then close. She sprang off the bed and out the door. No one was in the hallway so she slipped into Jak's room.

"Hey, babe." Torrin stopped short when Jak whirled around, gun drawn and pointed unwaveringly in her direction, her face contorted in a snarl. Torrin raised both hands. "Jak, it's me!"

Jak's face relaxed when she realized who it was, and exhaustion overwhelmed her face. "Geez, Torrin," Jak rasped, falling into her old patterns of speech. She was filthy, covered in mud from head to toe. Patches of dark red streaked her fatigues. The only time Torrin had seen her looking more dragged out was right before she had fallen into bed after abusing stims for weeks on end.

"Are you okay?" Torrin crossed the room and cupped Jak's cheek.

Jak briefly rested her face against Torrin's palm. "I'm fine." She pulled away abruptly and began stripping out of her combat fatigues. "None of the blood is mine. Watch the door."

Torrin was more than happy to watch Jak disrobe. She reached behind her and engaged the door's lock without taking her eyes off the sniper. Jak might be short, but she was perfectly formed. Her muscles were honed and defined to perfection. Torrin considered herself in good shape, but Jak's body made her feel like a slob. The six-pack of abs topped by perfectly shaped breasts and balanced by gently swelling hips literally dried her mouth. When Jak leaned over to pull the mud-encrusted socks off her feet, Torrin licked her lips.

"Enjoying the show?" Jak grunted.

"You know I am." Before Jak could get into the shower in the adjoining bathroom, Torrin stopped her. With hands on Jak's shoulders, she turned her and covered her lips in a searing kiss. Jak kissed her back with equal intensity, hands slipping behind Torrin's hips and pulling her closer.

"Oh Johvah," Jak groaned. "I wish I could take what you're offering, but I don't have time." She pushed Torrin away with a show of reluctance.

"Don't you have a few minutes?" Torrin wheedled. "I could wash your back."

Jak laughed. "If you wash my back it's going to take more than a few minutes. I need to clean up and go debrief."

"That's fine, I'll wait."

"I wouldn't." Jak shook her head in regret. "I don't know how long I'll be. There are prisoners to question."

Torrin's heart fell. She'd been looking forward to stealing some time with Jak and these short minutes just didn't hack it. It was true they needed to plan to get her back to the *Calamity Jane*. The closer they got to realizing her escape from the planet, the more her excitement waned. Jak was tying her to this place and to her.

"It's all right, I get it," Torrin said, trying to hide the disappointment.

"Hey, I'll have some time to spend with you tomorrow." Jak took her by the chin and gently pulled her face around. "And hopefully we'll be that much closer to getting you home." Her crooked smile held more pain than pleasure. Torrin was sure Jak didn't want her to go any more than she wanted to. Not that Jak would talk about it or any other feelings. The woman was hard to crack. Every time she tried to get at some personal details, Jak either had to go or fell asleep.

"I'll hold you to that," Torrin said and let herself out of the room.

Back in her own room she amused herself by surfing on the Internet with the crappy little computer. Out of boredom, she'd started looking into Haefonian history. From what she could see, the civil war that embroiled Orthodoxans and Devonites had been coming on since the colonists had left Earth. She could see in the recounting of the trip where the divisions were and centuries of isolation on Haefen had only exacerbated their differences.

She shivered. The Right Reverend Dobson sounded like a nightmare. He'd led the colonists away from the godless heathens on Earth. In his view, the proper worship of God had been abandoned. From what she knew of Earth from that time period, he was pretty much right. Years of secularism on humanity's home planet had almost entirely erased the worship of any deity. Only a few had clung to any kind of religion. Reverend Dobson had amassed a fairly sizable cult and convinced them that their salvation was to be found in the stars. They would start a new society that followed the tenets of the Christian Bible. Unfortunately, he'd had a marked preference for the tenets of the Old Testament. Once they'd set up their new colony on Haefen, he'd ruled with an iron fist, especially over the women. He had instituted polygamy and had begun systematically stripping women of the rights they'd enjoyed back on Earth.

One of his sons had disagreed with the severity of Dobson the elder's changes. Devon Dobson had preached a more moderate view of his father's teachings and had converted many colonists to his point of view. Father and son had a terrible falling out and Devon was excommunicated from Dobson's church and exiled into the wilderness. Dobson had probably meant that to be a death sentence, but Devon's followers went with him and they set up their own settlements hundreds of miles away. It was many generations before there was any intermingling between the two factions, but eventually the hurts of previous generations had been dulled by time and the two societies had been reintroduced.

Torrin smiled as she read. Of course it had been the merchants who had precipitated the fraternization between the two groups. Only a merchant would decide to try overcoming decades of hurt and division to make a profit.

Apparently, by the time the two societies started mingling again the divisions were so extreme that they never truly merged. The Devonites lived in their own enclaves near Orthodoxan cities. Aside from the merchants, Orthodoxans rarely set foot in Devonite cities. Many generations passed, though, before percolating tensions boiled over into the civil war that now plagued Haefen.

Torrin yawned and stretched. Her research had taken her into the wee hours of the morning. She scrubbed hands over eyes bleary with fatigue. There was still no sound from next door. Jak hadn't returned. She must still be heavily involved in the interrogation of those prisoners. Torrin decided she wouldn't inquire too closely after Jak's activities; there were some things she was happier not knowing.

It was funny. She'd always thought of herself as being quite worldly. There wasn't much that could shake her, but her time on Haefen had opened her eyes. It was amazing how much people could hurt each other. There was no greater falling out than that between families. She'd seen it happen before, but never on the scale in which it was happening in this conflict. The level of dehumanization was incredible. A whole society descended into madness on one side and on the other... Jak was a warm, caring woman, but she'd trained herself to be a dispassionate killer. Torrin shook her head. She despised the flip side of Jak's psyche. When Jak's eyes hardened, Torrin hardly recognized the amazing, passionate woman that she'd come to know.

Her jaw cracked on another giant yawn, and she returned her attention to the screen in front of her.

Torrin opened her eyes and stared muzzily at the blinking screen in front of her. She must have fallen asleep. A quick glance at the clock showed 0600 hours. Jak hadn't woken her like she'd said she would when she returned. That little... If Jak had come back without waking her, she was going to be peeved. Maybe she hadn't gotten back yet. For her sake Torrin hoped that was so.

She felt more than a little disgusting after falling asleep fully clothed. Running her tongue over her teeth, she grimaced. They felt fuzzy, and her mouth tasted terrible. She stopped to run a sonic toothbrush over her teeth in a hurry, then quietly let herself out of her room. The doorknob to Jak's room turned easily in her hand and she licked suddenly dry lips. It was good that she'd be able to get in there, but Jak was usually fanatical about making sure the door was locked whenever she slept. Something was very wrong.

Jak lay fully clothed on the bed. Her back was to the door and she lay on top of the blankets, curled toward the wall. She hadn't even bothered to take off her boots. Torrin stared at her back for a few moments and sighed. There was no use being angry at her. If she'd been too tired to even take off her boots, then Jak hadn't been in any kind of shape for the other entertainment that Torrin had planned. It would have been nice to laze around in bed with her and fall asleep together for the first time in days. She understood Jak's reluctance; the sniper didn't want anyone to discover them together.

Torrin sat on the edge of the bed, grasped Jak's shoulder and pulled back her hand with a sharp hiss. Jak was on fire; she was noticeably hot even through her jacket. Torrin laid the back of her hand on Jak's cheek.

"Jak, baby." Torrin shook her shoulder gently. "Wake up, babe." When Jak didn't respond, she shook her harder. Torrin's heart pounded out her anxiety. This was not good. The longer Jak failed to respond, the more worried Torrin got. She was about to get up for a glass of water when Jak's eyes opened a crack.

"T—" The dry husk of Jak's voice cut off. She swallowed with obvious effort and licked her lips. They were dry and cracked. "Torrin, I don't feel so good."

"I know, hon. You're burning up. You need to see a doctor."

Jak shook her head feebly but emphatically. "No. No doctors. I can't let them find out who—what I am."

"That doesn't make any sense. This can't be the first time you've gotten sick since you joined the army. How did you handle it in the past?"

"Bron would go to the doctors and fake the symptoms so I could get the right medication." Jak coughed weakly. "That won't work now. You have the same problem I do."

Dammit, but Jak was right. What the hell were they going to do? Torrin stood up, grasping at the stubble of her hair with both hands.

"Maybe this'll pass on its own," Jak offered in an attempt to be soothing. The effect was somewhat marred by the ghastly pallor of her face.

"Not bloody likely. You're sicker than hell and you're immune-compromised from those fucking drugs you insisted on taking." Torrin's anger was out of all proportion to the circumstances. Part of her knew that it wasn't really Jak's fault she'd gotten sick. Torrin was frustrated and couldn't see a way clear of the situation. Her fingers grazed the subdermal transmitter she used to talk to Tien.

"That's it!" She leaned down and started tugging Jak upright. The sniper tried to fend her off but was too weak.

"What's it? Leave me alone. Just let me lie here."

"My ship! It has a fully functional medical bay and autodoc. If I can get you there, I can get you treated. We'll find somewhere quiet to fix you up where we won't be interrupted." Jak wasn't sitting up in bed so much as she was leaning against Torrin. She was too weak even to sit up straight. With her this close it was evident exactly how high Jak's fever had gotten. Heat rolled off her in waves.

"That's fine," Jak replied with weak sarcasm. "We'll just walk up to the fence and ask to be let through, then take a nice little hike to wherever your ship is parked. Oh, wait, I don't think I can walk and the Orthodoxans will shoot us on sight. Do you even know how to get to your ship?"

Torrin blew out an aggrieved sigh. "It's better than your idea. Oh, wait, did you have one beside lying here and dying of fever?"

"Well, no," Jak admitted. She coughed dryly. "Still, there are things we need to do to get to your ship. We need to sneak out of here, sneak past the fence, then get to your ship."

"The last part is the easiest. Once I'm within range of her transmitter, she'll guide us in."

"Her? And what transmitter?"

Torrin tapped the bone behind her right ear. "I can communicate with my ship using an implanted transmitter. The ship is controlled by an Artificial Intelligence construct named Tien. I let her know when I was heading out of range after we left Hutchinson's compound. She'll be getting worried that she hasn't heard from me in so long."

"So that's one problem solved. All that's left is to get out of here and past the fence." Jak disengaged herself from Torrin's shoulder and slid back down to the bed. "First thing we have to do is bring my fever down."

"Sponge baths?" Torrin waggled her eyebrows lasciviously.

Jak tiredly flapped a hand toward her. "Ha, ha. There's an herb, we call it ligbane. It reduces fevers. You can find it growing along cracks in the pavement and along buildings. Get me some of that and I'll be fine. Then we can start tackling the other problems."

"Got it. I'll go pick some flowers so you feel better."

"Thanks." Jak started coughing again. Her cough was weak, but she shook like a ship with a loose engine. She struggled against the pillow behind her, rearranging it so she was propped up. "It has trefoil leaves and is topped by little flowers. Those are…"

"Blue?" Torrin knew she was being a pain but couldn't help it. Serious situations made her nervous, and she dealt better with them when she could make them into a joke.

"Yellow actually, but the leaves are blue. Pick as much as you can. We'll need it again later."

"Can I get you anything before I go?"

"No. I'll be fine. You don't have to get anything for me."

"I'm offering and you can barely move. If you need anything, let me know. It's not an imposition. The sponge bath offer is still open."

"Just some water then." Jak smiled up at her wanly. She really did look like hell. Sweat plastered what little hair she had to her forehead. The pounds seemed to be melting off her as Torrin watched. Jak had always been slender, but Torrin thought she could see her growing gaunter by the minute. She was trying to put on a lighthearted facade because she didn't want Jak to know how worried she was, but it was hard. Jak had only been sick for a few hours but already she looked like she was beating on death's door.

"I can do that." Torrin reached over and caressed the sniper's cheek tenderly. Jak reached up and captured her hand, cradling her head on their two hands.

CHAPTER TWENTY-THREE

After Torrin left, Jak lay in bed and confronted her fears. She couldn't remember ever feeling this sick before. The fever had come on suddenly, so quickly that she almost hadn't made it back to her room. There was no way she would admit this to anyone, but she was scared. Not of dying exactly, but of dying without having fulfilled her promise to take out her brother's killer. She couldn't die now.

She pushed down her blanket. The shivers were gone, and she was so hot that the covers felt like they were going to suffocate her. Even the sheet was too much to bear; she shoved it to the side. Her body ached, every joint was a dull mass of pain and moving the covers had exhausted her. She lay back and stared at the ceiling.

Much as it galled her, Torrin's suggestion was the only way out that she could see. Torrin was right. Her immune system was nearly nonexistent right now and she'd seen how bad the various trench-diseases could get. This one had come up on her so quickly and drained her so fast that she wasn't even certain they could make it to wherever Torrin's ship was.

And if they did... Would that mean leaving Haefen? If so, how did she feel about that? She wasn't sure. She'd never lived anywhere else and while the Devonites weren't perfect, they were the only people she'd ever known. They weren't exactly hers, but they were all she had. Torrin hadn't talked a whole lot about where she was from, though from what little she'd said, her planet sounded as different from Haefen as it was possible to get and still be in the same galaxy.

On the one hand, if she left now it would be a long time, if ever, before she would be able to take out Bron's killer. On the other hand, staying now would inevitably mean discovery or death.

Maybe they could go off and live in the woods until Torrin could nurse her back to health. Jak snorted. The idea of Torrin playing the nursemaid was ludicrous. Unless there was profit to be made the woman got twitchy when she had to stand still for too long. Jak had no profit for her.

And besides, Jak would be AWOL. At the very least, when she came back she would be reprimanded. Who knew what a court-martial might uncover?

Not to mention what would happen if Torrin ended up being stuck here. She'd made her opinion of Jak's planet well-known and in front of a great many witnesses. Torrin had no place on this world. Better that she be able to leave.

Getting Torrin off the planet was as important as her promise to Bron, Jak decided. As sick as she was, she still trusted herself to be the one most able to get her through Orthodoxan territory. She'd spent more time behind enemy lines than most of the other snipers combined. And if Jak had to go off world with her, well, maybe it would only be for a little while, just long enough to get healthy again. Better to survive for now, then come back later and do what needed to be done.

With all that sorted out, she felt better. Not physically better by any means, but mentally settled enough to work on how to get them past the fence and into Orthodoxan territory. If she hadn't felt like death warmed over she would have laughed. She wasn't sure she could make it to the door right now, much less make it three days across rugged terrain back to Hutchinson's compound and however much further it was from there to Torrin's ship.

With a fever this high and as much as she was sweating, Jak knew she had to get as much liquid into her system as possible. Pushing herself up on one elbow, she snagged the glass of water from the table by her head. Her hand shook so badly that she had to use the other one and brace her arms against her chest to take a drink. The water tasted really, really good. The cool liquid was a sip from heaven as it slid down her parched throat. She settled back on the bed and began considering their options.

First things first. They needed to get past the fence and the Orthodoxan border guards. She could see their way through once the fence was down, but how would they get the fence down?

* * *

A gentle hand shaking her elbow woke her. Jak shook her head; the move sent a spike of pain between her eyes. She must have fallen asleep while planning. Torrin sat on the edge of the bed and looked down at her with concerned eyes.

"I got you flowers," Torrin said lightly, holding up a bunch of blue and yellow blooms in a crude bouquet. Jak wished she had the energy to laugh, but the best she could manage was a meager smile.

"I need them chewed on a bit to work faster."

"How do you mean?"

"I need you to chew them a bit to break them down," Jak explained patiently. Torrin looked slightly dubious when Jak confirmed what she'd said. "You're not going to yak them up in my mouth like a mama bird. Just break them down a little. They'll start working faster." Torrin still stared at her doubtfully. "Don't tell me you're not feeling good about swapping spit now," Jak chided her. Her head felt really heavy. Their exchange was taking a lot out of her. She rested her head back on the pillow.

Torrin stuck a sprig in her mouth and chewed gingerly, grimacing at the taste. She pulled the vegetation out and hesitantly offered it to Jak. "Tastes like old boots," she complained, taking a swig out of the canteen at her waist.

"Yep." Jak took the half-chewed plant and immersed it in her water glass. "Get me a few more like that and I'll have a tincture to drink."

Torrin made a face at the prospect but complied, chewing her way through four more sprigs of the unimpressive flower. When she was finished, Jak had an extremely unappetizing glass of blue-green water and sludge. Her arms gave out when she tried to struggle to a sitting position. Torrin gently slid an arm around her torso and pulled her up. She picked up the glass and held it to Jak's lips while the sniper railed inwardly at her own weakness. Her first swig of the improvised tincture sent Jak into a sputtering fit at the flavor.

"You need to finish your drink," Torrin admonished.

"*Now* you're the voice of reason," Jak muttered weakly. "Nothing," she said more loudly when Torrin shot her a questioning glance. She took the glass with hands that trembled like leaves in a high wind and downed as much as she could without breathing.

When she had emptied most of the glass, Torrin lowered her back to the bed.

"The herbs should take effect soon," Jak told her. "I should eat while I'm still feeling good enough. Get us some food from the mess hall. We can't do anything before nightfall anyway, and that's hours away still."

Torrin nodded, then leaned over Jak to kiss her forehead. She grimaced at the heat that still radiated off her. "I'll be back," she said on her way out the door. "You should try sleeping."

The instruction really wasn't necessary, Jak thought muzzily. She was so tired that she didn't see how she could stay awake without trying. Trying sounded so hard; it was so much easier to let go and let sleep pull her under.

* * *

By nightfall Jak felt marginally better. The ligbane was doing its work, and while her fever wasn't gone, it was much lower. She still felt like crap, but it was a level of crap at which she could function. She'd eaten to get her strength up and had drunk what felt like ten liters of water to combat dehydration.

The two of them had crept out of the barracks and were now crouched outside the quartermaster's office. Torrin kept an eye out while Jak worked on bypassing the door's locking mechanism. She and her brother had been known to slip in and out of rooms and buildings all over camp during basic and sniper training. Typically, it had been Bron's idea; she'd only been along for the ride. He'd never taken anything; he'd just wanted to see what he could find. Still, it had been a while since she'd had to break through a locked door, and in her current condition she was having some problems getting back into the swing of things.

Finally the lock popped open. Jak slipped inside, Torrin on her heels.

"We need a couple of cloaks and enough food and water to get us there," Jak whispered. "You look for the supplies. I'll grab us some cloaking devices."

Torrin nodded and started rummaging through cabinets while Jak made a beeline for the technology lockers. It didn't take her long to locate the cloaks. She missed her ghillie suit, which was probably still in the shelter in the woods. Maybe they could pick it up on the way through. A rack of assault rifles sat next to the cabinet, and she grabbed one for Torrin. She, of course, already had her sniper rifle on her. In fact, she had two. Her favorite rifle was good for extremely long ranges and her second favorite was better over medium distances. Since there was a good chance it would be a long time before she'd be back, if at all, she wanted both with her. She also had a few items that weren't strictly necessary for their escape. A holopicture of her parents and her brother's custom-made pistol with the wood grips she'd whittled for him. There really wasn't anything else from her life that she felt absolutely had to come with her if she left the planet. It was sad, really. The fever must be making her sentimental, she thought. Now was not the time to be dwelling on such distractions. She grabbed a couple boxes of ammunition for the rifle and turned.

On the far side of the room, Torrin had a rucksack and was shoving rations into it. She'd also picked up a few flasks for water.

"You'll find stims on the top shelf," Jak whispered, coming over to stand next to her.

"Don't you think they've caused enough problems?" Torrin shot back, making no effort to get them. "We don't need them. By now, you should trust me enough to watch your back."

Jak didn't argue. Torrin had a point...or two. But it felt wrong to go on a mission behind enemy lines without stims. This was the first time she'd had any major side effects from taking the drugs, but this had also been the only time she'd taken them for more than a few days.

"I think we have everything," Jak said. "Let's go."

They were crossing the room toward the front door when a light caught them in the eyes.

"What do we have here?" asked a voice. Jak squinted but couldn't make out who it was at the other end of the flashlight. "This looks a little strange, Sarge. I'm sure you have a good explanation."

The voice was gruff but not angry. Amusement hid in its depths.

"Get that light out of our faces, Lambert." He obligingly shone the light at their feet.

"Seriously, Stowell. What are you doing? This looks really bad for you and the corporal."

Torrin started to slide forward, and Lambert held up a pistol.

"Stay where you are," he said. "I will shoot you. I'm not dumb enough to let you within arm's reach."

Torrin stopped in her tracks, and Lambert looked back at Jak.

"You're making a break for it, aren't you?"

"What?" Jak tried to bluster off the truth of his statement. Inwardly her mind raced. She didn't want to have to hurt him. He was one of the few men in the camp that she felt any connection with. They'd been almost-friends for too many years for her to casually consider injuring him. But she couldn't afford to let anything stop her, and she would do what she had to so they could both leave this place.

"I don't blame you," he said. "It's not easy being a girl and serving."

"How long have you known?" Jak asked as levelly as she could. She'd been so careful. How could he have possibly figured it out?

"Since the first day I saw you." Lambert looked her in the eye. "You didn't think you were the only woman serving out here, did you?"

The thought had never even crossed her mind. The day-to-day struggle of passing as a man had completely occupied her mind and left little extra for other considerations.

"My baby sister is on a long-range artillery crew. I see her as much as I can, but it's not usually more than a couple of times a year." He lowered the gun. "You're taking a lot of supplies just to head off into the woods for some unscheduled leave. If I had to guess, I'd say you were making a break for the fence. I can't figure why you'd want to do that, though. Unless you finally pissed McCullock off enough that he's out for you. The other side of the fence would be one place he couldn't reach you. Bit of frying pan into the fire, though."

The quartermaster looked at both of them. He wasn't threatening, but he wasn't going to move until he had some answers.

"Look, Jak's sick," Torrin said.

Jak tried to signal to Torrin not to say anything further, but she paid no attention.

"I can get her fixed up so she doesn't have to go to the camp docs. If she doesn't get help, she'll die."

"And you're going to do that in the woods?" Lambert looked skeptical. His face suddenly brightened. "Wait, you're the lady smuggler. I saw you on the vid. Wondered why they'd decided to kill you, seemed like a waste. First time I saw you, I thought you looked familiar."

"Then you understand why we need to go, and now."

Lambert shrugged. "So you do. You'll need some meds to keep her in good enough shape to get her to wherever you're going." He clomped over to the cabinet behind them and started rummaging through the top shelf.

"No stims!" Torrin's voice was sharp and Lambert glanced at her over his shoulder.

"Fine. I've got some painkillers, a fever reducer and an antiviral. Do those meet with your approval?" At Torrin's nod, Lambert turned back toward them, his hands full of small bottles. "As for the rest of this, I hope you've thought this through. If that's your plan, you'll need my help to get past the fence."

"What the hell do you know about getting past the fence?" Jak asked bluntly.

"I was on an insertion/extraction team when I was on active duty."

"Well, we don't need your help."

Torrin grabbed her by the arm. "Don't be an ass, Jak. We definitely need his help. You can barely stand up."

Jak dragged her arm out of Torrin's grasp, glaring at Lambert the whole time. "Fine," she admitted, voice grudging. "We have everything else we need. All that's left now is to get out of camp and past the fence. But if you rat us out, I'll kill you myself."

Trust had never come easily to Jak, and every fiber of her being screamed at her not to go anywhere with this man. What did he stand to gain by helping them? She felt hemmed in from all sides. She surreptitiously thumbed the safety off Bron's pistol and eased it in the holster as their small group headed for the back of the compound.

The camp was surrounded on all four sides by three-meter-high walls of duracrete-covered wire support. However, it had been built in a hurry in response to the Orthodoxan aggression. It had been anticipated to last fifteen years and had been serving faithfully for twice that time. Inevitably, the structure was showing its age. Decades of plants being watered at the produce garden in the back had eroded a section of wall. The weak point was well known inside the camp, but no steps had been taken to permanently fix the problem. Instead, a series of patches had been applied and reapplied.

Lambert started prying boards from the latest patch and laying them quietly to one side. Torrin pitched in after glaring Jak into keeping watch. The exertion was getting to her, so she put up only token resistance to Torrin's urging. She just needed to make sure that giving in to Torrin didn't become a habit.

The last board removed, the three of them slipped through the opening and into the forest beyond. Without transport, it was about an hour down the escarpment to the fence. Outside the camp, anyone they met along the way would assume they were just another late-night patrol.

They made their way down to the isthmus without running into anyone.

"We'll head to the insertion point at the third pylon," Jak told Lambert. "It's further away, but I know my way through the trenches there best."

He nodded and they kept along, though Jak chafed at the pace. Even Lambert, who was missing a limb and with his limp was slower than Jak, was faster and quieter than Torrin. They carefully made no reference to her clumsiness in the dark, but she slowed them down considerably.

"Take my elbow," Jak finally told her after Torrin stumbled for the third time.

"I'm fine," Torrin groused. "Give me a little bit for my eyes to adjust to the dark."

"If your eyes haven't adjusted enough by now, they're not going to. We have to be past the fence and deep into the woods on the other side before dawn." Jak knew how independent Torrin was.

She was just as independent, but at least she knew when to accept help.

Torrin grumbled a bit but eventually conceded, wrapping her fingers around Jak's elbow. After that they moved much more quickly. They navigated the darkness with ease and made their way to the tree line in front of Jak's usual insertion point.

"We'll go up to the fence as a group," Jak told Lambert. "That way we can slip through as soon as you bring it down."

"That's a bad idea, Sarge," Lambert argued. "If they see us, they'll take us all out with one mortar."

"I'm not going to put you in danger for any longer than I have to. You're already sticking your neck out for us." Jak fixed the quartermaster with a hard stare. "If we're all there, we'll slip through, then you can put the fence back up. If we're fast enough, the Orthodoxans won't even notice that it was down."

Lambert held her gaze a little longer before nodding. He broke from the cover of the trees at an unsteady run. Jak and Torrin came after him more slowly, hampered by Torrin's inability to see and Jak's inability to breathe. The air in her lungs felt like sand, and every breath was a herculean effort. Gasping for air would only alert Torrin to her distress, however, so she breathed as shallowly as she could.

She was lightheaded by the time they got to the base of the closest pylon. Lambert had already unearthed the power cable.

"Here," Jak gasped, handing Torrin one of the cloaks. "You activate it like this." Inert, the device looked like no more than a flexible rod about the length of her forearm. Each end had a cap on it, one with two prongs that fit into the other end. Jak curved the rod around her neck, put the prongs into the holes and twisted the entire mechanism. The air around her shimmered briefly. Her surroundings looked no different, but to the others she'd completely disappeared, save for an occasional shimmer in the air like a heat mirage.

Torrin attempted to follow suit, fumbling a bit. Growing impatient, Jak reached over and connected the two ends before twisting to activate the cloak. Torrin disappeared instantly from view. She felt Torrin's hands cover hers and give a quick squeeze. The display of affection brought a smile to Jak's lips. She kept one hand in Torrin's and waited for Lambert to finish.

"It's going down in three...two...one..." Lambert cut the cable and the blue light of the fence flickered out. "Go!"

Jak pulled Torrin behind her and they sprinted through the gap. Lambert had no way of knowing when they were through, but he was a seasoned professional. Moments later, the fence sprang back to life. As they ran, Jak listened for artillery or machine gun fire or any sign to indicate that their infiltration had been spotted. The night was eerily quiet.

Too soon she had to slow to a walk. The air in her lungs burned, each breath more painful than the last. They were still a ways from the trenches, but she could run no further. Moving as stealthily as was possible with Torrin in tow, she guided them to the head of the trench system. Torrin really did have a heavy tread. Jak made a mental note to show her how to move quietly through the wilderness.

Their descent into the Orthodoxan trenches was uneventful. As usual, the Orthodoxans had no more than a token number of sentries who either slept or chatted amongst themselves. They were able to navigate through the trench system with relative ease, coming out the other end in less than half an hour.

As they broke for the cover of the deep forest, Jak couldn't help but feel some sadness. These woods had been a second home for her, one that was easier to bear than the barracks she had called home. Once they made their way through the forest, she didn't know the next time she would see them.

CHAPTER TWENTY-FOUR

"Tien, do you read?" Torrin activated the subdermal transmitter. They were finally within transmitter range of the ship. Though the trip had been largely uneventful, it had taken an extra day to get in range of her transmitter. It was a definite contrast to the last time she'd been this way. Then she'd blown through on her bike; now she was forced almost to a crawl by Jak's illness. Her worry over Jak's condition had grown from low-level anxiety until she hovered on the edge of sheer panic. Jak grew weaker by the hour and the effectiveness of the meds were waning. There was only so much that Jak could take before she started vomiting uncontrollably.

Next to her Jak started into a wracking cough that shook her entire frame. She stood with her back against a tree. Torrin suspected that Jak thought she looked like she was lounging casually, but Torrin could tell the tree was all that was keeping her from tipping over. Jak leaned over and spat into the weeds. Torrin pretended, as she had been for the last day, that she hadn't seen the blood flecking Jak's sputum.

"I read you, Torrin," the AI replied. Torrin heaved a sigh of relief.

"Are you alone in there?"

"I am quite alone, Torrin." Tien sounded mildly perturbed. "As I have been for weeks, I might add."

"Yeah, sorry about that. I ran into some...complications."

"Is one of the complications the other human life sign I read with you?"

"That's right. We're both coming in. Is the area clear?"

"Negative, Torrin. There are a number of members of the Orthodoxan military establishment present." Smugness colored the ship's tone. "They gave up trying to get in after a week or so. They realized that short of a precision nuclear device, they would not be getting through my defenses. Apparently, they have been reluctant to destroy what they have been working so hard to attain."

"Good. I'm going to need you to guide us in and direct us around the Orthodoxans." Torrin slung Jak's arm around her waist and started forward again. For the last day and a half the sniper had been unable to move any significant distance without support. The amount of support Jak required had been increasing steadily. At this point, Torrin was almost carrying her. The heat radiating off Jak suffused her fatigue jacket until she was sweating almost as much as Jak did. Fortunately, it was still light out. Night would be falling soon, but there was enough sun breaking through the canopy for her to see by. Navigating at night was difficult since she had to rely on Jak's night vision. The sniper had slipped into hallucinations a day ago, and she had to work hard to keep Jak focused on reality.

"That will not be possible, I am afraid." Tien sounded regretful. "There is a group of soldiers camped out in front of the cargo bay doors. You will need to go through them."

"Shit," Torrin spat the curse out with venom, and Jak looked at her sideways. It had been too much to hope that they might have a clear path to the ship. "How many are there?"

The AI was silent for a moment. "There are fifteen camped out in front of the ship, and I read four more life signs patrolling the woods nearby."

Torrin groaned. There was no way they could take on nineteen men. Jak could barely hold her sniper rifle, let alone aim it effectively. She couldn't even walk unaided.

"Jak, we have a problem."

Jak took a breath to speak but choked as another coughing spasm shook her frame. The skin on her face was stretched too tight over her skull. Torrin had thought Jak had been whipcord over bone before. The whipcord was a fond memory. Her skin was almost translucent, and she weighed as little as a baby bird. The paroxysm went on far too long, and Torrin tightened her grip for support. Hanging from her grasp, Jak went still. Terrifyingly so.

"What's the problem?" Jak finally croaked.

"We have almost twenty Orthodoxan soldiers to get through to get to my ship." Despair filled her tone, and Torrin tried to modulate her voice so her desperation wasn't so apparent. She knew she was failing miserably. "Fifteen camped out in front of the ship and four patrolling the woods."

"That's not so bad," Jak whispered.

"Not so bad?" Torrin was incredulous. "You can't hold a weapon steady, let alone fight. I don't have your training. I'm your girl if you're in a back alley brawl, but I can't hold my own in this kind of fight. We barely have two of us to go in on this."

"What about your ship? Doesn't it have weapons and don't you have a fancy AI?"

Torrin tapped her lower lip with an index finger. "Of course we have weapons. Tien does have control over them, I didn't lock her out of that system. But there's no way they can be brought to bear on the men camped out by the ship. They're too close."

"But they don't know that." Jak snorted, then coughed weakly. "They're Orthodoxans. They're about as smart as aetanberani in heat."

"That's dumb?"

Jak grinned. Torrin wished she hadn't; it made her look like a death's head.

"That's dumb. I once saw an aetanberan try to fuck a stump because it was about the right height and had a hole in about the right place. Tore it apart with his bare claws when the stump spurned his advances."

"So your plan is to scare them off. How about the four already out there?"

"Your ship can keep an eye out for them and take them out if they come to investigate. The Orthodoxans aren't known for their bravery under fire, so they'll probably go to ground somewhere and stay down until things blow over." Jak paused and closed her eyes. "We can do this. We have no other choice."

"What about our cloak things?"

"I don't think it's a good idea." She paused and Torrin could see her wrestling with herself. "I don't know if I can stand without your help. If we get separated, you won't know where I am. Not to mention, I'm having problems tracking. If you sneak up on me wearing one of those, I might react first. I'd rather not put a bullet through you by accident."

If Jak was willing to admit that, she was doing even worse than Torrin thought. They had to move now. The faster she could get Jak into the autodoc, the better.

"All right, we'll do it your way." Torrin reactivated her subdermal transmitter. "Tien, we're coming in. It's slow going right now, so keep an eye out and let me know if we're about to trip over a patrol. When we're in place, I need you to open up with all barrels and scare the crap out of those soldiers."

"Affirmative, Torrin."

"Come on, Jak." Torrin reached over and slid the smaller woman's arm back around her waist. Jak could barely walk, but she struggled forward gamely, doing all she could to help Torrin.

They moved on through the falling dusk until dark. Relying on Jak's night vision was chancy, but it was all Torrin had to go on.

"Torrin, stop where you are!" Tien's voice came sharply through the transmitter behind her ear. She jumped and almost dropped Jak before freezing in place. "There is a two-man patrol heading toward you on an intercept course."

"Son of a bitch," Torrin cursed. "Jak, do you see a hiding spot? There are Orthodoxans coming our way."

"There's a small deadfall over that way." Jak tugged her to the right. Torrin followed her movements over to a jumble of trunks and branches. She disengaged her arm from Jak and deposited her by the pile. Jak pulled herself over the tree and settled behind the trunk. Torrin scrambled in behind her and curled herself protectively around the sniper. She wished they had their cloaks, no matter what Jak said, but they were in her pack. There was barely enough room to breathe in their hiding spot, let alone to start rummaging around. They were stuck.

Booted feet on hard earth came closer and closer. Torrin tensed, readying herself for confrontation. She slid her knife out of the scabbard. Jak muttered angrily to herself.

"Jak, shush," the smuggler hissed.

The sniper gave no indication that she'd heard her and kept speaking in a low, insistent voice. The footsteps drew closer; Torrin pulled Jak back against her body and slid a hand over her mouth.

"Jak, it's me," Torrin whispered when she started to thrash. At her voice, Jak quieted momentarily. She relaxed against Torrin, who cautiously removed her hand from Jak's mouth.

"I don't feel good, Mom," Jak complained quietly.

"I know, baby. But you need to be quiet or the bad men will hear us." With Jak clutched against her, Torrin could tell her fever had spiked again. The hallucinations were back, stronger than ever. She wasn't sure how much more of this Jak's body could take. It was amazing that she'd lasted this long. As high as her fever was, Torrin was astounded Jak hadn't yet gone into convulsions.

"Okay," Jak sighed. She lay quietly in Torrin's arms, restless movements twitching through her slight frame.

Through the branches, Torrin could barely make out two forms in the darkness of the clearing. She couldn't hear anything; the men had stopped moving. Had they stopped because they'd heard Jak or were they simply resting? Her hand hovered in the air over the sniper's mouth, in case she seemed ready to make another outburst. The sound of her heartbeat thundered in her ears, and she wondered why the soldiers couldn't hear it. Over the sound of her heart, she almost didn't hear them start walking again. Finally, after what seemed like days, the two men left the area. She lay there with Jak for another ten minutes before deciding the coast was clear enough to risk talking aloud.

"Tien, are there any life signs in our immediate vicinity?"

"Negative, Torrin. You are clear for the time being. I see no one between you and the camp."

"Good. I need to take care of Jak before we can start moving again. Let me know if anyone heads our way again."

Torrin sat up. There was only enough room under the branches for her to sit, albeit she had to do so hunched over. She pulled Jak against her and held her up with one arm while fishing out a water flask. She dug around a little longer before she found the pill bottle of fever-reducing pills Lambert had sent along with them. There weren't many left and she carefully shook two out into her palm.

"Jak." Torrin shook her lightly. "You need to take your medicine."

The face Jak made, eyebrows drawn down and nose scrunched over pursed lips would have been comical if not for the direness of their situation. "I don't wanna," Jak complained.

"It's important. Open your mouth."

Jak shook her head petulantly but was in no shape to resist Torrin when she put the pill in her mouth and forced her to take a drink from the canteen.

"That's awful," Jak gasped, retching dryly.

"I know." Torrin grimly administered another pill. "You need to take some more." Jak numbly accepted another swig from the canteen, then turned her head into Torrin's shoulder. Hopefully the pills she'd swallowed would take effect soon. Torrin hummed tunelessly and stroked Jak's sweat-laden hair away from her forehead as she rocked the sniper in her arms. Jak's fragility was terrifying. Torrin didn't know what she'd do if Jak didn't survive. In a frighteningly short period of time, Jak had set up shop in her head and in her heart. To have to let her go now when she'd only just found her was not something she wanted to face

Slowly, Jak began to perk up. Finally she opened her eyes and looked up at Torrin.

"Why are we stopped?"

"You were out of it. I had to get your fever down." Torrin handed her the canteen. "Have some more water."

Jak accepted the canteen and drank deeply. They were losing the battle with dehydration.

"That's probably enough. You don't want to drink all of it." Torrin took the container back and Jak nodded.

"Give me a few moments and we can get on with it," Jak told her. Pulling herself up, she was able to sit without support, but she kept one hand in Torrin's. Her flesh was still too hot to the touch and Torrin gently stroked the back of her hand. Keeping in contact with the sniper helped her stay calm over the rising panic she was feeling at Jak's deterioration.

"All right, let's go," Jak announced. "I'm as good as I'm going to get." Good was a relative statement. Jak still needed Torrin's help to crawl out of their hiding place. They started out at a walk, Torrin practically carrying her. Slowly they made their way through the trees until the light of a campfire was visible through the trees ahead.

"Tien, we're in place. Are you ready?"

The AI sounded mildly excited. "I am, Torrin."

Torrin looked over at Jak, who nodded back at her. "Fire when ready then."

The stillness of the night was broken by a mechanical whirring the two women could hear, even back in the trees as they were. Torrin could see movement between the trees as the Orthodoxans reacted to the unanticipated sounds. A sharp noise came up like a loud wind and ended with a concussive thud. Across the clearing, a stand of trees vaporized in a flare of plasma. Shouts filtered back to them through the trees. The Orthodoxans were extremely worked up.

Two more whooshes and brilliant flares shattered the night. Torrin could see all sorts of movement now.

"Tien, what's your status?" she asked urgently.

"The soldiers do not wish to leave what shelter they have here, Torrin. I think they are aware that I cannot shoot them. They seem to think I am shooting at some elusive enemy."

"Crap." Torrin turned to Jak. "We have another problem."

Jak quirked an eyebrow at her.

"The soldiers don't want to leave their shelter. They think Tien is shooting at someone else and they're hunkering down."

"I told you, dumb as hell." Jak shook her head. "I guess we need to make things a little less comfortable down there." She pulled the sniper rifle off her shoulder and started loading it.

"Are you sure you're up for that?"

"We can't afford me not to be. I need you to watch my back." The sniper surveyed the area and pointed off to the right. "There's a bit of a rise and a break in the trees off that way. We'll set up there." She put her left arm around Torrin's shoulders, and they skirted their way through the woods to the break in the tree line.

The clearing where the ship sat was lit by burning trees on three sides. Burn marks were visible on the surface of the *Calamity Jane* and Torrin cursed internally. She was going take every scorched centimeter of paint out of the hides of the Orthodoxans.

Jak assumed a prone position and was taking a bead on the soldiers grouped back against the ship. They'd erected a hasty barrier of crates and boxes and had their heads down, weapons bristling out of every cranny imaginable. With Jak ensconced, Torrin unlimbered her own weapon, thumbed the safety off the assault rifle and slammed a fresh magazine home.

"Let me know about those patrols," she radioed to Tien through the transmitter.

"Confirmed, Torrin. They are moving toward our position, but none are in the immediate vicinity."

That was reassuring. Even though she'd been expecting it, she still jerked when Jak took her first shot. The report shattered the silence and there was a shocked yell behind the flimsy barricade. Shots rang out in response, but the return fire was spotty, uncoordinated. The Orthodoxans were shooting blind. The sniper calmly lined up her next target. Torrin knew when Jak stuck her tongue out between her teeth that she was ready to take her shot. Sure enough, another shot rang out and more return fire came from the trapped soldiers.

"Torrin, there are two soldiers coming your way," Tien reported quickly.

She blistered the air with a torrent of invectives and kept her eyes open for the patrol.

"They are closing in at your two o'clock."

"Thanks, Tien," Torrin said as she caught sight of the first man. She raised her assault rifle and squeezed off a few rounds, catching the soldier in the torso and spinning him around. He dropped to the ground, but his companion ducked behind a tree.

"I'll be back," Torrin tossed over her shoulder to Jak, who was busily lining up her third shot.

The trees faded quickly into darkness the further she got from the clearing. She would be at a complete disadvantage there, but she needed to draw the soldier away from Jak. Working her way to the soldier's left, Torrin tried to flank him. He'd been expecting the move and a muzzle flash bloomed in the dark as he fired on her. She ducked behind a tree and crouched, wondering what she should do.

"He is moving toward you, Torrin," Tien informed her.

"Good, let me know which way he's coming." He might be able to see in the dark like Jak, but he didn't have an AI reporting her every move to him. Knowing his movements leveled the playing field a little bit.

"He has paused, Torrin. I do not believe that he is sure what to do."

She needed to bring him to her. Maybe if he believed she was wounded, he would let down his guard. She groaned loudly and listened closely for any movement.

"He still hesitates."

She let out another groan and followed it up with a sobbing cough.

"That has done it, Torrin. He is moving toward you, around the tree to your right."

The grin that spread across her face looked nasty, she knew. It was the first and last thing the soldier saw when he came into sight. His mouth gaped in surprise and her muzzle flashed. At close range, the slugs from the rifle tore his chest apart in multiple sprays of blood. Torrin paused long enough to put a bullet through his temple, then hurried back to Jak.

Below their low hill, several bodies lay half in, half out of the barricade. Still, the soldiers clung to their little bit of shelter.

"Are they ready to run?"

"I think they need a little something else to push them over the edge," Jak replied in a distracted tone. She was lining up another shot.

"I know just the thing." Torrin activated the subdermal transmitter. "Tien, let's give them something to really worry about. Lower the cargo bay doors." A breath later and the loud clunks of clamps releasing rang out through the clearing. Torrin could see consternation running through the group clustered below. The release of the clamps was followed by a rumbling groan as the ramp started to lower.

Unable to take it any longer, the soldiers finally broke. As one they scrambled over their barricade and headed for the dubious shelter of the tree line.

"Time to go." Torrin leaned down and scooped Jak into her arms. Adrenaline and Jak's fragile condition made her weight negligible. Forcing her way through the bushes, Torrin sprinted down the hill toward the lowering ramp. She was halfway to the ship before the Orthodoxans realized what was happening. Scattered gunfire rang out from the woods, kicking up the ground by her feet. She wove an evasive pattern, trying to avoid the ever more insistent bullets whizzing past her. Fire creased the back of her right calf; she stumbled, righted herself and kept on.

With a deafening whoosh and thud, a vast swath of trees disappeared in a searing fireball. The Orthodoxans had forgotten that the ship's fire could reach them in the trees. The sound of scattered shots was replaced by screams of men burning alive. Torrin tried not to think about them. She resumed her sprint and reached the ramp to the cargo bay just as it hit the ground. Without bothering to slow, she pounded up the ramp, which began to lift as soon as she hit it, and into the cargo area. Lights flickered on in front of her as she ran.

"The elevator is ready for you, Torrin," Tien informed her. The doors hissed open and she raced through, her lungs burning. Cradling her burden carefully, Torrin slid to the floor. Behind her the doors closed and the elevator whirred to life.

"Jak, are you all right?" Torrin maneuvered Jak around to get a better look at her face. Her heart stuttered to a stop in her rib cage when Jak's head lolled forward limply. She grabbed her by the cheeks and tilted her head back. There was no way to tell if the sniper still drew breath. Torrin bent and held her ear to Jak's chest.

"Dammit, dammit, dammit!" she breathed. "You'd better still be alive, or I'll…" Her voice trailed off. There. Yes, there it was. It was faint, desperately so, but there was a heartbeat. She raised her head and rubbed the back of her hand roughly across her eyes, angrily dashing tears away.

"Tien, power up the med bay!" Torrin yelled more loudly than she probably had to.

"It is already done, Torrin." The AI's impenetrable calm washed over her and she worked to pull herself together. "However, we have other problems."

What now? Would this never end? She wanted to leave and never come back. More than anything else, she wanted the little, complicated woman in her arms to be all right. Everything she'd been through since arriving on Haefen seemed destined to end in ruin.

"What kind of problems?" The elevator doors apparently had been standing open for a while. She gathered Jak back into her arms and stood, grunting with effort. The dash from the forest to the ship had burned away her last stores of energy. She needed to focus on getting Jak to the med bay, then she could take care of the latest wrinkle to her plans.

"They have a tank, Torrin" was the extremely unwelcome answer. "It is possible that our hull will stand up to what they can unload, but I make no guarantees."

"Fine," Torrin replied tersely, teeth gritted as she maneuvered through the medical bay's doorway while trying not to knock Jak's head on the doorframe. "Start up the engines. We'll take off as soon as I load Jak in the autodoc. You can start treating her while I find someplace on this planet not crawling with misogynistic, homicidal assholes."

"Are you certain, Torrin?" The ship's voice held a hint of uncertainty. "The League picket is currently in orbit almost directly above us. If I power up the engines, they will almost certainly see our power signature."

Unable to take it any longer, Torrin let loose a guttural shriek of anger. Her frustration, weeks of uncertainty, of forced dependence and confinement bubbled to the surface. "What the fuck!?" Chest heaving, she stood immobile in the middle of the med bay, Jak's form clutched to her chest and her head buried in the crook of the sniper's shoulder. Jak's hand slid over Torrin's head, weakly stroking the stubble of her shaved scalp.

"S'okay," Jak mumbled, barely audible. "S'okay."

Galvanized by Jak's actions, Torrin moved forward and deposited her on a low table that jutted out of the far bulkhead, monitors, displays and readouts blinking on the wall above it. Two arms unfolded from the table's side.

"Just start the engines!" Torrin ordered, her hands busy at the fastenings of Jak's fatigues. Fortunately, she'd gotten a lot of practice in undressing the other woman over the past week and a half. Quickly, she stripped Jak down to her skin. "I'll take care of the League ship when I get to it. Let's take care of the disaster we have in front of us."

She spared one moment to look over the woman lying naked on the table in front of her. Jak looked so vulnerable. Torrin knew she'd been losing weight rapidly, but to see her nude for the first time in days was a shock. Gaunt didn't begin to describe it; skeletal was closer.

The graze on the back of her leg wasn't anything to worry about, Torrin decided after a glance down. It still bled sluggishly but was already starting to clot. They had far bigger things to worry about than that scratch.

"She's all yours," Torrin snarled. "If you fuck this up, Tien, I'm permanently disabling you." She hurried out the door as more leaves unfolded from the side of the table. The whole contraption started reforming over Jak's form, obscuring her from Torrin's last backward glance.

"I will do my best, Torrin," the AI assured her solemnly.

Torrin tore forward, ducking her head to avoid bulkheads and sliding sideways through doors that had just opened in front of her. She entered the bridge and threw herself into the pilot's chair. The safety harness fastened itself around her, snugging her body into the chair. On the display she could see a large heat signature approaching them on the ground from the north. Orbiting above them, on another display, was the energy signature of the League's picket ship.

Her hands danced across the consoles, and both main plasma cannons swiveled. Two bolts of plasma lanced toward the oncoming tank as she redlined the engines.

Weeks of enforced idleness had taken their toll on her beloved ship. The engines whined and protested as she drove them ruthlessly past their safety limits. It was time to break the pull of the planet's gravity. She needed to bust out so desperately she could feel it in her chest. Steel bands tightened around her rib cage until she could barely breathe. She hated being tied down and now that she was so close to getting out of there, she felt the confinement all the more. The taste of blood, salt and iron, filled her mouth. She'd bitten through her lip.

The engines quit whining and flipped over, belting out a deep, throaty roar. Torrin slid her hands across the control panel and the ship hovered, rotated, then leaped forward. Behind them, the clearing erupted in a conflagration as the engines' exhaust heated the ground well past its flashpoint. Streaming backblast, the *Calamity Jane* clawed its way out of the planet's gravity. Torrin yelled exultantly as they broke out of Haefen's pull and the buffeting of their hurried trajectory through the atmosphere suddenly ceased.

She grinned wolfishly. She was back in her element, where she belonged.

Her excitement came to an abrupt halt when her comm crackled to life.

"Unidentified vessel. You have violated the League of Solaran Planets blockade of the sovereign planet Haefen. Heave to and prepare to be boarded in accordance with interstellar law."

CHAPTER TWENTY-FIVE

Torrin had known it was likely the League ship would notice a ship's power signature firing up on the surface, and of course it had. It was just the way her luck had been running lately.

There was no way that she could lose them before the jump to FTL. The League ship likely had enough shielding to slip between normal and peripheral space without requiring the crew to climb into heavily shielded pods. For her to do the same would be a death sentence. Exposed to the extremely high radiation levels of peripheral space she would have at most a year after coming out before dying of some exotic cancer. Some people never made it out the other side.

There had been a nearby nebula on her way into the system, hadn't there? Maybe she could lose the other ship in there. That she was still over Haefen made it unlikely that the League bastards would unload on her, not when they might hit the planet below. After all, they were going to play conquering heroes when the Devonites started to sew up their little civil war. Accidentally blasting a farm village into oblivion wouldn't play well when it came to that.

Running her hand over the command console, she slipped the *Jane* back into the planet's atmosphere. Her engines whined as Haefen's gravity well pulled against her. If she got the timing down, she could use the planet's gravity and rotation to slingshot out toward the nebula.

"Unidentified ship," the voice crackled over her comm again. Definitely female and definitely irritated. Torrin allowed herself a tight smile. It was a good day when she could piss off some League flunkies. "You are ordered to heave to." When Torrin didn't respond an audible sigh of irritation filtered through the comm. "You won't be warned again."

Torrin fiddled a bit with the comm. A few adjustments and her voice could sound like anyone's. She didn't have time to imitate anyone in particular so she just settled for deepening her voice into the baritone range.

"I'm having some engine trouble here," Torrin said, an edge of panic leaking into her voice. She cut the engines for a moment, just long enough for the League ship to see the engine exhaust dim and read a lowering of output. "We were down there for so long our engines have destabilized. I can't get out of the planet's gravity well!"

Her performance was met by a long silence. "Cut your engines and we'll offer assistance." The voice turned wry for a moment. "Don't think that 'engine trouble' will get you out of breaking through the picket."

"Are you kidding?" Torrin injected horror into her tone. "They're animals down there. I can't go back! All the credits in the universe aren't worth dealing with those savages again." She kept an eye on the monitor, lining up their position relative to the nebula. They weren't quite at the right angle, just a little further.

"That will of course be taken into consideration during your trial," the voice promised disingenuously.

"Oh, thank you!" *And thank you!* Their conversation had bought her just enough time. She punched the engines. The extra thrust combined with their orbital course shot them out of the grip of Haefen's gravity on a trajectory toward the nearby nebula. They flashed past the League ship close enough that Torrin could make out the name on its side. *Icarus*, was it? The League was fond of naming their ships after Earth ancient heroes. She hoped for their sake that the name wasn't an indication of any flight deficiencies on the ship's part.

The *Icarus* had been high enough above Haefen that it was outside the planet's orbit and couldn't match her speed. It was entirely possible that they couldn't have matched her speed to begin with. When she'd had the engines retrofitted, she'd demanded enough speed to outrun all but the fastest known vessels. Her engineers had packed in as much power and speed as the frame of the vessel could take without tearing it apart.

They flashed on, the nebula growing rapidly in the viewscreen. Purple and pink clouds of cosmic gases overlapped in diaphanous bands. Deep within the nebula, lightning flashed fitfully, silhouetting bands against each other. It was tantamount to suicide to venture too deep into some nebulae. It was easy to get turned around. The ionized dust obscured sensors and visual navigation was the only way to get through, but the dust clouds made it difficult to see. Hopefully she could lose them in the cloud and make a quick getaway out before jumping into peripheral space with the *Icarus* being none the wiser.

She plunged the ship into the nebula, bathing the interior of the bridge in its soft pink light. Before long, ionized gases and shifting magnetic fields had scrambled her sensors and she was forced to navigate by relying on her vision alone.

The comm crackled to life again but all that came through now was static. The *Icarus* was close enough to punch a message partially through, but it was hopelessly scrambled. That wasn't great news. If she was that close, they needed to go deeper into the cloud.

Torrin cut power to all systems except propulsion, life support and medical. The League ship most assuredly had stronger sensors than her little ship and minimizing her power footprint would allow the *Jane* to fade into background noise of the nebula.

A band of brilliant purple parted as she piloted through it, and cloud streamers flowed by the window. Deeper in the nebula, the colors also deepened as the ambient light of nearby stars and planets was sucked up by the bands of ionized dust. She coasted the ship further, eyes peeled for asteroids and other objects that could be hiding in the clouds of dust. Lightning flashed brilliant orange above them, lighting up the cloud as they passed through. An electric blue afterimage lingered on her retinas, and she blinked rapidly, trying to clear it out.

This was as good a spot as any. Torrin brought the ship to a stop, putting her propulsion systems into standby mode. It wasn't as power-efficient as turning them off altogether, but cutting them completely would require too much warm-up time when it came time to leave.

"How's Jak doing?" Torrin addressed the empty air of the bridge, knowing Tien had been monitoring her every move.

"She is stable, Torrin." She could tell from Tien's tone that the AI was hedging.

"But?" The smuggler leaned back in her chair, gripping the arms hard enough to press an imprint of its edges into her palms.

"She was more damaged by her illness than you may have realized, Torrin," Tien said, preoccupied. "I have halted the progression of the illness, but the virus that caused it is not in my medical databanks. It is most likely peculiar to Haefen. League medical information can be woefully incomplete for planets on the Fringes. The virus has ravaged her lungs. They are functioning at less than fifty percent of their full capacity. It is amazing that the fever has not done any permanent damage to her brain, but I worry that I will not be able to return her lungs to full capacity."

"What can you do for her?" Torrin had to work to get the words out past her clenched teeth. This was exactly the situation she'd been worried about.

"I have lowered the fever, Torrin. She is no longer in danger of permanent brain damage. The real danger is in her lungs." The AI was hesitant, which really worried Torrin. In all of their time together, Tien had rarely questioned her own conclusions, but she seemed to be doing so now. "She should be taken to a well-qualified doctor, one who is well-versed in Fringe diseases."

"Is she stable enough for cryostasis?"

"She is, Torrin," Tien affirmed. "At this point, it is probably best for her and will increase her chances of survival."

"So you're saying she could still die?"

"It is a distinct possibility. If she survives, physically she may never be the same."

Those damned stims. Without them there was no way Jak would be in this trouble now. Torrin felt a powerful pang of guilt. Jak had taken the drugs in part so she could protect her. Of course, if Jak had just trusted her to watch her back, this never would have happened. *Would you have trusted Jak if your positions had been reversed,* a niggling voice at the back of her mind wondered, *especially if you'd been unable to trust anyone else for years?* That wasn't the point. The point was that, when Jak recovered, Torrin was going to kill her!

"I'll move her over," Torrin announced as she released herself from the harness and pushed herself up. "Keep your eyes out for the *Icarus* and engage in evasive maneuvers if she finds us. Oh, and transfer power from the medical systems to cryostasis as soon as I remove Jak from the autodoc."

She strode down the hallway. Tien couldn't move Jak over to cryostasis, but that was fine since Torrin wanted to see her again. She wanted to touch her again. In her mind, she tried to avoid acknowledging the part that shrieked dimly at her. It might be her last chance to feel Jak's warmth. Frantic grief threatened to overwhelm her at the thought, and she wrenched her mind away from considering the idea too closely.

Jak looked so tiny on the table in the cramped medical bay. The diagnostic arms of the autodoc were gone, folded back along the side of the table and she was covered by a voluminous blanket that made her seem shrunken. Torrin cleared her throat roughly to ease the rapidly increasing tightness there. She stood for a moment at Jak's bedside, looking down on her, willing Jak to open her eyes and look back at her. She longed to see those intense blue eyes staring seriously back at her.

Torrin reached over and stroked Jak's short blond hair gently. The sniper always looked so surprised when Torrin was able to get a laugh out of her. Her life had been so grim and fraught that Torrin had been looking forward to showing her it was okay to let go. She lifted Jak carefully in her arms and cradled the sniper against her chest.

The cryostasis room was just down the hall. It contained four cryopods meant to protect their contents against the damaging radiation that was generated by the inhospitable atmosphere of peripheral space. Torrin had never had four people in the ship for anything other than short trips which hadn't required FTL travel. She was glad that she'd always insisted on keeping all the pods operational. Without her prompting, the lid of the closest pod swung open smoothly. This pod was meant to accommodate anyone, from hulking mountains of men to the tiniest infants. Jak would barely fill half of it. Gently, Torrin slid her into the receptacle. She stepped back as Tien took over preparing Jak for cryosleep. A face mask slipped down and over Jak's face while electrodes snaked out over Jak's chest. Torrin braced herself as large bore needles stabbed into the veins on Jak's arms. The pod's systems would inject chemicals that would replace her blood and keep Jak from becoming a frozen lump inside the pod. It hurt enough when she hooked herself in, but watching the needle's tip sliding under Jak's painfully translucent skin made her skin crawl.

The needles were sliding into the great saphenous vein that ran along the inside of Jak's thighs when she felt a hand on the arm she was resting on the edge of the cryopod. Looking up, she saw the blue of Jak's eyes. The whites of her eyes were more red than white, with barely any white left at all. Terror swam in her eyes and Jak clutched weakly at Torrin's forearm.

"Shhh." Torrin took Jak's hand and held it to her chest. "I know it hurts, but we need to do this."

Jak tried to speak but what came out around the face mask was too muffled to decipher. Quickly Torrin removed the mask.

"What's happening?" Jak's voice cracked painfully.

"We need to get you to a real doctor," Torrin explained, stroking her cheek. "You're being hooked into the cryopod so we can make the FTL jump. The pod will protect you while we're in peripheral space."

"What about you?" Jak shook her head. She clearly didn't understand the explanation but trusted Torrin enough to go along with it.

"I'll be in the pod right next to yours." Torrin pointed to the next pod down. "Tien will get us home and we'll find someone who can make you better."

"Scared."

"I know. But I know what I'm doing. You need to trust me."

Jak smiled weakly. "I do."

"It's about time," Torrin teased her. "Let's get your mask back on. We just need to finish up with your legs."

Jak nodded tiredly and laid her head back on the pod's hard plastic headrest. It was adjustable, and Torrin had slid it way down to be useful to her.

"I'll see you soon. Everything's going to be all right." After one last reassuring squeeze to Jak's hand, Torrin activated the pod's lid.

As it slid closed, Jak looked alarmed. Torrin held her gaze through the lid's clear glass. When Jak put one hand to the glass, Torrin covered it with her own. Jak's elevated vital signs dropped slightly when Torrin put her hand up. The rapid rise and fall of Jak's chest slowed slightly but noticeably. She nodded and Torrin activated the freezing cycle on the pod. As a powerful sedative flooded her system, Jak's eyes drifted shut, her head drooping to the side. Her hand stayed against Torrin's, separated only by the thin clear pane. When the pod's systems flash froze her in place her hand remained, still reaching out for Torrin.

Torrin stayed there for another moment, long enough to make sure Jak's vital signs stayed constant. There was no change, she was in cryostasis and the best course of action was for Torrin to get Jak to someone who could fix her. For one moment longer Torrin lingered, drinking in the sight of Jak lying there, quiet and serene.

With Jak taken care of in the cryostasis chamber, Torrin made her way forward to the bridge. As she strapped herself into the pilot's chair, she cast an eye over the displays. Nothing registered, which was only to be expected in the nebula. Still, it made her a little nervous. She needed to know if the *Icarus* had followed them into the cloud or was lurking just outside, waiting for them to emerge.

"Any sign of the *Icarus*?" she asked Tien.

"Torrin, I am effectively blind in here. The only sensors that are working are the optics in my hull."

"Then there's nothing to do for it but to get out of here," Torrin decided. "We can't just sit around waiting for them. I have a bit of an idea where we are, so let's navigate back out of here. I want to come out at a different point than we entered." Torrin entered a few points of reference into the navigation computer. The nebula shifted so rapidly that the points would only be useful for a few minutes, but they were all she had to go on. She grasped the ship's rarely used yoke and began steering them manually back out of the cloud, using the points she had just entered.

They crept slowly forward and lightning flashed fitfully around them in brilliant shades of orange and blue. Since Torrin didn't know exactly where the edges of the cloud were, she still needed to keep her power signature at a minimum. They skulked further forward, past towering clouds of chromatic lavender, through bands of blinding pink. She wished Jak was with her to see all of the fantastic display. Jak had never left her own world, and this nebula had a beauty that was impossible to find on any planet. When she'd recovered, Torrin would take her to see all sorts of sights. The sunrise over the twined rings of the sister planets Clotho and Lachesis, maybe. Or to the wastes for the beauty of a nebula born from the remnants of a long dead star system. There was so much she could share with her. All they had to do was get Jak to Nadierzda so she could be fixed up.

Between one flash and another, she caught a glimpse of the bow of the *Icarus* nosing out from between two lavender cloud banks. She hauled the *Jane* to a stop and reversed back into the band of pink they'd just passed through. Sitting there at a full stop, she cut power to all systems except the cryo-chambers. The lights dimmed, then went out altogether.

In the dark, lit only by the light from the nebula and the constant lightning, Torrin watched the faint outline of the League ship as it passed by the band in which they were hidden. The *Icarus* was moving at a glacial pace. Any captain who knew her stuff would know that nebulae could hide larger objects within the highly ionized gases. With the sensors not working properly, incautious flying could have very regrettable results.

She barely breathed as the other ship cruised slowly past their hiding place. It was stupid, she knew. She could have been jumping up and down while screaming at the top of her lungs and no one on the other ship would have had any clue. Quietly she sat, watching, waiting. Five minutes ticked by, then ten and still she could just make out the outline of the *Icarus* as it finally left their immediate vicinity. They were heading on a course almost opposite to their own, deeper into the nebula. At least Torrin knew where they were.

She waited another seven minutes after the *Icarus* left visual range before turning vital systems back on. They were now running under low power, with only propulsion and the cryo-chamber receiving any juice. She still had hours of breathable air, but it felt like it was getting harder to breathe.

She eased the *Jane* slowly out of the cloud, alert to any sign of the *Icarus*. The ship wasn't visible anywhere, and she let out the deep breath she hadn't known she was holding. She piloted the ship forward on a course she was only vaguely certain of. The markers she'd entered into the navigation computer were now completely gone, and she flew on instinct alone.

She craned her neck constantly, watching for the *Icarus* with single-minded intensity. With agonizing slowness, they passed through bands of purple and clouds of pink-hued dust while lightning illuminated the area with fitful flashes. Every dark cloud she passed pulled her heart up into her throat, making her think it might be the *Icarus*. Every second glance revealed only clouds.

Was it just her imagination, or was the sky getting darker in front of her? That would be a good sign. She leaned forward in her chair, willing the bands in front of her to part and reveal the star-studded, inky blackness of space. When she caught the glimmer of a star through a fuchsia band, she almost wept with relief. Unbearable tension oozed out of her shoulders and neck. The last band dissipated in front of her and they were free of the nebula. The readouts and monitors on the consoles flickered and pulsed before finally settling as the sensors came back online.

She would have to run some diagnostics; some of the sensors weren't reporting back as they ought to. The ionized dust they'd flown through had probably made its way into some openings in the ship's hull and dampened the reception. It was a little annoying but no big surprise.

"Tien, move us to a clear jump point," Torrin instructed, releasing herself from the chair's safety harness. "I'm going to put myself on ice."

"Affirmative, Torrin," the AI responded, but Torrin only paid her half a mind as she headed back to the cryo-chamber.

The pod closest to the door was the one she always used. It was custom-built to fit her and had a much-scaled down command console on the inside, complete with a monitor that showed the view from the main bridge screen. In it, she was able to monitor as many of the ship's systems as possible and direct the ship until the last moment before she slipped into cryosleep. She would also be able to assume control of the ship as soon as she came out of stasis.

She gave the pod a cursory examination before turning to tending to her leg. It was the work of a few moments to clean the graze on the back of her calf. Torrin hissed through her teeth when she sterilized the shallow wound. The faint smell of burning skin made her stomach flop. After a long examination, she didn't see any oozing blood. Tien would need to remove all the blood from her body when she was prepped for cryosleep. The frigid temperatures of cryostasis would crystallize any blood left in her body and could lacerate the inside of her leg. The wound wasn't that bad, and any laceration would do little more than give her a truly impressive bruise, but there was no point in risking complications.

Leg taken care of, Torrin checked the adjoining pod to view Jak one last time. She hadn't moved, of course, but Torrin felt better for having seen her again. She disrobed where she stood next to Jak's pod. When completely undressed, she gave the other woman one last, long look before she stepped into her own pod.

Tubes snaked toward her as she lay very still, waiting for the large bore needles to pierce her arms and legs. Tien maneuvered the needles expertly, if somewhat dispassionately and Torrin grimaced as the needles plunged into her veins all at once. She'd made literally hundreds of FTL jumps into the periphery, but she never got used to this part. Trying not to think about what Tien was doing, Torrin allowed her mind to wander. She needed some answers. Her presence on the planet hadn't been an accident, of that she was reasonably certain. Neal had a lot to explain and she intended to wring the answers from him, no matter what it took.

"Are you ready, Torrin?" The AI's cool tones pulled Torrin away from her thoughts.

"I've already laid in the course," Torrin instructed before Tien could start pushing the sedative that would precede the cryo chemicals. "Take us to Nadi using the third preset. The access code is zero zero five tango." The code would let Tien communicate with the probes set up in her home planet's system. Some of those probes were set merely to detect intruders; others were set to engage them. Using the wrong codes would cause an armed buoy to go on the offensive.

"Yes, Torrin," Tien said. "Pushing sedatives now. You will start to feel sleepy soon."

"I know that," Torrin shot back irritably. "This isn't my first…" She yawned hugely, jaws cracking. "…jump."

Just like that, it was too much effort to bicker with the AI. Her limbs were getting heavier and her eyelids slid inexorably over her corneas. She blinked and bright trails tracked the lights in smeared streaks.

Before she slipped under completely, Torrin felt a powerful surge of homesickness. They would be home before she knew it. She'd never brought anyone home with her before, not like this. Jak would love it there, she was certain of it. Things would be different, away from Haefen. They could get to know each other, make a life together. Things were about to look up.

EPILOGUE

Carefully, he made his way toward the burned-out clearing. Smoke still rose from the incinerated trees in and around the area. Here and there embers shone eerily in the darkness. At the clearing's edge, behind a charred bush, he knelt. Someone had lain prone here. He could see a large scuffed area where her torso had been, smaller areas where she'd braced her knees and elbows.

He crouched down next to where she'd laid, picking off his comrades one by one, and brushed his hand gently through the compacted dirt and ash. He brought his hand up to his nose and inhaled, imagining he could smell her once again. This was the closest he'd been to her in years, over a decade now. He'd been watching her, yes, but it was a poor substitute for being able to touch her. He imagined he could still feel the warmth of her body even though an hour had passed since she'd been there.

He stood and made his way into the middle of the clearing, slinging a sniper rifle over one shoulder, fingering the bright red cartridges in his bandolier. He gazed up into the night, toward the stars. She'd left that way not an hour before. Still, she would be back. He'd made sure of that two years ago. He would watch and wait, as he'd always done. When the time was right, she would come to him.

Bella Books, Inc.

Women. Books. Even Better Together.

P.O. Box 10543
Tallahassee, FL 32302

Phone: 800-729-4992
www.bellabooks.com